Nothing to Repent

Nothing to Repent

THE LIFE OF
HESKETH PEARSON

IAN HUNTER

HAMISH HAMILTON
London

First published in Great Britain 1987
by Hamish Hamilton Ltd
27 Wrights Lane London w8 5TZ

Copyright © 1987 by Ian Hunter

British Library Cataloguing in Publication Data

Hunter, Ian, *1945*–
    Nothing to repent: the life of Hesketh Pearson
    1. Pearson, Hesketh   2. Biographers—
    Great Britain—Biography
    I. Title
    828'.91208   CT34.G7

ISBN 0-241-11993-6

Typeset by Rowland Phototypesetting Ltd., Suffolk
Printed in Great Britain
by St Edmundsbury Press Ltd., Suffolk

To Alison and Colin

Contents

Illustrations

Acknowledgements

I must first express my gratitude to Michael Holroyd, a friend of Hesketh Pearson's later years and his literary executor. Without his encouragement I should have lacked the courage to begin this book; without his assistance (including placing at my disposal all of Pearson's letters, diaries and papers) I should have lacked the means to complete it.

Other people assisted by generous recollections of a generous friend; I should mention particularly Basil Harvey, John Wardrop, Alan Frazer, Richard Ingrams, and H. Montgomery Hyde.

To Malcolm Muggeridge I owe an incalculable and lifelong debt. It was through my acquaintance with him that I first came to appreciate his two close friends, Hesketh Pearson and Hugh Kingsmill. It was while writing Muggeridge's biography (*Malcolm Muggeridge: A Life*, Collins 1980) that I resolved to write Pearson's life. It would be difficult to put my debt to Muggeridge into words. I shall not try. Rather, I content myself with his own observation that literary obligations are the kind of burden which sails are to ships or wings to birds.

Two institutions deserve mention. Much of this book was written in the pleasant environs of Wolfson College, Cambridge which did me the honour of making me a Visiting Scholar in 1985–6. I was thus enabled to take up a sabbatical leave from my own University. To Western University for letting me go and to Wolfson College for taking me in, thank you.

Ian Hunter

CHAPTER ONE

Entrance

'When we are born, we cry that we are come to this great stage of fools.'
King Lear, Act IV, Scene VI

It is easy enough to say that all the world's a stage; the trouble is that the parts are not written out beforehand and no one knows, as he stumbles on the opening scene, who he is to portray. Edward Hesketh Gibbons Pearson was born at Hawford in Worcestershire on February 20, 1887. So sickly was he that his parents did not bother officially to register his arrival in a world he would revel in for the next seventy-seven years until three months later when, finally, the Registrar at Droitwich was informed of his birth.

A third son to his father and second to his mother, Hesketh came from what he called the 'squarson class', landed gentry whose younger sons routinely became clergymen. Sufficient ancestral oddity ran through his lineage to fire a latent biographical spark.

The Pearsons traced their immediate ancestry to one Omfrey Pearson who settled at Tettenhall in Staffordshire in the mid-seventeenth century. Both Hesketh's grandfather and great-grandfather were Church of England vicars with a strong sense of civic responsibility (an affliction notably absent from their grandson).

John Pearson, Hesketh's paternal grandfather, was Rector of Suckley in Worcestershire. In addition to clerical responsibilities, he was a Justice of the Peace and chairman of numerous philanthropic organizations and institutions, including the County Lunatic Asylum. Indefatigable in discharge of his parish duties, he often set out late at night to walk several miles to the home of some troubled parishioner who had requested assistance; solace rendered, he would then trudge back alone in the dark. Once John Pearson's stamina was taxed in a less spiritual way; he was challenged to fight by the champion boxer of Oxford. The reason for the quarrel had been lost, but the two men fought at Magdalen Bridge and Pearson decisively won a protracted bare-knuckle encounter. Hesketh liked to claim that his own levity and sloth had been atoned for by his ancestor's excessive contributions to deeds of earnest energy.

Like many public-spirited men, John Pearson's home face was considerably less genial than the one his parishoners saw. Hesketh recalled his grandfather as 'stern' and 'unsympathetic', a dour moralist and an authoritarian parent, lacking a sense of humour. His household staff was comprised of three sisters named Addis; years after his grandfather's death, Hesketh visited them, now elderly spinsters pensioned off and living behind the church. They remembered the Reverend John Pearson fondly, even 'reverentially'; but Hesketh was pleased after a short visit to depart their company so that 'it was no longer necessary to appear holy'.

When nearly fifty, John Pearson married a cousin, Elizabeth Harriet. Hesketh's father, christened Thomas Henry Gibbons Pearson, was an only child, born in the rectory on December 11, 1853. His mother never recovered from the birth and died sixteen days later. Whether from despair or a sense of helplessness, John Pearson packed his son off to the home of grandparents and seldom thereafter took any notice of him. In his memoirs Hesketh could not recall his grandfather even once displaying the least affection toward his son and, on his death, John Pearson bequeathed twice as much of his estate to charity as he left to Hesketh's father.

From the age of four Hesketh's father was brought up by an aunt named Fanny who lived at The Elms, Abberley. Fanny was the widow of John Pearson's younger brother who had been killed in the Indian Mutiny. Hesketh described her as 'well up in the coercive class'. For Henry Pearson it was not a happy childhood. On his deathbed, Hesketh heard his father murmur 'I'll sleep at the lodge tonight' which he took to mean that 'he found the social life of the gardener's family at the lodge more to his taste than any company that included his aunt'.

After schooling at Hereford Cathedral School, Henry won a scholarship to St. John's College, Cambridge. John Pearson had apparently hoped his son would follow his path to holy orders but Henry, at least as a young man, was no ascetic. Before graduation, Henry was removed from Cambridge and sent in disgrace to Australia. While never entirely certain of all of the details of his father's transgression, Hesketh believed that it arose from an amorous dalliance with a local girl, probably the daughter of an influential parishioner. The inevitable result was her confinement (which no doubt heightened the Reverend John's indignation if, as Hesketh thought likely, he had to pay the bills) and Henry's exile. In affairs of the heart, Hesketh Pearson was the least judgmental of men and he attached no disgrace to his father's conduct: 'I like to think that this was my father's indiscretion, because in that respect he and I had something in common, and I followed in his footsteps without being expatriated.'

If Australian exile was meant as stern punishment, it failed. It did, however, enable Henry Pearson to perfect his billiards game. He passed his days in the billiards saloons of Sydney, watching the best players and learning their strengths and weaknesses. His main source of income was from wagering, usually on himself. Once he was matched against the reigning Australian billiards champion; Henry bet £50 (a sum he could never have paid) on himself, and fortunately won.

In the late 1870s, Henry learned that his father was ill and, although perhaps his debt of filial obligation was slight, he immediately returned to England to offer moral and financial support. He enrolled in the agricultural college at Cirencester and, on graduation, worked as a land agent in Wales. This employment was not taxing and gave him time to indulge a passion for sports of all kinds, particularly shooting, fishing and cricket. It was in Wales that he met his first wife, Eleanor Fagan, whom he married in August 1881. Hesketh's half-brother, Harry, was born something less than nine months later. Alas, the tragedy of the father was to be visited on the son; Eleanor died seventeen days after Harry's birth.

In 1884 Henry remarried, this time to Amy Mary Constance Briggs, an attractive and intelligent twenty-nine-year-old daughter of a land-owning vicar. The couple settled in a spacious house built in the 1830s at Hawford near Worcester. A massive stone structure with six chimneys, a portico, and an adjoining coachhouse, it stood amidst acres of fields, gardens, orchards and woods. From the top of a tree on the front lawn, young Hesketh could catch a glimpse of the Malvern Hills. The Severn River meandered past the house and Hesketh was informed by a man named Turner who operated the horse ferry to Ombersley that, after the battle of Worcester, Charles II had swum across the river and scrambled up the opposite bank only to discover Oliver Cromwell waiting for him; in the nick of time, the King plunged in and swam back. 'Often in childhood I dreamt of this achievement, but later study has convinced me that the story was apocryphal.'

Henry Pearson would today be considered a gentleman farmer. He kept cows and pigs which supplied the family with milk, butter, cheese, bacon, beef and pork. There was a large kitchen garden for vegetables and an orchard for apples, pears and cherries. Henry raised pheasants and partridges, primarily for shooting. He had an annual investment income of about a thousand pounds and, if not actually rich, the family was comfortably off. Henry kept three carriages, two horses, and a pony. Ten servants, including a cook, parlour-maid, gardener and nurse, attended the family. In his memoirs Hesketh recalled evening parties in summer when a marquee would be erected on the front lawn and a band played for the dancers.

Henry Pearson possessed a rich, melodious voice which he could occasionally be persuaded to raise in song at a festival, wedding or concert. Later in life, he sang in a cathedral choir. But he read little. Any genetic inclination toward literature Hesketh derived from his mother. Amy was an incessant reader and her favourites were Shakespeare and Jane Austen. Henry's reading did not extend beyond the cricket scores, which for some reason he insisted on reading aloud to his wife. Not long before his mother died, she told Hesketh that she never had the slightest interest in sports, recreation, or outdoor activities. Remembering the attention she had always paid to her husband's daily bulletins, Hesketh was astounded at first but later concluded that 'she loved him, and so made his interests apparently hers'.

Hesketh was born one year to the day after his brother Jack which meant, to their chagrin, two birthday parties annually consolidated into one. Two sisters followed, Elsie born in 1890, and Evelyne born in 1892. Hesketh's memoirs reveal little of the fate of either sister, except that Elsie devoted a decade of her life to looking after her parents between her two marriages, the second of which proved happy; and that Evelyne was married to a man who spent much of the second world war as a prisoner of the Japanese in Singapore.

Hesketh's account of his boyhood years paints a happy, bucolic picture. He was close to his brother, Jack. Both boys were fascinated by the clanking steam engines of the railway station in nearby Fernhill Heath. They threw stones at birds; they huddled together in a branch fort in the hop fields near the Severn; they hid in the wagon shed to light dry leaves in clay pipes supplied to them by their hero, a coachman named Albert; they clambered on to branches in the orchard and shook fruit down on anyone who happened by; they walked proudly behind their father on shooting expeditions for partridge, pheasant and rabbit. Hesketh particularly loved the sounds and smells of woods; 'what thrilled me was the mysterious life in the woods, with its sudden outcries and its equally sudden silences.'

In his closeness to Jack was foreshadowed a lifelong pattern: Hesketh Pearson had a sensual disposition; he loved women and often they loved him. Tall, handsome, invariably well dressed, an attentive listener and a witty conversationalist, many women found the adult Hesketh irresistible. But always he reserved his closest companionship for men. Once, when he was ill, his parents took the family on a day's excursion to a cousin's farm; when the time came to leave and the carriage was waiting, Hesketh could not be found. Eventually his mother came upon him in a summer-house embracing a girl of about his own age and covering her with kisses. 'It seems I resented the intrusion of grown-ups but my feelings were not considered.' With women he strove for intimacy; with men for companionship.

Days at Hawford began at morning prayer with the servants in the dining room. Indoor activities were confined to the nursery. The outside world seldom intruded, although Hesketh remembered the day when his father burst into the nursery and announced: 'The Queen is dead.' Young Hesketh was intensely interested in the Monarchy and 'I went straight to my bedroom and burst into tears'. But usually the boys saw little of their parents during the day, one or the other appearing only to tuck them up in bed. Neither mother nor father was demonstratively affectionate. In fact, when Hesketh was about six years old, his father stopped kissing him entirely, preferring to shake hands instead: 'At first, I was rather dismayed; the new mode seemed so distant and formal, but I soon got used to it. I daresay it was his way of instilling manliness at an early age, and I must admit that I vastly prefer it to the Continental habit of indiscriminate male embracement, which parodies the relationship it is meant to symbolize.'

When Hesketh was eight his parents went for an extended visit to Bristol, leaving the children in the care of a nurse. Pearson's memoirs do not mention this, nor can the reason for the separation now be ascertained. However, a letter to his mother from 'your affectionate son, Hesketh' survives; it thanks her for all her past letters, reminds her to put money in his birthday cake (the letter was written on February 19, 1896, one day before Hesketh's and Jack's birthday), and informs her that 'Mrs Turner at the houseboat scalded her legs very badly' but 'the little calf is alright'. What scraps of correspondence to his parents survive reveal scant emotional intimacy with either one.

On Sunday mornings the family attended church. Since their house stood half-way between Claines and Ombersley, they alternated, walking one Sunday to Claines, riding the next week by cart to Ombersley. Hesketh preferred to ride. 'Jack and I, sitting behind with our backs to those of our parents, entertained ourselves by grimacing and making unseemly gestures at the church-going pedestrians we passed, until complaints were made to authority and correction was administered, father's position as vicar's churchwarden making it inadvisable that his children's high-spirits should upset the parishioners.' From a religious standpoint, these Sunday outings must be considered uninstructive. 'Religion made no impression on me whatever and my sole attempt to get in touch with God was unsuccessful. On being told that all reasonable requests would be granted by Him, I asked in my prayers for a large bowl of brown sugar to be placed under my bed during the night, ready for consumption in the morning. But apparently He considered the request unreasonable, and the absence of brown sugar when I looked under the bed shook my faith in His commonsense.'

Nothing in Hesketh's first nine years at Hawford gave hint of any literary aptitude. There was, however, one incident which may have presaged his theatrical inclination. After several weeks in bed with a nagging illness, he was allowed out of doors one morning before breakfast: 'I walked sadly across the wide front lawn, my head on one side, an arrow in my hand, to a strip of rough grass and trees called "the wilderness" which separated the lawn from the park. There I gravely stuck my arrow into the side of a tree facing the park. I then made the return journey in melancholy mien. After a stage pause, I repeated the performance in order to retrieve the arrow from the tree, slightly emphasizing my sorrowful deportment as I recrossed the lawn. If my memory is to be trusted, I did this to impress my parents, who I assumed to be watching me from their bedroom window, not only with the heroism of my recovery from illness but with the fact that I desired sympathy from my recent affliction. An odd example of exhibitionism, seasoned with self-pity.'

His last months at Hawford were memorable for the bitterly cold winter of 1896 when the Severn River froze and skaters pushed the nine-year-old boy back and forth across the ice on a makeshift sled. In the spring the Pearsons moved from Hawford to Bedford, a county town of thirty thousand inhabitants. It was the end of early childhood, golden memories recalled seventy years later as days when 'Jack and I were happy as children could be'; ahead was the worst unpleasantness Hesketh would ever experience, school.

The family lived at 31 Shakespeare Road and Hesketh was enrolled in the Orkney House School then run by a headmaster named Blake whom Pearson, in his memoirs, called 'the only individual who ever aroused my hate'. Blake was a gaunt, tall, thin-lipped bully whose primary satisfaction in life was caning pupils. 'He seized every possible excuse to thrash me, and I know he enjoyed the exercise because I occasionally heard him smack his lips. Something obstinate in me prevented me from howling over the pain and this made him pile it on. I can recall two occasions when he flogged me so hard that the cane went limp in his hand and he had to throw it away.' Pearson was not the only victim of Blake's sadism but he was one of the most frequent. Years later he told his friend, Hugh Kingsmill: 'On the very rare occasions when I have a nightmare, I imagine myself back at my preparatory school.' Time never mellowed the horror Pearson felt for school; at the end of his life, he wrote: 'I derived a single advantage from Blake's school: the worst things that have happened to me since leaving it have seemed relatively mild in comparison with those five years of helpless misery, and I would far rather have died at any period of my existence than go through them again.'

Outside school, Pearson was a normal adolescent delinquent, which is to say raucous, high-spirited, noisy and disruptive. Whether raiding vegetable gardens, puncturing bicycle tires, setting fire to hayricks, insulting tradesmen, clambering at night over neighbours' roofs, laying traps for pedestrians, or hurling rocks at anything mobile, this period of his youth was passed with 'a tender bottom and sturdy lungs'. One prank showed ingenuity. With a chum named Sidney Helmsley, Hesketh kept pigeons, including a dozen white fan-tails who settled one day on a neighbour's eaves which had just been painted red. The result was red fan-tails. Hesketh and Sidney transformed this misfortune to profit by convincing a classmate to buy what they told him were a dozen of the rarest fan-tails, the red fan-tail found only on the upper Amazon River. With a tidy profit secure in their pockets, they added that red fan-tails crave freedom and would pine if cooped up. The dupe duly took their advice and, as soon as the birds were released, they of course flew back to their original owners, who kept them caged until all the feathers were white again. When their classmate complained that his red fan-tails had disappeared, Hesketh and Sidney commiserated but suggested that the birds were probably now perched on the mast of a cargo boat steaming back to the Amazon and that he was at fault for neglecting to keep them warm enough. 'We then assured him that in this country white fan-tails were far more adaptable and home loving, showing him ours when they were back to normal, and he bought them again . . . this *coup* suggests that I might have been a successful stockbroker.'

At fourteen, Pearson escaped from the 'flagello-maniac' Blake and his 'hell-house' school and went to Bedford Grammar School to which he won an entrance prize for proficiency in spelling. The prize was a book called *Tad: Or Getting Even With Them*, though whether or not he ever read it Pearson could not recall. In fact, the only reading that appealed to him then were the *Sherlock Holmes* stories ('for me a real figure, not a figment of fancy') and novels by Stanley Weyman.

Although the atmosphere at Bedford School was less oppressive, Pearson's desultory academic performance did not improve. This was doubly galling since his older brother, Jack, also at Bedford, was a superior student and advanced several forms ahead of Hesketh. This temporarily estranged their friendship and, as Jack was a notorious tease, the two brothers frequently fought. Hesketh was interested only in history, French and literature; mathematics, Latin and Greek utterly bored him. He was lazy by nature and did not suffer tedium easily. He refused always to apply himself to subjects, scholastic or biographical, which failed to kindle an instinctive interest. Long after he had established himself as a biographer, Pearson turned down a lucrative offer to write a life of J. M. Barrie and another to write on Montagu Norman, Governor of the Bank of England; while he needed the money he could not bring himself to write about a subject which did not fire his imagination.

Even Shakespeare (who, years later, would be the subject of one of Pearson's finest biographies) was ruined for him by a schoolmaster named Yule (appropriately rhymed with fool), whose idea of teaching the plays was to force the boys to memorize and recite long speeches, and, when their recall inevitably slipped, to make them write the speech out by hand fifty times. When Hesketh tripped over Macbeth's: 'If it were done when 'tis done, then 'twere well/If it were done quickly . . .' he was compelled to copy this out 'until I loathed the name Shakespeare as much as I detested Macbeth'. This 'sin against the Holy Ghost', as Pearson considered it, nearly destroyed what would prove to be the greatest solace of his life, Shakespeare's plays.

His form-master, Rice, despaired of Hesketh ever becoming anything, particularly after he scored nought in an algebra examination. 'Many years later I met [Rice] on a golf course; we shook hands, and I asked if he remembered me. "Remember you!" he exclaimed: "you are the only boy in my experience who scored a duck in an algebra exam." I remarked that it was a distinction to be so freshly remembered. But he was furious at the time, and insisted on my being sent down to a lower form. In retrospect, I regard this algebraical o as an outstanding scholastic achievement. It signified an instinctive knowledge that for me algebra was a waste of time and would have no place in my life.'

Henry Pearson was advised of his son's academic weakness and it was suggested that Hesketh study classics with H. W. Barnes, an even-tempered and forgiving man, 'the most sensible master I ever met'. During a half-term holiday Pearson and another boy spent the day and early evening cycling near Kimbolton. Arriving back well after curfew, they were not surprised to receive a summons to Barnes's study. 'Before he could open his mouth, we presented him with a brace of rabbits. He frankly admitted that we had stymied him. Clearly a man with a noble nature.' Barnes later became the school Chaplain.

The headmaster at Bedford, James Surtees Phillpotts, Pearson described as looking like a combination of Zeus, Jupiter and an Old

Testament prophet, when with 'grey beard, flowing gown and mortar-board' he would mount the platform to lead morning prayer. Occasionally he would also deliver a brief homily and, when he chose as his text, 'Unstable as water, thou shall not excel', Pearson considered it specifically directed at him. 'Not only was my nature unstable as water, but I could not conceive myself excelling at anything.'

The Boer War was on and Phillpotts usually marked a British victory or the relief of a besieged town by declaring a half-holiday. Perhaps considering that victories were becoming routine, he neglected this practice and made no holiday concession after the relief of Mafeking. This upset a mob of townsfolk who marched on the school, led by a brass band, smashing the windows of those along the way who failed to display a flag. Not wishing to be lynched, Phillpotts decided to receive them. What happened next Pearson recalled in a Speech Day address sixty years later (only two years before his own death): 'The big central door was opened and the mob flooded in while we boys were sent to the galleries. The Old Chief then delivered an extempore harangue to a hall packed with patriots. It was received with yells of delight. After which he stooped down from the platform, shook hands vigorously with a thousand or more citizens, freed us for the day, and probably spent the rest of it having his arm massaged.'

Phillpotts retired while Pearson was at Bedford and was replaced by J. E. King, who had formerly been headmaster at Manchester Grammar School. Pearson had only one encounter with King. It came about when Pearson responded to a question asked by a clergyman named Massey, a small, red-bearded fat man, called 'Pot' by the boys because of his overhanging belly; whatever Pearson's answer was, it threw Pot into a rage to which Pearson responded by breaking into a nervous peal of laughter. Insensate with fury, Pot picked up an ink bottle and hurled it at Pearson. 'I caught it neatly and threw it back, catching him on the belly where it broke and deluged him with ink. He was so utterly confounded that he remained for several seconds with his mouth open, staring at me as if he could not believe his senses. Gradually he became conscious of what had happened, said nothing at the time, but at the end of the lesson took me down to report my behaviour to the headmaster . . .' King listened attentively to Pot's account and then asked Hesketh what he had to say. 'I simply explained that I had made a good catch, returned it, and could not be blamed for Mr Massey's failure in the field. King sent me out of the room and had a heart-to-heart talk with Pot, and I heard no more about it. From that moment I had complete confidence in the new 'head' who was so conspicuously fair.'

Rugger was the principal game at Bedford and Pearson hated it, a

reaction which he attributed to a combination of congenital claus-
trophobia and the fact that 'I usually found myself beneath a heap of
other boys when the scrum caved in'. He was proficient in rowing,
running (which he enjoyed because it was the only sport into which
team spirit could not be introduced), and cricket. His first form-master,
Rice, had been an excellent cricketer, playing for Gloucestershire. Rice
once required Pearson to memorize Scott's *Lay of the Last Minstrel*.
When called upon to recite, Pearson cast a forlorn glance through an
open window onto the playing fields, and began:

> The way was long, the wind was cold,
> The minstrel was infirm and old;
> His withered cheek and tresses grey
> Seemed to have known a better day.
> The bat his sole remaining joy,
> Was carried by another boy.

'"Bat!" exclaimed Rice: "Another boy!" He held himself in with an
effort and then spoke caustic words: "This is the Lay of the Last
Minstrel, not the Cry of the Last Cricketer. Minstrels usually play with
harps not bats."'

Pearson's father, Henry, excelled in cricket and was chairman of the
Bedfordshire Cricket Club. Henry had also become Vicar's Warden of
St Martin's Church and, perhaps in consequence, had adopted a stuffy,
censorious attitude which now carried over even into sport. He led the
fight, for example, against Sunday golf in Bedford. Hesketh recalled
caddying once for his father when a golfer miscued and exclaimed:
'Blast!' Henry jerked his thumb over his shoulder in the direction of his
son and gave the miscreant an admonitory, 'Now, now!'

The Pearson family regularly attended St Martin's Church, a flock
entrusted to the Reverend Mr Haig. This lugubrious but estimable
vicar had a habit of preaching for twenty minutes, which Henry Pearson
considered precisely ten minutes too long. The Pearsons occupied the
very front pew and, at the beginning of the sermon, Henry would
ostentatiously remove his gold watch from his waistcoat, note the time,
and shut it again with an audible click. Ten minutes later he would
again produce the watch, click it open, sigh loudly, and snap it shut,
repeating this process as often as was necessary until Haig subsided. 'I
remember a Cowley Father named Hollings who came to preach on the
Sundays of one Lent. He droned along for over half an hour, dead to
the sighs and snorts and watch-snappings from our pew, and after the
second Sunday father simply stopped going to church, becoming a
Christian again at Easter when Hollings had withdrawn to Cowley.'

Another idiosyncrasy of Henry Pearson was his determination to arrive late for church. Whether his motive was to gain attention as the family paraded up to its front pew, or to avoid admitting that he was among the 'lost sheep' of the General Confession, Hesketh was never able to determine. Henry also insisted on being first to drink from the chalice at holy communion which led to 'a slightly undignified sprint to arrive first at the altar rail'.

Although Hesketh was confirmed in St Martin's, the religious significance of this act never concerned him. The church was no more than an unvarying part of a weekly family routine. He attended regularly and, among his earliest writings, is this appeal for church funds: 'Much help is wanted for St Martin's church funds. Any reader who would like to contribute to these funds would kindly send it to: Master Hesketh Pearson, 31 Shakespeare Road, Bedford, who would promptly forward it to the Reverend A. Haig (Vicar of St Martin's).' At church Hesketh liked to observe the demeanour of the communicants as they came down the chancel steps: 'Some tried to look as if they had passed through a great experience, others were a little sheepish, others put on a nonchalant expression as though the occurrence were normal, a few were tight-lipped as if they had done their best and would do it again.' Hesketh was a 'natural sceptic' where religion was concerned; all his life he remained, like a recalcitrant virus, immune to any form of religious inoculation. He discovered early on that many professing Christians, including clerical schoolmasters, were 'the retributive type who enjoyed the act of punishing others for not being like themselves'. Nothing was more foreign to Pearson's tolerant, hedonistic nature. However, like all men with a spiritual temperament, Pearson's estrangement from institutional Christianity did not preclude experiences in which unpredictably, almost furtively, past and present seem to fade and, for a moment, all contradictions merge in one sublime realization of the joy and sadness of all creation. Such experiences border on mysticism. Pearson described one such experience which occurred 'on a tranquil Sunday evening' while he was paddling a canoe on the Ouse River: 'At a spot I can still see in the mind's eye I let the boat drift across the stream and sat for a while entranced by the deep shadows of the woods on my left, the rich green fields on my right with the line of pollards beyond, the violent sky, the clouds red and pink in the sunset, and the distant sound of bells from Kempston Church across the meadows. I was sixteen years old at the time, and when the bells ceased ringing I felt a little ashamed of an emotion that filled me with happiness and yet made me want to cry.'

Pearson's biographical interests were foreshadowed when, at sixteen, he and his sister Elsie began to publish bi-annual journals which were sent around to family relations and friends at the cost of a shilling. His was called *The Lightning*: Elsie's *The Thunderer*. Preserved among his papers is the first issue, dated 1903, a battered bound volume with blue boards covered in brown wrapping paper and proclaiming, in boyish scrawl, 'A right Royal magazine: under the patronage of HM King Edward VII and HRH The Prince of Wales'. The first page is devoted to 'signatures of those who have been looking at this book'; there are twelve signatures, most from family members. Then a Preface in which the author proclaims:

> This book contains much interesting and political news. It also contains pictures; dialogues; storys; *summarys of famous men's lives*; and comedies.
>
> It comes out every half-year and it is only for each member to read, and then to be sent back to the author. I think that it is worth it as I have spent many precious minutes or hours writing in it, whereas I might have been doing other things. When you have read this kindly say whether you would like one to be sent in regularly every half-year.

Although poetry is not mentioned in the list of contents, volume one begins with a poem entitled 'On the Occasion of the Battle of Austerlitz':

> Another year! – Another deadly blow!
> Another mighty Empire overthrown!
> And we are left, or shall be left alone;
> The last that have to struggle with the foe.

The Lightning chiefly consists of pictures, press cuttings, and short articles written by Hesketh about those who happened to be among his current pantheon of heroes and villains (for example, the convicted murderer Samuel Dougal, hanged in July 1903 and according to the author 'one of the greatest criminals in every respect for some little time'). The 'heroes' section is disproportionately comprised of generals, royalty and ecclesiastical dignitaries: Pope Leo XIII, Napoleon, Joseph Chamberlain, Queen Victoria ('a better woman never lived') and Edward VII. Of Charles II the sixteen-year-old editor wrote: 'He is the man whom everyone should know about;' half a century later Pearson took his own advice and one of his last biographies was of Charles II.

Looking back on these efforts six decades later, Pearson pronounced himself 'amazed by their immaturity and naivety'. He considered 'the opinions expressed of such an assertive nature that [I] cannot fail to notice the early appearance of a characteristic I have spent my life attempting to subdue'.

To his sister's competitor magazine, *The Thunderer*, the young editor tried to be charitable: 'The editoress (or rather author) of *The Thunderer* is my sister, so of course I would say nothing against it except that mine is the best.' But he was not receptive to editorial criticism; at the conclusion of the article on Napoleon, he appended this note: 'I don't want any letters from any of my readers saying that my language is a bit too eloquent on this most painful subject, because if I receive them, they shall be torn up and put in the fire without ceremony.'

The first issue of *The Lightning* concluded with a poem:

> Goodbye all ye who this magazine have read,
> And think of the contents when you go to bed,
> And when you have finished, to yourself sing,
> Love ye your country; God save the King.

The signature page of the second issue of *The Lightning* (1904) bears only four signatures, and the enterprise then petered out.

Pearson spent his final term at Bedford as a boarder in Merton House, rather pretentiously named after the master's Oxford college. This experience failed either to kindle school spirit or to initiate Pearson into the ways of homosexuality, those twin legacies so common in boarding school memoirs. His only experience in the latter vein was when a fellow resident offered him a practical demonstration on how to masturbate. The resident's demonstration was not successful; Pearson watched for a bit but quickly 'got bored' and left to find other recreation.

At the end of his final term, a dinner was given to honour the boarders who were leaving Merton House. The housemaster unexpectedly called upon Pearson to speak. Never good at impromptu addresses, Pearson pulled himself to a standing position only to sway back and forth in silence. 'At last I managed to utter one syllable. I said: "Er." That exhausted my eloquence. Our housemaster clapped his hands to help me along, and all the boys clapped theirs with ironic enthusiasm. Upon which I said "Thank you" and sat down. The laugh that followed lifted the roof, and perhaps explains why Merton House was shortly shifted to Pemberton Avenue and changed its name to Pemberley.'

At the age of eighteen, Hesketh Pearson left Bedford Grammar School 'with small Latin, less Greek, no Mathematics', a hatred of punishment and cruelty, a violent objection to routine, and an imagination 'half-famished by the paralysing curriculum of an English public school'. To show for his time he had acquired 'a scholastic education that had taught me nothing of value'. Fifty-seven years later he was invited to return to give a Speech Day address. He told the boys that if an 'average dullard' with a 'disgraceful' scholastic record, 'a complete flop' in every school endeavour, could stand on the platform to exhort another generation to high academic achievement, then truly 'there is hope for everybody'.

CHAPTER TWO

A Commercial Career

'In those days a fellow who was good for nothing went into commerce. I was good for nothing and I went into commerce.'

Hesketh Pearson

Eighteen years old and for the first time faced with the awkward necessity of earning a steady income, Pearson did what he would always do when confronted by obdurate economics, he chose the path of least resistance. A friend of his father's, Alfred Strover Williams, who was managing director of the Royal Mail Steam Packet Company, a shipping firm, arranged a job for Hesketh as a clerk. On a cloudless summer day, one that Williams told him 'augured well for his future in business', Hesketh first entered the Transfer Department where, for ten shillings a week, he was to keep track of customs specifications, share certificates, and bills of lading. Seldom have a position and an incumbent been so ill-matched. 'I could not apply myself to anything and developed a fatal facility for adding two and two together and making five or three'; worse 'I was (and am) quite content with the result'. Looking back on his first job, Pearson wrote: 'I must have been a serious menace to the heads of departments because I made a habit of cornering as many of my fellow-clerks as showed the least interest in matters unrelated to their work and discussing the literary and political figures of the past and present.' He considered his duties 'tedious interruptions in the real business of life' which was to hold forth about fascinating characters. Fortunately his immediate supervisor, a Scotsman named Mac-Kintosh, was a theatre-goer who enjoyed recounting the plays and imitating the actors he had seen, particularly Sir Henry Irving, until at the climax of some stirring scene he would suddnely remember himself and break off: 'Well, we must get on with our work.' But what exactly he was to be getting on with remained a mystery. Years later, when he was strolling with Hugh Kingsmill past the Custom House, Pearson mentioned that he used to frequent that building with 'specifications and things like that'. '"Things like what?"' Kingsmill inquired. '"Oh, specifications."' Which about summed up, Pearson considered, his combination of 'complete ignorance' and 'total lack of interest' in whatever it was he was supposed to do.

At first Pearson lived at home in Bedford and commuted to work, taking the 8:40 train in the morning and returning on the 5:45. Then, in November 1905, he rented a room in Hampstead where, each morning after breakfast, he could bathe in Highgate Pond or practise golf shots on the Heath. Pearson loved Hampstead Heath. He used to sit for hours on summer evenings listening to the bells of Christchurch. In all weather and seasons, he tramped miles over the Heath. 'Hampstead Heath is for me the most beautiful place on earth and I could never tire of its spring and autumn glories.'

The primary benefit of living in the city was proximity to theatre. Ever since an aunt had taken him to see William Gillette in *Sherlock Holmes* at the Duke of York's, he had been entranced. (The page, Billy, had been played by an unknown youngster named Charles Chaplin.) This passion for theatre may have been partly inherited. Among the few of his father's memorabilia which have survived are playbills from the 1870s and 1880s; Henry Pearson apparently saw original productions of Gilbert and Sullivan's *Patience* at the Opéra Comique, and *Othello* at the Lyceum Theatre with a young Henry Irving as Iago and Ellen Terry as Desdemona.

At work an acquaintance named Standage lent Pearson a copy of Oscar Wilde's *De Profundis*. This soon led to *The Soul of Man Under Socialism* (which Pearson maintained ought to have been called *The Soul of Man Above Socialism*). With its contempt for bourgeois authority and its idealization of the liberating effect of art, this extended essay 'performed the vital operation of making me think for myself'. In his biography of Wilde, Pearson concluded that it was this intense anti-capitalism, rather than Wilde's foppishness or even homosexuality, which so infuriated the British aristocracy, so that, in the aftermath of Wilde's trial and ruin, almost no one raised either a finger or a pound to assist him. But at eighteen Hesketh was still inclined to regard conservatism and the Church of England as part of the natural order, 'the sole channels of political and religious truth'. With a chuckle not a theory, with wit rather than logic, Wilde demolished such conventional and unexamined beliefs. 'For laughing my mind out of its rut and so enabling me to think freely with the aid of what inner light God had given me, I have always been grateful to Oscar Wilde.' In his memoirs, Pearson called the discovery of Wilde one of 'four major revelations of my life, as a result of which I grew up'. The other three revelations were Shakespeare, Herbert Beerbohm Tree and Bernard Shaw. Wilde and Shakespeare 'liberated my mind'; Tree and Shaw 'released my sensibility'.

Pearson made inquiries about Wilde's other books, but in that far-off time homosexuality was regarded as a perversion unmentionable in polite society. His questions were met by compressed lips and disapproving glances. In second-hand bookshops he loudly requested the works of that 'genius and rare human spirit, Oscar Wilde', and he professed surprise when 'shopmen used to blush, glance around fearfully, and make signs of protestation, while the customers used to disappear hurriedly behind the bookshelves'. When Pearson eventually learned the nature of Wilde's offence, the love which dared not speak its name, he was amused rather than offended: 'The idea of a man getting excited about a member of his own sex struck me as very funny.'

Pearson's memoirs reveal little of his own sexual development. He was now over six feet tall and sturdily built; he had an aristocratic face, clear complexion, blue eyes, a long aquiline nose, high forehead, and dark hair combed straight back. When stimulated by conversation, he was capable of immense charm. He spoke in a dry, slightly ironic manner and loved to laugh. He had a lean, well-coordinated body and great physical stamina, derived from his fetish for walking. Women found him attractive and their attentions were seldom unrequited. Yet at twenty-one he described himself as 'strangely innocent'. If this was true it was so despite a sensual disposition, a hedonistic outlook, and a congenital inability to work himself into a moral lather over any sexual peccadillo. His virginity must be attributed less to inclination than to the limited opportunities which an Edwardian society made available to a randy young man.

Pearson's 'revelation' of Shakespeare was as fortuitous as his acquaintance with Wilde. One summer weekend he was invited by a school acquaintance to Shrewsbury for shooting and golf. He arrived at a rambling manor house only to be greeted by 'cataclysmic rain'. While wandering idly from room to room, Pearson found only two books in the place, the Bible and a one-volume edition of Shakespeare's plays – 'an austere choice between the boredom of church and the anguish of school'. What happened was so etched in his mind that half a century later he recalled it vividly. 'I decided to be a martyr and began to read *Hamlet*. The opening scene held me and I galloped through the play with increasing excitement. I reread it immediately after lunch the same day. That did the trick. I entered a new world which expanded with every play I read and to such degree was I carried away that I sometimes wept with joy. Looking back on these days, I seemed to have walked on

air. My imagination was released, my sense of beauty set free. The City
was no longer a prison where I did purposeless jobs but a place of magic
where, sitting at my desk or wandering through the streets, I could
dream of Shakespeare's poetry and characters.' From that day forward
Pearson claimed never to have passed a week without reading
Shakespeare. He saw innumerable performances of the plays, preferring at first *Hamlet* and *Macbeth*, then graduating to *Julius Caesar*,
mellowing to *Twelfth Night* and *The Winter's Tale*, before finally
settling on his all-time favourite, *Henry IV*, the two parts of which '. . .
contain not only the soil and soul of England but the supreme character-
creations in all literature'. Looking back on his 'revelation' of
Shakespeare, Pearson wrote: 'The extraordinary thing about
Shakespeare is that, as you grow older and your understanding of life
deepens with the sorrow you have known and heightens with the joy you
have felt, he becomes less and less dispensable and more and more a
miracle. Other writers are for certain moods; he is for all moods . . .
other writers are exhaustible; he is inexhaustible.'

Flushed with Shakespeare, Pearson decided to start a Hampstead
branch of the British Empire Shakespeare Society. He made inquiries
and, in due course, a Society emissary appeared at his door, a tall man
with 'an impressive forehead and jaw, humorous eyes, and a slightly
crooked nose'. This was John Beamish, the Secretary, who successfully
dissuaded Pearson from any such notion, his reason being that it would
add to his labours. Beamish was a melancholic man given to bouts of
severe depression relieved only by stimulating talk, a dash of cynicism
adding to his native humour. He and Pearson quickly became friends
and Pearson later shared a flat with Beamish in Westminster.

His revelations did not enhance his usefulness to the Royal Mail
Steam Packet Company where he talked incessantly of Wilde and
Shakespeare to any who would listen. Even routine shipping inquiries
were now answered with rhetorical flourishes; a telephone inquiry
about cartage rates to Rio de Janeiro, for example, was met with
Shylock's observation: 'Ships are but boards, sailors but men; there be
land rats and water rats, land thieves and water thieves . . .'; at this
point '. . . the telephone was wrenched out of my hand by a fellow who
disliked the tone of my observations and the conversation was continued on a lower imaginative level'. On another occasion, when a
supervisor's request for six copies of a bill of lading was met with 'But in
them nature's copy is not eterne', the man studied Pearson quietly and
then sighed: 'Anyhow, six is the number I want.'

Pearson added indiscretion to indolence when he raised a fuss over
the discharge of a fellow employee, taking his protest over the heads of

supervisors and directly to the manager, his father's friend Williams. The employee was given more generous severance pay as a result of Pearson's intervention, but he had broken 'all the laws of sycophancy' and from then on he was a marked man. When he began to promote a trade union among clerks, this was the final straw. As soon as Williams left on holiday, Pearson was summoned to the office of the general manager, R. L. Forbes, who bellowed that Pearson might think or believe what he liked so long as he didn't *do* what he liked. 'Never act upon your convictions and you'll get on in the world,' Forbes concluded. With these words ringing in his ears, Pearson was fired. On his return from holidays, Williams reversed the dismissal but Pearson was shifted to Outward Freight (as it turned out, aptly named). Here too he proved 'an infernal nuisance to clerks who took their work seriously.'

Outside the office Pearson spent his waking hours at the theatre or playing golf or just walking about Hampstead Heath, 'my head in the clouds with Shakespeare'. To a golfer labouring under his bag of clubs, Pearson shouted: 'Set down, set down your honourable load,' and noted that this was received with 'an uneasy look'. To a policeman who came upon Pearson walking alone and declaiming *Hamlet* and inquired if he was in pain, Pearson replied: 'Yes, the pangs of poetry.' 'Better see a doctor about it,' the policeman admonished.

Pearson occasionally strolled through Hyde Park where on Sunday mornings the cream of society could be seen after church; ladies in long dresses, holding brightly coloured parasols, accompanied by gentlemen in black or grey top hats and frock coats, wearing spats and high stiff collars, perambulating up and down or driving in landaus. Once at this 'Church Parade' Pearson heard someone whisper that J. M. Barrie was in the crowd. Try as he might, Pearson could not get a glimpse of him. A few years later Pearson was to meet Barrie in a curious way. It was in 1920 and Pearson, now an aspiring actor, was engaged for a bit part in a revival of Barrie's play *The Admirable Crichton* at the Royalty Theatre. Pearson had envisaged the playwright as tall, with longish hair and a neat pointed beard, dandified in manner and dress. Determined to make a favourable impression, he arrived early for the first rehearsal and scoured the theatre for anyone matching this mental image. Seeing no such person, he assumed that the author was not present. Just before the rehearsal was to begin 'a stoutish, insignificant little fellow, smoking a large pipe and wearing an overcoat, bowler and woollen muffler', a man with the air of a 'disillusioned bookie' who Pearson concluded was probably a worried financial backer, sidled up and asked for a match. Pearson handed him a box. 'Keep your eye on me: I'm a match thief,' the man muttered. Thinking a backer was bound to know the author, Pearson inquired: 'Does the author ever turn up for rehearsals?'

'"Pardon?" he asked.

'"The author – does he ever come to rehearsals?" I repeated.

'"Oh, you mean Barrie?" he said in a surprised tone. "Yes, he is nearly always here."

'"I haven't seen him."

'"Well, he was here a minute ago," he said looking around.

'"What's he like?"

'"He's not unlike me."

'"You?" I exclaimed.

'"Yes, you could hardly know us apart."

'I laughed.

'"What's the joke?"

'"Oh nothing! I didn't picture him like you – that's all."

'"We are often mistaken for one another." I looked sceptical and he went on: "You may not believe it but I help him to write his plays."

'"Nonsense!"

'"Fact."

'But I wasn't going to swallow that, so I told him to try the other leg.'

'"You don't believe me?"

'"Well, if you helped to write his plays, why doesn't your name appear on the programmes?"

'"It does," he replied mysteriously. "Hush! Not a word to a soul," and he waddled off.

'"He must think me an absolute idiot," I said to myself, feeling convinced of it when I discovered that he had taken my box of matches. I asked an actor nearby, "Who's that little blighter in the bowler? He's pinched my matches."

'"That," said the actor, "is Sir James Barrie."'

With some difficulty Pearson recovered himself sufficiently to stumble through the rehearsal. Just as it ended the mysterious match-thief again sidled up to him.

'"I have discovered half a dozen boxes of matches in my overcoat pocket. If one of them is yours, you may take it."

'I took it.

'"Seen Barrie yet?" he asked.

'"Yes."

'"Good. I told you he was not unlike me," and he rolled down the gangway.'

Thirty years later, in fact just a few weeks before Barrie's death, Pearson happened to see him again passing through Leicester Square. Barrie's appearance now struck him as one of 'settled horror – the horror and self-contempt of a man who has spent his life kissing the bottoms of people he detests and for whom he has as deep a contempt as he feels for himself'.

Pearson's growing passion for the theatre soon led to his two remaining 'revelations' – Beerbohm Tree and Bernard Shaw, both of whose biographies he would later write. Pearson first saw Tree perform in Stephen Phillips's play, *Nero*, 'the first big artistic moment of my life'. Tree was then staging plays at His Majesty's Theatre where Pearson spent 'the happiest hours I have known', despite audible rumblings from his stomach, deprived of food to afford tickets. He and Charles Burt, an office companion whom he had managed to infect with Shakespeare, attended most opening nights and, when Tree made his first entry, they would clap and shout and set up such a din as visibly irritated other patrons.

Pearson was first introduced to Shaw's plays at the Court and Savoy Theatres where he saw early productions of *Man and Superman*, *John Bull's Other Island*, and *The Doctor's Dilemma*. 'The unique achievement of Shaw was that he gave his generation a good shaking, made them question everything and think for themselves.' Of all Shaw's plays Pearson preferred *Caesar and Cleopatra* with Johnston Forbes-Robertson as Caesar: 'Somehow I raked up the money to go three times and the play remains one of my favourites in all literature, enriched for me by the unforgettable tones of Forbes-Robertson's voice and the dramatic diction of Shaw, who read it to me at my request when he was past eighty and brought every character to life.' So successful was the run of *Caesar and Cleopatra* that there was talk of taking the production to America. That never materialized and, a few years later, Forbes-Robertson told Pearson why; the American producers had insisted that Shaw come along which he declined to do, saying that if he went to America he should immediately prove so popular with ordinary citizens that they would demand that he remain and become their president. This, said Shaw, would be a 'crashing bore', a tragic end to a life of genius.

With Shaw now added to his repertoire of speeches, Hesketh took to public declamation at the office, walking on Hampstead Heath, or while sitting listening to church bells. He often spent his lunch hour in St Paul's which he considered ideally located at the very heart of commerce, its spirit of permanence mocking the transitory pursuit of riches. 'Realizing that the city fathers worshipped nothing but success [Wren]

built their chief temple in the likeness of its bodily symbol; and the
fleshy men of business swarm about their dingy alleys, from the centre
of which rises a gigantic pot-belly.' How itinerant worshippers, seeking
a moment of silence away from the clamour of the city, reacted to
Pearson's soliloquies is not recorded. Half a century later, in a radio talk
on manners, Pearson would rail against 'detestable people' who carry
transistor radios and disturb 'places that should be sanctuaries of peace
and quiet.'

As Pearson's mind was stretched by theatre, his stomach shrank from
undernourishment. Once, having spent his last penny on tickets and
feeling ravenous, he encountered a fellow clerk just leaving for lunch.
Where was he lunching, Pearson inquired, and was told 'Tiffins', a
smart Cheapside restaurant. Confident that such affluence could stand
a friend to lunch, Pearson invited himself along. After lobster lunches,
the bill arrived. Pearson made a show of fumbling through his pockets
for money. Just as he was about to begin expressing annoyance at
having misplaced his wallet, he realized that his hoped-for benefactor
was exactly imitating his own actions. At just the same moment each
implored: 'I say, I left my money at home: can you lend me ten bob?'
When their mutual deception dawned on them, they both 'roared with
laughter'. Fortunately, the proprietor proved to be understanding,
although Pearson had to forego theatre for several weeks to repay the
restaurant.

It was as a result of the theatre that Pearson's education began in
earnest. He now read widely and counted among his favourite authors
Dickens, Thackeray, Smollet, Boswell, Hazlitt, Balzac, Fielding,
Kipling and Stevenson. He discovered music, particularly Wagner
('the idol of the adolescent, the perfect companion for the spiritually
immature') and his lifelong favourite, Beethoven. His sensibilities,
always acute for nature, deepened. He was happy to walk where there
were grass and flowers and to listen to the sound of church bells. Bells
had a 'queer hypnotic effect' on Pearson, so that he found it difficult to
pass by a church when the bells were ringing. 'They suggest the passing
of time, they imply also the continuity of things. Life is short, but it
goes on: here today, there tomorrow: Shakespeare in 1600, Beethoven
in 1800.' His fascination with the character of famous men intensified
and he continued to try his hand at biographical sketches. He had
purged his mind of the 'useless knowledge' and 'many factious opinions'
that had been drummed into him in school, and he was now free to
develop his own aesthetic and critical standards. Although too strongly
influenced by his four 'revelations', Pearson was beginning to put into
practice a dictum which he only consciously formulated at the end of his

life: 'The only person by whom the intelligent man is profoundly influenced is himself.'

On several occasions Pearson visited his great-great-uncle, Francis Galton, an anthropologist who is credited as the father of modern eugenics and was also the discoverer of fingerprinting as a means of identifying criminals. Hesketh was then nineteen; Galton was eighty-four. 'I expanded with self-importance; he was strangely simple and unaffected. I had begun to feel that I knew everything: he had long passed the age when he first felt that he knew nothing. In brief, I was a dogmatic prig: he was a tolerant philosopher.' Galton's marriage was not a happy one; his wife, Louise, was something of a martinet and a hypochondriac. Periodically, she would prepare herself for death, so much so that a constant saying in Pearson's family was 'Aunt Louise is dying again'. Then, when everyone was hoping for the best, she would make a slow and painful recovery. When her death actually occurred, 'no one believed it till after the funeral'. Hesketh was particularly annoyed at the way Louise would deny her husband the minor comforts that might have soothed his old age. When Pearson knew him Galton was quite deaf which necessitated the use of an ear-trumpet. Once Hesketh came upon Galton and Ralph Inge, later Dean of St. Paul's, bellowing away at one another about religion, not so much arguing (although Galton was an atheist) as shouting to make themselves heard. Galton had that unusual combination of a scientific mind coupled with an unfeigned interest in people. In conversation he was direct and unpretentious, with no side or vanity. 'Were you glad to be knighted?' Hesketh once asked him. 'Yes, and no,' Galton replied: 'Yes, because it has drawn more public attention to eugenics; no, because it has trebled my correspondence.' Curious about the outstanding personalities of Galton's day Hesketh asked whether he admired any politicians? 'I'm afraid that my interest in politicians has always been a phrenological one,' Galton replied: 'The colour of their views does not interest me as much as the shape of their heads. Gladstone had one of the finest heads of any man of my time.'

Galton loved gadgets and was forever inventing something new to make life easier. When Hesketh visited his home at 42 Rutland Gate he found that Galton had hooked up a device to warn those on the first floor when the second floor bathroom was occupied, thus sparing the prospective occupant a futile climb up a flight of stairs and the actual occupant the embarrassment of having the door-handle rattled. Another of his gadgets was a wooden brick wrapped up to look like a brown parcel and tied to a string, this he carried beneath his coat to a procession or other public gathering until, when required, it could be lowered on to the ground so that Galton could stand on it to see over the heads of a crowd, and then he would unobtrusively reel it back up. He also invented a 'Hyperscope' so that he could see round ladies' hats in the theatre.

It was at Galton's house that Pearson met the poet, Mary Coleridge. On one rather disappointing occasion, he also met Arthur Conan Doyle. At Bedford Grammar School, Pearson had read Sherlock Holmes. In the first issue of *The Thunderer* he had proclaimed Conan Doyle 'one of the greatest literary men of the present day' and 'my favourite of all book writers'. Pearson was expecting to meet a large, clear-eyed imposing figure and was rather disappointed to find a thick-set, broad-faced man 'who had no more mystery about him than a pumpkin'. Pearson began to pester Doyle with questions about Sherlock Holmes. At first Doyle responded enthusiastically. Then, as the barrage continued, Doyle became thoughtful, then curt, then glum, until finally he burst out: 'I loathe Holmes!' Startled, Pearson asked why? 'If I had never started on him,' Doyle muttered, 'my historical novels would have stood a chance.' Pearson considered this rather bizarre and attempted some placatory comments about his other works, but Doyle swept this aside: 'Holmes, curse the fellow! I should never have resurrected him. In England one gets a label. If I were to write a dozen masterpieces I would still be known as "the author of Sherlock Holmes".'

Shortly after meeting Doyle, Pearson's employment came to an end. Since his unsuccessful attempt to organize a trade union among the clerks, his days had been numbered; even the patience of the manager, Mr Williams, who in the past had protected Pearson from dismissal, had worn thin. Now he begged Hesketh to find a more suitable line of work. Pearson nursed a vague ambition to visit China so he applied for a job with an Oriental chartered bank which maintained a London office. He was cordially received by the manager who began the interview by asking why he wished to join the bank. Pearson replied that he did not care for his present job. 'But are you interested in banking?' the manager persisted. 'Not in the least' came the reply. 'Then, Mr Pearson, I do not think that I shall require your services.'

If interest was required for a job Pearson could think of only one suitable line of work and, with considerable trepidation, he composed a letter to Beerbohm Tree begging to be allowed to join his acting troupe. However, before he could post it, something better than a job turned up, in the form of a thousand-pound inheritance from the timely death of an aunt. With the smell of foreign air in his nostrils, Pearson triumphantly presented Alfred Williams with a letter of resignation from the Royal Mail Steam Packet Company, but not before extracting free passage on a company cargo boat bound for Mexico.

CHAPTER THREE

Revelations

'Any influence which a book or a human being is supposed to have had on a man is nothing more than a disclosure of what is latent in the man himself.'
Hesketh Pearson

Pearson was twenty-one when he set sail for Mexico. Before accompanying him on his grand tour, it is worth examining two of the four 'revelations', Herbert Beerbohm Tree and Oscar Wilde, responsible for transforming an impulsive, headstrong youth into an impulsive, ebullient man of letters. The other two revelations – Shakespeare and Shaw – figure extensively in Pearson's later life.

Hesketh's parents had little apparent influence on him. His mother scarcely rates a mention in either of his two autobiographical volumes (*Thinking It Over* (1938) and *Hesketh Pearson by Himself* (1965)), while his father is treated as a lovable humbug, an object of gentle derision. If anything, formal schooling had a negative influence, rendering literature in general and Shakespeare in particular less passions to be courted than aversions to be shunned. So it may be said that it was Hesketh's serendipitous discovery of Wilde, Tree, Shaw and Shakespeare which started him on a writer's path. 'In my twentieth year I made up my mind that some day I would write about Wilde.' In the event, Pearson would write biographies of all of his revelations and those books illuminate author as well as subject.

Pearson came to know Tree and Shaw intimately. Under Tree's auspices, his stage career began and it was as an actor that he first met Shaw. The actual circumstances of these meetings will be recounted later; our immediate concern is to assess the character and personalities of two of the four men who formatively influenced Pearson.

Remarkable parallels exist between Tree and Pearson. Herbert Draper (the ancestral name Beerbohm was adopted; Tree was added in 1887, the year of Hesketh's birth, when his father told young Herbert that acting was a tree up which few aspirants successfully climbed) was the second son of Julius and Constantia Draper, born in 1852. Along with his two brothers, he was sent to a German school which he hated. The combination of enforced learning and hamfisted discipline produced in Tree an aversion to education similar to Pearson's. When Tree had children of his own, he would occasionally burst out during their lessons: 'Education is useless – I don't believe in it.' What young Herbert Draper believed in was acting. At about the same age as Pearson was writing the lives of great men in *The Lightning*, Tree was appearing in school dramatics. A boyhood chum of Tree's, T. Murray Ford, described him as 'a lanky youth acting with amateurs . . . reserved, almost sullen, but keen and deep in love with his art.' When, near the end of his life, Tree laid the foundation stone for the Royal Tunbridge Wells Theatre, he spoke a sentence no less applicable to Pearson's career as a biographer than to his own as an actor: 'The works of our maturity are often but the games of our childhood.'

Tree's first job was as a clerk in Threadneedle Street in a mercantile exchange of which his father was a member. He spent eight miserable years there, chained to an exchange desk. When Pearson came to write Tree's biography, he sought out and interviewed clerks who had worked with him and their description could, without change of a word, be applied four decades later to a similarly restless clerk at the Royal Mail Steam Packet Company. 'Though fond of his father and anxious to please, [Tree] could not take the smallest interest in bills of lading, the price of corn, the shipment of cargoes, or the value of money. Given letters to post, he would sometimes put them into the letter box of a neighbouring office. Told to pay cheques into the bank, he would forget all about them as he walked the streets reciting a part or a poem, and find them in his pocket when he went to bed. To the end of his days he could not master elementary arithmetic, stating his opinion that 'the vagaries of finance have ever been a puzzle to me, and I know it is only hypocrisy on the part of mankind to accept the theory of an obscure mathematician who said that two and two make four".'

Pearson saw Tree perform in dozens of acting roles, first at the Haymarket Theatre where Tree's success as an actor-manager quickly rivalled that of Henry Irving at the Lyceum, and then as a bit actor in Tree's own company at His Majesty's. Pearson considered Tree's acting 'inspired but erratic'. His success came from an ability to adapt his individuality to the characters he was playing, relying on a gift for mimicry and intuitive cleverness to duplicate a person's mannerisms. To young actors, including Pearson, Tree's advice was: 'Project your being into the part you are playing, so that you unconsciously become the man without study.'

Tree lacked the emotional depth and grandeur to play classic tragedy. His most notable successes were in fantasy and comedy, particularly in parts that were sinister, macabre or extravagant – such as Svengali in

Trilby of which W. S. Gilbert wrote: 'We could smell him in the stalls'; as Fagin in *Oliver Twist*, and Falstaff in *The Merry Wives of Windsor*. He passed up a chance to play Captain Hook in J. M. Barrie's *Peter Pan*, a role Pearson considered ideally suited to his style. When Hesketh asked him why, Tree replied: 'God knows, and I have promised to tell no one else.' In deeper Shakespearian waters, requiring a grander sweep, Tree sometimes floundered; as Mark Antony in *Julius Caesar*, Shylock in *The Merchant of Venice*, and in *Richard II* which Tree staged complete with real horses whose behaviour occasionally proved to be unpredictable. In tragic roles Tree's acting was unfavourably compared to Henry Irving's. W. S. Gilbert once proposed that the Shakespeare-Bacon controversy be settled once and for all by opening both men's graves, having Tree play Hamlet, and observing carefully to see which one turned.

It would be tendentious to push comparisons between Tree's acting and Pearson's writing too far, and yet there are similarities. Pearson tended to climb into his subjects' skins, to see life and the world through his subjects' eyes, and to project his own attitudes and values on one no longer alive to object. He was particularly adept at drawing a portrait that depended on wit, gesture and nuance, but he too sometimes missed the tragic dimensions of a subject's character.

Pearson's attitude on first meeting Tree was one of reverential awe. By the time he came to write Tree's biography (published in 1956) the grosser elements of hero-worship had been purged. It was Tree's Puck-like character, his obvious delight in observing the effect his impudence had on others, which most appealed to Pearson. 'Tree's personality was all-dominant whenever he chose to exercise it. It was just as fantastical off the stage as on it, and just as wilful. The best part he ever played was Herbert Beerbohm Tree in the play of that name . . . he was a perpetual caricature of himself.'

One of Pearson's biographical duties was to sift the truth from the mountain of anecdotes, many apocryphal, which had gathered around Tree's name. Pearson resolved to use only incidents which he himself had witnessed, or for which there was other first-hand evidence. Even so, Tree's whimsicality shines through Pearson's portrait. Two incidents will demonstrate this. Once, while dining in the Carlton Restaurant, Tree called the waiter over to him and motioning toward a solitary diner he asked the waiter to convey Mr Tree's compliments and to ask Mr Henry Arthur Jones, the playwright, to join him. The lonely gentleman may have felt flattered, but advised the waiter that he was not Henry Arthur Jones. So informed, Tree said: 'Very funny, very funny indeed; he always did like his little jokes. But this is important. Please tell Mr Jones that I should feel most grateful if he would behave seriously for once. I am very anxious to speak with him.' The waiter again made his way to the putative Mr Jones who insisted, somewhat vehemently, that he had never heard of Henry Arthur Jones and that his own name was Wagstaff. On hearing this, Tree dismissed the waiter with a laugh and a gesture which implied that Jones was incorrigible. Mr Wagstaff finished his meal and, on the way out, confronted Tree: 'I don't see why you should insist on knowing me. Surely it was enough to point out your mistake once?' Tree feigned astonishment. 'Do you mean to tell me quite seriously that you are not my old friend Henry Arthur Jones?' 'I do, sir,' bellowed the other. 'Then you were quite right to deny it.' With this mild retort Tree resumed eating. Not the least amused spectator was Tree's dinner companion, Henry Arthur Jones.

On another occasion, while performing in Cardiff, Tree entered the local post office. After pondering his mission for some moments, he approached the counter and said to the clerk: 'I hear you sell stamps?' 'We do.' 'May I see some?' 'You may.' Tree stood carefully surveying a large sheet, then finally pointed to a stamp in the centre of the sheet and said: 'I'll take that one.' Tree was also notorious for thus addressing booking clerks at railway stations: 'Give me some tickets, please.' 'What stations do you want?' 'Well, what stations have you got?'

Often exasperating, occasionally infuriating, Tree was always interesting. Louis Parker said of him that he was 'the most lovable man I ever met – the most aggravating too'. To those who accused Tree of being a charlatan, Pearson wrote: 'All men are charlatans more or less, for they pretend to resemble the pictures they have formed of themselves or that other people have imposed upon them. The charlatanry of actors is more obvious solely on account of their profession, which is one of pretence.'

Malcolm Muggeridge, an intimate friend of Pearson's later years, observed a certain theatricality about Pearson. 'He could be a terrific fantasist and poseur.' For this trait, Tree was obviously the model, the iconoclastic actor transmuted into the irascible author. Pearson himself said of Tree that there was too much 'self-will, amounting in some instances to sheer perversity' in his make-up. Revealing words from one who was shortly to ruin his own stage career with a book, *Modern Men and Mummers*, and to follow that by nearly committing suicide as an author with another book which fraudulently purported to be the memoirs of a senior British diplomat (*The Whispering Gallery*) – an escapade that began in whimsy and ended in criminal prosecution.

Although there was forty years' age difference, Pearson and Tree had similar temperaments. Both were happy-go-lucky, by nature optimistic and ebullient, each enjoyed good sense and good nonsense. Both admired wit and loved to laugh; each possessed a sense of humour which originated in a recognition of the immense disparity between human aspiration and human achievement. The heartiest and most fulfilling laughter is touched off not by contrived jokes but by that momentary revelation of the intrinsic absurdity of human beings. 'The silliest and most insignificant episode can remove the blinkers,' Pearson wrote, 'disclose the panorama of life's folly and release the spring of laughter.' Tree and Pearson laughed no less heartily when the joke was against themselves. Tree 'cried easily and unashamedly' and 'laughed with abandonment', wrote Pearson. Both men loved stimulating company, good food and drink. Of the bottle, Tree remarked: 'It is better to drink a little too much than much too little.' Pearson witnessed many incidents of Tree's kindness and generosity to actors in what Tree called 'an advanced state of alcoholic decomposition'. When one such besotted thespian stole the box office receipts, Tree considered that he had to prosecute because others in the company knew of the theft. Privately, however, he arranged for the villain's escape and for his future financial support, wryly chuckling to Pearson over the fact that he was simultaneously paying detectives engaged in a search for the culprit. When others remonstrated that drunken actors were not conducive to box office prosperity and should be sacked, Tree's only reply was: 'If you drink too much wine you get drunk, but if you drink too much water you get drowned.'

Tree and Pearson were alike also in that neither man took himself seriously. 'It is part of my religion to endeavour not to be earnest,' Tree told him. Both men were content to play the fool and to derive amusement from their own performance. Once Pearson was walking with Tree when a man carrying an enormous grandfather clock staggered towards them. 'My dear fellow,' Tree trilled in his best falsetto, 'why not carry a watch?' Yet both men's geniality could give way almost instantly to violent, unpredictable rages. The storm would soon pass but it thundered in the heat. Pearson wrote that, in his rages, Tree was 'often inconsiderate and sometimes cruel to others'. Pearson was similarly notorious for a flashpoint temper, suddenly triggered by a seemingly innocuous incident or comment, raging violently, and then expiring as suddenly as it began. He called these rages 'red fizzes' and described the process as seeing 'red shutters going up and down before my eyes' and feeling 'something inside me about to burst'. Suddenly he would lash out 'by saying outrageous things in a virulent manner'. Half an hour later he would 'wonder why other people remembered what I said to them in a fury when I had not the faintest recollection of it'. Pearson considered temper as part of the hereditary baggage one was stuck with, although his own seems to have got worse after he received a head wound in the first world war. In the last decade of his life, Pearson told Michael Helnoyd that his 'red fizzes' had suddenly ceased. Recalling Pearson's temper, Malcolm Muggeridge wrote: 'Despite occasional explosions of rage, he had a singularly sweet disposition, incapable of nursing a grievance or harbouring resentment against a friend, and benevolently disposed towards animals and men, in that order.'

In 1882 Tree married Maud Holt, an aspiring actress of high ambition but lesser talent. From then on Tree had to survive not only the wear and tear which any marriage puts upon a sanguine temperament, but also Maud's importunate demands for leading roles in his productions. Such demands Tree countered as best he could, sometimes by ensuring his wife's unsuitability through pregnancy, sometimes by making off on European or American tours. Still, the marriage survived until Tree's death in 1917.

There are again striking parallels in Pearson's life. He, too, married an actress, Gladys Gardner (although she was already pregnant), and, despite some basic incompatibilities and considerable friction, they stayed together until her death in 1951. There can be little doubt that Pearson had his own marriage no less than Tree's in mind when he wrote this description. 'Like so many marriages, theirs was to consist of quarrels, reconciliations, infidelity, fidelity, tenderness, coldness, sympathy, hostility, the change of moods, the differing of outlooks, the inevitable clash of opposing wills. But through all their ups and downs she continued to love him and he never ceased to love her, if not exactly on the lines of the Church marriage-service.'

Of all the characters Tree had met in a long, eventful stage career he admired none more than Oscar Wilde. Not only were the two men friends, but Tree appeared as Lord Illingworth in the first performance of *A Woman of No Importance*. On opening night, Wilde made his way to Tree's dressing room and announced: 'I shall always regard you as the best critic of my plays.' 'But I have never criticized your plays,' replied Tree reproachfully. 'That's why,' said Wilde. Since Pearson had already decided to write about Wilde, he seized every opportunity to pump Tree for reminiscences.

Sir William Wilde, Oscar's father, was a gifted man. He was a renowned ear surgeon, consulted by Royalty from several continents, and author of the leading textbook on aural surgery. He was also short, ugly and slovenly in appearance and personal hygiene. 'Why are Sir

William Wilde's fingernails black?' ran a popular Dublin riddle; 'because he scratches himself' was the answer. Despite his appearance, he had an inexplicable fascination for women with whom he did his best to increase the population of Ireland. He had more bastard children than legitimate heirs.

In 1851 William Wilde married Jane Elgee, the fiery poetess of the Young Ireland Movement, later to become Sinn Fein. She had narrowly escaped prosecution for treason. From this improbable union sprang Oscar Fingall O'Flahertie Wills Wilde, a second son born in 1854. As Tree was adding to his names, Oscar was discarding his, like excess ballast, as he sailed through manhood. His mother had desperately hoped for a daughter (a hope fulfilled three years after Oscar's birth). Oscar was deputed to play the part and was dressed in frocks, fussed over, spoiled, petted and exhibited. In his biography Pearson doubted that his 'early frocks' were the sole explanation of Wilde's 'later fancies', but he did allow that such an effeminate up bringing could have had some effect on Wilde's sexual inversion.

Pearson portrayed Wilde as a lovable, fun-loving adolescent who never grew up, the witty bon-vivant who never graduated, a Peter Pan figure. In Wilde, Pearson wrote, 'an immature emotional half' combined with an 'intellectual half well developed at an age when those about him had hardly begun to think for themselves'. These separate, and often warring, halves produced an unmalicious self-dramatist, a man of spontaneous wit, essentially frivolous, who eschewed conformity and indulged eccentricity. Wilde's excesses often produced charges of insincerity which he answered by saying: 'What people call insincerity is simply a method by which we can multiply our personalities.'

Of Wilde's multiple personalities none became so rooted in the public mind as Reginald Bunthorne, the aesthete in Gilbert and Sullivan's *Patience* who walks down Piccadilly in knee-breeches carrying a lily in his medieval hand. When Wilde lectured in America, students at Harvard and Yale showed up dressed in the Bunthorne manner and marched down the centre aisle carrying sunflowers and lilacs. This spectacle Wilde observed in silence; then he began his lecture (on the English Renaissance) by saying: 'I am impelled for the first time to breathe a fervent prayer: God save me from my disciples.'

Pearson's biography deliberately plays down the Bunthorne–Wilde caricature. He mentions, but does not dwell on, the effete costumes, languid posturing, and the ravenous ego. He has chapters on Wilde as dramatist, artist, wit, talker and critic; none on the aesthete, poseur or homosexual. He took every opportunity to note Wilde's physical strength, his courage and fistic prowess, his demonstrated ability to drink a bunch of American cowboys under the table, and on one occasion in New York his willingness to spend a night going the rounds of brothels. All of this Pearson cites as a vindication of Wilde's essential masculinity, an important attribute for a heterosexual biographer who apparently had to admire every facet of his subject. This wears a bit thin when Pearson must confront Wilde's proven pederasty, his trial and final exile. Even here Pearson manages to leave the impression that all this was a tempest in a teapot, a temporary lapse, rather like a vicar whose previously unblemished life is ruined when it is disclosed that he once took a newspaper without leaving money in the box. In a classic example of pot calling kettle black, Pearson indicted Robert Sherard, one of Wilde's earlier biographers, as 'a born hero-worshipper'; Sherard's 'rose-coloured glasses', Pearson charged, meant that 'his loyalty to his heroes [was] so extreme that he could not or would not see them with a naked eye'. Yet one could read all but about a dozen of Pearson's four hundred pages without realizing that Wilde was a notorious, practising homosexual.

Hugh Kingsmill anticipated this flaw; he told Pearson that he must hold out against his natural inclination to deal with Wilde's exile along these lines: 'In 1897, after serving a sentence for bigamy, or some other trivial offence, Oscar Wilde made for France again, a despicable country except for its wine, which Oscar had always enjoyed. He was accompanied by two or three women, an old soldier who acted as his valet, and the old soldier's wife, who acted as lady's maid and accoucheuse to the women.' After Kingsmill had read the book in manuscript he added this cutting note: 'I don't mind being brought to Wilde, by Hesketh or anyone else, provided I may treat Wilde like royalty, and retire from his presence backwards.'

When Pearson considered writing on Wilde he sought George Bernard Shaw's advice. Shaw's reply was succinct: 'Don't.' Shaw considered that too much had already been written about Wilde's homosexuality and that the subject was stale. It was typical of Pearson to seek advice and, having received it, to ignore it. His reply to Shaw makes it clear that even before he began he had decided to play down Wilde's (in those days) perversion. 'My intention [is] to take him out of the fog of pathology into the light of comedy, to restore the true perspective of his career, to revive the conversationalist not the convict.' In this Pearson succeeded but not without some biographical licence.

All four of Pearson's revelations are larger than life characters, but none more so than Wilde. Wilde's effect on Hesketh was to give him dutch courage, to enable him to be himself. If Wilde could be so contrivedly different, so stagily shocking, then Pearson could defy a not very domineering father. If Wilde could scorn bourgeois morality, then Pearson could reject a conventional business career and follow his own interests, acting and writing. If Wilde could spit in the public eye, then Pearson could snub conventional opinion and live according to his lights. Pearson acknowledged this influence. '[Wilde] symbolized the spirit of youth's revolt against age, of frivolity against decorum, of irreverence against acceptance, of anarchy against institutionalism, of the individual against society, of beauty against ugliness, of art against commerce, of freedom against convention. In speaking for the rebellious spirits of his own age, he spoke for those of all ages, which explains his appeal to the intelligent youth of every generation.'

Wilde also influenced, fortunately only temporarily, Pearson's writing style. Normally Pearson wrote clearly and charmingly, lucid, unassuming, readable prose. But, in both the Tree and Wilde biographies, the reader notices an occasional dandyism, a striving for cuteness, and attempts to emulate Wilde's epigrams. Here are some examples, some quite good, but not in Pearson's authentic voice. 'Absence makes the heart go wander.' 'A snob who would cut his own children if they weren't in his set.' 'It is easy enough to pick up honours if one cares to stoop low enough.' 'The sort of present one is always trying to get rid of.'

During Wilde's American lecture tour in 1882 he was taken to see Niagara Falls. This seems to have been an obligatory pilgrimage for Pearson's heroes. Herbert Beerbohm Tree was to visit Niagara Falls a decade or so after Wilde, and Pearson a decade after Tree. Wilde was not impressed. He described the spectacle as 'a vast unnecessary amount of water going the wrong way and then falling over unnecessary rocks'. 'But at least you will admit that they are wonderful waterfalls?' asked a companion. 'The wonder would be if the water did not fall,' Wilde replied.

In 1883 Wilde became engaged to Constance Lloyd, the only child of a successful Irish barrister. Later it was commonly suggested that Wilde married her for her money, but Pearson effectively scotched that insinuation by the simple expedient of demonstrating how little she had. Wilde himself probably originated the rumour about marrying for money when he described how his wife's grandfather 'lying on what threatened to be his death bed, had no sooner joined our hands and given us his blessing than, for the very joy of the occasion, he suddenly blossomed out into new health and vigour'. Pearson preferred the simpler explanation that Oscar loved Constance, genuinely if evanescently, and she, sincerely and permanently, loved him. Two sons followed their marriage in 1884, but Oscar was already chafing at the chains. Several of his cleverest epigrams at this period are directed against marriage. 'The proper basis for marriage is a mutual misunderstanding.' 'In married life three is company and two is none.' 'One should always be in love. That is the reason one should never marry.' 'Faithfulness is to the emotional life what consistency is to the life of the intellect – simply a confession of failure.'

Although Oscar tried for a time to accommodate his wife, she was too provincial and dull for him. When Constance wanted to entertain, Oscar's conversational brilliance could be counted on to attract the guests of her choice to their dining room at 34 Tite Street. Constance had become a zealous Church worker, with a particular zeal for improving the lot of missionaries. Once when she introduced the topic at a dinner party, Oscar taunted her: 'Missionaries, my dear! Don't you realize that missionaries are the divinely provided food for destitute and underfed cannibals? Whenever they are on the brink of starvation, heaven, in its infinite mercy, sends them a nice plump missionary.'

Not surprisingly, Oscar soon began taking extended leaves of absence from the marital hearth, proffering explanations which grew increasingly far-fetched. 'When one is in love, one always begins by deceiving oneself, and one always ends by deceiving others,' he wrote. Pearson considered Wilde's oddest explanation to be that he had taken up golf; for Kingsmill and Muggeridge, Pearson used to recreate the scene as Oscar told Constance of his pressing need for exercise; he would then do an impression of Oscar, sartorially immaculate with a lily in his buttonhole, huffing and puffing his way to the Café Royal beneath a load of golf clubs.

Short of cash, in 1886 Wilde became editor of *The Woman's World*, a magazine given over to cookery, advice to the lovelorn, corsets and shorthand to servants. The picture of Oscar Wilde, failing husband, planting his sodomite bottom on the editor's chair of *The Woman's World* is as rich as the picture of Frank Harris, a decade or so later and at the height of his philandering prowess, occupying the editor's chair at *Hearth and Home*. Wilde's financial troubles ended when he wrote *Lady Windermere's Fan*, his first stage play and a dazzling success. From the first run alone, Wilde's royalties exceeded £7,000. He followed this with another stage hit, *A Woman of No Importance*. When *An Ideal Husband* opened at the Theatre Royal on January 3, 1895, the Prince of Wales was in attendance. Wilde's plays were now the toast of London and it was not uncommon for him simultaneously to have the two biggest box office draws. By the time of his crowning success, *The Importance of Being Earnest*, Wilde had become wealthy, vain and bored. Intoxicated with himself, he now prattled and preened where formerly he had listened and talked. The seemingly inexhaustible well of amusing epigrams, the flashing wit and spontaneity, dried up; what was left was a narcissistic pederast, an obese caricature of what he had once been. Wilde's own description of his fall, written from Reading Gaol, is instructive: 'I let myself be lured into long spells of senseless and sensual ease. I amused myself with being a *flâneur*, a dandy, a man of fashion. I surrounded myself with smaller natures, and meaner minds . . . tired of being on the heights, I deliberately went to the depths in search of new sensations.'

Beerbohm Tree was to play a bit part in Wilde's downfall and ruin. Sometime in the mid-nineties Wilde took as a lover, Alfred Douglas, the eldest son of a combative, pompous and exceedingly nasty man known as the Ninth Marquess of Queensberry. To 'Bosie' as Douglas was called by family and intimates, Oscar penned what he vainly called 'prose poems' although they were decidedly prose not poetry and the prose was execrable; for example '. . . it is a marvel that those red rose-leaf lips of yours should be made no less for the madness of music and song than for the madness of kissing . . . your slim gilt soul walks between passion and poetry . . .' etc. A packet of these letters was stolen from Douglas's coat and found its way into the hands of blackmailers who first sent an original copy of the letter quoted above to Herbert Beerbohm Tree, then rehearsing Wilde's *A Woman of No Importance*. Tree was told that the originals would be published if money was not paid. He passed the letter to Wilde with the characteristically offhand remark that perhaps the sentiments expressed might be open to misconstruction. Wilde paid the blackmailers thirty pounds for the incriminating letters but they double-crossed him. Unknown to Wilde copies of these and other letters eventually fell into Queensberry's vindictive hands, thereby, as Pearson put it, 'sending up his blood pressure without quickening his sense of poetry'. After unsuccessful attempts to goad Wilde, on February 18, 1895 Queensberry turned up at the Albemarle Club, produced a visiting card erratically inscribed 'To Oscar Wilde posing as a somdomite', handed it to a porter with instructions to deliver it to Wilde, and departed. Why Wilde did not merely tear it up, treating its author with the contempt he deserved, will never be known. Instead he consulted a barrister and commenced a libel prosecution.

On the best facts, a libel action is a dangerous undertaking, inevitably drawing public attention to the very allegations which the plaintiff resents and wishes to suppress; when the alleged libel is true, and justification is pleaded as a defence, it requires unimaginable folly to carry on. This is what Wilde did. Towards the abyss he floated, 'blowing bubbles of enjoyment', and actually relishing the approaching confrontation with Edward Carson, counsel for the defence, who had been with him at Oxford.

In his biography, Pearson described Wilde's performance in the witness box as 'triumphant, having scored off Carson in every move of the game'. This is arrant nonsense, ignoring the fact that this was a court not a drawing room, that Carson was not an actor trying to amuse an audience, but a barrister relentlessly shredding Wilde's case with consummate professionalism. When Carson finished cross-examining Wilde the case was irrevocably lost and Wilde had been exposed for the courtroom poseur (if not yet perjurer – that would come later) that he was. To call that 'triumphant' and to imagine that an English jury, whose sensibilities may be presumed to be less exquisitely acute than Wilde's, would actually be amused by Wilde's performance, reveals how Pearson's romanticism and his intense partiality for his subject could undermine biographical accuracy and the sturdy common sense he usually exhibited.

On the third day of the trial, Sir Edward Clarke, Wilde's counsel, conceded that the libel could not be proved. Later that same day Wilde was arrested in Bosie's rooms at the Cadogan Hotel in Sloane Street. He was refused bail. Unable to raise money he saw his possessions seized and sold for a song to satisfy creditors. His Tite Street house was broken into, his desk rifled, and manuscripts were stolen. His publishers withdrew his books from circulation. His children were removed from school, presumably because their presence might contaminate the other boys. For a period of time *The Importance of Being Earnest* became a play of immaculate conception; Wilde's name was removed from the placards outside the St James's Theatre and on the programme slips of paper were pasted over the author's name. Booksellers took his books from their shelves. Acquaintances burned his correspondence and pleaded for their own letters back. Fairweather friends (like Alfred Douglas and Reginald Turner) hightailed it for France. All of this occurred before trial when, according to England's proudest creation, the common law, Wilde was presumptively innocent. Pearson wrote: 'There is but one step from popular success to popular obloquy. The moment a man who has been petted and spoiled trips over the law and falls from favour, he receives no mercy. Those who once praised him feel that he has betrayed them, and hurt vanity more than anything else makes them kick him when he is down.'

Wilde's trial on charges of gross indecency opened at the Old Bailey on April 26, 1895. The first jury was unable to agree and a second jury was empanelled. For several specious reasons Pearson maintained that

the trial was unfair. His biography belabours the fact that the prosecution witnesses were mostly male prostitutes, blackmailers and swindlers; yet, given the charge, Pearson could hardly expect the witnesses to
be chartered accountants and churchwardens. Pearson also wrote that
the trial judge summed up unfairly to the defence, an assertion refuted
by more objective commentators like H. Montgomery Hyde (himself a
lawyer). Pearson's description of the trial is inaccurate and unconvinc-
ing, a determined effort to portray the accused as 'a wounded lion being
worried by a pack of mongrel terriers'. It is a fair question whether
consenting homosexual acts between adults should have been subject to
criminal prosecution; but, given the law as it was, Wilde's trial was fair
and he was unquestionably guilty of the charge, as the jury concluded
on May 25, 1895 after only two hours' deliberation. Wilde was
sentenced to two years hard labour.

After Wandsworth Prison and Reading Gaol, he was released in 1897
and went into exile. Penniless, cut off from familiar haunts and
associates, he wandered from hotel to hotel in France, registering under
the name Sebastian Melmoth and usually being unceremoniously
evicted as soon as the hotelier learned his true identity. Men who had
known of his sexual proclivities in the days when his star was rising, and
had prided themselves on his friendship, now cut him, avoided him, or
disowned him. One honourable exception was Herbert Beerbohm
Tree. With characteristic generosity, Tree stood by his friend and sent
him money with a letter which said: 'No one did such distinguished
work as you; I do most sincerely hope . . . that your splendid talents
may shine forth again.'

Wilde informed anyone who inquired that he would begin writing the
next day, but he told Laurence Housman that 'in my heart – that
chamber of dead echoes – I know that I never shall'. Misfortunes and
humiliations Wilde bore with a stoical nature, never indulging in
recrimination, never lashing back. In exile and disgrace, he tried to
continue the role of aesthete and raconteur. Perhaps it was this innate
love of showing off, however improbable the circumstances, which so
attracted Pearson. From boyhood, Pearson loved actors and acting; in
Tree, and even more so in Wilde, he saw his own inclinations and
passions magnified. In none of his other biographies does Pearson so
closely identify with his subject, so abandon his objectivity, as with
Tree and Wilde.

Shortly before Wilde died, Laurence Housman recorded some conversations with him in Paris. Perhaps the most important lesson
Pearson learned from Wilde's life (one apposite when he, like Wilde,
stood in the dock charged with criminal misconduct) was conveyed in

this comment of Wilde's to Housman: 'The artist must live the complete life, must accept it as it comes and stands like an angel before him, with its drawn and two-edged sword. Great success, great failure – only so shall the artist see himself as he is, and through himself see others.'

Drinking excessively, idle and liverish, Wilde passed his days. In October 1900 Reginald Turner visited him. 'I have had a dreadful dream,' Wilde told him, 'I dreamt that I was dining with the dead.' Turner replied: 'My dear Oscar, I am sure you were the life and soul of the party.' In fact, Wilde was dying of cerebral meningitis, perhaps complicated by syphilis. On November 28, when he lay almost comatose, a priest was summoned to administer Holy Baptism and Extreme Unction. Wilde was unable to speak and, when the questions were put, he could only make gestures of affirmation with a hand. Two days later he was dead.

In the twentieth century which he did not live to see, Wilde's plays have obtained a popularity exceeded only by those of Pearson's other two revelations, Shakespeare and Shaw. Wilde would have been affronted by the greater success of Shaw and amused by the comparison with Shakespeare. He was fond of maintaining that his own plays consisted solely of style because Shakespeare had stolen all the subjects. 'Originality is no longer possible – even in sin.'

CHAPTER FOUR

Vagabond

'I drink to vagabondage, the only bondage of the free'
Herbert Beerbohm Tree

In the spring of 1908, Pearson took leave of his family, talking quite convincingly of finding suitable, secure employment in the New World. This story was given a shred of plausibility by the fact that his company friend, Standage, had recently gone to Mexico City and found work. However it is likely that Pearson's destination owed more to a book, Prescott's *History of the Conquest of Mexico*, which had impressed him than to the dubious enticement of employment.

Pearson sailed on a cargo steamer which made stops at Bilbao, Santander, Coruña, Vigo, Las Palmas, Tenerife and Havana, before finally docking at Vera Cruz. Almost immediately he had a foretaste of the mixture of slapstick and terror which was to be his lot in Mexico. Pearson had travelled with a knapsack containing a few clothes and those books he considered indispensable; a one-volume Shakespeare, Shaw's *Plays for Puritans*, Boswell's *Life of Johnson*, Wilde's *The Soul of Man Under Socialism*, Dickens's *A Tale of Two Cities*, and Thackeray's *Vanity Fair*. He also carried with him a bulky, portable gramophone with an old-fashioned horn which customs officials mistook for a new-fangled weapon. No amount of pleading could convince them of its innocent purpose; oblivious to all Pearson's offers to demonstrate how it worked, the gramophone was impounded. For twenty-four hours he was kept hanging about the customs office in Vera Cruz, free to leave but reluctant to abandon his gramophone. Then, without explanation, the customs officials levied a 'fantastic sum' as duty and ordered its immediate removal. Pearson observed that the guards 'vanished from the scene of action during this process'.

From Vera Cruz Pearson travelled by train to Mexico City noting the differing scenery and vegetation that accompanied three distinct changes of climate, tropical, sub-tropical, and temperate, all passed through within a twelve-hour period. As the train chugged up mountains, it moved so slowly that he could get off, stroll around, and then catch up his carriage on foot. 'I remember one place, at the foot of an enormous chasm, we saw what looked like a toy village almost lost on a plain that stretched to the horizon but what was really a large town through which we had passed some hours before.'

On arrival in Mexico City he discovered that Standage had moved out to the village of Orizaba about thirty miles away. Pearson spent a fortnight 'lazing and gazing' in the city, during which time there were two small earthquakes which 'more thrilled than terrified me' reminding him of the rocking motion of a ship at sea. The second tremor occurred while he was asleep and propelled the bed across the room. 'I waited eagerly for the return journey, which however it refused to accomplish.'

Near Orizaba, Pearson found Standage living in a cottage next to a newly-built American factory, an oasis of industry cut out of the surrounding jungle. For some reason that Pearson never discovered, a Spaniard living in an adjacent hut had taken a dislike to Standage which he exhibited by taking potshots at his cottage. As he and Standage shared a tin of meat for supper the first night, without warning – phut!, a piece of window frame whizzed past Pearson's ear. Standage immediately doused the candle and took cover. 'Aren't we a bit overexposed here?' Pearson inquired. 'Doesn't matter where we are,' Standage replied, 'he can't hit a haystack in a passage. You're safe as long as he *tries* to hit you. I only feel uneasy when he's potting at something else.'

After three more shots Pearson announced that it was time 'to pay the dago a visit'. In the dark he crept out of the back door and, by a circuitous route, gradually approached the other's hut. From a clearing in the woods, he caught a glimpse of a man in short sleeves, leaning out of an opening that had once been a window, cradling a long-barrelled rifle in his arms, and grunting like a pig. It took Pearson twenty minutes more to creep from the clearing to the back door of the hut, exactly behind the window opening through which the shots were being fired. 'Taking a revolver from my hip pocket, I stepped into the centre of the doorway, braced myself, covered my antagonist, and let out a yell that would have awakened the entire settlement if its inhabitants had been sober and asleep. The dago dropped his gun through the window, spun around and flung his arms skywards simultaneously. With a coolness that surprises me when I look back upon it, I then solemnly fired four shots to right and left of him. The amazement on his face during this operation was wonderful to see. He simply didn't know what to make of it and just gaped. He was standing in exactly the same position, stupefied, when I strolled around to the front of the hut. Here I picked up his rifle, levelled it at his back, and let out another yell. Again he shot around to face me, and this time I really thought he was going to have a fit. His features worked convulsively and his colour changed to a sickly white. I felt I had done enough for one evening, so I marched straight back to our shack, his rifle in my possession.' A few weeks later Pearson heard from Standage that the trouble had ceased.

While at Orizaba, Pearson made an attempt to climb the mountain from which the town took its name. Disdaining the services of a guide, he set out on a scorchingly hot morning, taking for provision only a sandwich, six bananas, and a bottle of wine. All day he climbed until, at dusk, he had reached the snowline. Realizing now that he could neither go higher nor return before dark, he settled in under a projecting rock, devoured his last banana, and berated his own impracticality. 'Sitting there in the dark, ten thousand feet up, I came to the conclusion that for sheer stupidity my latest exploit made the average certified lunatic look like a master of calm logic and common sense.' As the stars came out, the cold intensified. Unable to sleep for shivering, he alternated between smoking a pipe and declaiming *Hamlet* and *Macbeth*, both of which he knew by heart. Towards morning the cold made him vomit and, as it became light, he could see that he had brought up blood. At first light he began to scramble downwards and, heedless of the change in atmospheric pressure, his head began to swim and his nose to bleed. 'After a terrible descent, punctuated by periods when I lay flat on my back in spasms of vertigo, I got back to the hotel late in the afternoon, more dead than alive.'

For two days he recuperated in bed but Pearson's perils at Orizaba were not over yet. Four or five days after his mountain adventure, he set out on foot to explore the densely-treed district north of the village. After a mile of heavy going he came to a clearing in the trees and, walking easily now, his attention wandered. Drifting along, listening to the pleasantly buzzing hum of insect life, he lost all track of time and direction. He came suddenly to his senses in a dark tunnel of trees. 'A pathway stretched behind and ahead of me, losing itself in a gloom of green. On either side of it was thick bush. The foliage met above my head, but looking down the tunnel I could see occasional shafts of light where the covering parted and let in the sun.' He tried to retrace his steps. In whatever direction he pursued the light at the end of the arboreal tunnel, it seemed only to recede. The path forked. He had no idea which fork he had come on. He pressed on 'conscious of the dank, sickly reek of sunless vegetation' which pressed down and in upon him.

What happened next Pearson described twenty years later in a *New English Review* article which Hugh Kingsmill praised as 'a perfect reflection in the physical world of a spiritual experience'. Its allegorical significance, Kingsmill maintained, was of 'young Mr Love-Life' straying from a path in a pleasant wood and suddenly overcome by spiritual despair ('Where was the sun?') when he realized the essential isolation of each human soul. The passage is not only one of Pearson's finest pieces of descriptive writing but also, as with his boyhood experience on the Ouse River, mystical:

I could feel my heart thumping with the exertion. Would this tunnel never end? It was like a maze. Perhaps I was going round in circles? At the thought I came to a standstill. Suppose I was just going round and round. Surely there must be some way out. How did I get into it? Where was the sun? I looked up at the green roof above me, but no ray came through it. Where I stood was twilight; but it was brighter farther on. I pressed on to the light but it seemed to recede. Always it was twilight where I stood and brighter farther on. I stopped again. And this time I strained my ears for the sound of anything human that might direct me. I listened and listened, but no sound penetrated the everlasting hum, the shrill song of the insect world.

With an appalling suddenness I was seized with a feeling of utter isolation. It came upon me while I was listening breathlessly for a human voice, for the bark of a dog, for the sound of anything that could break through the all-enveloping tic-tic-zz-zz of insect life that wrapped me about and drummed and buzzed in my ears. It was not merely a feeling of solitude, of which I am fond. It was as if I were cut off from all human relationship, from the life of my kin and my kind; as if I were surrounded by a blank wall of impenetrable darkness and invisible horror.

For a while I fought against this feeling with all my might. I started off again down the path, but I could not shake it off. I hurried, I ran, but it grew upon me. Again I stood still, telling myself aloud that the feeling was idiotic and meaningless and if I wanted to escape from this maze I must use my intelligence, not give rein to my imagination. And while I stood there, fighting down my fear, I became aware of a sound, scarcely audible at first, unmistakable at last. It was the sound of something or someone moving in the bush to my right. I faced around and held my breath, staring into the thick growth a few feet from where I stood. The sound was intermittent. It ceased-continued-ceased again-went on again. Was it a man or an animal? A footstep, possibly, but a dragging, uncertain footstep? A rustle of leaves, a snapping of branches, a dull thud as if someone or something was falling, then silence – and for me suspense.

My heart was beating unevenly, now loudly, now imperceptibly; there was a kind of prickling about the top of my head; and I noticed that my throat was dry. I tried to call out something in Spanish, but no sound came. I held myself in and tried again. A hollow croak issued from my lungs, which frightened me as much as the silence it broke. Up to now I had been controlling my breath, either stifling altogether or letting it go in sharp staccato bursts. Now I could control it no longer and I realized the terrible strain that had been put upon it by the hoarse, long-drawn, half-sobbing sighs with which it came and went.

How long I stood there choking and gasping I cannot say. The dread of the unknown was upon me and the limit of my endurance was almost reached. A crash in the undergrowth not twenty yards away shook me through and through and left me quivering. Sheer panic gripped me. I turned and ran, ran, ran, not knowing why, not knowing where, conscious only of some immense and elemental horror at my heels.

I was found the next morning by a *peon*, bruised, bloody, insensible, crumpled up at the foot of a tree that must have cut short my wild escape from my own imagination . . .

After this experience, Pearson immediately left Orizaba and went to Mexico City. Thanks to a confusion of names (with a prominent financier, Sir Weetman Pearson, then operating in Mexico), a confusion he did nothing to discourage, Hesketh secured an interview with the President of Mexico, Porfirio Diaz, at the castle of Chapultepec. Diaz was a swarthy man of medium height with a large strong body and short legs, a former bandit or, in contemporary jargon, a 'freedom fighter'. As soon as he seized power, Diaz installed himself as a dictator, albeit a relatively benign one. When Pearson met him, Diaz was nearly eighty but still vigorous and fit. He spoke abruptly and with little animation, making a few words go a long way. Pearson asked him about the Vera Cruz rebellion when, at Diaz's express instruction, nine men were summarily shot. To satisfy protocol, the party line was that nine prominent citizens had valiantly laid down their lives while defending the government against insurgents. However the party line frayed, and there was a public outcry and later a judicial inquiry, when the bodies were disinterred and it was discovered that the nine had been roped together and shot through the head. Pearson asked Diaz how he accounted for this? The President sat impassively for several moments and then said that the governor had told him that it was done by 'an absent-minded gravedigger'. Another long silence followed. Then the

President added, almost wistfully: 'Possible, but not probable . . .' Despite the awkward question, Diaz treated Pearson with 'the utmost courtesy and cordiality'.

At a villa a few miles from the capital, Pearson met a young, pretty Spanish girl who seemed amenable to his attentions. However, her Spanish suitor discovered them embracing and threatened to kill Pearson. When it became evident that he was serious, Hesketh returned to the capital and wrote asking the girl to join him. She replied that she dared not take the risk. Pearson decamped without further ado. 'My senses had been so much excited that the only thing I remember doing in Mexico City after receiving her letter was to walk into a brothel, where I was shown into a room in which a naked girl was washing herself. I turned around immediately and walked out. There were limits to the means of gratifying my senses.'

Pearson travelled to Vera Cruz and then, by boat, to New York City. After a 'stuffy fortnight' there, he moved on to Canada visiting Montreal and Toronto, then like his hero, Oscar Wilde, making a special trip to Niagara Falls. 'I was disappointed with Niagara Falls . . . I had expected to be deafened with the sound of falling water from the moment I got out at Niagara station, and was sadly disillusioned to find that one could hear people swallowing their soup at dinner in the hotel within a stone's throw of the Falls.' Herbert Beerbohm Tree had been similarly unimpressed when he visited Niagara Falls with Gilbert Parker, a member of his acting troupe. Parker made all the appropriate noises of awe and astonishment. Tree stood immobile. 'Well?' prompted Parker at last. 'Well,' muttered Tree, 'is that all?'

In Quebec Pearson stayed at the Château Frontenac, the most traditional and expensive hotel in the city, where he met a self-styled inventor who inveigled him into parting with one hundred pounds to complete an invention that would be of everlasting benefit to mankind. Always an easy mark for an improbable story, Pearson not only gave him a hundred pounds but also bought his ship's fare so that the inventor could accompany him back to England to market the device. Exactly what the invention was, Pearson could not recall. 'I have a vague notion that it had some connection with saddles or stirrups or spurs or bits, which, in view of the fact that motors were rapidly displacing horses, ought to have made me think twice before investing in a bad or decaying industry; but were I now to be told that I had sunk my money in a new kind of musical-box, I should not feel certain enough to deny it. If the world depended upon me for inventions, we would still be dressed in skins, living in wattle huts, and eating berries.'

Pearson and the inventor sailed from Quebec City to Liverpool. He described his feeling on docking in England as one of 'joy and relief . . . a poignant sense of coming home to my own people'. He would only leave England for an extended period twice more in his life. Never again would he doubt his essential Englishness. 'I am an Englishman through and through, insular, irascible, inhibited, iconoclastic, intelligent, ignorant and individualistic.' His first day back in London was foggy and wet yet, half a century later, Pearson remembered 'as if it were last week, how I walked down the Strand inhaling the fog with gusto and buying a number of quite unnecessary things for the pleasure of talking to the shopmen'. As for the inventor, Pearson advanced him several more loans from his now dwindling inheritance until, having no money left, 'he vanished from my life'.

With his money gone and neither a job nor any training for one, it was his brother Jack who came to Hesketh's rescue. Jack had used his inheritance to buy a car sales and hire business in Hove and he now planned to open a Brighton showroom. In a singular display of brotherly affection over business acumen, he asked Hesketh to manage the Brighton operation. 'Knowing nothing whatever of motor cars or their accessories', Hesketh accepted, and from 1908 to 1910 'I mismanaged that business for him, bringing it safely and surely through periods of accidental prosperity into liquidation'.

Hesketh always considered his two years in Brighton 'among the happiest of my life'. Although he refused to learn anything about motor cars, he enjoyed driving them fast down country lanes. He also loved the countryside, the walks along the cliffs, and inland over the Sussex weald dotted with tiny, picturesque villages. Always a prodigious walker, Pearson considered a twenty-mile hike as an afternoon's entertainment. On one occasion his passion for walking and his boastful nature produced painful consequences. It began when he was sitting in the bar of the Royal York Hotel as some men came in who had just completed the London to Brighton walk. Annoyed at their boastfulness and self-satisfaction, Pearson announced that any fool could walk that far with a bit of practice. His bluff was called by a man named Asher who bet him five pounds that he could not walk to London in under twelve hours. On condition that he be allowed two hours for refreshment on the road, Pearson took the bet and the pair agreed to set forth at midnight. On the stroke of twelve they started from the Royal York. Several walkers accompanied them along the Old Steyne but turned back after Preston Park. Pearson had never done more than thirty miles and that on grass, not road. 'I did not even bother to change my light shoes for heavy boots, and was idiotic enough to wolf two pounds of strawberries and a pint of cream shortly before starting. There is no need to enumerate my many agonies, which began with a terrifying stitch before I got to Crawley, where we knocked up someone at the George Inn and had a breakfast of eggs and bacon soon after 5.00 a.m.' Asher was a keen theatre-goer and the talk was at first of plays and players. However, by Reigate, conversation had subsided. 'I vaguely remember that Asher tried hard to find out who in my opinion was the best actor on the stage at that time, while my thoughts were solely concerned with the best shoemaker.

'Tree?' he asked.
'Perhaps.'
'Forbes-Robertson?'
'I dare say.'
'Lewis Waller?'
'M-yes.'
'Martin Harvey?'
'Possibly.'
'George Alexander?'
'Oh, shut up!'

By the time the two men reached Reigate the soles of Pearson's feet were raw and blistered. In Sutton they had a hasty lunch. 'The last part of the journey would have been sheer torture if I had not been so exhausted that my movements were automatic and the pain in my feet almost numbed. We reached Charing Cross just before two o'clock and I received five pounds.' Hesketh used the money to treat his companion to a matinée at the Adelphi Theatre; in the evening they attended Conan Doyle's play, *The Fires of Fate*, at the Lyric. 'I left London by the midnight train for Brighton, and passed the next two or three weeks supinely, with enough blisters on my feet to arouse the doctor's admiration.'

It was at about this time, while on a weekend visit to his parents in Bedford, that Pearson accidentally met again his sadistic school head-master, Blake. He had accompanied his mother to church and, follow-ing the service, she had stopped to talk to Blake. Hesketh did not acknowledge his presence. Finally Mrs Pearson said, 'Surely you remember Mr Blake?' Hesketh replied: 'I remember him so well that if I saw him drowning in the river I would throw stones at him from the bank.'

Under Hesketh's supervision the car business sputtered. Of elementary motor mechanics he knew nothing; even a tire puncture stumped him. Once he and his showroom manager, Robinson, were delivering a car from Brighton to Margate when the engine gave out near Canterbury. They left the car at a garage and went for lunch. When they returned the mechanic informed them that 'the big end was gone'. 'Who's taken it?' was Pearson's reply. Robinson had some difficulty convincing the mechanic that his partner was indeed in the motor business.

When sales were quiet, which was most of the time, Pearson and Robinson repaired to the Seahouse Hotel to play billiards, a game for which Pearson had inherited from his father 'an excellent eye, a steady hand, and sensitive fingers'. To his employees, Hesketh was an ideal manager; he never sacked anyone and his managerial style could best be described as *laissez-faire*. Jack felt constrained to point out to his brother that drunkenness during working hours was not conducive to efficiency and that if mechanics were allowed to come or go as they pleased it was difficult to meet repair schedules. 'I saw his point and passed it on, with apologies, to the men; but they had views of their own on the subject and did not let it affect their lives.'

Jack accepted all this with equanimity, asking only that Hesketh give the business a fighting chance by taking frequent, extended holidays. On one such holiday to Brussels, Hesketh met a girl '. . . not pretty but attractive . . . with lively hazel eyes and a quizzical expression'. He was reading the newspaper in the sitting room of a hotel on the Boulevard Anspach where she was staying with relatives; she told him that her name was Julie and that she was from Paris and asked if he went there. Hesketh replied that he would make a point of going there, whereupon she produced a card, wrote her address on it, and told him to let her know when he would come. A fortnight later, thanks to a small loan from Jack, 'in a frenzy of expectation', Hesketh set out for Paris. It was autumn 1908. He was twenty-one and a virgin. 'A fortnight in Paris at the age of twenty-one in the company of a vivacious girl, much of it spent in learning how to make love, is "paradise enough". She told me that no Englisman understood the sexual side of love unless taught by a French woman, and I think she was right . . . We parted with protestations of undying devotion and an oath on my part that I would be back in Paris as soon as I could beg, borrow, steal or even earn some money. And so I would have been if, a few weeks later, I had not been captivated by another girl.'

His new flame was a dark-eyed brunette 'whose face and figure made my heart gallop', a chorus girl he first saw in a pantomime production of *Robinson Crusoe*. It was in early January 1909. At the interval, Hesketh sent her 'the largest box of chocolates I could buy in the theatre', together with a note saying that he would wait for her at the stage door. A bribe induced a theatre attendant to convey the message backstage. When scene followed scene with no reply, Pearson found the suspense unbearable and sought out the attendant who confirmed delivery of the chocolates and the note. Then what was her reply? Pearson demanded.

'Well, she asked a lot of questions about you.'

'About me?'

'Yes. She wanted to know if you were good-looking and nicely-spoken!'

'Good-looking and nicely-spoken?'

'Yes. And whether you looked as if you wanted anything for it.'

'For what?'

'For the present, silly!'

'Oh!'

'Then she asked where you were sitting. I told her and she had a squint at you through a hole in the curtain.'

'Oh!'

'After that she said you could wait for her at the stage door if you really wanted to.'

Trembling with anticipation, Pearson waited by the stage door and was mortified not to recognize the girl when she came out, her face now without make-up and partly obscured by a fur muffler and a velvet hat. They strolled arm in arm along Marine Parade to Black Rock, then to her parents' house in Hove, parting only 'after a final hurricane of kisses'. Thus began a passionate love affair that lasted for two years. In his memoirs, Pearson did not name the chorus girl, but she was Dolly Cowles. Together Hesketh and Dolly tramped over the cliffs, explored the villages dotting the coastline, splashed on the beach, and revelled in one another's company. Once they took a bus from Castle Square to Rottingdean, despite the cold wind preferring to travel on the top so that they could be alone. 'The Downs were on my left, the sea on my right, and Dolly close beside me. It was as if I saw, felt, heard the outward world for the first time in my life.' Pearson eventually rented one of the small 'arches' beneath King's Road, little apartments that opened on to the beach, so that they could be alone. After a suitably intricate *pas de deux* ('she was always begging me to have patience; I was forever begging her to have courage') courage as usual triumphed over patience, and their union was complete. 'Of course, I thought myself in love with her, but later experience has taught me that my feeling was ninety percent lust. I doubt if one can tell the difference before the age of forty.'

It must have been a curious affair. Pearson loved literature and Dolly had read only one book, *Alice in Wonderland*. Yet she was sensual, vivacious and full of fun. Imaginative men often fall in love with women whose inclinations seem most at variance with their own, perhaps even marry them, seduced by the Pygmalion illusion that they will shape the beloved to their own mould. Pearson was to experience this, but not with Dolly. By the time he left Brighton (in September 1910) their love was cooling.

Pearson's two years in Brighton marked not only his initiation into the capricious pleasures of sex, but also release from what had become a morbid fear of death. Just why he experienced 'acute discomfort' about the future of the soul and everything connected with death is unclear. Pearson was inclined to attribute it to his 'religious upbringing', but this seems rather wide of the mark. Although descended from a line of clerics, his father and mother were not notably devout and it seems unlikely that any of the churches his family frequented were hotbeds of evangelical zeal or apocalyptic preaching. Once, at the urging of a friend, Pearson attended St Bartholomew's Church in Brighton where the vicar, Father Cox, was holding forth about hell, 'tying himself into knots in his efforts to reproduce the physical torments of the wretched victims cast into it'. Since this single incident was sufficiently un-pleasant for Pearson to write of it half a century later, it seems likely that it, rather than his religious upbringing such as it was, was the source of his fear about 'the apparent meaningless of mortality' which so troubled him in Brighton. In any event his doubts and fears were sufficiently troublesome that he sought counselling from the Reverend Felix Asher of Holy Trinity Church in Brighton; 'Though he did his best to help me, I became more and more uneasy.' Typically, it was literature, not rationalism, psychology or faith, that cured him. While walking on the top of the Downs, Pearson was attracted by the small church of Poynings at the foot of Devil's Dyke. He went down and wandered through its graveyard, reading the mostly depressing inscriptions on the tombstones. As the doleful texts piled up, he was overcome by melancholy. 'To be at the mercy of Fate in this world was bad enough, I thought, but to be forever condemned to an inescapable subjection in the next was too horrible to contemplate.' Just as he was about to leave, 'full of foreboding and uncertainty, fearing yet doubtful', he came upon the tombstone of a man named Tabor Cunliffe who he later learned had been killed by lightning in 1899 at the age of twenty-seven. Inscribed on his headstone were lines from the dirge in *Cymbeline*, worn faint in places, which Pearson recited aloud:

> Fear no more the heat o' the sun,
> Nor the furious winter's rages;

Thou thy worldly task hast done,
Home art gone and ta'en thy wages;
Golden lads and girls all must,
As chimney-sweepers, come to dust.

Fear no more the lightning-flash,
Nor the all-dreaded thunder-stone;
Fear not slander, censure rash,
Thou hast finished joy and moan;
All lovers young, all lovers must;
Consign to thee, and come to dust.

As he recited, Pearson was overcome by a flash of insight, a 'revel-ation', which he described thus: 'In a moment my apprehensions seemed to vanish. What I had previously regarded as merely a perfect lyric now appeared as a spiritual illumination, and I clearly perceived, what I must always have felt obscurely in my bones, that one's life could be a blessing or a curse without the least reference to what might or might not happen beyond the grave; that it was all-sufficient, an end in itself; that it would close either in the peace of cessation or in the peace beyond human understanding; and it did not matter which, since both meant the annihilation of the human mind with its cares, the human body with its tribulations. A mood of extraordinary serenity followed my phase of difficulty and doubt, and I have never since worried about the mystery of the universe, the ultimate truth, the nature of God, or any other insoluble problem.'

One insoluble problem then dividing the Church was the doctrine of trans-substantiation. Brighton was at the centre of the controversy, and Pearson knew clerics on both sides of the issue. His own attitude to such religious zealotry was one of amused derision, as he made clear in a short story called *The War of the Wafer*. He begins by describing how the Church of England had sold its birthright and become a citadel of the upper-classes, how 'in a world panting for the light and groaning for belief' its leaders had embraced materialism, 'hope had gone howling into the wilderness', and the Church become moribund. 'Several great men realized – with that opportune intuition as of divine revelation, which has so often distinguished the princes of the church – that unless the congregation were made to keep awake, they would almost infallibly go to sleep.' Knowing that worshippers crave mystery, these innovators gave them mystery in the form of candles, chants, incense, vestments and, in the boldest stroke of all, 'the belief that, after an appropriate incantation, God could be turned into a biscuit'. Protestants and traditionalists immediately denounced such practices as 'Romish' and,

after several feints of a slightly dubious order in the course of which
each side called the other every name they could think of except
Christian, 'the war of the wafer (or, in the more vulgar parlance of the
day, the Battle of the Biscuit) was begun'. On one front were mustered
the theologians and dons, experts in Greek and Aramaic, who scruti-
nized Holy Writ for proof texts; over against them the hard-headed
empiricsts, men of practical reason and common sense, much given to
the simple slogan that 'Biscuits are biscuits'. In the middle were the
compromisers, clerics who, while conceding that in a cosmic sense God
could be said to have made biscuits, also acknowledged that some credit
must in fairness be given to Huntley and Palmer and McVitie's. 'Much
heart-burning was caused by cynical levity. Some of the waferites
expressed their amazement that the sky did not open and rain fire on
these blasphemous unbelievers. The latter retaliated by calling down
the wrath of heaven on all papistical idolaters. In point of fact there was
a great deal of wonder in both camps at the continued placidity and
serenity of the firmament.' The spectacle of the Church of England thus
preoccupied, while masses of hungry, unemployed men and women
marched through the streets of London and other industrial cities,
baffled Pearson; beneath the cool satire is a current of anger and a sense
of betrayal. In all his writing, this is perhaps the closest Pearson ever got
to political exhortation:

> Had the church been of this world, had she been of mortal clay, had
> her sons been mere opportunists and materialists, she would have
> risen in wrath and told the country that it had a duty towards its
> citizens, they they should be well-fed and decently-housed, work or
> no work, that according to Christ there was no special grace attaching
> to manual labour, which was at best a brutal necessity. But the
> church was above such base expedients. She flatly declined to spend
> her reserves of energy and cash on the cause of the unemployed.
> Resolutely she locked her doors against their possible depred-
> ations and shut her ears to their impious appeals. She was about
> her Founder's business. No man could doubt her sanctity or her
> sanity. In a world driven crazy by want, her ministers crossed
> themselves devoutly – and grandly pursued the metamorphic
> Wafer.

Brighton offered Pearson meagre theatrical pleasure. Its single
theatre, the Grand, formerly the Eden but known locally as 'The
Bloodtub', was mostly given over to melodrama with titles such as *The
Sign of the Cross*, *Women and Wine*, *The Sorrows of Satan*, or *The
Ugliest Woman on Earth*. There were music hall shows at the Alhambra

and the Hippodrome, but classical theatre meant a trip to London by train. Three plays, each of which Pearson attended several times, were Tree's production of Sheridan's *School for Scandal*, George Alexander's revival of *The Importance of Being Earnest*, and Lewis Waller's *Henry V*. On June 30, 1909 Pearson heard the news that Tree had been knighted. He fired off a congratulatory telegram (which forty-five years later he was to discover preserved among Tree's papers), adding that he had recently seen Tree's *Hamlet* as His Majesty's and noted that the production did not end until nearly midnight. Knowing Tree's propensity to stretch scenes out, Pearson's telegram concluded: 'Can you play Hamlet in a business-like manner next Thursday so as to enable me to catch the midnight train from Victoria?' His brash presumptuousness was rewarded by an immediate reply. 'Cannot alter my conception of the part to fit midnight train,' Tree wired, 'but will cut a scene if you'll run to Victoria.' Tree kept his promise and omitted a scene; Pearson ran to Victoria and made his train.

Hesketh may not have been the only cause of the demise of his brother's car business, but he was unquestionably a contributing factor. Although in title he was Manager of the Brighton operation, he managed little and understood less. 'Occasionally, I signed orders, probably for the issue of petrol or the commission of jobs in the workshop or the hire of cars, but the drivers drove, the fillers filled, the turners turned, and the retreaders retrod, without much oversight on my part.' Nor was his attitude to accounts conducive to solvency. He employed a clerk named Walker to deal with such irksome financial details. Some indication of Walker's tact may be gleaned from an occasion when an irate creditor rang up demanding payment of an overdue account. 'What's your name?' Pearson overhead Walker inquire. 'Walker.' 'So's mine,' was the reply and then the clerk hung up. Pearson 'bellowed with laughter' at this exchange but ruefully conceded that 'trade conducted in this fashion was not likely to flourish'. In the spring of 1910, Hesketh temporarily staved off bankruptcy by obtaining a loan of £300 from an aunt, but that money was soon exhausted. In September, Jack was forced into liquidation. 'Following a somewhat uneasy session with the company's debtors, we drank to our demise at the Royal York Hotel.'

After the wake, Hesketh and Dolly spent a blissful week together in a rented cottage in the village of Bramber. They walked along the ridge of bare hills between Washington and Amberley; they lay in the long grass of Arundel Park and listened to the doves. They talked of marriage as soon as Hesketh had found secure employment; they parted with declarations of undying love of the kind which only lovers can give or receive without acute embarrassment.

A few weeks later Hesketh received this letter from Dolly: 'My lover: Oh, how can I write what I have to say with the memory of our heavenly holiday so fresh upon me! Yet it must be done. I owe it to you, to our love. Before the month is out, I (how *can* I say it) will be another man's wife.' The letter went on to assure Hesketh that she loved only him, that she 'never cared' for her betrothed but married him only because 'he is rich and my family is poor', that she was unworthy ('a common little beast, really') of Hesketh, and that marriage would only 'bring a blight' on a love that had been 'the most marvellous thing in my life'. The letter concluded: 'You couldn't bear a lifetime of me; and I couldn't bear your not bearing it. So this is the end of it all, the end of my happiness, the end of love. Love is too good for life, or life is too hard for love. Which?'

Pearson's reaction to this unexpected letter was 'a curious, irrational sensation, something between irritation and relief'. Perhaps the shock was mitigated by the fact that he too had met someone else and was beginning to realize the truth of Oscar Wilde's dictum – that each time one loves is as the only time one has loved.

Fifteen years later, after the first war, he saw Dolly Cowles again, quite by accident, in a lift in Leicester Square tube station. At first he did not recognize her. Not until the lift emptied and the commuters crowded out into Charing Cross Road did Pearson realize who she was. 'She had altered greatly, yet not, I think, as much as I had altered. She still carried herself proudly and the years had not added to her figure; if anything she was slimmer than of old. But her face had hardened; the eyes were shrewd and critical, the mouth had tightened, and the lips were a little cruel.' Before Hesketh could speak to her, she crossed the road and disappeared around the corner '. . . while I remained, lost in my memories, on the edge of the pavement'.

CHAPTER FIVE

Player

'All the world's a stage
And all the men and women, merely Players;
They have their exits and their entrances,
And one man in his time plays many parts.'
As You Like It, Act II, Scene 7

Lacking money and a job, Pearson returned briefly to his parents' home in Bedford where, in the fall of 1910, Sir Frank Benson brought his Shakespeare Company to perform *Much Ado About Nothing*. Pearson wrote for an appointment, got it and, after a performance, was taken backstage. Benson was standing on the stage with his back to the curtain in discussion with the stage manager but the moment Pearson appeared he came over, shook hands, and told him to come back for an audition the next morning. Pearson was struck by Benson's courtesy and perfect manners. The next morning, 'horribly nervous', he was led to 'a tiny room near the entrance of the theatre where one couldn't swing a cat'. Here he declaimed Henry V's 'Once more into the breach' speech; '[Benson] stood a yard away, looking out of the window so as not to confuse me as I shouted the lines in a room where I ought to have chosen "To Be or Not to Be" and whispered it.' However, Benson offered him an unpaid training position with a salary to follow after one year's apprenticeship. Elated, Hesketh begged his father to finance him. Henry Pearson, who considered the stage 'a sort of licensed brothel', refused, and relations between father and son quickly deteriorated, a process exacerbated when Hesketh ceased attending church. A final break came over a casual remark; Henry Pearson had been discussing Christianity, when Hesketh interjected that if Christ were anything like the average Christian he must have been 'a pretty poisonous person'. After a shocked silence, Henry Pearson said: 'I shall have to assume that I heard you incorrectly or order you out of the house.' After 'a sorrowful farewell of mother' Hesketh caught the next train to London. This estrangement from his father foreshadowed a more tragic future estrangement from his own son. For the next four years, Hesketh and his father did not communicate, a truce only being declared on the homefront to coincide with the declaration of war in August 1914.

Pearson moved into a tiny, two-bedroom flat at 81 Regency Street, Westminster shared with his friend John Beamish from the British Empire Shakespeare Society. Beamish was then acting bit parts at the New Theatre, but Pearson's lack of stage experience hindered his attempts to obtain similar employment.

In January 1911 Sir Francis Galton died at the age of ninety and Pearson spent several weeks at 42 Rutland Gate sorting through Galton's extensive papers, reading exchanges of correspondence with eminent Victorians, and pumping his Aunt Eva, Galton's last house-keeper, for information. It was she who gave Hesketh an account of Galton's death. He had moved for the winter to Grayshott House, Hindhead where, on first reaching the top of the stairs leading to his bedroom, he had remarked: 'This will be an awkward corner to get my coffin around.' Increasingly, he had trouble dressing, washing and walking, yet he remained cheerful and serene. On the day he died, January 17, 1911, some food was brought to him and he tried to eat it, but gave up and, smiling, quoted Burns:

> Some hae meat and canna eat,
> And some wad eat that want it.

His nephew, Edward, entered the room and Galton said cheerfully: 'My dear fellow, I am standing on the precipice.' 'A little later,' Pearson concluded, 'he fell into a coma, and with the coming of night passed into the darkness.'

For a time Hesketh toyed with the idea of writing a biography of his great-great-uncle. Ten years later, in his first book *Modern Men and Mummers*, he did include a short sketch of Galton. But, for the moment, it was the stage, not biography, that attracted him. He wrote letters requesting auditions and one found its way to Sir Herbert Beerbohm Tree. 'Come and see me,' Tree replied, 'but don't be too optimistic. You should have independent means or relatives in Court Circles to be successful on the stage nowadays. If you have the former, why go on stage? If the latter, the Kings and Queens of real life should satisfy you.'

On receipt of this reply, Pearson went to His Majesty's Theatre where Tree was appearing as Cardinal Wolsey in *Henry VIII*. Speechless with anticipation, Pearson was led down a corridor to the legendary actor's dressing room. There before him was Tree, dressed in Wolsey's red silk robes and sitting morosely behind a desk.

'He rose, shook hands, said "How do you do? Take a seat," and sat down again. I took a seat. He leaned back in his chair and stared hard at me for about two minutes without speaking. I became fretful. Suddenly he said: "Don't bite your nails. It's a sign of mental stagnation." I ventured a remark about one of the pictures in his room. He ignored the remark. There was another long silence. After which he said: "Don't suck your thumb. It signifies lack of stamina." This irritated me and I asked whether he would like to write me a prescription. He immediately took up his pen and wrote some words on a slip of paper. Then he rose, handed me the paper, murmured, "Come again after the next Act," took me a few steps along a corridor outside his room, and pushed me through a door that opened into the dress circle. I read the paper:

DISEASE: Want of philosophic calm, typically modern.
CURE: One performance of Henry VIII, to be taken weekly.
H.B.T.'

At the end of the first Act, Pearson was again taken to Tree's dressing room where an even more bizarre exchange occurred. Pearson was then in the habit of writing down such conversations immediately after they happened and, since he had an excellent memory, the freshness of events justified his assertion that these are 'almost verbatim' reconstructions.

'Who are you?' he asked the moment I entered.
I told him who I was.
'What do you want?' he demanded.
'Surely you can't have forgotten that –' I began.
'Answer my question,' he interrupted; 'I forget everything I don't wish to remember.'

Pearson now realized that he was dealing either with a maniac or with a man who carried his profession into his private life. The conversation continued in this strain:

Pearson: I want a job.
Tree: Can you speak German?
Pearson: No; but does one have to speak German to go on the stage?
Tree: It would certainly be useful if you wanted to go on the German stage.
Pearson: I don't.
Tree: Well, that settles it, doesn't it? Can you speak French?
Pearson: Yes.
Tree: Fluently?
Pearson: No.
Tree: What a pity!

Pearson: Why?

Tree: Because one should always swear in a foreign language at rehearsals.

Pearson: Is there any necessity to swear at all?

Tree: No necessity, but a great relief. Are you fond of your wife?

Pearson: I haven't got one.

Tree: Yes, but are you fond of her?

Pearson: How the devil can I be fond of a wife I haven't got?

Tree: Ah, I hadn't thought of that . . . have you read much?

Pearson: It depends upon what you call reading much.

Tree: I mean the perusal of a vast quantity of words printed on paper and bound in books.

Pearson: Yes, yes, of course I knew you meant that; but to what class of reading do you refer?

Tree: Oh, the kind that teaches facts and figures.

Pearson: I know nothing of facts and figures. They don't interest me.

Tree: That's right, quite right. Beware of the encyclopedias. A little knowledge is a dangerous thing, but a lot ruins one's digestion.

At this point the theatre manager, Henry Dana, interrupted their conversation to discuss some financial matters relating to the production. Pearson noticed that Tree appeared not to have the haziest idea of what was being explained to him but he would occasionally put his finger on some figure on the ledger books much as a child might exclaim, 'Oh, look at that lovely big one there.' When Dana left, Tree was called for the next Act. But, just as Pearson was leaving, Tree padded back down the corridor, his Cardinal's silks billowing: 'Have you ever been in Jerusalem?' Tree whispered. Pearson replied that he had not. 'How interesting!' Tree said and then drifted off down the passage.

When the play was over, Pearson trudged backstage once more, determined this time to press his claim. Tree was now removing his make-up and changing his clothes, utterly oblivious of Pearson's entreaties, but engaged in a disjointed, stream of consciousness monologue:

. . . How did you like the play? Wonderful production, isn't it? Have you read my brochure on *Henry VIII*? Quite a charming little essay. I wrote it during my holiday. It's always useful to have a job on hand during one's holidays; it saves one from bores who insist on interrupting one's dreams with tedious prattle about politics or mixed bathing. Did you ever see old Irving? A strange personality, but hard . . . hard . . . I couldn't get on with him at all. Quite unlike his two boys, Harry

and Laurence. Such nice lads; I like 'em both . . . Don't forget to
remember me to your wife . . . The English public doesn't really like
Shakespeare; it prefers football . . . Shakespearian scholars say I'm
wrong in tempting people to come to the theatre and giving them a
spectacle instead of Shakespeare. But I prefer a spectacle on stage to
spectacles in the audience . . . Some day you will tell me how it was
you didn't go to Jerusalem. It must have been a delightful experience
– not to have gone after all . . . Winkles! – Yes, that's a fine
occupation – picking winkles out of shells on a frosty night in Pimlico.
Are they in shells, by the way? Take my advice: don't go on the stage
– pick winkles out of shells . . . Do you believe in God? (Where's that
damn stud?) Perhaps you aren't old enough. The reason older people
believe in God is because they have given up believing in anything
else, and one can't exist without faith in something. Besides, after
sixty, one hasn't the vitality to combat the instincts of the majority.
God is a sort of burglar. As a young man you knock him down; as an
old man you try to conciliate him because he may knock you down.
Moral: don't grow old. With age comes caution, which is another
name for cowardice and both are the effects of a guilty conscience.
Whatever else you do in life, don't cultivate a conscience. Without a
conscience a man may never be said to grow old. This is an age of very
old young men . . . Never neglect an opportunity to play leap-frog; it
is the best of all games, and, unlike the terribly serious and conscien-
tious pastimes of modern youth, will never become professionalized
. . . Have you ever been in love? That is the greatest thing in life.
Don't confuse love with matrimony. Love keeps you young, matrimony makes you old. Love should never be allowed to disturb the
excellent economic foundation of the domestic hearth. Love is more
precious than life, but a silver wedding speaks for itself . . . Why is it
that we have to go to Germany for grease paints? . . .

Throughout this soliloquy, Tree floated up and down the room,
picking up and then discarding articles of clothing '. . . in a state of
complete uncertainty as to where he was, whom he was talking to, and
what he was supposed to be doing'. Finally dressed, Tree made for the
door, held out his hand in Pearson's general direction, and muttered,
'Goodbye. So nice for you to have seen me,' and disappeared.

Two weeks later Pearson was surprised to receive an unsigned wire
telling him to report at once to His Majesty's Theatre. It was, although
he did not know it, a Tree audition. Pearson arrived to find 'a general
feeling of vague expectation in the air', while about the stage hovered a
nondescript crowd which broke down into two groups; the old actors

'whose deeply-lined faces, permanent frowns and flashing eyes spoke of the halcyon pasts and dismal presents', and the young aspirants, all 'as self-conscious and uncomfortable as I was'. Among the latter, Pearson first met Douglas Jefferies who was to become a lifelong friend. (Pearson's biography of Tree, published in 1956, is dedicated: 'To my friend Douglas Jefferies who walked on with me at His Majesty's Theatre in 1911–12.') During the *Whispering Gallery* trial it was Jefferies who volunteered to come forward as a witness and testify that Pearson was mad and should not be held criminally responsible for any of his actions.

Eventually, Pearson was led through two pairs of swinging doors by an attendant with a foghorn voice. On stage were three chairs, two occupied, and foghorn settled himself on the third.

'Name,' bellowed foghorn.

'Pearson,' I meekly responded.

'Experience,' boomed foghorn.

'I beg your pardon?' I queried, not quite certain what he was driving at.

'I like his legs,' purred Sir Herbert Tree who I now noticed was sitting in the centre chair.

'But you can't see them through his trousers,' objected his companion.

'That's why I like them,' returned Sir Herbert.

'What parts have you played?' Foghorn had to repeat the question twice before I was conscious of it.

'None,' I replied.

'Splendid!' said Sir Herbert Tree, who gave no hint by his manner that he had ever set eyes on me before; 'You will have nothing to unlearn. We must give him something really good, nothing must be allowed to stand in his way. He has a fine nose. He has a most becoming modesty. Moreover I like his legs. We will do everything in our power to help you, Mr – er –' (he referred to the paper) 'Mr Hesketh Pearson – if you will promise not to hyphen your two names. I will speak to Mr Dana about your contract, and you shall play the part of Bottom in *A Midsummer Night's Dream*.'

At these words the other two began to roll about helplessly in their chairs, almost choking themselves in their frantic endeavours to keep laughter within the bounds of moderation. As soon as his companions had obtained a fair hold over their emotions, Sir Herbert proceeded:

'My God! I owe you an apology, Mr Pearson. I had completely forgotten I have already promised the well-known actor, Mr Arthur

Bourchier, that he shall play Bottom. It is therefore casting no reflection upon you when I say that he has the prior, not to mention the posterior, claim.' (Here he had to pause while his friends performed a further series of contortions.) 'But do not despair. You will get a far wider and more valuable experience by not playing it than by playing it. For you will be able to watch Mr Bourchier's performance night after night, and after a careful study of his manner and method of acting you will always know exactly what to avoid . . . In conclusion, Mr Pearson, I cannot do you a great honour – much though I admire your legs – than to engage you to walk-on at my beautiful theatre for a salary of one guinea a week – extra for matinees.'

Within the hour, Pearson was rehearsing *A Midsummer Night's Dream* which opened at His Majesty's Theatre in April 1911. Pearson was a courtier whose only responsibility was to laugh merrily at Theseus's feeble jokes. He must have laughed heartily for he was given a speaking part in the next Tree production, *Julius Caesar*. Pearson was an ancient Roman Senator, Publius who, in the Tree version, had only three words to speak: 'Good morrow, Caesar.' Determined to make his first speaking part a memorable one, Pearson spent hours studying the voice and walk of old men, quietly piping to himself and learning to totter. After some days he had achieved a flawless falsetto with an old man's quaver and crack. He had followed aged men through the streets of London, aping their gestures and duplicating their shuffles; 'when one day I tripped over a kerbstone and fell into the gutter, I felt sure that I had at last got the correct gait'. For two hours on opening night, Pearson busied himself putting on enough wrinkles to match his long white beard. Up until the very moment of his entrance, he stood in the wings practising his falsetto voice until a sympathetic stagehand inquired if he had always been troubled by asthma?

'The great moment arrived; I braced myself to meet it, and marched on to the stage, which was the cause of my undoing. In my anxiety to reproduce the accents of senility, I had temporarily forgotten the motions of senility and I strolled into Caesar's room with the gait of my age. Realizing my error, I stopped abruptly and was about to return in order to make an entrance more consonant with my make-up when Caesar said, 'Welcome, Publius', which in the text followed my words, 'Good morrow, Caesar'. Shattered by the deprivation of my greeting, I collapsed into the palsied condition necessary for the part; but at the same instant I forgot the piping tones that had been so carefully rehearsed and replied with an audibility of a young man whose lungs

were in good order: 'Hullo!' Antony, Brutus and the rest followed me
into Caesar's apartment, and I tumbled off somehow, horrified by my
ghastly exhibition. Naturally I expected instant dismissal and shook in
my sandals as Tree came up to me at the conclusion of the scene. 'What
did you say to Caesar?' he asked in the rather fearsome guttural tone he
put on for special occasions. 'I'm afraid I said "Hullo!" Sir Herbert',
was my miserable admission, and I was about to stutter some feeble sort
of excuse when he went on: 'Oh! I beg your pardon. My mistake. I
thought you said "WHAT HO!"'

This inauspicious debut was soon followed by another disaster. Cast
as Balthazar in *The Merchant of Venice*, Pearson's opening address to
Portia required him to say: 'The four strangers seek for you, madam, to
take their leave; and there is a fore-runner come from a fifth, the Prince
of Morocco, who brings word the Prince his master will be here
tonight.' There had been little time for rehearsal and the 'noises off'
were not available until the first performance. On opening night
Pearson confidently strode on to the stage carrying his wand of office,
took up a stately position before Portia, threw back his head and opened
his mouth to commence his address, when suddenly came three shrill
trumpet blasts which, unknown to him, were supposed to herald his
arrival. Balthazar leapt startled into the air and landed again, confused
and disordered.

> Once more I threw back my head and again I opened my mouth. But
> the managerial requirements were not yet satisfied. I had not uttered
> a word before another and closer blast of trumpets, which unknown
> to me, should have heralded my speech, finished what the first had
> begun. At its conclusion I was speechless. I was not going to be made
> a fool of a third time, so I held my peace. But that second outbreak
> really had concluded the programme from a heraldic point of view
> and Portia and I remained for an appreciable period gaping at one
> another in dead silence. She was the first to speak; and if Shakespeare
> had failed to provide for such a contingency, she was forced to take a
> liberty with the text:
>
> 'Well, Sirrah?' she said.
> By this time I had completely forgotten what my speech was about;
> but I had to say something, so I retorted: 'Well, Madame?'
> This cornered her but did not advance matters. Suddenly I heard
> an angry hiss from the stage manager: 'Get off the stage, you bloody
> idiot!'
> I did as he suggested.

Such was Pearson's initiation into repertory theatre. With very little amateur experience, he had become a member, however bumbling, of England's leading company. But any vagrant inclination he might have had to self-importance was dashed by the rigid caste system which operated in the theatre. The certified stars sometimes condescended to speak to the medium part players, but never to the bit players; the medium part players spoke occasionally to the bit players, but never to the walkers-on; the walkers-on, like Pearson, spoke to anyone who would listen.

In the autumn of 1911 Tree produced *Macbeth* in which Pearson carried a warrior's shield and once inadvertently dropped it on Tree's foot. Nevertheless, Tree remained friendly and accessible. One night as Pearson was leaving the theatre, he heard Tree's voice calling to him. Grasping his arm, Tree propelled him into a taxi and said to the driver: 'Drive us slowly round and round the West End until we tell you to stop. If you see a man in green trousers, a top hat and spotted waistcoat, blow your horn three times and increase your speed.' Pearson considered that the driver must think Tree was a Scotland Yard detective and for some period of time they careened up and down narrow streets. Had the driver been able to overhear Tree's soliloquy he would have concluded that his fare was an escaped lunatic. It went like this. (The 'Crippen' to whom Tree refers had recently been hanged for the murder of his wife.)

'I used to believe the world was round. Nowadays I am sure it is flat . . . poor old Crippen! . . . Why? You naturally ask.' (I hadn't, but it didn't matter.) 'I don't know. Possibly because I can't believe that God plays football with the planetary system. The idea is outrageous. It is horrible that a man of your intelligence should support it.' (I hadn't uttered a word in its favour, but that was neither here nor there.) 'You have what I may call a Crystal Palace mind. I don't mean to suggest that your mind is as clear as crystal. It isn't. No Crystal Palace minds are. That is the paradox of the Victorian era. . . . Poor old Crippen! . . . Don't talk so much. Talking hinders thought. I always think aloud, and I can't stand people talking when I am thinking at the top of my voice. Do you really imagine that anything you say is of the smallest importance? Your tongue was given you to hold it. . . . Poor old Crippen! . . . Once, many years ago, while I was witnessing my own impersonation of Hamlet – a beautiful performance – a thought struck me that I would sometime or other, produce one of Shakespeare's plays. But alas! – Don't interrupt me – all our ideals escape us. . . . Does your eye ever roll in a fine frenzy?

No, of course not. You would be in Hanwell if it did. As I said before, you have a Crippen Palace mind. . . . Poor old Crystal! . . .'

At this point Tree lapsed into silence for about ten minutes. Then he commenced to murmur, but Pearson only caught one phrase – 'She probably deserved it' – referable no doubt to the late Mrs Crippen. Then silence again. Eventually the driver tired of his fruitless pursuit and demanded a specific destination. Tree was non-committal. 'Are you going to tell me where you want to go, or shall I fetch a bobby?' demanded the driver. 'Whither thou goest, we will go,' said Tree, 'but whither thou lodgest, we certainly don't intend to lodge.' Pearson eventually soothed the driver and persuaded him to take them back to His Majesty's Theatre where Tree borrowed money to pay the fare. As Pearson turned to leave, Tree muttered: 'Goodnight, my boy . . . why in heaven's name can't they use the Lethal Chamber?'

Pearson next went on tour in a play by Alfred Sutro called *The Builder of Bridges*. Another member of the company was an actress, Gladys Gardner. She was the daughter of a German father and an English mother; her mother had died giving birth to a sixth child when Gladys was young. She was quite tall and dark, with a clear complexion, and a whimsical smile which revealed perfectly formed teeth. She liked walking, she loved Shakespeare, and she was entranced by the theatre. They became sexually intimate, which Pearson considered 'a prudent preliminary to a satisfactory marriage'. The tour took them to Scarborough where 'late one night, sitting on the sands in the moonlight, I asked her to marry me'. She accepted. After five weeks on the tour, Tree summoned Pearson back to London to perform at His Majesty's. Shortly afterwards he heard from Gladys that she was pregnant.

On June 6, 1912 they were married at the Westminster Register office. The only witnesses were Pearson's roommate, John Beamish, and an actress acquaintance of Gladys's named Amy in whose Regency Street flat Pearson and Beamish had often talked the night away over pots of tea. 'To soothe the two families we antedated the ceremony by two months when making the announcement, our caution being justified when Gladys gave birth to a son who weighed ten pounds, a trifle overweight for a seven month baby.' At the insistence (and expense) of an ageing aunt of Hesketh's they repeated the ceremony a year later in the church of St Stephen the Martyr. The same witnesses stood up for them and this time Beamish forgot to give the bride away. Hesketh and Gladys were simultaneously seized by the ridiculousness of the spectacle and chortled so loudly they could not get through the responses. After a moment of silent recuperation, the ceremony carried on and

Aunt Adele was satisfied. By then their son, Henry, had already been born.

Several of Hesketh's friends were puzzled by Gladys. She was neither beautiful nor unusually intelligent and, as Hesketh confided later to Basil Harvey, he and Gladys ceased having sexual intercourse after Harry's birth. However, Gladys was placid, a keen walker, and willingly devoted her life to looking after Hesketh (whom she called 'Ned'). Hesketh, meanwhile, did not lack for extra-marital opportunities. Harvey once introduced a woman to Pearson and afterwards she said: 'You hadn't told me how good-looking he is.' Another woman, still alive, who had an intense affair with Pearson during the second world war, described him as 'a charming fellow, handsome, amusing, full of fun, kind – he was irresistible'. Still, Hesketh's marriage to Gladys survived until her death in 1951 and, looking back at it, he wrote: 'I could not have had a better wife than Gladys from the moment we laughed our way into marriage until her death nearly forty years later. Our love and mutual dependence on one another grew with the years, and despite certain sexual irregularities on my part, which produced unhappy emotional tensions, we never wished to separate.'

CHAPTER SIX

Secretary

'As in a theatre, the eyes of men,
After a well-graced actor leaves the stage,
Are idly bent on him that enters next . . .'
Richard II Act V, Scene II

Supporting a wife and child on a guinea a week would have proved impossible had not Hesketh's friend John Beamish decided to go on tour. He relinquished his position and persuaded the Shakespeare Society to hire Pearson as his replacement at a salary of two pounds a week. For a short time the Pearsons also lived rent-free in Beamish's flat, until they found diminutive but permanent quarters in St John's Wood.

Pearson now lived within walking distance of 8 Clifton Hill, the residence of Acton Bond, Honorary Director of the Shakespeare Society. To that address, he repaired each morning to take dictation, arrange readings, and generally attend to Society business. The patron and nominal President of the Society was Princess Marie Louise, a grand-daughter of Queen Victoria, but policies were set and decisions were approved by a Committee which comprised all the leading actor-managers. Such contacts gave Pearson's acting career a boost and brought him into contact with Sir Johnston Forbes-Robertson, Sir George Alexander, Sir Frank Benson, Lewis Waller, H. B. Irving, Laurence Irving, Sir John Martin-Harvey, Oscar Asche, and Harley Granville-Barker. The curtain fell on these giants of the stage after the 1914–18 war, so Pearson knew them in the twilight of their greatness.

The Shakespeare Society, whose motto was 'Using no other weapon but his name', had, in theory at least, far-flung branches throughout the Empire, but the only one whose existence appeared to be more than mythic and which therefore appeared on the letterhead was in Wellington, New Zealand. Pearson had some doubts even about this one: 'I doubt if we really believed in this antipodean branch, though we occasionally corresponded with a fellow who claimed to be Secretary. My own opinion was that he had a small circle of friends who met at his house on Sunday evenings and read Shakespeare together.' Pearson was astonished when a man named Joynt, claiming to be Vice-President of the New Zealand branch, turned up in London. Without over-zealous checking of his credentials, Pearson pressed him into regular service, proposing toasts, distributing prizes, bearing greetings from abroad, and generally disporting himself as a distinguished Imperial representative. Pearson even accompanied Joynt to Stratford to lay a wreath on Shakespeare's grave; the heading in the paper next morning was 'Distinguished New Zealander pays tribute to Shakespeare'.

As secretary of a society devoted to the bard Pearson read everything about Shakespeare he could lay hands on. This experience proved 'distressing' and he concluded that 'as a rule only the half-dead write about Shakespeare'. One exception, though few would use the adjective 'honourable', was Frank Harris whose book, *The Man: Shakespeare*, 'came like a gale . . . into this atmosphere of stagnant scholarship'. Pearson considered Harris the first of Shakespeare's biographers to make it clear that the plays were written by a man not a committee. With typical impetuousity, Pearson tried to ram Harris down the throats of his fellow Shakespeareans. The situation became sticky when Princess Marie Louise was called upon to distribute the prizes for the Society competition held annually at the Haymarket Theatre. From a dwindling stock of books she presented to each successful male competitor a copy of Harris's *Shakespeare: The Man*, and to the female winners Harris's *The Women of Shakespeare*. 'In choosing the prizes I had allowed my personal taste to get the better of my secretarial judgment and I was gravely, perhaps justifiably, reprimanded.'

Pearson wrote Harris an admiring letter. Not a man to overlook praise, Harris replied that his letter exhibited 'an astonishing mastery of words and rightness of judgment' for one so young. In due course Pearson got an invitation to Harris's flat at 67 Lexham Gardens in South Kensington where the master paced up and down holding forth in a reverberant bass voice 'that made platitudes sound like profundities'. For all his guile, Harris had the virtue of not talking down to a young man and as he was also a born actor with the full emotional spectrum from fiery scorn to melting pity at his command, Pearson came away convinced that 'I had spent an evening with the only man who could put the world right'. Closer aquaintance undermined this expectation.

The Shakespeare Society's primary activity was to sponsor readings. Some were put on in West End theatres by famous actors who were persuaded to donate their services by Pearson's confidential assurance that 'Her Royal Highness will be most grateful'. Less successful were the regular Sunday evening readings at the Passmore Edwards Settlement. Sundays were usually the actors' night off and critics seldom attended these readings. Consequently Pearson had to find beginners who often doubled up on parts. At one reading of *Richard III* Pearson had no fewer than six parts and the two little princes were played, one by an actress approaching seventy, the other by an actress in an advanced state of pregnancy.

For its theatre performances the Society depended on the generosity of the managers. Having virtually no budget, the theatre and the actors' services had to be donated. Pearson was once deputed to approach Tree for the loan of His Majesty's Theatre. He broached the topic in Tree's dressing room after a performance of *David Copperfield,* while Tree was still in his costume and make-up as Micawber. 'Have you seen my *David Copperfield?*' replied Tree taking no notice of Pearson's request.

Pearson: No.

Tree: Then you must see it.

Pearson: I should like to.

Tree: So should I.

Pearson: (After a pause) Do you think you will be able to lend us your theatre?

Tree: Have you seen *David Copperfield?*

Pearson: I said 'No'.

Tree: Then you must see it.

Pearson: Yes, I said I should like to see it.

Tree: So should I.

Pearson: Will you please give an answer to my question?

Tree: (in Falstaff's voice) Upon compulsion? Never.

Pearson: I said 'Please', Sir Herbert.

Tree: I heard you.

Pearson: Am I to understand . . .?

Tree: Silence! Conduct this gentleman to the dome and give him a drink.

Tree's dresser then accompanied Pearson to a lift leading to the theatre dome where Tree maintained an apartment which had, in effect, become his permanent London residence, a sanctuary frequented by his wife only on Tree's invitation to one of his elaborate dinner parties. Tree's marriage had become a sham; he wrote: 'Of all the laws the marriage law is the most immoral (not excepting that relating to income tax) for it is productive of more subterfuge, lying and hypocrisy than any law that governs us.' As Pearson was about to enter the lift, Tree poked his Micawber head round the corner and said to the dresser: 'Explain to the gentleman after he is pacified with a drink, that if he had seen *David Copperfield* he would not have come at the fall of the curtain to ask for a thing I am too tired to refuse . . . take great care of him. The last man who used this lift was killed instantaneously, owing to the unaccountable habit it has acquired of dropping quite suddenly from the top floor to the bottom, just as one is about to step out of it . . . Good luck.'

The dome consisted of two rooms, one large and reeking of mediaevalism with tapestries, armour, swords and baronial objects decorating the walls, and a long refectory table occupying the centre of the floor; the other room was smaller and airy, with a desk and a bed, fitted up in the latest drawing room fashions.

Twenty minutes later Tree appeared and wearily seated himself at the desk while an American newspaper reporter tried to interview him, a process made difficult by Tree's refusal to answer any questions beyond the occasional murmur of 'Oh, God!' and 'Oh, Manhattan!' He did, however, launch into unrelated soliloquies on topics as diverse as Chicago, pigs, porcupines, and trouser buttons. Then, with a curt nod, Pearson and the American reporter were simultaneously dismissed from his presence. Tree's last words were, 'How curious . . .padded pavements . . . the orange-peel would lose its terror.' The Society was given use of Tree's theatre.

In the autumn of 1912 Tree offered Pearson a part in his production of *Drake*. Secretarial duties being then rather onerous, Pearson declined. But by now 'having gained a wide experience in silent parts' he soon accepted another offer, this time to join Granville-Barker's company at the St James's. It was the most fashionable playhouse in London. As Pearson later described it: 'The most expensive seats were occupied by Society with a capital "S", the less expensive seats by ones who longed to be in Society, the least expensive by those who wished to see what Society looked like.' The drama served up reflected the pedigree of the audience and there were about as many peers on stage as in the stalls.

Granville-Barker's methods were as unlike Tree's as night and day, although the resulting productions were not necessarily superior. Granville-Barker never bullied his actors but took them aside as friends in whom he hoped to instil some of his own enthusiasm for whatever character they were playing. He would sketch for them the life history of their character, his habits and tastes, joys and woes, his waking thoughts and his sleeping dreams, thereby forcing the actor to think his way into the skin of a character. 'The method he employed was purely biographical, which may explain why I found him the most helpful and inspiring of all the producers I have known. What he did in effect was to make an actor conceive his part from within, not study it from without . . .' It was a technique Pearson would adapt to biography.

Pearson's first play with Granville-Barker was George Bernard Shaw's *Androcles and The Lion*. Pearson was Metellus who, in the last Act, reproves Lavinia for addressing Caesar in a presumptuous manner. Granville-Barker had been at pains to teach Pearson to do this with restrained hauteur, 'a kind of scandalized dignity'. Through four weeks of rehearsal, Shaw had not put in an appearance. Then, at the final dress rehearsal, he appeared and immediately proceeded to 'transform the play from a comedy to an extravaganza'. When Pearson said his lines, Shaw leapt on the stage and shouted: 'Good gracious! You mustn't behave like an offended patrician. You must treat her as one who has committed sacrilege. Jump at her! Fling yourself between them! Shut her mouth! Assault her!' Shaw then proceeded to undo all that Granville-Barker had laboured to achieve. The dress rehearsal ended at three in the morning. 'Long before that Barker had retired from the contest and was looking on the destruction of his month's work with a face that registered amusement and annoyance in about equal degree.' Thus began for Pearson an acquaintance with Shaw, yet another of his 'revelations'.

After *Androcles* Pearson appeared in repertory in plays by Molière, Ibsen, Galsworthy, Maeterlinck and Masefield. His next Shaw play was *The Doctor's Dilemma*. When he muffed a line in rehearsal, Shaw took him aside and said: 'If you must alter my words, for heaven's sake improve them.' Pearson acknowledged that he was never able to reconcile Shaw to any of his improvements.

His first leading role was as Marlow in Galsworthy's *The Silver Box*. In one scene Marlow must clear away a breakfast table while carrying the dialogue. Until dress rehearsal all went smoothly. The scene required quick execution. For the first time Pearson was confronted by a table laden with what appeared to be the remains of a six-course State dinner. The moment he tried to gather things up, he forgot his lines; when he paused to recollect, the prompter began to shout and Pearson began to drop things. 'By the time I was due to leave the stage, I had emptied the teapot over the son, dropped the bacon and eggs onto the carpet, swept the crumbs into the lap of the mother, drenched the table cloth with hot coffee, poked the leg of an entrée dish into the left eye of the father, and taken delivery of nearly everything else down my own trousers and waistcoat. I then marched out with some of the minor crockery on the tray, banged into a female who was waiting just beyond the door to make an entrance, and fell into the arms of Granville-Barker, who not wishing to speak until he had found the precise words he wanted, knelt quietly by my side and helped to collect the shattered fragments.' After two days' practice of clearing and reclearing, he managed the job in performance with only an occasional sprinkling of crumbs to mark his passage, but 'never afterwards had I the slightest desire to play butler parts'.

Pearson enjoyed his time in Granville-Barker's company and stayed with them when they moved from the St James's to the Savoy. Granville-Barker's productions were conservatively cast and tastefully staged but they lacked the excitement and unpredictability of Tree's spectacles. Granville-Barker was a cautious man who, in the twenties, abandoned the stage for the safer groves of academic life, thenceforth lecturing at universities and writing about, rather than producing, Shakespeare. When he died in 1946, Pearson wrote that '. . . thirty years of comfortable living without care and without incentive, produced a man who would scarcely have been recognized by the actors who remembered their great producer'.

Pearson's most notable success in Granville-Barker's company was in a play called *The Basker*. At first he understudied Sir George Alexander for the lead and then, when Alexander became ill, Pearson took it over and got more critical plaudits and curtain calls than ever Sir George had done. Lesser men might have been envious. But Alexander rejoiced in Pearson's success and thereafter became a kind of patron, putting his name forward for parts and once paying him full salary when a play was cancelled at the last minute by the censor. Pearson later said that Sir George's patronage too frequently took the form 'of introductions to royal or noble personages whom I had no wish to meet', but then added: 'I shall always remember him with feelings of gratitude and affection.' Genevieve Ward, then an ageing star, returned to the stage especially for *The Basker* and, although she was annoyed when Pearson inadvertently took another actress's hand at a curtain call, she praised his performance and predicted 'a great future' on the stage.

So it might have been had not Britain declared war on Germany on August 4, 1914. Pearson immediately enlisted in Kitchener's Army. For a year before this he had been troubled by recurrent nose bleeds; Gladys had urged him to see a doctor but he had stubbornly refused. Now six weeks of drilling and physical training transformed occasional blood stains on the pillow into regular, prolonged bleeding. When this was discovered Pearson was sent for medical tests, diagnosed as tubercular and, early in 1915, invalided out of the army. He had by now been reconciled to his father and returned home to Bedford, skin loosely hanging on his tall, gaunt frame, to rest and recuperate. When he was well enough to return to London, he called on Acton Bond but was advised that the Shakespeare Society was closing down for the duration. Bond suggested that Pearson might act as Secretary to the Actors' Committee established to plan for the Shakespeare Tercentenary celebrations the following year. Although Pearson continued to make efforts to get into the services (in 1915 he successfully enlisted in the Kite Balloon section of the Army until doctors discovered his medical history) the next two years were divided between acting and committee work.

His acting was now done as a member of Sir George Alexander's company at the St James's. His first play was Pinero's *His House in Order*. In the two decades since the opening night of *The Second Mrs Tanqueray*, Pinero had established himself as the most successful contemporary playwright in England. A man of magisterial opinion and autocratic temperament, no theatre-manager dared cross him. Pearson first glimpsed Pinero at a rehearsal, black homburg set on his head, hands gloved, smoking perpetually, 'sitting in solitary majesty in the front row of the stalls'. At intervals he would bark out commands which the recipient would obsequiously follow. 'Scratch your nose reflectively at that point, Alec,' Pearson heard him shout, and Sir George Alexander dutifully and reflectively scratched.

Alexander invited Pearson to meet Pinero at a dinner party, together with Austin Brereton who was Henry Irving's biographer. Being many years younger than the others, Pearson felt 'nervous and diffident' and held his peace at first. Then Pinero happened to mention, to the usual nods of agreement, that Henry Irving reached his peak playing Macbeth and he misquoted 'Thou clarion set for Shakespeare's lips to blow'. Pearson could not resist the temptation to correct so punctilious a playwright and, under his breath, muttered 'trumpet'.

'Pinero looked at me as if I had just appeared from somewhere and said "Eh?" Aware that I had the attention of the table, I quoted boldly: "Thou trumpet set for Shakespeare's lips to blow!" "Oh!" said Pinero disapprovingly. Alexander asked who had written it. Becoming over-bold, I said in a rather challenging manner: 'That genius Oscar Wilde.' An atmosphere of constraint fell upon the table, for although Wilde's name had come back into circulation by that time it was still mentioned with economy. There was a long and pregnant pause. Everyone waited for someone to speak. At last Pinero growled: "No. Not a genius. No." "Clever," murmured Brereton. "Brilliant," suggested Alexander. "Talented . . . yes . . ." said Pinero and then to settle the question beyond all dispute, he added: "But *not* a genius, definitely not." I had been put in my place firmly and finally, but I would not abandon my position without a passing shot. "Then who is a genius?" I asked. "Well . . ." said Alexander and stopped there. We awaited the oracle and looked at Pinero who leant back in his chair, folded his hands, smiled graciously, and spoke: "Perhaps Shakespeare . . ."'

In addition to the Tercentenary Committee, at Alexander's suggestion Pearson had become Secretary to the Arts Society, the Arts Fund and the Laurence Irving Memorial Trust. But his most time-consuming obligation was to plan for the Shakespeare celebrations which were to culminate in a performance of *Julius Caesar* at the Savoy Theatre on May 2, 1916. All the leading actor-managers were on the Committee. Tree was the President but took to heart his own admonition that 'a committee should consist of three men, two of whom are absent' by going on tour in America, so that most of the work fell to the secretary (Pearson) and the Chairman (Sir George Alexander). Committees, Pearson ruefully concluded, were 'self-admiration societies', while the main purpose of meetings seemed to be for each member to exhibit his unbounded love for himself and his own ideas. Each of the actor-managers was eager to have the best part in the production while not appearing to wish to do so. This produced elaborate protestations about selfless devotion 'to the cause' and many opportunities for wounded pride. 'What a man would shrink from doing as an individual,' Tree told Pearson, 'he would not hesitate to do as a member of a committee.' Pearson had to sail through these egotistical shoals as best he might, aided by Sir George Alexander's adroit diplomacy. 'My secretarial experiences did not make me warm to my fellow Shakespeareans, but I doubt whether Shakespeare himself would have liked Shakespeareans any more than Christ would have liked Christians.' Finally the production was cast with, thanks to the efforts of Pearson and Alexander, most members still on speaking terms. Apart from drenching rain outside, the production was a success. King George V was to be in attendance and Pearson was to be in the official party. 'Receiving royalty was not much in my line and I did my best to lose myself in the auditorium just before the royal party was expected.' However, Sir George Alexander spotted him and dragged him into the vestibule where he was presented to the King. 'This is Mr Pearson, the secretary of our committee.' The King: 'Oh! (shaking hands) Very nice weather we've been having.' Pearson: 'A bit damp about the knees today, Sir.' For a moment, Pearson did not realize that everyone around him had 'turned to stone'. Then the King smiled a little grimly and passed on down the receiving line while Pearson found himself shaking hands in silence with Queen Mary. 'Passing me on the stairs . . .

Alexander stopped, frowned, and remarked: 'You should have said: 'Yes, sir.' I looked downcast and replied 'Sorry'. But the incident must have tickled him because he smiled, put his hand on my shoulder, and said: "You stand rebuked but forgiven."'

One cloud darkened the Shakespeare celebrations for Pearson. His friend John Beamish had enlisted at the beginning of the war and had been wounded in France. He was first hospitalized at Millbank where Pearson frequently visited him. Then, when he was able to leave hospital, he had stayed with the Pearsons in St John's Wood. While waiting to rejoin his regiment, Beamish had met a girl and soon after he married her. For some reason which was never clear to Pearson he had left his wife almost immediately and, on November 1, 1915 he shot and killed himself in a public lavatory in Edgware Road. A policeman came to Pearson's flat (now at 14 Abbey Gardens) and he was taken to the mortuary to identify the body. Beamish had left a letter to Pearson but he never revealed its contents. Since the letter is not among Pearson's papers, he probably destroyed it. There was an inquest at which Pearson testified, but he either could not or would not throw light on the tragedy beyond saying that Beamish was subject to 'severe fits of depression'.

As soon as the Shakespeare Tercentary was completed, Pearson again tried to enlist. He had heard that the Army Service Corps was notoriously lax in its medicals. Feigning a late-blooming conscience which had only gradually overborne deep-seated pacifist convictions, he presented himself on June 16, 1916 at the recruiting office from which, after a few perfunctory questions and a formal tap on the chest, he emerged as Private Pearson. 'To spare the authorities the mental effort of finding me a job for which I was totally unqualified, I volunteered for the Motor Transport, knowing nothing whatever about motorcars except that they were liable to break down and was immediately accepted.' He was issued a special driver's licence authorizing him to drive motorcars or motorcycles through the streets of wartime London. The only thing lacking was a vehicle of either description, an oversight not corrected until long after he had left wartime London.

He was sent first to Pennington Camp near Grove Park where his motoring skills were honed by marching up and down a parade square. He was then posted to the Quartermaster's Department at Shepherd's Bush which allowed him to sleep out. Gladys and Henry moved to a flat nearby. Although his days were 'a pure waste of time for the country and myself', they could walk in the evenings, attend plays, and generally enjoy each other's company. In later years Pearson would write: 'Most women pine for bondage, most men for vagabondage, and the two desires are irreconcilable'; but, in the first, fresh days of marriage and fatherhood, he was content with bondage.

An innate aversion to politicians and to rhetoric shielded Pearson from the jingoism of that time. He had read George Bernard Shaw's *Common Sense About the War* when it first appeared in 1914 and he was not surprised by the obloquy heaped upon Shaw for keeping his head while all about him *soi-disant* statesmen were losing theirs. 'Jackals,' Pearson wrote, 'invariably howl when they scent a thoroughbred.' He considered that Shaw's pragmatism embodied 'the sane instincts of the men who fought in the trenches and on the deserts', the Englishmen who won the war as opposed to the Englishmen 'who talked twaddle about how it ought to be won'. Perhaps he had in mind here Horatio Bottomley, journalist, editor, Member of Parliament and orator who toured the country giving patriotic speeches. Pearson went to hear him at the Kursaal at Harrogate. To an auditorium packed 'floor to ceiling' Bottomley proclaimed that there were three reasons why Britain must inevitably win this war. First, 'Munitions'. Applause. After several words on munitions, he revealed the second reason: 'What will help us through this terrible ordeal is that we are Englishmen.' Thunderous, prolonged applause. When this storm tapered off, Bottomley reached his peroration: 'And the last thing, ladies and gentlemen, that will beyond cavil or question, give us Victory triumphant is THAT THERE IS A GOD IN HEAVEN.' At these words the audience 'rose as one man and nearly lifted the roof off'. Bottomley stood bent before the roar, and then bashfully disappeared from public view. As he made his way off the back of the platform, he turned to an acquaintance of Pearson's and said: 'That fetched the buggers – what?'

Pearson's own attitude was that the war was an unfortunate, but probably unavoidable, nuisance. 'I had long since ceased to feel that there was anything romantic about soldiering.' True to form he neither lamented his fate nor puffed up his importance; he just tried to make the best of it.

Late that year the remnants of the Shakespeare Society met at the St James's Theatre to honour Pearson for his work on the Tercentenary celebrations. In addition to Pearson, only three of the original Committee were present and all three would soon be dead. Sir George Alexander and H. B. Irving died within two years. Sir Herbert Beerbohm Tree, who presented Pearson with a silver cigarette case, had even less time. Tree asked Pearson how he liked army life? Pearson replied in the negative. 'Do you want to go to the front?' Tree asked. 'Does anyone *not* want to?' Pearson countered. 'I don't,' Tree said, and then added: 'At least I shan't pretend to.' In those days of elderly

men sitting about insisting 'If only we were younger . . .', Pearson
found Tree's honesty refreshing. He would never see Tree alive again.
On July 17, 1917 Tree was convalescing after minor surgery. After
eating his dinner that night, he talked and laughed with a nursing
attendant, then asked her to open a window. She did so and, when
she looked around, Tree was dead. He was sixty-four years old. When
Pearson heard the news, he wrote: 'London has not been the same
place to me since Tree's death. A link with my youth has been snapped.
The great theatre which he loved and lived in will remain, but the
genius which made it great is gone.'

   Pearson soon tired of quartermaster's duties and decided to try for a
commission. Armed with papers signed by Princess Marie Louise, late
patron of the Shakespeare Society and now patron of Private Pearson,
he was sent on a six-week training course from which he emerged
as Second-Lieutenant Pearson bound, within forty-eight hours, for
Mesopotamia.

CHAPTER SEVEN

War

'I am not among those who find virtue in war, which settles nothing, unsettles everything, and is a silly, boring occupation for a grown man.'

Hesketh Pearson

On March 15, 1917 Pearson was handed a terse written order to proceed to the Embarkation Dock, Devonport, by noon the following day 'for embarkation for Mesopotamia'. The intervening hours were taken up with inoculations, documentation, and packing and allowed little opportunity for an emotional leave-taking of his wife and son.

He sailed on the S.S. *Kenilworth Castle*, a Union Castle passenger liner which had been recently converted to a troopship. Their destination was Durban, with stops at Sierra Leone and Capetown. Submarine scares enlivened the first days at sea. For the remainder of the voyage, Peason amused himself, and perhaps few others, by editing a shipboard magazine called *The Eastern Enterprise*. The first issue was thus launched: 'From the pinnacle of the poop we make our bow before a disorganized, though necessarily immobile, public.' There followed gossip, poetry, quizzes, 'Courteous Thanks of the Day' to Officers whose ministrations had been appreciated, satire, deck sports results, special events and 'Things we Simply Must Know'; for example, 'Whether waiting in a queue three and a half hours for a bath is better than not washing? Whether that periscope of the mind, the monocle, is not as unnecessary as anything else beginning with "mo" – monogamy, monomania, monotony, monophysitism, for instance?'

Pearson's actual shipboard duties were minimal although he was once posted as Orderly Officer to receive complaints. Receiving none, he took it upon himself to inspect the men's mess. After inspection, he made this entry in the day book: 'The men's meat is uneatable, while their butter is disgusting and not fit for pigs. I suggest that the men should be given the officers' food, the officers the men's, alternately. At present the officers are fed like aristocrats and the men like animals.' Next morning he was summoned to explain his 'stupid and offensive' entry. His explanation was that it was true. At least since the time of Pontius Pilate this has proved a feeble defence and Pearson was disciplined for 'insolence' and 'frivolous comment tending towards insubordination'. His shore leave in Capetown was cancelled. The second (and last) issue of *The Eastern Enterprise* recorded Courteous Thanks of the Day to 'nobody in particular'. But the editor smugly announced that the first issue had 'hit the mark of our high calling'. Some shipboard critics had charged that the paper took too serious a tone; such critics, Pearson suggested, ought to repair to the ship's library 'wherein may be found "Paradise Lost" and "Pilgrim's Progress" both of which should afford endless joys and shrieks of merriment by the hour'. He also claimed to have received wireless messages of support from George Bernard Shaw ('Stupendous. Congratulations from Self and Kaiser') and from Lord Northcliffe ('Colossal. Raise the price at once').

Pearson sailed from Durban to Bombay aboard the *Aragon*. He spent a comfortable fortnight in Watson's Hotel, a gracious six-storey Victorian frame building looking out on a shaded boulevard. Here he had his first rickshaw ride. From Bombay he went to Basra, arriving in the middle of one of the hottest summers on record, when daytime shade temperatures regularly exceeded 120 degrees. The dry heat cured his tuberculosis but he soon contracted sandfly fever and colitis. He was moved to Beit Na'ana Hospital where an amorous dalliance with a nurse prolonged his recovery.

After the war Pearson wrote a short story about the nurse. She had black hair and eyebrows, large brown eyes 'with a light that came and went', and a mouth 'made for rapture'. He met her on his eighth day in hospital and her effect on him was instantaneous. 'The whole of his world came toppling down the moment he felt her touch and looked into her eyes.' The story describes Pearson's boldness in declaring his infatuation and his astonishment when, instead of rebuffing him, she proposed that they meet in the garden the next day. There, after some initial reticence, she gave herself to him. 'The sudden birth of an uncontrollable passion, following a long period of enforced celibacy, had whipped him to a delirium.' This experience, the most sexually intense of Pearson's life, left him 'leaning weakly against the stump of a tree'.

Within a week, the nurse was transferred to Baghdad and Pearson was discharged to his camp. On infrequent occasions over the next three months, he was able to get permission to go into Baghdad. However he was soon transferred to another camp and never saw the nurse again. The most revealing aspect of his account is the comparison Pearson makes between the nurse (called 'Dolly' in the story) and his wife Gladys (called 'Mary'):

Dolly was unlike his wife, to whom he wrote pleasant, homely letters once a week. Dolly was dark-browed and had a quick wit. Mary, his wife, was fair, resigned and domesticated . . . He was fond of Mary – he kept telling himself that – very fond of her. She was a good wife and would make an excellent mother. But in his heart he rather pitied her. She was so very – what was the word?? – so very humdrum. She had never kindled in him the spark of passion. Not that she could help that! It simply wasn't in her to be anything more to him than a companion and a good housekeeper. Still, he had been quite satisfied in a dull, comfortable kind of way – until Dolly arrived in the ward . . .

For most of his life, Pearson would be torn between conflicting feelings of loyalty and love. At least from the time of his son Harry's birth in 1913, he was not in love with Gladys. He told Basil Harvey that. On certainly two occasions Pearson had love affairs sufficiently intense that he considered leaving Gladys (he once actually did leave). Yet, after his fashion, he remained doggedly loyal to her. He appreciated her kindness; he genuinely cared for her; he felt responsible for the pregnancy that had necessitated their marriage and thus indissolubly bound to her. Dr Johnson once observed that kindness is within our power, fondness is not. In his conduct to Gladys, Pearson tried to exhibit kindness but his heart followed its own course.

In the desert east of Kermanshah Pearson was stationed at a camp at the head of a large valley flanked by rugged hills. The one tolerable aspect was the view. On the northern valley flank he could see twenty-five miles of mountains rising gaunt and cadaverous to heights of 1,200 feet above sea level. The varied effects of light and atmosphere were dazzling. 'At sunset these colossal billows of rock changed from one tint to another – now bronze, now indigo, now almost pink, now cavernously black with an eerie rapidity . . . and right down the centre of the valley we could see the wide white road – the oldest road in the world – the road that had seen the birth and death of a dozen civilizations and had heard the pant of humanity from unrecorded times.'

In the constant heat and sand of the desert, Pearson developed septic sores on both legs. In the morning and again in the evening fresh poultices had to be applied, a process of 'inexpressible torture'. The doctor ordered total bed rest and advised Pearson to prepare himself for amputation because of gangrene. Major operations in Mesopotamia in 1917 usually meant death. Pearson's rueful solace was to marvel at how much the doctor's appearance resembled Falstaff's description of

Shallow: 'A man made after supper of a cheese paring; when he was
naked he was for all the world like a forked radish, with a head
fantastically carved upon it with a knife.' Only Hesketh's congenital
unwillingness to accept orders saved his legs. Although exercise had
been forbidden, each morning he dragged himself out of bed, at first
just hobbling to the tent entrance and back, then daily lengthening the
distance. 'Each movement caused so much pain that my greatest
difficulty was not to yell.' After a week the doctor noted slight improve-
ment; within a month the sores had all dried up. 'The MO was highly
satisfied with his treatment. I hadn't the heart to tell him what a fool he
was.'

Pearson's unit, 784 Company, was posted next to Baqubah on the
Diala River, an oasis of palm trees and vegetation thirty miles north-east
of Baghdad, from which convoys trekked across the sand to deliver food
and supplies each day to infantry at the front. Through the month of
July 1917 the afternoon shade temperatures exceeded 130 degrees. In
camp men would bury their heads in wet towels which, within a quarter
of an hour, would be bone dry. Vehicles broke down and had to be
repaired only after buckets of water had been sloshed over them;
the least touch of metal would blister flesh. Hale, fit men suddenly
fainted, sometimes died from heat prostration and were buried in
sandy graves.

For nearly a month, Pearson led a daily convoy of forty Ford vans
from Baqubah to Beled Ruz. The distance was only about sixty miles
but in the desert the trip often took twelve hours. The convoy set out
from camp at five each morning. On July 27, Pearson was accompanied
by a driver named Hope. As the first rays of sun illuminated the vast
wasteland of sand, the sand grouse greeted the dawn with shrill,
rook-like cries. At this hour, the desert was cool, stark and primeval.
Pearson was suddenly caught up in one of those transcendent experiences where for a fugitive moment all creation seems in harmony, where
the blinkers fall from one's eyes and the animating spirit behind and
within all life is briefly apprehended, moments which are the hallmark
of a mystical temperament. 'The whole of nature, or what there was of
it, seemed to be trembling with ecstasy,' he wrote later, 'on tiptoe with
excitement to greet its master, full-tongued. For perhaps half an hour
every scrap of discernible life in that colossal land of dust appeared to
lift its voice in praise of the Life-giver.' As the vehicles continued to
slink forward, the only life became crows and hawks overhead and an
occasional hyena prowling at a distance, the desert's air and land
scavengers. Suddenly the convoy was enveloped in a dust storm.
Unable to see the vehicle ahead, Hope cut the engine. Every crevice of

body and vehicle quickly filled with sand. 'It was like being buried alive. To breathe was to be suffocated. The world was a chaos of flying filth.' In an hour the storm had passed and the convoy regrouped, a tapering line of vehicles like a column of ants on a slow pilgrimage through sandhills. Mahrut was reached and passed. By mid-morning the convoy had reached Beled Ruz and the provisions were off-loaded and radiators and canteens were refilled. By noon they began retracing their path. The shade temperature now registered 133 degrees. Tyres punctured as though made of paper and repairs were excruciatingly difficult in the blast furnace conditions. Worse, to get the vans to Mahrut, the men had to pour their water canteens into the steaming radiators. Six drivers had to be left behind in the tiny tent hospital at Mahrut. The men begged Pearson not to attempt the final stretch to Baqubah that afternoon but he reminded them that if they failed the next day's convoy would not set out and men at the front could starve. In early afternoon the depleted convoy set forth. Within an hour, Pearson was delirious and saw visions of God 'dancing and clapping his hands and singing a song with this refrain: "Got you now! Got you now! Got you now!"' Then he blacked out entirely, recovering semi-consciousness with 'blackness and whirling spots' in front of his eyes but with a distant vision of the Diala River. The driver, Hope, was slumped over the steering wheel babbling incoherently, the vehicle still lurching forward. Then the van swerved, Hope's head lolled forward on the wheel, and the van pitched jerkily to a stop. The convoy halted and Hope's dead body was lifted into the back. 'Through the blinding glare of the afternoon sun I drove the dead man into Baqubah. At the entrance of the camp I noticed three enormous hawks wheeling slowly in the airless void above us.'

In September Pearson was sent to the Euphrates front where it was slightly cooler. He was soon back in hospital, this time suffering from dysentery and malaria. For two days he was delirious, then semi-consciousness gradually returned, although he was unable to speak or respond even to the simplest question. But he could hear, and through a fog he caught a nurse telling a doctor: 'He's got honour on the brain. Something about honour setting arms and legs.' The comatose Pearson mentally echoed the doctor's surprise. 'The words were wholly out of character, yet they were vaguely familiar. Suddenly it all became clear. In my delirium I had been quoting Falstaff's speech on honour. The humour of the situation seized me, and in spite of the pain in my head, the top of which seemed to be opening and shutting, I was convulsed with silent, helpless laughter, in which condition I again passed out. The doctor told me later that my recovery had begun, when for no apparent reason my body had been shaken by successive spasms, which were followed by several hours of peaceful sleep.' Pearson concluded that, in the most literal sense, Shakespeare had saved his life.

He was transferred next to Amora and was given command of a detachment. His first order of business was to put a stop to what he considered 'all the childish and degrading formalities of army life' such as field punishment, and unnecessary parades and fatigues. He shared the men's labours and closely attended to their rations. He treated them as adults not recalcitrant schoolboys. The men responded by diligent work and high spirits so that 'whenever anything really difficult had to be achieved we were invariably chosen for the job'. Sometimes Pearson's disdain for discipline produced a sticky situation; one of his men, Tasker, had carelessly damaged a vehicle, and Pearson received a direct order to discipline him. He attended to duty by carrying out the order and to conscience by emulating Tree's handling of the light-fingered actor who had made off with the box office receipts. 'Having no option, I reprimanded him, King's Regs making it necessary that the cost of the damage should be deducted from his pay. I did what was required of me in a very half-hearted apologetic manner, afterwards taking the lad on one side and giving him the money which in my official capacity I had been forced to tax him.'

It was in Amora that Pearson received a head wound. Under fire, a piece of metal from a car sheared off and knocked him unconscious. The wound was never properly cleansed, although after the war some shards were surgically removed. Pearson was inclined to attribute his flash-point temper and sometimes erratic behaviour to this head wound.

On April 15, 1918, Pearson was cited by Winston Churchill, then Secretary of State for War, for 'gallant and distinguished services in the field'. After the war (now Captain) Pearson received several medals, including the Military Cross, although he characteristically omits to allude to this in his memoirs. Basil Harvey claimed that he would have forfeited Pearson's friendship ever to mention the MC. 'Hesketh considered everything connected with the war, including the MC, to be senseless and boring.' Pearson once told Harvey the circumstances leading to the MC, laughing about it as 'a big joke'. During a fierce battle, an English soldier broke ranks and ran. Pearson confronted him, punched him on the jaw, and knocked him out. The other men held their positions and the battle was eventually won. His rage, Pearson told Harvey, sprang not from patriotism but from pique; he was offended that a moment so fraught with peril that it froze him on the spot should have induced so contrary a reaction in another human being.

Since Pearson believed that war settled nothing, he entertained scant hopes for peace. 'International peace will never come while there is turmoil in the heart of man,' he wrote; 'to expect peace between nations is to believe that sparrow hawks can lay dove's eggs.'

Early in 1918 a British expeditionary force reached the Pai Tak pass in the mountains which divided Persia (now Iran) from Iraq. Their commander, General Dunsterville, was not prepared to risk the journey through Persia to the Caspian Sea without knowing whether the route was passable to motor transport. Pearson was selected to find out. Persia had been ravished by both Turks and Cossacks and the population was decimated and starving. As Pearson and his guide, Tully, bumped along mountain trails and through quagmires, famished men and women appeared and threw themselves in their path begging for scraps of food. The more robust men were sometimes threatening and Pearson often had to fire above their heads to clear the way. Eventually they reached Kermanshah where several days were spent repairing damage to the vehicle. Pearson was warned to avoid the market bazaars where uniformed British soldiers were not welcome, but the merchants there had a peculiar fascination for him. 'Monstrous to think of these "fat and greasy citizens" sleek and capon-fed, with their double chins and swollen purses, sitting at the receipt of custom, their fellow men drooping from want on every hand. How many skeletons go to make up their cupboards?'

He made inquiries of the British Consul whether it would be safe to visit a school acquaintance named MacMurray who was now managing the Persian Bank in Kermanshah. The Consul advised against it, but warned that if he must go he should go armed, in uniform, and be accompanied by at least one other person. In any event the Consul could assume no responsibility for his safety. Pearson latched on to a burly Australian who was willing to act as his bodyguard and guide. But in the central marketplace they became separated and Pearson found himself being followed by a gang of six men 'sunburnt, hairy, tall, their teeth gleaming between dark moustaches and beards, their bodies taut and upright, their clothes held in by girdles, from which descended a miscellaneous display of death-dealing instruments'. No matter how he quickened or slowed his pace the men pursued him, neither gaining nor falling back. Eventually he ducked into a sweet shop where the owner sat cross-legged and impassive on the floor. When Pearson selected a sweet and attempted to pay, the owner gazed at him without moving. As he turned to leave, the six men stood blocking the exit. For several seconds they stared at each other in silence. 'Then something within me snapped. The sense of solitude that had been creeping over me through these mortal minutes became acute; the feeling of being shut in was more than I could bear. My courage ebbed from me; I felt frightened and helpless; I began to look about me, wild-eyed, to right, to left; the sweat broke out on my brow, and suddenly my fear turned to terror.' Pearson vaulted over a counter and through an open rear exit, falling down a short flight of steps. Always a powerful runner, he was lent wings by fear. Down winding alleys leading only to more alleys he ran, insensible to people around him, twice firing his revolver at those who obstructed his path. At some point, he was slashed by a knife. Suddenly one alley seemed to widen and he found himself panting for breath at the front entrance of the Bank of Persia. 'I hadn't my cheque book on me, but I went in all the same.'

After the vehicle had been repaired, Pearson and Tully left Kerman-shah for Hamadan. There was no road, only a rough track among boulders but, in four days, they reached their destination. Famine in Hamadan was, if anything, worse than elsewhere, and Pearson picked his way over dead and dying, young and old, in corners and doorways, 'through a veritable hive of stinking lanes'. Groans and the stench of death hung over everything. 'I hurried through these pest-holes as fast as their human obstructions would permit.' Tully padded along be-hind, plucking at his right or left arm when he wished to signify a change of direction. As they proceeded deeper into what seemed a rank maze, Pearson became conscious of a sound, 'a long drawn-out murmur which rose and fell rhythmically', gradually increasing in volume until it became 'a roar of angry, brutal voices'. Where the lane widened, Pearson and Tully were caught up in a phalanx of humanity and hurtled several hundred yards into an open square. Pearson fought free, bolted for an open doorway, drew his service revolver and turned to face the mob. 'I was amazed beyond words that no one was taking the slightest notice of me, that no one indeed seemed aware of my presence. I had, of course, had no time to consider the position, and it was only natural under the circumstances that I should have regarded the incident as a direct assault upon myself.'

The square was now filled with a surging, shouting mob. From his vantage point, Pearson watched as a clearing was made by about twenty men, taller and stronger than the rest, who formed a kind of gauntlet down which they propelled two half-naked women. The women ran in a crouching position, with their arms over their heads to ward off blows. Encircled in the middle of the mob they cowered, bent and shaking, while the pack howled like wolves. Horrified, Pearson barely noticed a wrench at his wrist and his service revolver was gone. 'The scene in the square held me spellbound and I could think of nothing else. Without troubling to follow up my loss, I besieged the fellow with questions. What was going to happen? Why were the people shouting? What was the trouble? Why were the two women there? And so forth. In a few words he told me the truth. I gasped and went cold all over. I think I would have dropped if I hadn't been held upright by the pressure of the crowd. These two wretched people had gone mad with hunger and eaten their own children. They had been dragged here by their fellow citizens to be stoned to death.' Pearson was brought back to reality by a shrill scream from one of the women. A tall man held a stone over his head. 'It struck the woman on the breast and a thin spurt of blood streaked the tattered gown with which she tried to ward off the cruel blow. A demoniacal howl rose from a thousand throats, and the writhing form of the helpless victim was pounded with a hail of bricks and dirt.' Pearson was seized by 'a murderous fit – had I kept possession of my revolver several in the crowd would have gone to join the miserable object of their wrath'. Tully tugged at his sleeve: 'No good, Sahib – pistol gone!' Pearson and Tully pushed themselves away from the carnage and, in a few minutes, found themselves in a courtyard. As Pearson collected his breath, Tully begged him to follow. Realizing their danger, Pearson followed. 'At the gate of Tully's house he handed me a revolver. "Where did you get this?" I inquired. "It is yours, Sahib. I took it from you. It was safer with me." I looked at the man's impassive face, but said nothing. He had probably saved my life.'

The stoning incident had a grisly sequel. Just before demobilization, Pearson passed through Hamadan again and was invited to dine with Tully and the local police chief. The conversation turned to the famine, by then much alleviated. The Chief said: 'Those women – you remember them, Mr Tully? – They were unlucky.'

'How unlucky?' I asked.

'Well, you see, it was so general,' replied the Chief. 'They were caught in the act you might say – but there were plenty more.'

'I suppose they were both killed,' I said, more from a desire to end the subject than from uncertainty.

'Killed? Yes, and cooked, my dear Sir.'

'Cooked?' I cried.

'Naturally,' he answered, lifting his eyebrows in mild surprise: 'Cooked and eaten . . . but what would you . . . the people were so hungry . . .'

It is scarcely surprising that Pearson hated the East in general and Persia in particular. Throughout his war service he had been sending dispatches and features articles back to the *Star* and the *Manchester Guardian*. These articles, on topics as varied as Egyptian archaeology and an Oriental version of *Hamlet* performed in Baghdad, have one

consistent theme running through them – a deep, passionate loathing of
the region and its inhabitants. In one article, 'The Glorious Orient',
Pearson summed up the three main features of the East as he saw it.
One, smell; a pungent, unmistakable smell compounded of roughly
equal parts dirt, dung, decay and death. 'Globe-trotters talk chiefly of
the Spell of the East. I was chiefly impressed by the smell of the East.'
Two, random cruelty to man and beast. Pearson was once disciplined
by a Military Court of Enquiry for shooting a donkey whose Arab
master had beaten and cut it until its bones stuck through its skin and its
back was one large, festering sore. He made matters worse by saying in
his written deposition that his only regret was that he had not also shot
the Arab. Third, flies, omnipresent and voracious. Flies that bit
through clothing and clung to food until it was inside the mouth. 'I
longed for a certain thing with an unnatural intensity. That thing was a
vast churn in which I could put all the flies of the Universe, and while I
turned the handle I wanted to hear the scrunch and squelch within
during the soul-animating process of converting them into a gelatinous
mass.'

The highpoint of Pearson's tour of duty came on a hot July day in
1918. A tall, thin man wearing a pith helmet entered his tent at
Khanikin and demanded transport. As Pearson was making arrange-
ments, the stranger began to talk expansively of poetry and painting.
Starved of real conversation for over two years, Pearson listened with
interest. Thus began his acquaintance with Colin Hurry, 'the only
first-rate intelligence I encountered during the war', a man who, along
with Hugh Kingsmill, would become one of his two closest and lifelong
friends. Later that year Pearson and Hurry were stationed together at
Kermanshah, and long after the camp was in darkness they would stroll
up and down between the tents 'discussing everything in the universe,
from the Creator to the protozoa'. Both men sympathized with the idea
of a God who assisted the needy, but neither could understand why the
universe, unless dismissed as a cosmic joke, should so resemble an
obstacle course with God as the celestial umpire. Hurry's view tended
to creative evolutionism; that is, that a benevolent force was behind the
scenes at work towards some inconceivable destiny, but Him or It was
unreachable and uninterested in the daily human drama. Hurry sent
Pearson several drafts of a poem in which he tried to articulate a joint
view; the poem was only completed after the war, when the two men
spent a walking holiday at Arundel. Pearson removed the whisky bottle
and told Hurry that his next drink would follow completion of the last
line. Hurry settled to it, producing 'Him Declare I Unto You'; the
concluding stanzas sum up both men's religious view.

His starry speculations
No finite mind can guess
No human science measure
That wider nothingness.

The sparrow falls unheeded,
Unseen the lily blooms;
All living things are speeded
Each to their several dooms.

No patriarch bestowing
Now kisses, now the rod:
Unknowable, unknowing,
Unconscious . . . He is God.

Colin Hurry was a patient, imperturbable, meticulous man. After the war, he established a successful public relations business. He frequently lent Pearson money and eventually gave him a job at a regular salary for few specific duties. After one display of Hurry's generosity, Pearson was moved to say: 'Colin, you really do have certain Christ-like qualities.' 'Unfortunately not the most important one,' Hurry replied: 'I cannot turn water into wine.'

After the war Pearson tried to interest publishers in Hurry's poems. In 1923 Constable published a tiny volume called *The Lost Illusion*. Pearson later persuaded Cecil Palmer (whose only defect as a publisher, Pearson used to say, was that he scarcely ever paid royalties) to publish Hurry's *Premature Epitaphs* which appeared under the pseudonym Kensal Green. Colin Hurry loved writing premature epitaphs and he would often send them to his subject, expressing apologetic hopes that they might long remain prematurely in print. Some are quite fine, particularly this one written for G. K. Chesterton.

Chesterton companion,
His companions mourn.
Chesterton crusader
Leaves a cause forlorn.
Chesterton the critic.
Pays no further heed.
Chesterton the poet
Lives while men shall read.
Chesterton the dreamer
Is by sleep beguiled;
And there enters Heaven
Chesterton . . . the child.

On the flyleaf of Hesketh's copy of *Premature Epitaphs* Hurry wrote:

When Hesketh Pearson passed away
God gave all Heaven a holiday.
But not from joy nor yet from sorrow
. . . THEY NEEDED STRENGTH TO FACE TOMORROW.

Pearson wrote two books based on his wartime experiences. The first, *A Persian Critic* (1923), purports to be a record of conversations with a mysterious Persian sage named Bahram to whose tent in the garden suburbs of Kermanshah Pearson ostensibly makes his way to lie on carpets, drink tea, smoke cigarettes, and talk of English literature. Not surprisingly Bahram holds forth in a Pearsonesque manner on all manner of Pearson's favourite topics. The overall result is predictably soporific, rather like listening to a ventriloquist engaged in earnest dialogue with himself. Two small points about this otherwise forgettable book deserve notice. One is that Colin Hurry was pressed into writing a not very convincing Introduction which begins: 'The internal evidence of the essays themselves . . . is heavily against the so-versatile philosopher and poet who is made to seem like an etherealized and orientalized Dr Johnson,' and concludes: 'On the larger issue which to some will be important – namely the accuracy of Pearson's reporting – I am frankly indifferent.' The other point of interest is that nowhere else does Pearson make so explicit a statement of his religious faith as the words he puts into Bahram's mouth: 'I cannot understand the people who ask me whether I believe in God. They might just as well ask me whether I believe in life.' Whether or not Pearson's intention was to stake out more orthodox theological ground than Colin Hurry, that is the result. The very last words of the book are a rhapsody of divine praise: 'God is so easy to find . . . think of the enchanting world we live in! Think of the divine power vested in us to make it fine! Think of God's creation of Life – that superb example and never-ending miracle, set before our very eyes, day by day, hour by hour, minute by minute – which we have but to apprehend in order to establish the kingdom of heaven on earth . . . God is so obvious that He cannot be sought . . . in a sense, then, it is wrong to say that one *finds* God. It would be truer to says that one divines Him. In an instant, as it were, one receives second-sight. And in that instant one perceives that He is Everywhere and Everything.'

Pearson's other wartime book, *Iron Rations*, is an account of some of his experiences plus a collection of his articles and dispatches. At first he had trouble getting it published, partly because war memoirs had flooded the market, partly because publishers were put off by the irreverent note Pearson appended to the customary disclaimer: 'When I say that the characters and episodes in this book are imaginary and have no relation whatever to real people and actual happenings, it will of course be understood that both characters and episodes are taken straight from life and are strictly true in every detail.' *Iron Rations* appeared in 1928, published by Cecil Palmer, minus the offending note. Neither book sold well, although *A Persian Critic* garnered a few favourable reviews, and an anonymous reviewer in the *Morning Post* compared *Iron Rations* to the Old Testament in recommending it as a salutary corrective to the jingoistic bilge which had poured forth about the war. This pleased Pearson 'as much as anything I have ever read about myself . . . except for the fact that I resent the Bible dragged in when anything of mine is being discussed'.

Early in 1919 Pearson was sent again to Baghdad. While driving a van on Maude Avenue he struck an Arab pedestrian. Pearson took the man to the civilian hospital where the doctor on duty assured him that the injury was only a trifle and a French nurse turned the air blue with perfervid denunciations of 'the dark species in general and Arab mankind in particular'. All the while blood oozed from the man's nose and ears. 'Just as the sister was in the middle of a heart-felt phrase at the coolie's expense, the latter relieved us and obliged everyone else by claiming his kinship with the dust.' Pearson was strangely cavalier about this incident, to the point even of sending back an article called 'On Killing a Man' in which he claimed to care less about the Arab's life than that of 'an alien dog or a moderately unattractive cat'. Three years of desert warfare, years of heat, disease and death, had corroded his sensibilities.

July 19, 1919 was given over to celebrating the Peace Treaty. There was a morning parade in the desert east of Baghdad, followed by speeches and a ceremonial thanksgiving. As the day wore on the celebrations became liquid and boisterous. By evening all but the stupefied or the phlegmatic had gathered on the banks of the Tigris river. Searchlights played over the crowd of white-robed men, women clutching children, desert nomads and uniformed Tommies. Guns were fired in the air. British cheers went up from hoarse voices. Ships on the river were lit from stem to stern. Tooting their horns, launches darted in and out between the bigger ships. On a raised dais military and local officials sat together while a brass band serenaded them with patriotic anthems. The day's events culminated in a salvo of red, white and blue rockets sent up by the Royal Flying Corps. Captain Pearson took in the spectacle from the river's edge, drinking whisky and soda. 'While I drank I reflected upon the probable meaning of the Peace we had just been celebrating. Would it, like every other "Peace" in history, merely be a prelude to another war?'

It is fitting that Pearson's army career ended as it began, in farce. Perhaps because of his acting experience, he was asked by GHQ to lecture on demobilization. To this end, he was provided with a stack of pamphlets, documents and memoranda, most of these conflicting and all unintelligible. Finding little inspiration here, he brightened on learning that a Major from GHQ would come to Baghdad to share his expertise. Pearson went to the Major's lecture only to discover that whatever abilities he possessed, public speaking was not among them. The Major stammered, coughed and stuttered his way through an hour of drivel. 'At last he gave it up in despair, declared that he would write articles in the *Baghdad Times*, which he hoped would answer all the points raised, and retired from the stage to the accompaniment of groans, hoots, jeers, and a fusillade of ear-piercing whistles.' About the only fact Pearson could extract from all this was that demobilization was to be carried out by an Industrial Group system which meant that soldiers would return home in accordance with labour demands in England for their particular occupation. To men who had spent years on the desert front, most without any leave, this was distinctly unpopular, particularly as English politicians had been promising that all soldiers would come home within six months.

In his first lecture on demobilization, Pearson attempted a shaky defence of the Industrial Group scheme. However, he was pressed hard during a question period about the politicians' promises. He replied: 'The man who believes a politician ought to be pickled and embalmed as a prime specimen of imbecile credulity.' He was then asked why British teachers with jobs in India were going home before teachers with jobs in England. Pearson said he didn't know. The questioner persisted. Finally Pearson said: 'It is probably merely another instance of the British government sucking up to the Indian government.' This reply was greeted by 'shouts of appreciative merriment' but GHQ was not amused. Pearson was disciplined for 'making a mockery of demobilization' and court martial proceedings were even rumoured. However, within a month, the Industrial Group plan was officially abandoned and Pearson escaped with a terse telegram from GHQ: 'Cease lecturing.'

He left Baghdad by ship in November 1919. As they sailed up Plymouth Sound on a clear, sunny December day 'the sight of green fields and hedges tugged at my heart and brought tears to my eyes'. Gladys and Henry, now six years old, were waiting for him on the quay. He weighed 130 pounds (50 pounds below his regular weight), skin and bone on his six foot, two inch frame. He received the usual army gratuity for his rank (Captain) plus a small pension for what was believed to be incurable malaria and dysentery. Actually, both ailments soon disappeared under the ministrations of an unregistered health practitioner named Raphael Roche who was recommended to Pearson by George Bernard Shaw. He was again without a job but at least he was alive.

CHAPTER EIGHT

Contemporaries

'Having realized that humanity is thoroughly shoddy, laugh at it, don't scream at it; and let your laugh be rich like Shakespeare's, not withering like Swift's. Perhaps the ideal stage in human development is that at which one is always "taken in" by humanity, and always aware that one is being "taken in".'

Hesketh Pearson

The postwar literary scene to which Pearson had returned was dominated by five men: G. K. Chesterton, Hilaire Belloc, H. G. Wells, Bernard Shaw and Frank Harris. Either through the theatre or the Shakespeare Society, Pearson became acquainted with each of them. Yet it was none of these, but rather a struggling novelist and critic, Hugh Kingsmill, who became Pearson's closest friend and literary mentor.

Pearson first caught a glimpse of G. K. Chesterton in 1913 in the Cheshire Cheese, a pub off Fleet Street reputed to have been a favourite haunt of Dr Johnson's. 'One should always drink port from a tankard,' G.K.C. was saying to a young man with yellow hair, 'because one does not like to see that it is coming to an end. Also it takes on a richer hue in a tankard. Also it has a mellower taste. Besides one can *grasp* a tankard and *drain* it . One can only *sip* a glass.' To each statement the young disciple gave affirmatory nods but Pearson observed a furtive guilt on his face as he was then drinking from a glass. Chesterton continued: 'Glasses are made to be smashed. It is said that those who live in glass houses should not throw stones. But what man, living in a glass house, would do anything else? It is the simplest way of getting out of a glass house. Indeed if he throws a sufficient quantity of stones, it ceases to be a glass house.' To this the young man made no response but appeared thoughtful. After a silence, Chesterton boomed out: 'I do not need to look, but my other four senses tell me that there is no more port in this tankard of mine.' Anxious to seize the moment, the young man leapt to his feet and asked the barmaid for two tankards of port. 'No, no,' interposed Chesterton, 'it is my turn. One tankard of port for me, and one glass of port for this gentleman who is, by birth and training, a sipper.' All of which turned out to be mock bravado because, the next time Pearson spotted him in licensed premises, G.K.C. was sipping Horlicks.

Pearson was not introduced to Chesterton on this occasion but, a year later, he was, and he amused G.K.C. by parodying a debate between Shaw and Chesterton. Chesterton considered the parody brilliant and urged Pearson to have it published. It was later published in the *Adelphi* magazine, from which it has taken on a life of its own, often being reprinted as though it were a transcript of an actual debate. The parody is lengthy but the gist of it is G.K.C.'s demonstration that G.B.S. is a soulless puritan.

G.K.C.: You puritans, I say, fashion God in your own image. You conceive the truth to lie in yourselves. You would not be content merely to remould the world nearer to the heart's desire; you would recast it entirely to the highbrow's dream. The magnificence of uncertainty, the splendour of ignorance, the sublime impossibility of Nature, the marvel and mystery of this miraculous and ridiculous thing called life – all this is lost on you.

G.B.S.: I think I catch your drift. If a manure-heap close to your front door were fouling the neighbourhood, you wouldn't remove it because God might have placed it there in order to test your sense of smell.

G.K.C.: I couldn't overlook the possibility that my next door neighbour might be a Socialist; in which case the manure-heap would have its uses.

G.B.S.: You are evading the point.

G.K.C.: Points are made to evade. Consider the history of the rapier.

G.B.S.: There is no getting at you. You are as bad as Dr Johnson. When your pistol misses fire, which it usually does, you knock your opponent down with the butt-end. Why will you never come to grips?

G.K.C.: The art of argument lies in the ingenuity with which one can hide and seek simultaneously.

G.B.S.: But what is your philosophy?

G.K.C.: My philosophy is in the thrust, not in the parry.

G.B.S.: I don't see that. You must be able to hold your own field while you are advancing on the enemy's territory.

G.K.C.: Not necessarily. If my attack is strenuous enough, the enemy will require all his strength to hold his own fortifications.

G.B.S.: And if he succeeds in holding them?

G.K.C.: Then I retire, bring up my reserves, and attack him again at a totally unexpected quarter.
G.B.S.: But if he attacks you while you are retiring?
G.K.C.: I go to ground.

And so on. The debate ends with G.B.S. stalking off in disgust at his inability to pin Chesterton down. When G.K.C. saw the published version of the debate he wrote to Pearson saying that he had parodied his style so convincingly that he ought to produce his next book for him.

Two Chesterton anecdotes were told to Pearson by his friend, Edward Fordham, who had been at St Paul's School with Chesterton. In the midst of a vehement debate about whether some social policy was good or bad, Chesterton said: 'The word "good" has many meanings. For example, if a man were to shoot his grandmother at a range of five hundred yards, I should call him a good shot but not necessarily a good man.' Chesterton was seldom stumped by an unexpected question. Following a school debate on eugenics, he was approached by an elderly woman who, in a rather affected manner, inquired: 'Mr Chesterton, I wonder if you could tell me what race I belong to?' 'Madam,' returned G.K.C., adjusting his glasses: 'I should certainly say one of the conquering races.'

Pearson admired Chesterton's virtuosity as a writer and talker. With a pun or a paradox or a play on words, he could expose pomposity and deflate humbug. His zestful enjoyment of life, 'a sort of Falstaff in bulk and wit' as Pearson described him, mirrored Hesketh's own vivacious temperament. Even after Chesterton's verbal juggling and weakness for paradox had become silly, Pearson retained an admiration for him. Just before going to tea at Chesterton's, a young girl was told by her mother that she would learn a lot from Mr Chesterton who was a very clever man; afterwards the child revealed the nature of her lessons: 'He taught me how to throw buns in the air and catch them in my mouth.'

Pearson once went to lunch with Chesterton at Beaconsfield, arriving to find another guest, a Roman Catholic priest, present; although Pearson does not identify the priest it is probable that it was Monsignor John O'Connor, the original of Father Brown. After lunch, the three men sat in the rose garden and the conversation drifted to religion. Chesterton had not yet converted to Roman Catholicism but he demanded to know why Pearson was not a Catholic? Wishing to evade a subject which always took second place to literature and speculating on the lives of famous men, Pearson muttered some vague and inconclusive reply. The priest then interjected: 'Is there anything in the teaching of the Church that stands in your way?' 'Everything,' Pearson replied. 'You do not believe in God, then?' 'Indeed, I do. But I think the subject too big for Popes, Archbishops, Convocations or Cardinals. You cannot reduce God to a formula or a doctrine. And I think theologians are the last people to understand God, just as scholars are the last people to understand Shakespeare.' 'What is your conception of God?' demanded G.K.C. By now rather rattled by this persistence, Pearson replied: 'If I could give you my conception of God, I might have conceived Him, and I assure you I didn't. But my private opinion is that he is a combination of oxygen, hydrogen and carbonic acid gas, with other substances thrown in to make him solid.' 'Well, well,' said the priest, 'we are getting nowhere. But you will come around to us in time.' Pearson said: 'If only you realized that in admiring those lovely roses you were nearer to God than when saying your masses, I should be with you in no time.' At this point, the priest left and Pearson's account concludes: 'I spent a very pleasant evening with G.K.C.'

Pearson wrote several articles for the *New Witness*, then edited by G.K.C.'s brother, Cecil. However, he turned down an opportunity to be their fiction reviewer at a salary of three pounds a week. Although he needed the money, Pearson could not work up sufficient interest in novels. It was GKC who saved Pearson's writing career. After the *Whispering Gallery* fiasco, it was Chesterton who approached publishers on Pearson's behalf to convince them that, however impetuous or irresponsible he might be, Pearson was a writer of merit who deserved a second chance. Twice Chesterton lent Pearson money with little expectation of repayment. And, most important, he contributed an Introduction, *gratis*, to Pearson's biography of Sydney Smith just at the moment when it was most required.

The last time Pearson saw G.K.C. was at the Savage Club in January 1929. Thinking that Chesterton might have forgotten him in the interval, he reintroduced himself. Chesterton protested: 'I remember you well. In fact you appear in one of my Father Brown stories.' Pearson naturally inquired which one but Chesterton would not be drawn. 'It is a detective story and the least you can do is detect yourself.'

The occasion was a dinner party to honour G.K.C.'s contribution to the cause of Distribution. Pearson sat close to Chesterton and kept him under observation, later reporting to Kingsmill: 'There is only one word to describe G.K.C. He looked unutterably *wretched*. It was as if he absolutely *had* to believe, but simply couldn't. The horror of the man who sees the pit and shuts his eyes to it – a sort of knowing ignorance.' Among the other guests was the man whose name became so inextricably linked to Chesterton that Bernard Shaw invented the term 'Chesterbelloc' – 'a quadruped, twiformed monster'.

In many ways, Hilaire Belloc was Chesterton's opposite; belli-cose where G.K.C. was playful; pompous where G.K.C. was in-souciant; skinflint where G.K.C. was generous. Even in physical appearance they were contrasts: Chesterton, a billowing blimp of a man; Belloc, squat and severe, looking like a medieval cardinal with mutton-chop whiskers. 'I used to see Belloc in a bar near Ludgate Circus, debating, reciting in his high-pitched voice, laughing, telling Rabelaisian stories, and improvising lines of poetry that would not have been received with such shouts of merriment in a company of tea-drinkers.'

In the mid-Twenties Pearson attended a cricket match at Rodmell in Sussex and afterwards accompanied Belloc to a reasonably stately home on the village green. In full voice Belloc declaimed poetry, club room yarns, banter and philosophy until the recently defeated Liberal candi-date for a near-by constituency showed up. Immediately the conversa-tion was deflated with political drivel. 'He told us of his life struggles, of his attempts to liberalize the community, of his friendships with the eminent.' Belloc, who was inured to the tedium of politicians by a stint in the House of Commons, took this for a long time and then, when the politician paused to catch a breath, he looked innocently at the ceiling and interjected: 'Have you ever heard the story of the male and female contortionists on their honeymoon?' The politician admitted that he had not. 'Oh,' said Belloc. This did not advance matters and the politician, by now successfully side-tracked, felt compelled to inquire further. 'They broke it off,' said Belloc. So, Pearson noted, did the politician.

In 1947, when Belloc was seventy-six and in failing health, Pearson and Kingsmill visited him at King's Land, his Sussex home. In the last of their three talk and travel books, they included an account of their conversation. Pearson asked Belloc if he had influenced Chesterton? Belloc didn't think so particularly, except on property where he said that all of G.K.C.'s ideas had come straight from his books. Pearson asked if Belloc would write an autobiography?

Belloc: No. No gentleman writes about his private life. Anyway, I hate writing. I wouldn't have written a word if I could have helped it. I only wrote for money. *The Path To Rome* is the only book I ever wrote for love.
Pearson: Didn't you write *The Four Men* for love?
Belloc: No. Money.
Pearson: *The Cruise of the Nona*?
Belloc: Money.

Kingsmill: That is a wonderful passage in *The Path to Rome*, about youth borne up the valley on the evening air.

Belloc: Oh-yes.

Kingsmill: I love the poetry in your essays, especially in the volume *On Nothing*.

Belloc: Quite amusing. Written for money.

It was dusk as Pearson and Kingsmill left, Pearson remarking that he was grateful Belloc had never come into an inheritance and was compelled always to write for money. As they considered the old warrior, solitary and in ill-health, living on while the four human beings who had mattered most to him – his wife, mother, eldest son Peter, and G.K.C. – were all dead, Kingsmill quoted a verse Belloc had written as a young man:

> A lost thing could I never find,
> Nor a broken thing mend:
> And I fear I shall be all alone
> When I get towards the end.
> Who will there be to comfort me
> Or who will be my friend?

Pearson was never a close friend of H. G. Wells whose work (particularly *Kipps* and *Mr Polly*) he admired but whom he considered 'a lesser Dickens, small, tubby and easily offended'. Pearson experienced Wells' thin skin when, in an article, he referred to his squeaky voice. He immediately received a long letter of complaint from Wells, the gist of which was that if ever his voice had been squeaky it was not so now, that he had trained himself to be a platform speaker and a broadcaster, and that he might now almost be considered a baritone. In any case, the letter finished off, why fuss about a man's voice? It was what the voice said that mattered. Pearson replied in a placatory fashion but noted privately: 'I could tell from the querulous tone of the letter that the writer still had a squeaky voice.'

In August 1939 Pearson called on Wells at his house at 13 Hanover Terrace, Regent's Park. When he mentioned that he was contemplating a biography of Shakespeare, Wells said irritably: 'Why must people live in the past?' 'Because the past which we know is more interesting than the future which we don't know,' Pearson replied. 'Isn't the present good enough for you?' Wells asked. 'Yes, quite. But one of its principal charms is that it enshrines the past.' Observing that Wells was becoming agitated, Pearson tried to move the conversation to another topic by asking Wells what he thought of Frank Harris? 'Harris,' replied Wells, 'was a blackguard, a blackmailer, a liar and a bore, who would have murdered his own grandmother for sixpence if he had the courage to do it.' Thinking this rather strong, Pearson demurred. Wells than related this glimpse of Frank Harris's methods. Shortly before the war Harris went to stay in Essex with the Countess of Warwick who solicited his advice in confidence concerning some correspondence of an intimate nature which she had received from the Prince of Wales (later King Edward VII). When Harris left, the letters could not be located. When he was eventually tracked down in America, Harris admitted to having taken the letters and claimed that they were placed at his disposal with a view to publication. A King's ransom was paid for their return.

By exactly what means the pint-size, unattractive and unscrupulous Harris became editor of half-a-dozen leading newspapers and magazines (including the *Saturday Review*) remains a mystery. Certainly Wells was partly correct in attributing his success to extortion and blackmail. A story Harris tells of himself suggests that he learned the basic techniques early in life. At the age of four, Harris says, he surprised his nurse in bed with a man and he threatened to tell unless she gave him sugar on his bread and butter. His skills were considerably refined when he became editor of the *Candid Friend*, about which Bernard Shaw said that it was candid about everyone who declined to be financially friendly. When Pearson got to know him, Harris often boasted of his unscrupulous methods. He told Hesketh how he once happened to be driving past the office of Horatio Bottomley when he observed coming out the chairman of a company which Bottomley had been ripping apart in his paper. 'Stopping my cab, I walked straight into Bottomley's sanctum. I hadn't been announced and his surprise at my appearance turned to amazement when I said: "I want five hundred pounds of the sum your recent visitor has just paid to you." He knew me and knew that I knew him. Without a word he opened his safe, took out a bundle of bank notes and handed me five hundred pounds. "How did you know about it?" he asked. "I didn't," I replied, and left him to think that one out!' While all of Harris's stories must be presumptively considered apocryphal, at least this one is consistent with his character and his methods.

Before the first war, Pearson saw a good deal of Harris. One evening they went on a pub crawl during which Harris related an interminable tale of his early days as a commercial traveller in America trying to sell copies of the Bible. 'The point of the yarn, reached some three hours after its beginning, was that the housewives on whom he called refused to purchase Holy Writ but proved more pliable in other respects, and something more lively than the Gospel had been propagated in foreign parts.' The evening ended in a drunken brawl after a patron took offence at the conversation and hurled a cuspidor at Harris which narrowly missed hitting Pearson.

When Harris was committed to Brixton Jail for contempt of court, Pearson wrote to the prison authorities requesting permission to visit him. His request was turned down. As soon as he was released, Harris went into self-imposed exile, first in France then in New York, where he worked on his lewd autobiography, *My Life and Loves*. For many years this 'autobiography' (which Malcolm Muggeridge suggested be re-titled *My Life and Lies*) was available only under the counter; obscenity prosecutions were taken in most countries in which the book appeared. Harris's account demonstrates how he had been born in various countries at different times and educated at different schools at the same time. At the end of his life, Harris took to wearing an Old Etonian tie and claimed to have been at Rugby; however one could not reliably infer from that, Pearson noted, that Harris had been at Winchester.

Once Harris was settled abroad, he began a regular correspondence with Pearson; indeed during the first war Pearson was Harris's only regular English correspondent. At this time Pearson tended to lionize Harris whom he considered fearless, truthful and alive. 'His appeal,' Pearson wrote, 'is to men and women who have lived, not drifted, through life.' Some idea of the eulogistic nature of Pearson's side of the correspondence may be gleaned from this letter: 'You seem to be gifted with something very like divine insight,' Pearson wrote. 'Pray God that you will someday be acknowledged for what you are . . . your whole personality, embracing as it does an unmatched loving-kindness and complete understanding is beyond compare and to consummate everything you have been given the crown of thorns.' The tenor of Harris's reply suggests that he regarded such effusiveness as little more than his due: 'Your praise makes me think of Meredith when he says in one of his letters that too much praise is not good for us; we want just enough to incite us to do our best – enough, if you will, to do better than our best, but never enough to make us persuade ourselves than in us humanity has reached its zenith.'

Most of Harris's letters to Pearson are self-pitying laments of the injustice which drove him from England, the critical neglect which reduced him to penury, and the diminished opportunities to gratify flagging appetites. Two examples will suffice. 'All my life I have been an exile,' Harris wrote to Pearson in November 1915: 'But as age comes on transplanting is like amputation, one is apt to bleed to death. Shakespeare says "Tis honour with most lands to be at odds". I have always felt at odds with every land, and now, were I given to self-pity, I could arrange a moving tale: friends and money lost; health shaken; universal contempt; unpopular opinions; exiled and old.' A year later, Harris wrote: 'It's the devil to begin again at sixty when you are practically unknown and altogether unappreciated; but whom the gods love, they chasten, and I don't complain. Every such experience enriches one with new knowledge and I'm being taught in order to teach the more efficaciously.'

Like everything else about him, Harris's loyalty was suspect. He was considered to have pro-German sympathies, although he was at pains to deny this to Pearson. As a result, his letters were opened by the censor. After Pearson entered the army in 1916 he was advised to stop corresponding with Harris but he refused, saying that Harris was neither pro-German nor anti-British but simply pro-Harris and anti-anyone who was not. After the war Pearson received a letter stamped 'Confidential' from Scotland Yard's Special Branch warning him that Harris was a pro-German propagandist (a claim apparently based on the fact that Harris had visited the German submarine *Vaterland* when she docked in New York) and that he was a member of Sinn Fein.

In 1916 Harris posted Pearson a copy of his biography of Oscar Wilde inscribed: 'To Hesketh Pearson, best of critics, truest of friends, from the author, gratefully.' Pearson treasured this inscription until he found another copy in a second-hand bookshop inscribed to someone else as 'truest of critics, best of friends'. It then dawned on him that for Harris this was an all-purpose inscription subject to minor variations. With the book came a letter urging Pearson to spare no effort to arrange for reviews in the leading English papers. Pearson's efforts to this end brought only stinging rebukes from Arnold Bennett, Joseph Conrad, James Barrie, Hall Caine, Edmund Gosse, and Rudyard Kipling, each man outdoing the other in calumniating Harris. Only Bernard Shaw put acquaintance above respectability and wrote a detailed account of his relationship with Harris which he permitted to be used as a Preface, thereby enhancing sales of later editions of the book.

When *My Life and Loves* appeared, Pearson had a personal visit from Scotland Yard. Customs authorities in England and America had confiscated the book for obscenity, but Pearson's four volumes had arrived in the post concealed in dust-wrappers bearing the titles: 'The Family Companion'; 'Elizabeth Barrett Browning'; 'Theological Essays'; and 'St Francis of Assisi'. In due course an Inspector called and accused Pearson of procuring obscene matter. Pearson pointed out that the inscription (this time: 'Best of critics and of friends') proved that the volumes had been sent *gratis* and unsolicited, and that he had no commercial intentions. In any case, he went on, if the Inspector were at all serious in his mission to stamp out inflammatory reading matter, he might start with the brothel scene in *Pericles*, and move on to *Troilus and Cressida*. Compared to those the fevered outpourings of Harris's imagination were scribblings of a schoolboy on a lavatory wall or, as Kingsmill put it, 'a school hero telling a group of pubescent friends how he felt the housemaid during the holidays'.

By far the most sympathetic portrait in Pearson's first book, *Modern Men and Mummers*, is of Frank Harris. He is described as 'the most dynamic writer alive' and his work as 'a gospel for the great'. That Pearson was beginning to entertain twinges of doubt about the master's character and veracity is also apparent. 'He is indeed a monster according to all conventional standards,' Pearson wrote, 'but his monstrosity only offends the shallow people who can't see beyond it – and they are people who simply aren't worth propitiating.' Despite the fulsome praise, Harris was not satisfied and relations between the two men temporarily cooled, although they did continue to correspond.

In a letter dated September 5, 1919, Harris professed world-weariness: 'I want to pull the curtain down and go out. I have had enough of the show. The last act that I thought would crown all has turned the great drama into the commonest knock-about farce, and the taste of it is in my mouth and will be until I die.' In which case the taste lingered for a decade since Harris did not go to his final rest until August 21, 1931. When Hugh Kingsmill heard that Harris was dead, he wrote to Pearson: 'A vein of sadness was touched by the news, but one feels that the old boy has had a good run for everybody else's money, and that old age is depressing him, and he'll be better in his last, and for the first time, otherwise untenanted bed.' Pearson replied: 'I will not go so far as to echo Harris on Wilde: "The world went grey to me when Oscar died", but I did definitely feel that a bit of colour had left the universe and that we wouldn't be likely to spot that particular tint again.'

Although youthful admiration waned, Pearson always remained fond of Harris, seeing in his bluster and bravado a pygmy Glendower, in his licentiousness a lesser Boswell, and in his misdeeds a shadow of Falstaff. In a letter to Kingsmill, Pearson once referred to Harris as 'a monumentally impossible and wildly imagined being'. Harris could quote Shakespeare, Keats and Browning by the yard, his voice trembling with emotion and his eyes melting with tears. While scorning the moral and religious precepts on which Pearson had been brought up, he claimed to be a true disciple of Jesus Christ. When Pearson scoffed at the notion of Christ's divinity, Harris wrote to him: 'Jesus [was] the man who first discovered the soul and brought love into life, made it the principle of all our actions, the Sun of all our seeing.' But Harris was prepared to allow that Jesus may have succumbed to those temptations which he himself found irresistible. 'He had imperfections enough. I always see his hands in the hair of Mary Magdalene, and she is not at his feet but on his heart. Where else did he learn "much shall be forgiven her, for she loved much"?' Nor was Harris uncritical of Christ's tactics. 'He made lots of mistakes, and then that final mistake, the going up to Jerusalem heralded by triumph on all the sunlit ways – "Blessed is he that cometh in the name of the Lord". Was there ever such a divine blunder?'

For what (referring to the plot of *Cymbeline*) Dr Johnson called 'unresisting imbecility', these passages are admittedly difficult to match. Yet Hugh Kingsmill recounted to Pearson and Muggeridge an experience he had with Harris which comes close. It was in the spring of 1912 and Kingsmill was staying with Harris in Nice, neither man doing much except going for long country walks by day and visiting the roller skating rink in the evening. One night Harris proposed a visit to a brothel. Although not exactly innocent in such matters, Kingsmill was a neophyte compared to Harris. When they arrived, Harris and the proprietress spent some time selecting an appropriate recipient for Kingsmill's attentions. This accomplished, Kingsmill and the lady retired, but as they did Kingsmill noticed that Harris now seemed reluctant to engage in anything more strenuous than conversation. A few days later the two men were strolling along the Promenade des Anglais when Kingsmill became aware of certain distressing consequences of his indulgence. As the symptoms became more acute, Harris boomed out his considered opinion that 'Jesus Christ goes deeper than I do, but I have had a wider experience'.

It was thanks to Frank Harris that Pearson met Hugh Kingsmill Lunn (he dropped the surname for writing purposes). Kingsmill was intrigued by Pearson's portrait of Harris in *Modern Men and Mummers* and wrote to him about it. They met on November 18, 1921 at 5 Endsleigh Gardens, the touring agency office of Kingsmill's father, Sir Henry Lunn. The date can be fixed with certainty because afterwards they strolled to Mudie's in New Oxford Street and Kingsmill presented Pearson with a signed and dated copy of his first novel, *The Will to Love*, whose philandering protaganist, Ralph Parker, is a thinly-disguised portrait of Frank Harris. Kingsmill, too, had been an early disciple of Harris, but now regarded him only as an astounding human oddity. 'From the moment I met Hughie,' Pearson later wrote, 'I began to see

Harris from a new viewpoint, and gained far more than I lost from the change of angle.' Some critics have contended that this change of angle produced distortion or disloyalty. In his biography of Frank Harris, Robert Pearsall alleges: 'Like Kingsmill, Pearson atoned for his early discipleship with reams of attack and innuendo.' Since Pearson did little more than publish the text of Harris's letters to him this criticism is difficult to accept. If the result of publishing a man's own letters is considered incriminating, it surely falls in the category of confession, not accusation. In any event, Pearson's admiration for Harris was already waning when he met Kingsmill who hastened, but did not initiate, the apostasy which Pearsall resents. One example will demonstrate this. Already gathering material for a life of Oscar Wilde, Pearson had discovered that, prior to Wilde's release from Reading Gaol, Harris turned up and magnanimously promised Wilde £500. Within four days he reneged on his promise and Wilde wrote to an acquaintance: 'Harris has no feelings. It is the secret of his success.' After Wilde's release some friends did rally around and Harris was shamed into making good his promise; he sent along a cheque which, Pearson noted, resembled £500 as closely as possible except that the final zero was missing. However, Pearsall is correct in deducing that Pearson's exaggerated opinion of Harris did not survive Kingsmill's mockery. The opening sentence of one of Harris's letters to Pearson became a favourite comic quotation: 'Another milestone on the dreadful road . . .', which meant only that another issue of the monthly magazine Harris was then editing had been brought out. Kingsmill discovered another favourite in Harris's memoirs: 'It must not be understood that I became a Saint;' Kingsmill wrote to Pearson: 'This sentence is surely as good as ever he has given us. One can taste it indefinitely without losing any of its original flavour.' Recalling their frequent discussions of Harris, Pearson wrote: 'I fancy we must have laughed more boisterously and more frequently over some of Frankie's seriously intended but unconsciously comical sentiments and phrases than over the finest passages in the works of the greatest humourists.'

From their first meeting in 1921 until Kingsmill's death in 1949, Kingsmill and Pearson were inseparable companions. When they could not see each other (and sometimes when they could) they wrote, and both sides of this correspondence have been preserved. They collaborated on three books, several plays and scripts. To the discerning eye the influence of Kingsmill is apparent in the best of Pearson's biographies. Before Kingsmill, Pearson had read widely but he lacked systematic standards for evaluating what he read. Kingsmill, whose literary principles are best illustrated by his brilliant *New English*

Review essays published under the title *The Progress of a Biographer*, became the tutor Pearson never had. In a sane world Kingsmill would have been a don, Malcolm Muggeridge is fond of saying, 'but in a world as sane as that, there wouldn't be a need for dons'.

The cornerstone of Kingsmill's view was the inevitable conflict between the will and the imagination; only by subordinating the will and learning to dwell in the imagination could one hope to realize King Lear's ambition – to take upon us 'the mystery of things, as if we were God's spies'. The pursuits of the imagination, Kingsmill believed, were love, truth, and understanding; the pursuits of the will were power, greed, and all panaceas for creating better human societies through collective action, a view Kingsmill scorned as 'dawnism'.

Nor was the influence entirely one-sided. It was Pearson who first proposed to Kingsmill that he write a biography of Frank Harris which, with consummate skill and humour, Kingsmill did in 1932. Years before publication one may observe the book take shape in their letters back and forth. Pearson frequently urges Kingsmill to get on with it; Kingsmill, in his leisurely and ruminative way, takes time to fix the correct proportions between the subject and his work. 'The great difficulty will be not to be carried away with mirth. I want to pick out what was really good in the old boy's work and character; perhaps I might devote an Appendix, two pages in large print, to this part of my subject.' Kingsmill so valued Pearson's criticism that he sent him his books in manuscript (sometimes chapter by chapter) for comment. Once when Pearson made a suggestion to which Kingsmill had come independently, Kingsmill wrote: 'It is as if God and the Holy Ghost (pick which you like and I'll take the left-over) had independently hit on the principle of sexual intercourse, and on meeting at the club had burst forth simultaneously with – "About this population impasse –"'

Pearson provided more than inspiration for Kingsmill's biography. He related his fund of Harris stories; he gave Kingsmill their complete correspondence; he wrote to Harris's acquaintances urging them to co-operate. Kingsmill referred to Pearson 'wet-nursing me through the job'. Curiously enough the Pearson-Kingsmill letters, which through the Twenties are full of analysis of Harris, reveal Kingsmill (already an established author) as tentative, insecure and needing encouragement. Pearson, by contrast, is the sounding board, critic and cheerleader. Their primary disagreement about Harris concerned his work, which Pearson was still inclined to overestimate, particularly the short fiction to which he applied superlatives like 'incomparable' (*Sonia*) and 'amazingly well done' (*The Bomb*). Among living writers, Pearson told

Kingsmill that he ranked Harris ahead of all but Shaw and Lytton Strachey. Such veneration did not survive Kingsmill's debunking. Kingsmill considered Harris's non-fiction so unreliable as to be absurd, and his fiction 'four-fifths fudge'. When Pearson wrote pleading for an exemption from this verdict for Harris's short stories, Kingsmill replied: 'Some powerful force is trying to get itself expressed. An elephant playing the piano would convey a real sense of power – here, one would say, is someone who matters; true, he is mattering rather outside his proper sphere, but he is not negligible. Somewhat similar is the effect produced by Harris when he writes of heroic self-sacrifice.'

In exchange for Pearson's assistance, Kingsmill proposed that he should receive a quarter of all royalties. From an acting engagement on the Isle of Skye, Pearson replied to this proposal on June 22, 1923: 'I am quite willing to snap up one quarter of what you get, though I think you are rather unnecessarily quixotic in suggesting it, since you know perfectly well that I would do anything in my power to help you, money or no money. I insist, however, upon being mentioned in your Preface as one of the prime Judases who contributed to your masterpiece. I don't want to go down to history as the best-loved disciple I have made myself out to be in my own book. I cannot wash out that self-inflicted stain myself, so you must do it for me.' In the result, the book earned too little to be significant, even for Kingsmill. Pearson received nothing. Indeed by the time the book appeared, it was Pearson who was frequently lending money to Kingsmill.

Kingsmill was also a healthy corrective to Pearson's adulation of Shaw. With his retentive memory, Pearson had practically memorized many of Shaw's plays and, for a time, considered him a genius greater than Johnson and equal to Shakespeare. Kingsmill nudged Pearson on to more realistic ground, but not without bellows of resistance. Pearson's first letter to Kingsmill consists of a truculent defence of Shaw as 'the biggest, clearest mind that ever graced this modern world of ours'; it concluded: 'Let us meet again and often by all means, but I don't think we had better discuss *Caesar and Cleopatra*.' In another letter Pearson advised Kingsmill that Shaw is 'immensely superior to Johnson – in wit, in humour, in dialectic, in fancy, in repartee, in personality, in everything'.

Kingsmill was sensitive and adept at handling discordant personalities. He would later be the linchpin between Pearson and Muggeridge, two fiery and often discordant temperaments; Kingsmill managed not only to retain the affection of both men but also to make possible a wary friendship between them, albeit one which only blossomed after

Kingsmill's death. To Pearson's immature adulation of Shaw,
Kingsmill found just the right tone. 'My Dear H.P.,' he replied,
'the great thing is not to arouse my combativeness as that will
distort my judgment. I value your criticisms very much and you
have already done me good, but I suggest (b) not (a) as the right
method:

(a) My God, Lunn, your puke about *Androcles* makes me sick.
    Shaw as a religious teacher wipes the floor with your flat-
    bottomed Buddhas, Assisis, and the rest of the addled goat-
    bearded rabbit-toothed bunch of mouldy rag-pickers whom for
    some inexplicable reason you are pleased to favour with your
    cock-eyed approval.

(b) I don't quite agree with your careful but in my opinion not quite
    complete estimate of Shaw as a religious teacher. It seems to me
    that you have, I won't say missed, but not altogether seized the
    full force of the second paragraph on p. 8702 of Shaw's introduc-
    tion to that, in my view, supreme play 'That Remains to Be
    Seen'; etc.

What could Pearson do but call a truce? 'In future,' he wrote back,
'let us leave out Shaw. If, at any time, I am moved to mention His
Holy Name, cross yourself reverently, raise your lips to Heaven and,
if the place permits, fall on your knees in silent prayer. But God
help you if you open your mouth . . . yours, till Shaw do us part,
Hesketh.'

Over time Kingsmill's influence was highly beneficial. Although
Pearson never lost his enthusiasm for his literary heroes, his biographies
became more balanced, mature and objective. Kingsmill moderated
Pearson's immature partisanship, and Pearson mitigated the self-doubt
to which Kingsmill was prone, particularly when he was the subject of
unfavourable reviews. Of reviewers, Kingsmill once lamented: 'The
silly buggers seem to be all corns, and I seem to be all feet.' Pearson
taught him to ignore critics; he wrote back: 'I am quite indifferent to
hostile reviews of my own work, or favourable ones for that matter, but
I am human enough to realize that other people aren't.' Kingsmill's
second wife, Dorothy, once asked him why he found Pearson so
attractive? 'Lack of vanity,' Kingsmill said. Kingsmill's understanding
of literature was deeper and more catholic than Pearson's. But
Hesketh's self-confidence and courage were contagious and Kingsmill
needed both to keep going. They never did agree on Shaw. 'What the
hell does it matter?' Kingsmill wrote: 'Surely two people who can rush
along underground subways roaring and bellowing profundities and

obscenities at each other should present a united front to the indignant millions who would certainly annihilate them at the first sign of disunion.'

CHAPTER NINE

A Saucy Roughness

'This is the same fellow
Who, having been praised for bluntness, doth affect
A saucy roughness, and constrains the garb
Quite from his nature.'

King Lear, Act II, Scene II

The Pearsons now lived at 88 Abbey Road, a location which recommended itself to Hesketh because of its proximity to Regent's Park where he tramped from early to late afternoon most days covering ten to fifteen miles. His acting was done at the Royalty Theatre where an acquaintance, Dennis Eadie, had gone to bat for him. His parts ranged from Chekov's *The Seagull* to light comedy. A glance through old theatre programmes reveals that Pearson had roles in stage productions whose casts included such luminaries as John Gielgud, Tyrone Guthrie, Ralph Richardson, Leon Quartermaine, Phyllis Nielson-Terry and Mrs Patrick Campbell.

In *The Blue Lagoon* Pearson played L'Estrange, guardian of two young orphans who are marooned on a desert island where they amuse themselves in vaguely suggestive ways. L'Estrange appears only in the first and last acts with a long stretch in between which Pearson, still in make-up, usually spent in a nearby bar. L'Estrange carried a wide-brimmed panama hat which he never put on his head; the night Pearson knew that Malcolm Muggeridge would be in the audience, he promised to put it on. With a flourish appropriate to the climactic rescue of the two orphans, Pearson swept the hat on to his head, only to discover that it was several sizes too small and remained balanced only if he walked like an African bearing a water jug. Six months into a successful but boring run, Pearson was responsible for a memorable fluff. In the opening scene on board ship he was supposed to relate the children's sad story to the Captain, beginning: 'Little Emmeline's father, Captain, died before she was born; her mother died in giving birth.' Instead he started: 'Little Emmeline's mother, Captain, died before she was born . . .' Unaware of any error, he was 'surprised to observe the distorted look on the Captain's face, and anxious to steady him I

emphasized my next remark: "Her father died in giving her birth."'
The audience might just have taken this howler in its stride had not
some bored musician in the pit let out a bellow which the audience then
took up, while the Captain 'turned his back to the audience, and shook
from bow to stern'.

By all accounts Pearson was a competent actor, 'spirited rather than
star quality' according to Muggeridge, but he found the job increasingly
tedious. If the character intrigued him, his acting was accomplished;
when the character bored him, his acting ranged from erratic to
atrocious. Too much time was spent at rehearsals, which he described
as 'resembling a zoo with most of the wild animals at large'. Also, the
pointlessness of most successful plays chafed him. Then there was the
excruciating banality of some of the lines one was expected to declaim.
Godfrey Tearle told Pearson that the most humiliating line he ever had
to utter was: 'It is not the way of an eagle to swoop twice.' Pearson
countered that this was Augustan compared to this line (from *The
Basker*) referring to the hair of a girl who has just broken the hero's
heart: 'All little shiny, goldy gleams and dear little blow-away curls.'
Kingsmill was called upon to arbitrate on the issue of banality and, in
due course, rendered his decision. 'After giving the most protracted
consideration to the rival agonies involved, I felt that I personally would
rather have had the curls, because with my almost morbid consciousness of not being equipped à la Kipling-Bennett, I could not give "It is
not the way of an eagle . . ." with the passionate conviction necessary,
for fear of someone shouting from the gallery – 'Shows what a bloody lot
you know about eagles". I don't think I could have committed myself to
more than "I'm very much inclined to doubt if a normal eagle would
swoop more than once".'

Dependent on the vagaries of acting, money was a constant pre-
occupation. In 1924 Pearson and Godfrey Tearle played in *The Fake* at
the Apollo Theatre. Since Pearson was then desperate for what he
called 'scratchit', Tearle suggested that he might put his experience
with the Shakespeare Society to use by becoming secretary to the Stage
Guild, which had recently been set up to counter the trade unionist
tendencies of the Actors' Association. Pearson went to an interview but
soon became embroiled in an angry exchange with Percy Hutchinson, a
member of the selection committee. Pearson was about to walk out
when Sir Frank Benson intervened in a conciliatory manner. 'I forced
back the words which were about to flow from me and the interview
concluded harmoniously. However I had upset the committee too
much to get the job.'

Pearson's first book, *Modern Men and Mummers*, consisted of

portraits of contemporary actors, directors and men of letters. Pearson
later acknowledged the accuracy of one reviewer's comment, 'a libel on
every page', but at the time he considered it no more than exuberant
honesty. Publication provoked howls (in one case, a writ) from the
wounded. A few examples will convey the pungency of Pearson's style.
Dean Inge is dismissed as 'simply a class-prejudiced clergyman . . .
[whose] hatred of trade unions is founded on the ineradicable belief that
the rest of the world is in a conspiracy against him'. Mrs Patrick
Campbell is said to suffer from 'true histrionic afflatus', while H. G.
Wells is described as 'a fat boy gorged on plums . . . the literary
Weather-Cock of the Age'. The Wells portrait goes on: 'There was
never a more heroic fighter – on the winning side. The moment the
enemy turns tail "the world's greatest writer" (as the advertisements call
him) will jump and shout and shake his fist and put out his tongue –
until it is time to spin around and exhibit his gifts in another direction.'

Reviewers proved kindlier than the subjects. *The Times* considered
the book 'excellent and suggestive reading', the *English Review* called it
'most quotable', and the *Daily Express* 'grotesque, caustic, humorous
and quite unforgettable'. In the *Daily Telegraph*, W. A. Darlington
wrote: 'He writes freshly and well, and he has mixed with his ink a touch
of vitriol which makes you chuckle and find somebody to read the
passage aloud to.' Entirely overlooked by all reviewers was this biting
prophecy (written in 1921) in a short portrait of Winston Churchill:
'Nothing short of death will prevent Winston from becoming Prime
Minister of the country for which he has so nobly sacrificed all his
principles . . . he has the supreme gift of plausibility and this, in the
ordinary course of things, should lead us into several dozen minor
campaigns and possibly one or two spanking big wars before he is laid to
rest by a sorrowing and grateful nation in Westminster Abbey.'

Had Pearson deliberately set out to destroy his stage career, he could
scarcely have done so more effectively than by writing *Modern Men and
Mummers*. Most of the actors and managers, whose vanities and foibles
he paraded so amusingly, were alive and capable of kicking furiously.
Offers of employment to so indiscreet a chronicler dried up. Pearson
went through a difficult period when all that stood between his family
and penury was a bank overdraft, a loan here and there from a friend,
and pawning of household effects. First to go was some Queen Anne
silver bequeathed to him by Aunt Adele (she who had demanded and
paid for a proper church wedding); then some ornamental saddle-bags
and carpets which Hesketh had brought back from Persia, finally a gold
watch which had been a present from his friend, Charles Burt, who had
died in the war. Pearson had been warned. Before publication he had

shown a few pages of the manuscript to George Bernard Shaw. Shaw told him that to publish in its present form was a one-way ticket to the workhouse. 'The more candidly you criticize,' Shaw wrote, 'the more delicately you must draw the line between what may be said and what may not. In short, your manners must be as good as your brains if you are to make good your claim to criticize.' Pearson's manners fell short of his brains and he paid the penalty.

Author and publisher received letters and threats. Horatio Bottomley, an account of whose Harrogate speech ('That fetched the buggers – what?') Pearson had included in *Modern Men and Mummers*, issued a writ for libel. However, before any trial, he became involved in another protracted law suit which eventually resulted in his imprisonment and ruin.

With no stage work available until the storm blew over, Hesketh was reduced to working as a minimally-paid chauffeur for his father who had recently bought a Mass car. Relations between father and son had never been close; frequent contact rendered them less than cordial. Once Hesketh asked his father the function of the Chancellor and Vice-Chancellor of Cambridge? His father laboured earnestly to explain, then gave up with the confession: 'When I was up there, it was not a topic that exercised me greatly.' When Hesketh greeted this remark with prolonged laughter, his father seemed hurt. In a friendship spanning thirty years, Basil Harvey never once heard Hesketh speak of his mother and he mentioned his father only with disdain.

Rescue from servility came in the form of an unexpected offer to write biographical sketches for the magazine *John Bull* at seven guineas an article; this, plus occasional books sent his way for review by D. L. Murray of *The Times*, enabled the family to stay afloat until the theatre blacklist gradually lifted. Even so, Pearson accepted this financial godsend with ill grace; he wrote to Kingsmill: 'I have been abominably hard up of late – even to the watch-popping stage – and have literally been living on credit. Suddenly, last week, like a bolt from the blue, a job was offered me to write weekly articles in a new and reformed "John Bull". I simply couldn't refuse. Clamorous creditors made my acceptance inevitable. The matter had simply gone beyond my power. I was at the mercy of the first body-bidder and soul-scrounger who came along.' By the mid-Twenties, Pearson again received acting parts, at first mostly touring roles in the provinces, later leading parts on the London stage.

During the run of Frederick Lonsdale's play. *The Fake*, a woman whom Pearson had known in Tree's Company at His Majesty's

Theatre, came backstage to renew acquaintance. After desultory conversation, she invited Pearson to tea at her flat to talk over old times.
Such conversations have a way of becoming horizontal and this was no
exception. As terms of endearment passed between them, the woman
suddenly burst into tears and claimed that she had loved Hesketh from
their first meeting but that it was now too late. Thinking she referred to
his marriage to Gladys, Hesketh maintained a discreet silence. After
taking to heart King Lear's admonition – 'Let copulation thrive' – they
lay peacefully sated in each other's arms. When the doorbell suddenly
rang, Hesketh observed a look of alarm pass over her face. 'Do you know
who it is?' he whispered. 'My fiancé,' came the reply. Now he understood why she had said it was too late. Her flat was at the top of the
building and, in muted tones, she urged Pearson to take refuge on the
roof. 'I covered up my sense of being slightly ridiculous by a display of
temper and angrily refused to do anything of the kind.' Eventually the
bell ceased ringing, parting footsteps could be heard, and silence
descended. However, 'romance had vanished and I left by the back
door'.

In his memoirs Pearson was reticent about his affairs, claiming no
more interest in them than for 'other less romantic forms of evacuation'.
He was similarly tight-lipped with his friends, although he told Basil
Harvey about an affair he had with Pola Negri, an actress of quite
stunning beauty with whom he had been on tour. He also told Harvey,
though not apparently in the boastful way that the story might suggest,
that he once took Gladys to the theatre in the Thirties and, during an
interval, decided to go backstage to greet an actor he had known.
On his way he observed, coming down a flight of stairs, 'the most
beautiful woman I had ever seen'. Although he did not know the
actress's name, he followed her to her dressing room, talked to
her, made love to her, and was back in his seat midway through the
next act. Gladys, of course, discovered some of Hesketh's liaisons,
which produced unavoidable domestic heat, so well described by
Shakespeare as 'the hourly shot of angry eyes', invariably followed by
protestations, inventions and excuses, and succeeded by inevitable
coolness.

Having nearly destroyed a stage career with *Modern Men and
Mummers*, Pearson spent 1925 writing a book which nearly finished
him as an author. In a letter to Kingsmill two years earlier he had
mentioned working on a series of sketches, 'slices from life' all of them
'essentially libellous'. In November, 1926 The Bodley Head published
The Whispering Gallery, which purported to be leaves from the diary of
a senior British diplomat. The title likens diplomatic and social circles

to a gallery where 'no secret can be breathed without the startling reverberation of rumour from an unexpected quarter'. In the Preface the diplomat-author explains that he kept a diary more or less constantly from the age of twenty-one, but that extracts are only now to be anonymously published. The anonymous diplomat-author turns out to have known practically everyone from Kaiser Wilhelm to Tsar Nicholas II ('Nicholas was a cad, a coward, a butcher, and a blackguard. If any man ever deserved his fate, he certainly did'), Cecil Rhodes, Lord Kitchener, King Edward VII, Lenin, Mussolini, and most authors. Only writers are portrayed as something better than half-wits; for example, Thomas Hardy, who confides to the visiting diplomat this gloomy but characteristic view of life: 'Fate stalks us with depressing monotony from womb to tomb, and when we are least expecting it, deals us a series of crushing blows from behind. Though the rays of intermittent happiness are permitted to play upon us for our greater undoing, we are marked down for miserable ends.' The kings, warriors, Empire-builders, statesmen and financiers are all shamelessly undressed; their reported conversations reveal nothing but commonness, banality and ignorance. To the sceptical reader who might doubt that such mediocrities are capable of achieving eminence, the diplomat-author gives this assurance: 'Thirty years in the diplomatic service and a more than nodding acquaintance with these makers of history have convinced me that the majority of these self-made famous men achieved their eminence by virtue of their excessive ordinariness, by the extremity and intensity of their reactions to the commonest impulses; and that the rest of them, those who were born eminent, obtained whatever popularity they possessed by their defects rather than their finer qualities.'

In his posthumous autobiography Pearson claimed, almost in defence of his conduct, that the eminent were so obviously parodied and so histrionically exhibited that 'by no stretch of the imagination could a page of it have been written by a member of the British diplomatic corps'. This justification is disingenuous in the light of the repeated assurances the reader is given that, however improbable the dialogue, the diplomat-author was present and heard it and made a written note of it. Indeed the book falls flat unless the reader believes this.

First to be convinced were the publishers. Claiming to be acting as an intermediary for the anonymous diplomat-author, Pearson first took the completed manuscript to Odhams Press who made an offer to publish but conditional on him divulging the diplomat's identity. He refused. The Bodley Head, however, were prepared to publish if Pearson would confidentially assure a single company director of the diplomat's identity, on condition that the name would never be revealed. Pearson must have realized that no publisher would risk his reputation on less assurance.

In September 1926 Hesketh and Gladys were on holiday in Sussex. Allen (later Sir Allen) Lane was the company director who undertook the secret mission. Pearson and Lane met at the Norfolk Hotel in Arundel and, after yet another assurance that the name would remain strictly confidential, Pearson gave Sir Rennell Rodd as the diplomat-author.

Rodd had by then retired from the diplomatic service, after a career that included being British Ambassador to Rome. Pearson's choice of Rodd as putative author is intriguing. As a young man, Rodd had been a minor poet and a friend of Oscar Wilde's. Wilde arranged publication of a volume of Rodd's poetry, contributed a Preface to the volume and, without consulting Rodd, dedicated the book to himself in these terms: 'To Oscar Wilde – Heart's Brother, these few songs and many songs to come.' Understandably, Rodd considered the dedication effusive, and he requested his publisher to remove it from future editions. This led to a rift with Wilde. Typically, Pearson championed Wilde's side. By fingering the hapless Rodd as the author of *The Whispering Gallery*, it is likely that Pearson's irrational partisanship for one of his literary heroes had once again clouded his judgment.

When the book appeared, press reaction was immediate and hostile. The *Daily Mail* led off by calling *The Whispering Gallery* 'monstrous' and 'a scandalous fake'. The first chapter of the book (called 'The Napoleon of Fleet Street') is an unflattering portrait of Lord Northcliffe in which Pearson none-too-subtly suggested that Northcliffe was not above bribing government officials in order to obtain 'inside' secrets for his newspaper. Northcliffe's brother, Lord Rothermere, was the proprietor of the *Daily Mail*, which may explain the sustained virulence of that paper's attack. Others quickly scented blood and the hunt began. In the *Observer* J. L. Garvin denounced both the author ('an imposter and a cad') and the book ('an unscrupulous farrago') in a leader entitled 'Ghouls and Garbage'. *The New Age* damned Pearson's 'double offence', although their grounds for doing so seem quaint: 'It gave away some of the secrets of the financiers . . . it also disparaged the intelligence and sincerity of the statesmen class as a class in their relation to public affairs.'

With such publicity the book's print run of three thousand copies immediately sold out. When the storm broke the publishers initially issued a press release defending the book's authenticity but, as pressure intensified, they panicked. When the *Daily Mail* announced that advertisements from The Bodley Head would henceforth be rejected and called for criminal proceedings, they caved in. Pearson was summoned to a directors' meeting where he made matters worse by sticking to the story that Sir Rennell Rodd was the author.

Why? What could Pearson have thought to gain by perpetuating the fraud? It was by now obvious that the book would be exposed. Sir Rennell Rodd was alive and able to repudiate his 'diary'; most of the subjects were alive to deny the reported conversations. The explanation cannot be that Pearson was utterly insensitive to the different constraints on candour when discussing the living and the dead. In a letter to Kingsmill penned shortly before *The Whispering Gallery* was published, he wrote: 'One may say: "Gargantua's farts were elemental, like claps of thunder, and their stink was prodigious, a combination of excrement, armpits and unwashed feet." But if you substitute King Edward VII for Gargantua, your remarks are (as Asquith would say) liable to be misinterpreted as personal.'

There is no explanation for Pearson's conduct except panic. Looking back on his actions with the benefit of thirty years' hindsight, he wrote: 'Had I been in possession of my wits I would have told them squarely that I had written the book, and that they could no more have believed it to be the work of a real diplomat than of a real dinosaur. Instead I kept up the fiction of a man behind the work possibly with the confused notion that the director who had negotiated with me would get into trouble if I did not brazen it out. But on this point I am vague, and my behaviour on that crucial day is as mysterious to me now as it must seem to the reader.'

The *Daily Mail* went next to Sir Rennell Rodd who naturally repudiated any connection with the book and called for the prosecution of those responsible. Meanwhile The Bodley Head had met privately with the *Daily Mail* and claimed to have been innocent dupes of a hoax perpetrated entirely by Pearson. Under the heading 'A Case For The Public Prosecutor' the *Daily Mail* denounced Pearson as 'an impudent literary forger', and took up Sir Rennell Rodd's call for criminal proceedings. No doubt fearing that if they waited for the decision of the public prosecutor they too might end up in the dock, the publishers seized the initiative and swore an affidavit charging Pearson with attempting to obtain money by false pretences. The charging of an inchoate offence (attempt) rather than the completed offence (obtaining money) is a curious legal footnote. Pearson had obtained £250 for the manuscript. The offence, if any, was therefore complete. On the other hand, he had returned the £250 to the publisher when the storm broke and before criminal charges were laid. The attempt charge was presumably designed to acknowledge this fact, but it was unsound in law, foolish in policy, and unavailing in result.

On November 25, 1926 Pearson returned to London from an acting engagement in Cardiff. A warrant had been issued for his arrest and he surrendered himself into custody at Marlborough Street Police Court. His brother-in-law, Colonel Dane Hamlett, arranged bail of £1,000 and took charge of the defence. The case was set down for hearing at London Sessions. Sir Patrick Hastings, a man devoted to the theatre and the ablest barrister of his day, was briefed for the defence.

Family and friends rallied around, but almost all urged Hesketh to plead guilty. Hugh Kingsmill was particularly adamant that this was the only sensible course of action. Kingsmill was one of those men who, while making a shambles of their own affairs, are most dogmatic about how other people should arrange theirs; he once added, under his signatures, 'Adviser and Consultant on other People's Business'. George Bernard Shaw wrote in support of Kingsmill's view: 'Poor Hesketh (damn his folly) has to choose between the heaviest sentence the court can give him and a lenient one. If he puts up a defence he will get the heavy sentence . . . but if he pleads guilty and throws himself on the mercy of the court, apologizing to Sir R. R. and the Lane Firm, and saying that, difficult as it may be for the court to believe that a man could be such a fool when it is easier to set him down as a knave, the truth is that he did not think that the thing would be taken so seriously, or that the Lane Firm really believed that it was anything worse than the fictitious memoirs and travels which have so often been published as genuine, he may get off lightly – or comparatively so. Nobody, he can say, was more taken aback than he when the *Daily Mail* avalanche descended on him. He did not defend his conduct: he exonerated everyone but himself; and he could ask for no more consideration than to be treated as a fool rather than as a scoundrel.'

The near unanimity of advice to plead guilty must have been harrowing. No less worrying, perhaps, was the fact that almost the lone dissenting voice was Frank Harris's, and his grip on reality and truth could at best be described as precarious. From Nice, Harris wrote advising Pearson to give evidence that '. . . memoirs are a well-known form of fiction. Say that a widely known literary man told you this. It will make the court laugh.'

On December 14, 1926 Kingsmill called on Lord Beaverbrook at Stornaway House to see if anything might be done to save Pearson. However, Beaverbrook behaved 'as a man who has established himself in the social order and looks on all outside criticism as very reprehensible'; beyond expressing an 'abstract sympathy' for Pearson, he refused

The Pearson Family. Standing: Hesketh's father (Henry) and
Harry; seated (left to right): Jack, Hesketh's mother, with Elsie
on her knee, and Hesketh, aged five.

Hesketh, aged 21, at Niagara Falls, 1908

Hesketh in uniform, 1917

Gladys in *The Miracle*

Hesketh (second from right) in *The Blue Lagoon*

Hilaire Belloc

G. K. Chesterton

Hesketh in 1923

Hesketh and Gladys in the 1920s

Hesketh with Hugh Kingsmill

Hesketh with Bernard Shaw

Malcolm Muggeridge

Colin Hurry

Hesketh Pearson

to become involved. It is interesting that, years later, when Pearson was respectable, Beaverbrook wrote several fawning letters about his books. Kingsmill also discussed strategy with his father, Sir Henry Lunn, and wrote to Pearson: 'He again reiterated his conviction that [you] must not fight, and the opinion of my father, who has built a big business up out of nothing and who has had to decide dozens of important matters every year involving a working knowledge of the law, is of some weight.'

Pearson, meanwhile, was deaf to all such advice. He was determined not to capitulate to what he considered an unfounded accusation. 'I am afraid poor old H.P. will get it in the neck,' Kingsmill told John Holms, 'he is fighting the case instead of caving in. I am very sorry for the poor old boy . . . he will probably get six months.' The sternest test of Pearson's resolve came the night before the trial. In his Inner Temple chambers Sir Patrick Hastings told Pearson that the case was virtually hopeless. If he pleaded guilty he would probably be bound over to keep the peace and then released; if he fought and lost, he would face three to six months in prison. Pearson later painted the scene for Kingsmill: 'Pat gravely warned me to go home and talk matters over with my wife who, next to myself, would suffer most if I went to prison. I answered that if the prospect was from three to six years I would still refuse to confess I had wronged a pack of cads, cowards and humbugs like the Lanes. Gladys, I am glad to say, did the Roman-wife touch and backed me up. So together we face the prospect of Pentonville. It was all done in the finest classical-heroic style and I haven't yet regained my natural plasticity. I shall not pretend for a moment I didn't piss myself pretty frequently during the process of being classical, but that does not affect the sculptural superbness of the pose.'

The trial opened on January 26, 1927. The courtroom was packed, 'many of the public being women' according to the *Daily Mail*. Sir Patrick Hastings displayed that talent for obscuring weak facts by going on the offensive which is the trial lawyer's technique. When the company directors testified about fraud, Sir Patrick cross-examined them on the morality of publishing. He asked Allen Lane to compare *The Whispering Gallery* which, however imaginary, contained nothing lubricious, with other company titles, such as Ovid's *Art of Love* and Apuleius's *Golden Ass*. While denying that these were obscene books, Lane refused to read aloud certain passages. Worse, they had been published with erotic illustrations not in the original. 'The judge looked at the illustrations through the fingers of a hand which covered his face, and the jury (barring the two women) inspected them so closely that I felt their interest was temporarily abstracted from the case.'

Sir Patrick: Did you think the *Daily Mail* would attack the book because of what was said about Lord Northcliffe and that everybody would buy it?

Lane: No.

Sir Patrick: Did you start these prosecutions because you were called a disreputable firm of publishers?

Lane: No.

Sir Patrick: You have heard the vulgar expression 'carrying the baby', have you not? That is the position this man [Pearson] is in, is it not?

Lane: No.

When the prosecution's case was concluded, Hastings's cross-examination had left no doubt that, despite misgivings about authenticity, the company had published the book, pocketed the profits and, when the wind blew, tried to shelter behind a criminal prosecution of their own author.

Hastings now called Pearson to the witness box. Prosecuting counsel, Sir Henry Curtis-Bennett, asked him why he had mentioned Sir Rennell Rodd's name? 'I think it was because I couldn't think of anyone less likely to have written a book.' Question: 'So you started the lie by taking the most unlikely person in your view?' Answer: 'Yes, to show that it was a lie.' Question: 'Do you realize what you are saying?' Pearson answered that he fairly acknowledged that he had lied and he would now save the prosecutor's breath by admitting to double the number of lies he was about to be taxed with. The flummoxed Curtis-Bennett concluded his cross-examination. Question: 'Why did you keep up the pose after the book was exposed?' Answer: 'Because I was mad.'

The jury retired to consider its verdict. Apparently, little consideration was required. In less than half an hour the jury filed back into the court, the foreman rose in his place and pronounced the prisoner at the bar 'Not Guilty'. 'Pearson was then discharged,' reported the *Daily Mail*, 'and on leaving the court was warmly embraced by his wife, who had been present throughout the trial, and congratulated by a number of friends.' When Pearson went to congratulate Hastings on his defence, Hastings said: 'Nonsense. You got yourself off by your evidence in the witness box.' At a celebration in a nearby pub, Pearson was told by several jurors that the prosecution was going nowhere but that his engaging candour in the witness box had earned their sympathy.

In retrospect many aspects of *The Whispering Gallery* affair are puzzling. Pearson's initial folly was to have tried to pass off the diary as the work of Sir Rennell Rodd. Such a palpable lie must be easily disproved and eventually shown up. It may also have been unnecessary. The book might have been published as parody. The dialogue is amusing and the portraiture skilful. In *G. K.'s Weekly*, W. R. Titterton wrote: 'Whatever be the origins of the book, it compels me to the conclusion that if it is not written by one who participated in the scenes he described, then it is written by a genius.' It was foolhardy, near madness, for Pearson to have perpetuated the lie at the company directors' meeting when exposure was certain. The parallel between Oscar Wilde pursuing his libel action against the Marquess of Queensberry to his own inevitable destruction and Pearson persisting in his fraud until criminal charges were unavoidable is obvious.

It was extremely cowardly of the publishers to have tried to escape their complicity by prosecuting Pearson. Would the Bodley Head immediately donate all proceeds, Hugh Kingsmill inquired, to the Society for the Encouragement of Refined Prose Style in Ex-Diplomats? After the trial, *The New Age* came around to this point of view: 'Messrs John Lane have got to shore on a raft which they had lightened by pushing Mr Pearson over among the sharks of the criminal law, from which he escaped by the skin of his teeth.'

Under pressure, Pearson's behaviour was exemplary. He neither lamented his misfortune nor sought to fix the blame elsewhere. As he would later write of Oscar Wilde, the ordeal of a criminal prosecution was self-inflicted, gratuitous and quite meaningless, and 'he suffered the torments of one who cannot reasonably complain of his sufferings'. His courage in refusing all advice to plead guilty is self-evident. 'I wish to God (delete) I had been present at your victory,' Kingsmill wrote: 'It was extremely stout of you to go through with it against them all.' Pearson's candour in giving evidence contrasts with his own description of most testimony in court as consisting of 'lies, half-lies, contradictions and prevarications'. Also to his credit, Pearson never tried to conceal his folly. Of Oscar Wilde he would later write: 'The temptation to ease themselves of bitterness by making others responsible for their sufferings is one which human beings rarely resist.' Pearson resisted this temptation and, thirty years afterwards, his memoirs describe the events fairly and in detail. His final verdict on his own conduct – 'imbecile to the last degree'.

'A nodding acquaintance with his Majesty's judges,' Pearson later wrote, 'is not favourable to an acquaintance, however slight, with His Majesty.' Nor, he discovered, with publishers. *The Whispering Gallery* fiasco had blotted Pearson's copybook, and for some years he was received in literary circles with something less than enthusiasm. A series of 'Parallel Portraits', tracing similarities between writers and politicians, went the rounds but never appeared. 'A publisher is sitting on the book like a frightened hen, hardly daring to hatch yet longing to bring it out,' Pearson wrote to Kingsmill; 'my own opinion is that he'll funk laying what may cause a bit of a stink.' Similarly, an autobiographical volume sank without trace. Pearson became unusually discouraged. He told Kingsmill that publishers lacked 'the spunk of a boiled rabbit'. He said he would waste no more time posting off a manuscript he knew would be rejected, only to feel disappointed when it came back.

Instead, he obtained a small commission to assist with the Polish translation of three of Bernard Shaw's plays. And, with Colin Hurry as collaborator, he wrote four plays; two comedies, a farce, and a drama called *A Writ for Libel*. When Pearson again became respectable, this play was broadcast by the BBC and was performed by several repertory companies.

The protagonist of *A Writ for Libel*, Donald Hartling, is an angry young writer and recently nominated Labour Party candidate who has published a book exposing corruption in high places. One of his targets is a sanctimonious prig named Sir Kenneth Oakley, his Tory opponent in the forthcoming by-election, who is shown up in the book as a notorious womanizer and adulterer. Sir Kenneth sues for libel. Hartling is pressured from all sides to withdraw his allegation to avoid a trial, but he tells his wife: 'I would rather my career were wrecked at the outset than compromise on a lie.' The twist comes when it is revealed that one of Sir Kenneth's mistresses, indeed the only one who could testify at the trial and vindicate Hartling, is Hartling's own mother-in-law, Mrs Rydal. Hartling's wife, Doris, now joins in urging him to give up. No doubt the play is an accurate depiction of the strain and sense of isolation Pearson experienced during the build-up to the *Whispering Gallery* trial. But the theme of the play is hypocrisy and, curiously enough, Pearson leaves no doubt that the most hypocritical person is the protagonist, Donald Hartling. It is his stubborn pride, his determination to seize the moral ascendancy, his necessity always to be vindicated, which has the greatest potential for destroying people's lives. Mrs Rydal calls Donald 'an earnest moralist' and laments: 'No one will ever know the harm done to our peaceful English home-life by earnest moralists.' So perhaps Pearson had learned a measure of humility from the trial. But he had not yet learned how to live without colliding with those around him. When Mrs Rydal is asked what is to be done with the Donald Hartlings of this world, she replies: 'There is only one place for them . . . they should be at the outposts of the Empire, hacking paths through trackless jungles, irrigating boundless deserts, converting thousands of idle happy natives into busy wretched ones, and working off their superfluous energy in a healthy, primitive manner. They are far too simple for a civilized community.'

It is fitting that Pearson spent most of 1928 touring as the villain in a melodrama called *The Acquittal*. In 1929 he toured in John Galsworthy's last play, *The Roof*. At a rehearsal Galsworthy came up to him and said: 'You remind me very much of an actor who once played Marlow in *The Silver Box*.' Pearson replied: 'That is odd, because you remind me very much of the author of *The Silver Box*.' Galsworthy looked displeased and answered loftily: 'But I *am* the author of *The Silver Box*.' Pearson replied: 'And I *am* the actor who played Marlow in it.' Despite this bond, Galsworthy looked displeased and Pearson 'derived no feeling of fraternity'.

In January 1930 Pearson received an unexpected offer to tour the United States in G. B. Stern's *The Matriarch*. He sailed from Tilbury to New York aboard the *Scythia*. To his surprise Pearson discovered that he liked the country but found the natives strange. 'Practically everyone in America is a lunatic,' he wrote to Kingsmill. 'They wouldn't live here if they weren't. I find them very amusing, but rather tiring. Fortunately, one can always get drunk. I have never been so tight in my life as I have been here. There being a law against drink, it stands to reason that there is more drunkenness here than in any other country in the world.'

In Chicago Pearson gave several lectures on drama to women's clubs, observing that American women tended to be more literary than men. The men seemed content to spend their spare time attending burlesque, 'a futile attempt to recreate the spirit of Paris in the sterner climate of Illinois'. One night Pearson went along. The show consisted of stale vaudeville routines, worn jokes 'mostly of a sexual or faecal nature', and bored, unattractive women making spastic gestures as they partially disrobed to the accompaniment of unmelodious music. 'When the last flimsy draperies were seemingly to be removed, the excitement of the audience reached fever-pitch, and the ladies were recalled again and again in the hope that they would expose every inch of their nudity; but they never did quite. Possibly their discretion was due to a feeling on the part of management that, with nothing left to see, the audience would not pay to come and see it.'

A month each in Philadephia and New York completed the tour. In Philadelphia Pearson gave a series of lectures and radio broadcasts on biography. Although he had not yet written a biography, he had written a book about writing biographies, called *Ventilations*. J. B. Lippincott, a Philadelphia publisher, released the book to coincide with his visit.

When he became an accomplished biographer, Pearson would reject most of the precepts so confidently advanced in *Ventilations*, particularly the book's central thesis that a biographer may justifiably tamper with the facts in order better to get at 'the essential truth' about his subject. The biographer's imagination, he came to realize, has full play in his selection of material, presentation of subject, and skill in delineation and narrative. When Pearson wrote *Ventilations* he was unduly influenced by Lytton Strachey (to whom one sycophantic chapter is devoted) and his approach was abstract and theoretical. With actual experience would come judgment and maturity. 'It is only after one has experienced the labour and anxiety of searching for the truth that one knows how to value it.'

Ventilations introduced Pearson to that Via Dolorosa of authors, the signing party. A local store, Wannamakers, invited him to autograph. He arrived to find shelves stocked, clerks at the ready, but of buyers there was none. The fault was diagnosed as inadequate promotion. A fortnight later, after whatever sordid rituals publishers and booksellers engage in under the name of promotion, Pearson re-attended and took up his place next to a stack of copies which he tried to persuade himself had diminished. The only interruption of his solitary vigil came from a lady who wanted to insult him. She had heard him lecture and had read his book and she wanted to know how a man with so kindly a face could say such cruel things? 'I tried to explain that there was nothing cruel in my book, only a little honest exposure of pretentions. The explanation did not interest her.'

CHAPTER TEN

Biographer

Hal: 'I did never see such pitiful rascals.'
Falstaff: 'Tut, tut! Good enough to toss; food for powder, food for powder. . . . Tush man, mortal men, mortal men.'
Henry IV, Part I, Act IV, Scene II

Pearson was forty-two when he abandoned the stage to write biography. It was Kingsmill who showed him how. 'Being entirely broke,' Kingsmill wrote on November 21, 1928, 'and seeing that G.B.S. had recently advised people to sell his letters, while at the same time threatening proceedings if they were published, I thought I could, without prejudice to anyone concerned, sell G.B.S.'s inaccurate forecast of your trial which he sent me. I got four pounds ten at Sotherans. Why don't you sell some of yours?' A week later Kingsmill wrote again, advising against trying to play one dealer off against another ('they are always in touch to swindle the seller') and advancing a specific plan: 'Go into Sotherans with your letters, say you wish to sell them, say a few words about their importance and interest, and leave them there, as they will want to test them with acids, TNT etc.' By now Pearson had accumulated a considerable collection of Shaw's letters and first editions; acting on Kingsmill's advice, he sold them for £200. Thus enabled to settle to writing he was doing what he had wanted to do since the age of sixteen, writing biography.

For his first subject he considered Cecil Rhodes, but eventually decided upon Erasmus Darwin, grandfather of Charles Darwin by his first marriage and of Sir Francis Galton by his second marriage. Darwin had occupied Pearson's mind for some time, as is shown by a reference in this letter to Kingsmill in 1923: 'I am not saying that the real Johnson hadn't wit of a kind. But it was of the bludgeoning, common sense variety and I will match it, and beat it, with a few of the scattered sayings of Erasmus Darwin, Johnson's contemporary.'

Through his mother and the Galton estate, Pearson obtained unpublished letters and papers. Even so, biographical material was scanty. Pearson accommodated this difficulty by devoting considerable space to the members of the Lunar Society (unflatteringly called 'the Lunatics'),

a circle of scientists, inventors and philosophers of whom Darwin was
organizer, patriarch and dominant personality. In devoting attention to
the Lunatics Pearson exemplified his credo that 'to know a man well one
must know his friends . . . a man's friendships tell us more about him
than his love affairs'. Thus the book is not a chronological narrative of
Darwin's life but rather is shaped as a circle, with Darwin in the centre,
glimpsed through his friends from their vantage points on the
circumference.

And what friends they were! Anna Seward, the Swan of Lichfield,
whose biography Pearson would write in 1936; Samuel Johnson, who
resented the fame not only of a rival Lichfeldian but of a religious
sceptic. Darwin maintained that all that one could know came through
the five senses: 'All else is vain fancy, and as for the being of a God, the
existence of a soul, or a world to come, who can know anything about
them? . . . These are only the bugbears by which men of sense govern
fools.' Darwin's closest friend and fellow Lunatic was Dr James Keir,
author, inventor and scientist. There was Richard Lovell Edgeworth,
inventor, experimenter, recipient of the gold and silver medals from the
Society for the Encouragement of the Arts, whose prodigious scientific
attainments nevertheless left time for four marriages and twenty-two
children; Josiah Wedgwood, potter and founder of the china firm which
still carries his name; Thomas Day, poet; William Withering, physician
and botanist, who lived out his final years in a library maintained at a
uniform temperature of 65° fahrenheit, prompting one wag to remark
that 'the flower of physic is indeed Withering'; James Watt, inventor
of the steam engine; Dr Joseph Priestley, cleric, philosopher and
discoverer of oxygen; John Baskerville, publisher and printer.

Erasmus Darwin graduated in medicine from St John's College,
Cambridge and from Edinburgh University. As a young man it is
recorded that he was 'fond of sacrificing to both Bacchus and Venus'.
When he discovered with age that one cannot sacrifice indefinitely to
both, he became a teetotaler; an acquaintance records that 'his affection
for Venus was retained to the last period of his life'. In 1756 he set up
medical practice in Lichfield and became known for his unorthodox and
risky treatments (he inadvertently killed one of his own daughters by an
inoculation against measles). His services were available to all classes;
King George III asked Darwin to become his personal physician but
Darwin declined because it would have meant living in London. His
services were often provided without fee. In appearance he was unprepossessing; 'a large man, fat, and rather clumsy, but intelligence and
benevolence were painted on his countenance' according to a contemporary account. He had a severe stammer. A young man inquired

whether this had been an impediment. 'No, sir,' Darwin replied, 'it gives me time for reflection and saves me from answering impertinent questions.' He married twice, both times happily. By his first wife he had five children; their third son, Robert, was Charles Darwin's father. By his second wife, he had seven children; one daughter, Violetta, was the mother of Sir Francis Galton. In addition, he fathered several illegitimate children.

It was not as a physician but as a poet, philosopher, naturalist, inventor and founder of the Lunar Society (so called because its meetings were held at the full moon so that members might have its light to return home) that Darwin achieved eminence. Besides assisting his friends with their ideas, Darwin invented a new type of carriage and a rotary pump. He made a speaking machine, but as its vocabulary was limited to the letters p, m and a, its words – mama, papa, map and pam – were of limited utility. He designed and built a horizontal windmill for grinding flints, an artesian well, candlesticks mounted on telescopic stands, knitting looms, weighing and surveying machines, ploughs, and a 'manifold writer' (an early model of a copying machine). He was the first to perceive that the spokes of a carriage wheel could be made to act as springs. He never stopped making experiments, particularly on wind and weather; each day he measured and recorded wind current and velocity. He wrote a plan for improving climatic conditions by navigating 'the immense masses of ice in the polar regions into the more southern oceans'. He was absorbed with ideas of perpetual motion and luminous music. It was Darwin who put James Watt on track for his discovery of the steam engine, and it was Erasmus Darwin, not his grandson Charles, who first conceived a theory of evolution and of the survival of the fittest in this 'one great slaughter-house, the warring world'.

Pearson's biography is fascinating on several counts: as a portrait of a grandfather whose extraordinary achievements were to be unjustifiably eclipsed by a famous grandson; as an account of the Lunatics, whose fate it was to be eclipsed by the more famous eighteenth-century Club which Darwin's rival, Samuel Johnson, gathered round himself; also as a glimpse of the stock from which Pearson sprang. Pearson is, after all, writing about an ancestor. No genetic trace of the scientific or inventive Darwin appears in Pearson's make-up. But of Darwin's individualism, the intensity and diversity of his interest in his fellow creatures, and a religious outlook oscillating uncertainly between Christianity and Creative Evolution, there are discernible traces.

Dr Darwin was published by J. M. Dent in 1930. Whether because the subject was too obscure or the author too much a literary pariah, it was shunned by reviewers and ignored by readers. Two years after its publication, on Darwin's bicentenary, the *Times Literary Supplement* 'discovered' the book and praised it as 'one of the models of sensitive ancestor worship'. This came too late to affect sales which were meagre. In 1964 an American publisher (Walkers) re-issued the book. This time it was extensively and favourably reviewed; the *Washington Post* called it 'vastly entertaining'. 'An agreeable ramble among the lunatics brought happily to life,' wrote Alan Pryce-Jones in the *New York Herald Tribune*; *Time* magazine praised book and author; the *Illinois Star* said it was 'a splendid book to read – Biography at its best'. Again notice came too late; Pearson died that year.

Whatever the financial disappointment of *Dr Darwin* – severe enough to force Pearson back on the stage and to necessitate the sale of half his library (a calamity mitigated, he told Kingsmill, by the fact that it consisted mostly of books he had borrowed from other people) – Pearson knew that he had found his vocation. 'I perceived that the writing of biography was the only occupation that could ever completely absorb me. Money or no money, reputation or no reputation, I would go on writing until, as Hamlet says, "my eyelids could no longer wag".'

His next book *The Smith of Smiths* (the title is Lord Macaulay's succinct tribute to the nineteenth-century cleric, wit and essayist, Sydney Smith) was to prove Pearson's most durable biography. Since first publication in 1934 it has rarely been out-of-print. It was an early Penguin paperback. It has appeared in a variety of editions (including a Folio Society volume graced with an affectionate Introduction by Malcolm Muggeridge) and in several languages. But, though the course was to prove smooth, the launch was troubled. With the book unfinished, Pearson sent chapters off to several publishers soliciting a contract and an advance on royalties. All returned the chapters with excuses; the subject was unknown, worse a clergyman; there was little drama and no love angle; it was too full of quotation; it was not written in the popular Lytton Strachey style of the moment. The publishers' letters invariably concluded with an expression of hope in placing the book elsewhere, a hope which reveals publishers at their most solicitous. In April 1933 Pearson told Kingsmill that he was now sending the first third of the book to publishers; as each rejected, he added a chapter for the next. 'By the time ten have turned it down, it ought to be ready for publication.' Finally Hamish Hamilton agreed to publish but, because of Pearson's track record, only if a reputable figure would supply a Foreword. Pearson approached G. M. Trevelyan who had written praising his Darwin. Trevelyan replied on July 31, 1933, advising Pearson to change the title of the book on the ground that *The Smith of Smiths* was too jocular for the scholar and too obscure for the general reader ('a playful title hardly does it justice'). Trevelyan suggested *Sydney Smith: His Life, Wit and Humour* or *Life, Wit and Wisdom*. Pearson consulted Kingsmill who replied that Trevelyan's suggestion was 'a little cloistral. It smacks a bit of a professor pacing an antique quadrangle with the blood coursing madly through his head – "I have it! I have it!" he shouts. "Life, Wit *AND* Humour – Ah!"' Pearson stuck to *The Smith of Smiths* but gratefully accepted Trevelyan's Foreword which praised Pearson as 'an honest biographer . . . [who] exercises his right to agree with his hero perhaps more often and completely than his reader will always be able to do'.

With the publisher's condition met and the book set to appear, Pearson was shattered to receive another letter from Trevelyan stating that he had only now discovered Pearson's true identity as the author of *The Whispering Gallery*; since Sir Rennell Rodd was a personal friend, the Foreword must be withdrawn. Pearson replied, berating Trevelyan for lack of intestinal fortitude. But Trevelyan proved generous, if not courageous. Although the Foreword was withdrawn, he assuaged his conscience by giving Pearson £300, exactly three times the amount of the advance. G. K. Chesterton then manoeuvred his substantial bulk into the void, supplying an Introduction to replace Trevelyan's. However Chesterton forgot to mention Pearson or the book, producing instead an essay on Sydney Smith. Pearson wrote G.K.C. a letter of 'dignified protest'. Chesterton replied apologetically saying that no slight had been intended, that he had become so interested in Sydney's character that he had got carried away, rather like a chairman who gave a lecture but forgot to introduce the guest speaker. The deficiency was soon corrected, and the volume appeared in January 1934.

Without exception the reviews were good. Desmond MacCarthy informed readers in *The Times* that 'everyone who reads it will enjoy it'; James Agate counselled *Daily Express* readers: 'Get it. Don't write to me a month hence to say you intended to but forgot and now can't. I shan't sympathize.' *The New York Herald Tribune* said: '*The Smith of Smiths* is a book of books, in which an irresistible subject has found the perfectly attuned biographer.' But for some papers a stigma still clung to the author. 'The *Morning Post* has quite a good selling notice,' Pearson wrote to Kingsmill, 'though the writer seems to assume that the book was immaculately conceived – that is to say he doesn't mention that it was written by anyone.' And Pearson learned that one paper had killed a long, laudatory review when the editor discovered that Pearson

'. . . had committed the crime of being found innocent by a British Jury'.

In his memoirs Pearson summarized the four qualities he sought in a friend or in a biographical subject: 'Good nature, good humour, good sense and good nonsense.' In Sydney Smith he had hit upon a subject who embodied all these qualities. The second son of Robert and Maria Smith, Sydney was born at Woodford in Essex (not Woodbridge in Suffolk as Pearson unaccountably says, a fundamental and uncharacteristic slip from an otherwise meticulous biographer) in 1771. Of remoter ancestors, Sydney would say only: 'My grandfather disappeared about the time of the Assizes, and – we asked no questions.' At Winchester he endured the usual public school humiliations so that, as an old man, he shuddered at the very word school. He was useless at games. 'Of what importance is it,' he wrote, 'whether a boy can play well or ill at cricket, or row a boat with the skill and precision of a waterman? If our young lords and esquires were hereafter to wrestle together in public, or the gentlemen of the Bar to exhibit Olympic games in Hilary Term, the glory attached to these exercises at public schools would be rational and important.' Faced with a choice of Oxford or Cambridge ('two enormous hulks confined with mooring chains, everything flowing and progressing around them') Sydney chose New College, Oxford. Faced with a choice of holy orders or the law, he chose the church as the profession best suited to a lazy man of scholarly bent and little means. He was ordained in 1794.

In 1802 Smith launched the *Edinburgh Review*, a risky undertaking at any time, but particularly for a cleric of liberal opinion in a time of orthodoxy, a reformer in an age of senseless bigotry. Nevertheless the *Review* throve, becoming the leading organ of public opinion in Britain, its independence alone causing it to be feared and respected. For a quarter of a century Smith held forth in its pages, usually upon serious subjects lightly treated; 'by making his countrymen laugh,' Pearson wrote, 'he made them think.' The Society for the Suppression of Vice was a favourite target of Smith's: 'It must be obvious that the fear of God can never be taught by constables, nor the pleasures of religion be learnt from a common informer.' Yet the moral busybodies of the Society assumed the opposite; class prejudice was their driving force and the effect of their zeal was to spread, not suppress, vice. 'Men, whose trade is rat-catching, love to catch rats; the bug-destroyer seizes on the bug with delight; and the suppresser is gratified by finding his vice.'

Missionaries, or at least those 'Goodies and Noodles' of the evangelical Methodist strain, also earned his contempt: 'Why are we to send out little detachments of maniacs to spread over the fine regions of the world the most unjust and contemptible opinion of the Gospel? The wise and rational part of the Christian ministry find they have enough to do at home to combat passions unfavourable to human happiness.' Smith also attacked hereditary wealth, class distinction, temperance campaigns, slavery, blood sports, and ill-treatment of prisoners. Despite his advocacy of the poor, he never romanticized; in response to some sentimental cant about the 'virtuous ploughman', Smith replied that 'a ploughman marries a ploughwoman because she is plump; generally uses her ill; thinks his children an encumbrance; very often flogs them; and, for sentiment, has nothing more nearly approaching to it than the ideas of broiled bacon and mashed potatoes'.

Such unorthodox views did not enhance Smith's chances for ecclesiastical preferment. In 1803 poverty compelled him to move from Edinburgh to London. Even in that freer, cosmopolitan air, he was a rebel. 'The greatest part of my congregation thought me mad,' he told a friend, 'and the clerk was as pale as death in helping me off with my gown, for fear I should bite him.' In declining to conform his opinions to the prevailing wind, he paid a penalty. His elder brother had to lend him money to keep going. When he was invited to preach in the Temple Church, Smith chose an explosive topic, Catholic Emancipation, and infuriated almost everyone who attended. Lord Henley said Smith deserved the Star Chamber. Lord Stowell advised him to change his politics. To his friend, Francis Jeffrey, Smith wrote: 'You ask me about my prospects. I think I shall remain long as I am. I have no powerful friends. I belong to no party – I do not cant – I abuse canting everywhere – I am not conciliating – and I have not talents enough to force my way without these laudable and illaudable auxiliaries.'

Smith's reputation had a brief revival when he delivered a series of lectures on Moral Philosophy at the Royal Institution. Although he did not take it seriously ('the most successful swindle of the season,' he told Jeffrey) the audience did, and the lectures were packed. In recognition of new respectability, the ecclesiastical superflux was briefly shaken in his direction. In the year 1806 Smith was presented with the living of Foston-le-Clay in Yorkshire. The village had been without a resident clergyman for more than a century. The parsonage was a hovel. The church was a little better. Preaching his first sermon, Sydney thumped the cushion on the pulpit and could not see the congregation again for several minutes until the dust had cleared.

Over the next twenty years Smith designed and built a Rectory, an imposing stone house whose windows commanded a view over the Yorkshire wolds. The building consumed most of his energy and all of his money, driving him several thousand pounds into debt. In 1954 Pearson fulfilled an ambition by going to Yorkshire and staying in 'Sydney's house', as the guest of its owner Mr R. F. Wormold. In 1962 the house was destroyed by fire.

In addition to clerical responsibilities, Smith farmed, doctored the poor of the parish, became a Justice of the Peace, and conducted experiments. He invented a set of armour for rheumatics, complete with a hollow top helmet to be filled with hot water. He appointed himself cook to the village, and he alternated the men's diet to see if they could be fed or starved into virtue or vice. Next to the front door of the Rectory he built an enormous speaking trumpet, through which he could shout directions to labourers in the fields, and a telescope through which he could keep them under observation. In the middle of the pasture he built a universal scratcher so that animals of any size, from lamb to bullock, could rub luxuriantly against it.

As a man of urban tastes, he was restless without the 'wits, chemists, poets, splendid feasts and captivating women' of the city. As the years accumulated and he was repeatedly passed over for a city living, he reconciled himself to rural life. When Lady Holland commiserated with him, Smith replied: 'If my lot be to crawl, I will crawl contentedly; if to fly I will fly with alacrity; but, as long as I can possibly avoid it, I will never be unhappy. If, with a pleasant wife, three children, a good house and farm, many books, and many friends, who wish me well, I can't be happy, I am a very silly, foolish fellow, and what becomes of me is of very little consequence.' Eventually Smith got a promotion, first to Combe Florey, then as Canon of St Paul's, London.

Neat parallels could be worked out between Sydney Smith and Hesketh Pearson: for example, their disdain for rural life; a sense of humour inclined to lewdness; an insatiable appetite for laughter; a temper which, when provoked, showed that neither man was altogether free from the tyranny he condemned in others; a droll manner in recitation which made other people laugh until they cried; the fact that the greatest tragedy in each man's life was the premature death of a son.

It is interesting that Pearson's most sympathetic biography should be of a cleric. Malcolm Muggeridge has recalled that many of Hesketh's own gestures were parsonical: for instance, a habit of pressing the tips of his fingers together and a sermonic timbre in his voice. In 1939 Muggeridge and Pearson collaborated on a play, *Harvest Thanksgiving*, in which the coming of the war is seen through the eyes of a milquetoast provincial vicar, the Reverend Wilfred Bree, the embodiment of what Pearson feared he would have become had he followed his ancestors into holy orders. 'Hesketh reduced me to a state of helpless laughter,' Muggeridge recalled, 'by speaking the vicar's lines as we went along.' Like Sydney Smith, Pearson believed that Christianity was made for man, not man for Christianity. Jesus Christ was a perfect specimen of man, one who showed us how we should live, but not God, nor a third part of some incomprehensible Trinity. Once Smith heard an atheist speak scathingly about a Supreme Being over dinner. He listened in silence, then said: 'Very good soup this.' The Frenchman agreed: 'Oui, monsieur, c'est excellent.' Said Sydney: 'Pray, sir, do you believe in a cook?' Beyond that neither Smith nor Pearson would venture into the quicksands of theology. When Muggeridge suggested to Pearson that Smith was Mr Worldly Wiseman in a clerical collar, that London loomed larger on his horizon than Golgotha, and that 'the resemblance between Smith and St Francis of Assisi was no more than a passing one', Pearson agreed. However, he maintained that Smith's credentials were impeccable and his discharge of clerical duties above reproach.

In 1977, forty years after first publication of *The Smith of Smiths* and thirteen years after Pearson's death, Muggeridge wrote these words about biographer and subject: 'They were, indeed, kindred spirits despite the century or so between their births, Hesketh being a throwback to the eighteenth century, and Smith the voice of one crying amidst the fleshpots to make straight the way for the twentieth. I cannot believe that Smith could have hoped for a more sympathetic biographer or Hesketh for a more sympathetic subject for a biography. They suited one another perfectly, and I trust that by this time they have met and compared notes in the celestial precincts reserved for Anglicans who in the days of their mortality were given to laying up treasure on earth, and regarding the Ten Commandments as like an examination paper, with seven only to be attempted.'

William Hazlitt, Pearson's next biographical subject (*The Fool of Love*, Hamish Hamilton, 1934), was chosen for reasons both literary and personal. The personal reasons had their source in a love affair, the most serious of Pearson's life, which made Hazlitt's doomed love for Sarah Walker, his landlady's daughter, especially poignant. The literary reason was a desire to rescue an essayist whom Pearson considered unjustly neglected. At his best, Pearson thought Hazlitt was unequalled; at his worst, readable. Next to Shakespeare and Boswell, Pearson chose Hazlitt for a desert island library.

With each of his biographical subjects, Pearson tried to get into their skin, to appreciate their oddities, to feel their emotions and antagonisms. 'Hazlitt provided me with more of these sudden unexpected but strangely revealing glimpses into his character than anyone I have ever known or read about, with the result that I was so much absorbed in him, so completely carried away by the excitement of discovery, that I do not think I was more than half-conscious of the outside world while I was in his company. I seemed to be living his life, and I often had the feeling that he was walking just ahead of me in the streets, a weird lonely figure whom people turned to stare at . . .' Despite, or perhaps because of, this intensity, *The Fool of Love* is not among Pearson's best books. Missing is the deft humour and irony that make his *Darwin* and *Smith* so readable; instead there is repetition, melodrama, and a pervasive *ennui*. The book was not a success. It was ignored by critics and readers. Total sales never exceeded 700 copies.

For his next book, Pearson chose the Victorian tag-team of comic opera, Gilbert and Sullivan. Two less compatible temperaments are difficult to imagine. Yet they produced appealing music, a variation in humanity somehow producing a fusion in art. It was this that intrigued Pearson. He discussed the idea of a dual biography with Bernard Shaw who counselled against it, saying it was a job for a musician. Why Pearson continued to solicit Shaw's advice when it was invariably negative is a mystery; had he paid attention to Shaw, few of his biographies would have been written. 'I explained to [Shaw] that one did not have to be a musician in order to write the life of a musician, that the art of biography had suffered from being in the hands of specialists, and that, as a biographer's main job was to recreate a human being, his primary qualification was a knowledge of human nature.'

Gilbert and Sullivan was published by Hamish Hamilton in May 1935. A few weeks later Pearson wrote to Kingsmill: 'As my future biographer (if I am not yours) you will be interested in the following duologue between myself and a total stranger at the Highgate Ponds today:

> Stranger (sitting by me on a seat): Excuse me, sir, but haven't we met before? I seem to know your face.
> Self: Indeed?
> Stranger: Yes. Would it – would you think it impertinent of me to ask your name?
> Self: In the ordinary way I should think it most impertinent of you, as I prefer to take my recreation incognito. But circumstances alter cases, and as I want to sell you a book I look upon your request as not only reasonable but polite. My name is Hesketh Pearson. I am the author of a biography of *Gilbert and Sullivan*. Advertisements appear in today's *Observer* and *Sunday Times*.
> Stranger: (after an embarrassed laugh) Then I don't think we *have*

met before. (A pause; then with a rush) Of course I know your name.

Self: The book is published by Hamish Hamilton. The price is ten/six net and it is very reasonable at the price. (Getting up) Having met me in the flesh, I am sure you will want to meet me in the spirit. Buy it. Good-day.

Reviews were extensive and favourable, although one or two reviewers accused Pearson of subjecting Gilbert to 'Freudian psychoanalysis'. A less plausible criticism is difficult to imagine. Pearson had not read a word of Freud when he wrote *Gilbert and Sullivan* and he never did thereafter. Clearly he would have found Freud, to put it mildly, an imperfect sympathy. Sales of *Gilbert and Sullivan* were poor which, given the reviews, puzzled author and publisher until a rival publisher confided his opinion that the vast majority of Gilbert and Sullivan addicts were illiterate.

Pearson returned to the subject in 1957, producing a full-length biography of W. S. Gilbert (*His Life and Strife*, Methuen). The representatives of Gilbert's estate had invited Pearson to undertake the book, giving him access to Gilbert's papers and hitherto unpublished letters. Unfortunately, what might have been a pleasant assignment was marred by a niggardly dispute over royalties. The estate representatives initially demanded 40% of the author's royalties which, after the agent's fee, would have left Pearson labouring for a year to eighteen months for half of an uncertain royalty. Eventually the estate agreed to 10%, but only after protracted negotiations and tiresome correspondence.

The subjects of Pearson's next three biographies – Henry Labouchere (*Labby*, 1936) *Tom Paine* (1937), and John Nicholson (*The Hero of Delhi*, 1939) – were all men of action. This posed a problem for Pearson who preferred contemplation to action, literature to both, and whose attitude to politicians and statesmen was Lear's:

> Get thee glass eyes
> And, like a scurvy politician, seem
> To see the things thou dost not.

Henry Labouchere, the radical politician, was not Pearson's choice. He wanted to write on Thackeray but Hamish Hamilton doubted there would be a market. Having reluctantly settled to Labby, Pearson came to admire his combination of ruthlessness and candour, political single-mindedness and personal charity, which meant that Labby did and said exactly what he felt like doing and saying, even in that temple of lies, the House of Commons. 'He was in reality that very remarkable phenomenon, a perfectly plain and simple man, who spoke exactly what was in his mind, careless of the consequences, and was completely free from conventional standards of thought, behaviour and speech.' In the smug years from 1880 to 1905, when England was adding to her Empire and business was booming, it was Labouchere who criticized Imperialism, exposed profiteers and swindlers, and thumbed his nose at Victorian morality. Born rich, he spent his life working for the poor. Gambler, diplomat, jester, reformer, journalist (founder and first editor of *Truth*, which Labby had wanted to call *The Lyre*), he had idiosyncrasies enough to attract Pearson.

Several ex-politicians who had known Labby were still about and Pearson sought them out. They rattled on about his views and theirs, but it was character and anecdote that Pearson was after. When Lloyd George wrote offering to tell Pearson all he knew, this seemed a stroke of fortune. 'In a state of suppressed excitement but doing my best to look calm on the surface', Pearson took a cab and met Lloyd George at the Reform Club. 'He gripped my hand, took me into the smoking room, ordered drinks, said "Come now let us talk about Labby" and began a sketch of his own career which lasted all through lunch and carried us as far as the coffee, when, quite by accident, the subject of my study cropped up. Pouring his diminutive jug of cream into his coffee, he idly remarked: "Labby never wasted the cream. First of all he emptied it into the cup, and then he rinsed the cream-jug with coffee and poured that into his cup. Millionaires never throw anything away. Of course Labby's ancestors were French. Now I always say . . ." He went on saying it until he had finished his cigar; after which I was well-equipped for writing the Life of Lloyd George but had learnt nothing of Labby except that he was frugal, which I already knew.'

When Pearson had nearly finished the book, he wrote to Algar Thorold who had previously written a Life of Labouchere to ask for an account of Labby's death. Thorold was a superstitious Catholic and, although he supplied the story, he begged Pearson not to use it. Apparently a lamp near to Labby's bed had been accidently overturned; Labby's eyes opened and he said: 'Flames? Not yet, I think . . .' and lapsed back again. Pearson wrote to Thorold that it was such a characteristic story he could not forebear using it but that he would take full responsibility for its use in the next world. 'Though I suffered a twinge of remorse when Thorold died a week or two after the publication of *Labby*, I would refuse such a request again and again.'

Labby attracted considerable attention. Reviewers who had known him (like Catherine Radziwill) claimed that Pearson had brought him exactly to life; in the *Daily Telegraph*, Sir John Squire wrote: 'This book is exactly right in length, shape and tone. It is well and humorously written; its author has made himself thoroughly familiar with the events and people of his period; and he has the gift of displaying his hero without analysing him. Labby, small, puckish, debonair, hand in pocket, head on one side, monocle in eye, cigarette in fingers, strolls through these pages as he used to stroll through the purlieus of Westminster, throwing quips right and left at all the world's expense. It is a book to keep.' Though sales were never spectacular, there was a steady demand and *Labby* ran through six printings in a decade.

Only one of Pearson's biographies was a *pièce d'occasion*, its subject owing more to the times than intrinsic interest. After Hitler's rise to power and the absorption of Austria, Pearson realized that war was inevitable and he set about to find a subject who embodied the virtues Britain would need to survive. He hit upon John Nicholson, the hero of Delhi, a ruthless fighter who proved during the Indian Mutiny that courage and tenacity could surmount military odds. 'Wars and revolutions,' Pearson wrote, 'are caused by greed and superstition, or, in more imposing terms, by statecraft and priestcraft.' Collins published *The Hero of Delhi* in September 1939. Unfortunately international events were considered more newsworthy and consumed all available newsprint. The book was ignored. Only a single review exists among all of Pearson's papers, a short favourable notice in *The Listener*. Sales were meagre. It is nearly impossible to find a second-hand copy today, one of the scarcest titles (along with *A Persian Critic* and *Iron Rations*) among all of Pearson's books. This is regrettable because, like all his biographies, it is thoroughly researched and highly readable.

It was Malcolm Muggeridge who suggested Pearson write on Tom Paine. Muggeridge, Pearson and Kingsmill were drinking at the Horseshoe when Muggeridge let fall Tom Paine's remark on the House of Commons: 'There is no body of men more jealous of their privileges than the Commons – because they sell them.' This tickled Pearson who, after a few days of preliminary reading, resolved to tackle a full-length biography of Tom Paine. He repaid the favour by dedicating the book to Muggeridge. But when Muggeridge reviewed the book, favourably to the author but not the subject whom he called 'poor, besotted Tom Paine', Pearson flew into a rage. Muggeridge responded in a conciliatory manner and Pearson's temper subsided. He wrote:

Dear Malcolm,
I hasten to tell you that there is not a grain of grit in our friendship as far as I am concerned. I like you because I like you, not because I agree with your opinions . . . when I read your 'poor, besotted Tom

Paine' I realized at once that you and I admire quite different things, but it did not alter my feelings of personal affection for you by a gram (whatever a gram may be) . . . You are one of my very few friends. Please remain so in spite of Tom Paine.

Perhaps warned off by Muggeridge's experience, Kingsmill decided not to review Pearson's next book, *A Life of Shakespeare*, which appeared in 1942. Kingsmill had only recently become literary editor of *Punch* and, since the book was dedicated to him, he may have feared a charge of favouritism. On May 5, 1942 Kingsmill wrote to Pearson from *Punch*: 'As the Shakespeare is dedicated to me, I thought it better to send it to another reviewer, and the only intelligent reviewer on the staff is a fierce old lady who is a fanatical Catholic. I told her to send the book back if she couldn't bear it, but she has greatly enjoyed it except for your concluding comments on W.S. as God the Father, Son and Holy Ghost. This got her, and she has had a crack at you on that score.' This innocuous letter touched off the only acrimonious row to mar a thirty-year friendship. Up until then, each man had freely reviewed the other's books. Pearson exploded, firing off three splenetic letters, all of which Kingsmill ignored. Unfortunately Dorothy Kingsmill entered the fray and wrote to Pearson:

Hugh has barely settled in his *Punch* job and yet you have already succeeded in thoroughly upsetting him. He came home last night white and shaken with his weekly article, already overdue, still unfinished. How can you behave like this to a man who, whatever his faults, has given you twenty years of devoted friendship . . . I have known for some years now that with increasing confidence in your literary ability would come increasing criticism of Hugh and irritation with him, and knowing too all the love and confidence he had for you and in you, I have watched this development with increasing distress.

Resentful at his friend's silence and stung by Dorothy's insinuation, Pearson replied:

Your letter displays a mind so distorted by rage, hatred, and spite, that I cannot even believe your statement that Hughie is upset. Your hysterical animosity, which must be due to my having quite unwittingly wounded your vanity, carries you beyond all bounds, and you hold Hughie up to ridicule in a manner that his worst enemy would envy . . . now be a good girl; and tend to your clothes and your cooking; and in future do not meddle with things you cannot understand. I have already forgiven you, and shall have forgotten the nonsense you wrote before you read this.

The row might have ended here had Kingsmill not felt compelled to rise to his wife's defence. He wrote to Pearson:

I saw a copy of Dorothy's letter on the evening of the day she wrote to you. It is of course true I was upset. You had accused me of letting you down in my own interest, and you have repeated this in a second letter. And in a third you were talking of dirty tricks. You cannot insult a friend of twenty years who has never in any way let you down, and then having relieved your own feelings, expect him to behave as if he had none himself. Dorothy was naturally angry at seeing how much you had upset me . . . I don't want to break our friendship, but as this trouble was started by you it is for you to end it, not bluster and bluff and pretend nothing has happened, but by admitting for once that you have gone too far. If anything solid remains in your affection for me, you will do this, but if I have become indistinguishable from the publishers and other people you fly out at whenever you want to relieve your feelings, you won't.

Pearson was not yet ready to concede. He replied:

I have wounded Dorothy's feelings, how or why I of course cannot say, as I have never given her a thought except when you have borrowed money from me for the necessity of your establishment, when I have occasionally wondered whether she was being as economical with my money as Gladys was forced to be without it. You must not complain if I add that quite apart from the sums of money you have borrowed from me when I could ill afford them, but which your rich friends would not spare you, I have never asked you to pay your whack at any bar or restaurant whenever we have met in the last fourteen years or so. I have never worried you to pay back a penny you owe me: in fact, when you offered to repay one loan, I told you to keep it until you could return it without hardship to yourself . . . I have merely to add that I bear you no malice; that if ever I have an opportunity of doing you a good turn I shall do it with the utmost pleasure; but that if you imagine I am going to apologize for expressing irritation over your shabby treatment of my Shakespeare book, you have learnt very little about me in twenty years of companionship.

Whatever justification there may originally have been for Pearson's annoyance, this letter was a low blow; Kingsmill was naturally sensitive about his poverty and only with difficulty had accepted the reality that he would never be a commercially successful writer. By bringing up his own generosity, Pearson had struck at Kingsmill where he was most vulnerable. Kingsmill replied with considerable dignity and restraint:

It is not true that you have been the host at our meetings for fourteen years. When we were both hard up, our meals were simple, there were no drinks, and each paid for himself. When, relatively to myself, you became rather better off, your meals became less simple, and you started to pay for me. I ought never to have drifted into this, but of course I had no premonition of the day when you would use your hospitality against me . . . I did not expect you to apologize for your abusive letters. I only hoped you might. You ought to have learnt by now that the truth always comes out in the end, and if you had expressed your regret the story of our friendship would have had a very different conclusion.'

As quickly as it erupted, the row ended. On June 10, 1942 Pearson's diary records: 'Feeling in a mood of seraphic serenity, I have written a letter to Hughie, proffering the olive branch.' Pearson expressed contrition. Dorothy expressed regret. Kingsmill was benign. All three resolved, in Prospero's words, not to burden remembrance with a heaviness that's past. Pearson's account of this single unpleasant episode concludes on a happy note: 'Our future friendship was untroubled by any memory of my petulance.'

CHAPTER ELEVEN

Vicissitudes

'In the general spectacle of life there is more to laugh at than to cry over.'
Hesketh Pearson

Royalties on Pearson's early biographies were meagre. Colin Hurry came to the rescue. In exchange for minimal, irregular services he put Hesketh on the payroll of Carlton Studios, his advertising and public relations firm, from June 1932 at a salary of £5 a week. 'I do not know how long it will go on,' Pearson told Kingsmill, 'I cannot even begin to pay off my tradesmen's debts on it, but it keeps me in food, so they can go hang themselves.' The salary kept Pearson's family while he spent his hours researching and writing in the British Museum. Once while waiting for an attendant to locate a book ('considering the time they are taking [it] is clearly being rewritten and reprinted') he wrote to Kingsmill: 'A woman is, beyond any reasonable doubt, making eyes at me from a distance of five feet. But I shall be firm. Women are out of place in the British Museum, except among the Mummies.' In reply Kingsmill proffered this excerpt for H.P.'s memoirs: 'I found after a time that I had to give up the B. Museum. When they began to rush me as I came out of the lavatory, I, frankly, threw in my hand (a dubious phrase).'

Colin Hurry proved an undemanding employer. Once he invited Pearson to join him for lunch with a visiting American Rotarian. By way of making conversation Hurry asked the man what he was doing in London. 'We come over here . . . to be loved' came the earnest reply. The artlessness of this remark convulsed Pearson who broke into fits of laughter. 'Colin, always in command of his emotions, grasped me by the arm, led me from the room patting my back sympathetically, took me to the long bar, ordered a drink for me, and hurried back to the Rotarian, whose astonishment he assuaged by saying that I suffered from shell-shock, upon which the other expressed much sympathy and the interview concluded harmoniously.' Another time Pearson was dining with a newspaper magnate, an important client, who had recently returned from Germany. The man launched into an interminable monologue on the benefits of the Hitler Youth Movement to which

Pearson made the necessary gurgles and sounds of affirmation. At last the man paused, gulped a drink of wine, and said to Pearson: 'Makes yer think, eh?' 'My reply was out of my mouth before I knew it was on the way: "Nothing could make you think." Thereafter his attitude to me cooled . . .'

As Pearson's biographies multiplied and achieved modest commercial success, he went off Hurry's payroll. But they remained intimate friends and more than once Hurry lent Pearson money. Hesketh, in turn, was no less generous to friends. From 1932 onwards he regularly gave Kingsmill money. In the Thirties when Basil Harvey was particularly skint, Hesketh lent him £300. When Harvey attempted to repay, Hesketh refused, telling him to lend it to some other struggling writer in similar circumstances. Harvey's autobiography, *Growing Pains* (Hamish Hamilton, 1937), which is dedicated to Pearson, includes this tribute: 'Hesketh was the first man I had known who had a point of view, a system of mind which enabled him to form clear judgments. I have grown rapidly in the years since I met him, and I attribute my emergence from a morass of muddled thinking, unsound opinion, insane beliefs, into some sort of coherent philosophy of life, largely to his friendship.'

Pearson and Colin Hurry (sometimes also with Basil Harvey and another close friend, a Scotsman named James Mitchell) spent many evenings drinking together, often at the Café Royal. Pearson was a considerable drinker, but Basil Harvey never recalled seeing him drunk. Pearson once summed up his attitude to drinking this way: 'It is important in an age of cant and humbug to claim every so-called vice and call it a virtue. I don't really regard drinking as a virtue, but then I don't regard abstention from drink as a virtue. I think that people should do exactly what they want to do, without being subject to the moralizing of all the prigs and hypocrites in the universe.' When, for some reason or other, Pearson had to quit London temporarily, Colin Hurry would write, on one occasion, lamenting 'the loss of the more agreeable landmark' and urging Hesketh's speedy return for 'a binge'. When Pearson was still touring, Hurry wrote: 'I need eight hours tramping, talking, boozing and ruminating with you as a purgative tonic and general spiritual aphrodisiac.' As with Kingsmill, Pearson filled the role of Hurry's muse, praising his poetry and prodding him to write. Once when strolling through a cemetery they came across an unengraved marker; Hurry composed this (for once not premature) epitaph on the spot:

> Pity one who lies alone
> Underneath this heavy stone,

Who so often in his life
Lay as heavy on his wife.

Though the Pearson-Hurry friendship was deep, Hurry lacked the breadth of Kingsmill's literary interests and, when faced with a choice, Pearson invariably sought 'Hughie's' company.

Pearson and Kingsmill enjoyed talking, laughing, quaffing, tramping, and letter-writing in roughly that order. Their correspondence is voluminous. Either Pearson did not retain Kingsmill's earliest letters or they have been lost. Pearson's side of the correspondence is complete from 1921; Kingsmill's from 1925. In the beginning Pearson's literary partisanship tended to be irksome. But Kingsmill's equanimity was not easily ruffled. In an early letter Pearson inquired: 'Why do you and I, who have so much in common as human beings, differ so widely in our artistic tastes? Why are we at one (more or less) in our attitude to life and at six's and seven's in our attitude to the reflection of life – literature?' Kingsmill replied: 'As a matter of fact, I think I do understand your frenzy. It's pure religious fanaticism, a very fine quality, but out of place in the realm of literature . . . the last word in wisdom is not to desire disciples but to keep friends, and here Falstaff – Shakespeare is the model and Christ the warning example . . . Your hatred of Christianity is proof that your religious sense is still active, and you pour it into your literary affections. My view of literature is that a man appreciates what he can, and should keep his appreciations supple by not conceiving fanatical hates and loves, and also by not straining it where it doesn't arise naturally. Writers who don't appeal to me I don't bother about, but I don't mind my friends liking them.'

Whatever their literary differences, each man took unbridled delight in the other's company. 'I am by nature a bit of a hermit,' Pearson wrote to Kingsmill, 'but I'd always quit my cell for a frolic (as Johnson would call it) with you.' In the Twenties Pearson frequently pleaded with Kingsmill to abandon Switzerland and return to London; Kingsmill, whose first marriage was then cracking up, regretted that he was tied to Switzerland. 'I wish I could see more of you at present,' he wrote, 'so that we could withdraw together to "that high hill of the muses, always calm and clear".' Kingsmill's last book, published posthumously, was an anthology of his favourite passages of English literature called *The High Hill of the Muses*. On August 5, 1926 Kingsmill wrote to Pearson: 'I always feel about you that beneath a rough and somewhat unprepossessing exterior there beats one of the kindliest of human hearts.' Pearson replied: 'You are quite wrong about my having a heart of gold beneath a somewhat forbidding exterior. I have many redeeming vices, but not a single abandoned virtue. I believe in profligacy, immorality and all the enobling and enduring qualities of unmentionable sin.'

Frank Harris dominated their early letters. Since both had known and worked with Harris, each had an inexhaustible interest in his sheer oddity and a plentiful fund of anecdotes. In 1926 one Florence Smith, spinster of Ramsgate, Kent began writing letters to Pearson expressing her anxiety about Harris and wondering if plans could not be made to smuggle him out of Nice until the furore over *My Life and Loves* died down. Pearson sent one of her letters to Kingsmill who replied on August 30: 'Florence Smith is developing into something rather big. The idea of "smuggling him out of Nice till the agitation has died down" lifts her out of the rank of minor grotesques . . . I should like her mental image of F.H. being smuggled out of Nice – Florence Smith in an enormous crinoline walking with stiff circumspection along the *Promenade des Anglais* – with F.H. under the crinoline trying not to disconcert his accomplice by following the sweet way of love according to routine.'

After Harris's death his widow, Nellie, wrote to Pearson suggesting that they collaborate on an official biography. Kingsmill who, unknown to Nellie, was then completing his own debunking study, sniffed a romantic interest: 'Is Nellie in love with you?' he wrote. 'This has occurred to me as a possibility for it seems strange, unless she is blinded by love, that she should not have spotted a certain weakening in your allegiance to the master.' Pearson replied by recalling an occasion in 1922 or 1923, when he was showing Nellie around London, and she '. . . took me up to her room in the Savoy, showed me her bed, and implied that it was rather large for one person'. When Nellie proposed that Pearson go to stay with her at the Harris villa to sort through materials, Kingsmill warmed to the scene: 'I hope you will remember that history contains some fine instances of chastity being sacrificed to the general weal, and oysters are ridiculously cheap in France.' When Nellie finally tumbled to the fact that Pearson's view of Harris was now well shy of idolatry, the plan was dropped.

In the days when Pearson was touring he concluded each letter with a list of landladies and addresses where he would be lodging; to one such list, Kingsmill responded: 'Your list of landladies stimulates my fancy. Can't you do some pen portraits to slake my curiosity? Miss Lyle (May 6) – a virgin? Mrs Webster Cairns – one of *the* Webster Cairns, I suppose? Mrs Brown – any relation to the other Mrs Brown? Miss Hobson – Hobson's necessity?' 'I cannot gratify your marked curiosity in regard to my landladies,' Pearson replied. 'A note on each must be allowed to close the subject. Miss Lyle is not only a virgin but, if faces count for anything, *virgo intacta*. Mrs Webster Cairns is distantly connected with marmalade, I believe. Mrs Brown is related, on her father's side, to Mrs Jones, and on her mother's side to Mrs Robinson. Mrs Hobson had no choice.'

While touring in *The Acquittal* in 1928 Pearson brought his son Henry, now nearly sixteen, to Halifax. Introduced for the first time to wine-bibbing, Henry delivered himself of the view that Shakespeare was 'a blasted old fool'. He followed this with the assertion: 'All literature is balls.' To Kingsmill, Pearson wrote: 'The next few thrusts in the argument will not bear repetition. Suffice it to say that his Rabelaisian vocabulary proves that he has not lived fifteen years under my roof for nothing. At the moment he is stretched out on the sofa sleeping off the effects of "Falstaff's advice" and snoring like a hog. Quite a sweet domestic idyll, is it not?' Kingsmill replied: 'Your son shapes well. Why don't you do his autobiography with yourself as the villain?' This incident, however lightly treated, foreshadowed what would be a permanent estrangement and the deepest tragedy of Pearson's life.

On May 21, 1928 Pearson was on a train from Edinburgh to London when he read the obituary notices of Sir Edmund Gosse, who had been among the literary critics howling for blood during the *Whispering Gallery* affair. He immediately dispatched this scene to Kingsmill:

[*Scene*: Heaven. Enter St Paul, doyen of Christian critics, leading Sir Edmund Gosse, doyen of English critics, by the hand.]

St Paul: Let me introduce myself. I am Paul of Tarsus.
Sir Edmund: (Nervously) *Saint* Paul?
St P.: (Confidently) The same.
Sir E.: Then I am in . . . ?
St P.: Exactly.
Sir E.: You know me?
St P.: We know everyone.
Sir E.: (Confused) Of course, of course. You must excuse me, it takes some time to . . .
St P.: Naturally. It is difficult, even for a critic of your eminence, to comprehend omniscience.
Sir E.: (Pleased) Tell me: am I, then, appreciated in . . . in . . . (coughing slightly) . . . here?

St P.: We take in 'The Sunday Times'.

Sir E.: Good! (St Paul frowns) I mean . . . well . . . it is not a bad
paper.

St P.: We have formed our own opinions as to that.

Sir E.: Of course, of course! I have no wish to influence . . .

St P.: Don't be a fathead!

Sir E.: I beg your pardon!

St P.: You needn't. In Heaven, when a thing's said, it's said. No one
takes the slightest notice, anyhow.

Sir. E.: (Relieved) Then we *are* in Heaven . . .

St P.: And where the hell d'you think *I'd* be?

Sir E.: (Distressed) Forgive me, I . . .

St P.: Rubbish! Have you read your obituary notices?

Sir E.: (Trying to conquer his eagerness) No; who has written them?
Did Squire – I mean, may I borrow –?

St P.: You will find them all in the waiting room.

Sir E.: Waiting room?

St P.: Yes, first to the right, second to the left, next to the lavatory.

Sir E.: (Fretfully) But I thought you said we were in Heaven? (St
Paul frowns) Sorry. (St Paul makes a hissing sound between his
teeth) But you mentioned the lavatory . . . rather a shock, you
know . . . I mean does one . . . in Heaven?

St P.: If you think you can hold your water for eternity, you'd better
think again.

Sir E.: (Crestfallen) Please don't be peevish. I am only too willing to
learn.

St P.: Ah! That reminds me. I've been detailed by 'SUPPERS' to ask
you a few preliminary questions.

Sir E.: 'SUPPERS'?

St P.: Oh that is what we call Him among ourselves. The Supreme
Being.

Sir E.: (Horrified) Good God!

St P.: Yes, that is what you call him. But we know better.

Sir E.: (Weakly) What sort of questions?

St P.: Well, to be precise, only one question of moment. SS Peter and
Co. will ask you the less important ones – about the Trinity and
what not. But it is my duty to warn you that not a little of your
future comfort up here will depend upon your answer to this major
query of mine.

Sir E.: (Faintly) Go on.

St P.: (Touchily) At my own leisure, thank you. (An awkward pause, during which Sir Edmund commences an apology, remembers it is useless, and subsides into silence.) Now, attend to me, please. (Sir Edmund makes an affirmatory gurgle.) What is, or was, your honest opinion of the works of Hesketh Pearson?

Sir E.: (Holding up his hands) My dear sir!

St P.: I am *not* your dear sir! Be so good as to answer my question immediately.

Sir E.: Are you referring to the scurrilous author of '*The Whispering Gallery*'?

St P.: Don't hedge! You know perfectly well who I mean. Incidentally '*The Whispering Gallery*' is thought very highly of in Heaven. Our librarian, Luke, complains that he is always having to replace stolen copies.

Sir. E.: *Stolen* copies? Look here, are we in heaven or H?

St P.: Take care! We don't allow people to question our credentials.

Sir E.: But I didn't.

St P.: You did!

Sir E.: (Plaintively) Pardon me, but –

St P.: Be quiet! You are wasting my time. Answer the question.

Sir E.: About Hesketh Pearson?

St P.: (Firmly) I am waiting.

Sir E.: Well, to tell you the honest truth . . .

St P.: I should strongly advise you to tell it.

Sir E.: I never seriously considered his claim to be regarded as an author of standing . . . no one on earth takes the smallest interest in him; and, if I may say so, I can hardly believe that God –

St P.: 'SUPPERS' reads him every night before turning in and has copies of all his first editions.

Sir E.: (*Triumphantly*) For that matter, I very much doubt even *He* could obtain any *second* editions.

St P.: A fact that does not redound to *your* credit, Sir. Why did you never write about him in the Sunday Times? What is the use of being a critic if you don't pick out the mastermind of the age?

Sir E.: (on his mettle now) Mastermind! Huh! Come, sir – St, I mean – let me have the names of these masterpieces; they have escaped my memory.

St P.: *Modern Men and Mummers*.

Sir E.: Ghoulish garbage!

St P.: *A Persian Critic*.

Sir E.: Wish-wash!

St P.: *The Whispering Gallery*.

Sir E. Garbish ghoulage.

St P.: *Iron Rations*.

Sir E.: Wash-wish.

St P.: Very well. You shall spend the next ten thousand aeons reading and re-reading his works. As each new work is published, you shall be supplied with a copy so that time need not hang too heavily on your hands. The following ten thousand aeons you shall spend writing and re-writing criticisms of his works. After that, I hope you will be in fit condition to meet your maker. (A bell rings) And now you must excuse me. 'SUPPERS' gets quite snappy when I am not there to mix His morning appetizer.

[EXEUNT severally – St Paul hurriedly, Sir Edmund heavily].

Next to Frank Harris, Shakespeare ('Shakers' to Pearson) is their favourite correspondence subject, particularly when Kingsmill was at work on his perceptive but neglected novel, *The Return of William Shakespeare*. In his dogmatic, opinionated way Pearson insisted upon ranking Shakespeare's plays and characters, giving pride of place always to Falstaff. Like Johnson, Pearson considered Shakespeare's tragedies to be skill, his comedies pure instinct. 'At moments of excessive vitality, when copulation is thriving (Lear), when spring is in the air, when life is rosy and care is not, when in fact all's for the best in the best of all possible worlds, and God (whoever he may be) is in his Heaven (wherever that may be) – Falstaff reigns supreme.' Pearson once met Charles Laughton and urged him to play Falstaff. 'No,' said Laughton, 'I dislike the type. I've seen too many Falstaffs in a hotel where I used to live.' Pearson replied: 'I'd rather live in that hotel than anywhere else in the world. Where is it? If you'll guarantee *one* Falstaff I'll book a permanent room there.' Pearson's ranking of the plays was *Henry IV*, *King Lear*, *Othello*, *Antony and Cleopatra*, *Macbeth*, and *Hamlet*. But Kingsmill urged a more catholic view: 'There is not much point in preferring [Falstaff] to Lear or Lear to him. One is the finest expression in the world of joy in life, the other of despair at the undeniable gulf between desire and satisfaction.'

Despite Pearson's explosive temper, Kingsmill promised to send him proofs of *The Return of William Shakespeare* but well in advance of his own return to England, 'so that the physical violence stage will be over'. Even so, he envisaged standing well back when ringing Pearson's doorbell; Kingsmill's letter concluded:

Mr Birdley, a retired accountant, testified as follows: 'I was returning home from Marlborough Road station on foot, according to my usual practice, at about 7.15 pm when I observed, without giving him special attention, a man walking a few paces ahead of me. He appeared to be of solid build and was dressed like a gentleman (well?). As I passed No. 88 the door was opened to this person, whom I had observed ring the bell. The person opening the door used the following words (consultation in court, words written down) 'You bloody swine! Would you! Lear! You fucking shit! Take that!' The person addressed, grappled with his interlocutor, and a desperate struggle ensued. On returning with a policeman, I was distressed to find the assailant and his victim at the bottom of the steps. Both were in a dying condition, and profusely covered with blood. Their speech was somewhat indistinct, but I distinctly caught the following words from the assailant – 'Hope teach lesson' to which the victim responded, expiring immediately afterwards 'Can only repeat . . .'

It was in 1932 that Malcolm Muggeridge came on the scene. Muggeridge was then living in Manchester writing editorials for C. P. Scott's *Manchester Guardian*. Kingsmill came to visit him for a weekend in the hope of scrounging some book reviewing from the *Guardian*. This did not materialize but a friendship, which Muggeridge later called 'half the joy of living', took root. Thereafter, what had been a duo became a trio, with Kingsmill in the centre, Muggeridge and Pearson on the flanks.

On the Sunday morning of his first visit, Kingsmill had the idea that Pearson would be passing through Manchester on his return from an acting engagement in Newcastle and he proposed meeting him at the station. Kingsmill's expectation seemed, as far as Muggeridge could gather, to be based on faint premises, but they went along to the station all the same. Muggeridge recalled the scene: 'It had about it that air of desolation which only a railway station in the north of England on a Sunday morning can produce. There were no trains and no expectation of any trains, then, or, it seemed, ever. We walked up and down the long platform, still talking, with a vague notion that Pearson would somehow appear, though by what means was not apparent.' Finally Kingsmill reached the conclusion that what he had imagined to be a carefully arranged rendezvous was not as definite as he had supposed. Muggeridge wrote to Pearson: 'We went off, however, feeling quite satisfied. If we had not met you, we had gone to meet you; and anyway, in [Kingsmill's] company I discovered, for the first time, that Stockport station was full of interest.'

Pearson finished his acting career in 1932 in a play called *The Challenge*, written by the author's agent David Higham. He told

Kingsmill it was 'quite the worst play ever written' and that the dialogue in this love scene was responsible for driving him from the stage forever:

> She: I think I ought to tell you, Adrian, that I am a virgin.
> He: I wouldn't have asked you that.
> She: But are you glad to know?
> He: Yes.
> She: And you? I am not the first?
> He: No. Do you mind?
> She: I am glad. You give your skill for my virginity.
> He: You are pleased that I am fledged? etc. etc.

Kingsmill wrote to the literary editor of the *New English Review*, who agreed to commission several short biographical sketches from Pearson. In exchange for this courtesy, Pearson promised to keep Kingsmill posted on developments at the Eucharistic Conference which was then underway in Dublin ('the funniest thing that has happened since the war'). In due course, he reported on one hellfire and brimstone sermon in the midst of which the preacher bellowed: 'And in that place there shall be weeping and gnashing of teeth.' One old lady in the front row slowly raised her hand and asked: 'How can I gnash my teeth when I haven't got any?' 'Make no mistake about it,' the parson shouted: 'Teeth will be provided.'

In 1933, when Pearson was casting about for an appropriate biographical subject, leaning toward Henry Fielding but unable to kindle any interest from publishers, he came upon a *Times* announcement of a new series of monographs 'On the unrecognized activities of genius'. Pearson suggested some prospective titles to Kingsmill:

> *A New Life of Shakespeare*: will deal primarily with his really remarkable talents as an actor.
> *The Virgin and the Virginals*: an intimate study of the musical temperament of Queen Victoria.
> *Gibbon as Guardsman*: unsuspected sidelights on the military genius of the well-known historian.
> *Clive the Climber*: recounts an early episode on the church steeple of Market Drayton, which had a profound influence on his afterlife.
> *Napoleon as Traveller and Ethnologist*: no one has done justice to this revealing side of the emperor's nature.
> *Oscar Wilde: His married Life*: neglected by the biographers.
> *Dickens the Dancer*: on the authority of Jane Carlyle he excelled in the ballroom.

Dr Johnson: Gentleman: the commentators on this author, from Hawkins to Kingsmill, have failed to lay stress on his politeness – a quality the doctor himself drew attention to.

Kingsmill, who was then immersed in writing a life of Johnson, surfaced long enough to lay claim to two additional titles:

Swinburne the Swimmer: a contribution to the theory that the great Victorian balladist would have swum the Channel but for the counterclaim of authorship.
Lord Clive: Numismatist: a monograph no coin collector should miss.

Kingsmill, Hurry and Pearson shared more than a love of laughter and literature. Each man was also involved in a love affair, one that threatened to destroy a precarious marriage. In Hurry's case, the woman was named Priscilla. In one letter, Hurry described her to Pearson as 'alternating between a nymphomaniac and the Virgin Mary'. Although Hurry's marriage survived this affair, in 1939 he told Pearson that he wished he had been 'a shit' and ended the marriage years before.

Kingsmill's first marriage (to Eileen Turpin) had been a mistake from the beginning, although he had fought stubbornly against admitting this. In 1927 he met a young women in Switzerland, Gladys Runicar. For some months Kingsmill endured the anguish of trying to prolong a dead marriage while trying also to snatch what few happy days with Gladys that he could. On one occasion they were seen together in a Lausanne hotel and this was duly noted in the social column of the *Continental Daily Mail*. Pearson wrote to him: 'I must really enter a caveat, as I believe it is called, against these reckless movements of yours. Why not, while you are about it, write a Sonnet with her name at the top and get it published in the centre page of the *Times*? . . . It seems to me, dear fellow, that as things are at present you are running a grave risk of keeping your secret from quite 10% of the world's population.' Kingsmill remained unrepentant about what he called 'the most agonizing but wonderful days of my life'. He had finally admitted to himself, if not yet to his wife, that the marriage was over in all but name. 'Those four days were so incomparably the best in my life,' he wrote back to Pearson, 'that everyone who cavils or criticizes can go to hell, always excluding you, to whom, in the matter of hell, I would say – "Tarry, sweet soul, and we shall fly abreast". You and I winging it side by side to hell is a fine subject for the now extinct school of historical painters.'

The strain Kingsmill was under, and the whimsical humour with which he bore it, are illustrated by a letter of April 23, 1927: 'I wonder if I shall go completely to pieces. One's private affairs should not be obtruded on others, but as you were within friendly hail of me from the beginning . . . perhaps you won't mind a restrained extract from my *Calvary at the Cross*, or *Through Golgotha on a Push-Bike* or *Gehenna and After* or *Hell and How to Heat It*, or *Straw and Why I Wear It* . . . ' Kingsmill lamented that he was about to lose his wife and child and, as a divorced man, be summarily dismissed from his father's business; meanwhile he was holed up alone in a hotel trying desperately to finish a biography of Matthew Arnold that almost no one would read. Pearson's reply took the form of a postcard, bearing a picture of Anne Hathaway's cottage at Stratford-upon-Avon, inscribed: 'I feel you should meditate on the sanctity of the marriage tie. Hence this picture. Be ye therefore faithful even as Shakespeare was faithful.'

Eventually Kingsmill's wife learned of his tryst in Lausanne, discovered Gladys's identity, and the final explosion occurred. By this time Kingsmill had become resigned to the inevitable. 'No one can reasonably object to being blown to bits if he sits on a cask of powder, but to have the fragments carefully re-assembled, and then be blown to bits again, is trying work.' No sooner had Kingsmill's marriage ended than Gladys's family forbade her ever to see him again. Even so, he told Pearson: 'Life has no value except the inestimable value of a few immortal hours, and one must endure the rest for their sake.' For a long time Kingsmill could talk of little else. Years later he took Pearson to see a house in which Gladys had once stayed with her guardian; when Pearson referred to it as 'a dinky little domicile', Kingsmill chuckled: 'Just what Mercutio might have said if Romeo had pointed out the mansion of the Capulets.' Though he later remarried (Dorothy Vernon), it was this brief interlude in Switzerland with Gladys which came to embody Kingsmill's ideal of romantic love. He once compared love to a fire which flickers harmlessly within the grate of marriage, but flares up, wonderful, terrifying and all-consuming, outside it.

Throughout the Thirties what Pearson called 'the most vital part of my life' was a dark, vivacious Jewish actress named Dorothy Dunkels. She was nearly twenty years younger than he and, because of that, he at first avoided sexual intimacy. But after six weeks of 'a gradually weakening resistance' they became lovers and remained intermittently so for nine years. 'Fascinating, infuriating, seductive, aloof, shameless, sensitive, cruel, tender: she could play all the emotional notes in quick succession, and leave me quivering with lust or quiescent with love or tingling with admiration or coldly critical.'

Gladys could no more help making scenes over Hesketh's infidelities then he could help repeating them. She eventually found out about Dorothy which led to 'agonizing emotional scenes' when Hesketh swore that he would break it off. There followed the cowardly letters trying to rupture from a distance what one wishes only to nurture when together; the feeling of utter emptiness when all the lights seem to have gone out and only one person can illuminate the darkness; the desolating loneliness in which he would see her or telephone her or write to her once again, and the cycle would start over. Although capable of decisiveness (as his military record attests) he was irresolute when at the mercy of sensuality. Like many men, when lust was in the ascendancy, common sense flew out of the window. His usual ebullience at times gave way to melancholy. He wrote to Kingsmill: 'I wish to God you were in England . . . I am between two fires and need a screen to keep the sparks off.' Kingsmill, who knew the predicament only too well, responded with concern: 'I wish you would explain the whole situation to Gladys. You can't go on bearing the double strain of acute money worries and two women in a state of misery about you.' Pearson did not take this advice and continued to be riven by ecstasy and despair.

Though normally the least suicidal of men, Pearson once gave way to such thoughts. He was rehearsing a play, alone in Cambridge, missing Dorothy and increasingly desperate. 'Life seemed hopeless, everything in it futile, the mere sight of my fellow-beings sickened me, a load of misery weighed upon me, and even the autumn beauty of "the Backs" was obliterated by the cloud of my depression.' Unannounced, and totally unexpected, Dorothy arrived. Even writing from a distance of forty years, Pearson regarded that moment as 'a miracle'. 'For the first time I fully understood how people could apparently be changed by a moment's revelation. We walked in "the Backs" late that afternoon and they never looked so beautiful. My spirit was free, careless, happy, confident. I remembered a passage in the Book of Job: "When the morning stars sang together, and all the sons of God shouted for joy." On my return to the theatre that night the evening stars were singing, the world was transformed and my soul shouted for joy.'

When Hesketh was in London, he and Dorothy met several times a week. They took few precautions to keep their affair secret. It was known to all Hesketh's friends. Malcolm Muggeridge recalled that Dorothy frequently turned up at the Horseshoe in Tottenham Court Road where he, Pearson and Kingsmill met for talk and drinks. 'Dorothy would breeze in and ruffle Hesketh's hair or straighten his tie,

as much as to say: "You two may be his friends, but I *own* him."'
Muggeridge knew that Gladys knew of the affair but did not think she
was unduly troubled about it. Basil Harvey met Dorothy several times,
considered her 'extremely attractive' and 'the only true love of Hesketh's
life'. When Hesketh was on tour, Dorothy quite often accompanied
him. For years they kept a room in London and they managed several
holidays away together. But there were also nasty rows, occasioned once
by Pearson's suspicion that Dorothy was seeing another man. He told
Kingsmill how, on approaching the flat, he thought he heard someone
within. Kingsmill replied: 'Mr Smith was not one of those feeble-
minded persons who suspects the fidelity of their mistresses. Returning
home unexpectedly one day, he heard a sound from his bedroom which,
at first blush, was remarkably like the creaking of a bed tenanted by two
persons of opposite sexes who are anxious to demonstrate their mutual
sympathy in a fashion which will preclude any alternative explanation
being placed on their activities. Entering the room, Mr Smith perceived
the rosy face of his beloved, partially hidden by the right shoulder of his
intimate friend, Major Browne, who appeared to be in convulsions of
laughter. Resolving to hear the joke at the earliest convenient moment,
Mr Smith returned to his study, where he was joined by the other two in
twenty minutes or so. As they seemed in rather quiet humour, he did
not trouble them to pass on the joke, feeling that it might lose some of its
flavour in an altered setting.'

The inevitable showdown with Gladys came in 1939. For years
Dorothy had demanded that Hesketh leave Gladys and marry her.
Whether from loyalty or cowardice, he had been unable to tell his wife
that their life together was at an end. Finally Dorothy tired of Hesketh's
vacillation and became engaged to another man. In desperation
Hesketh told Gladys he wanted a divorce. Although heartbroken, she
agreed. That evening Hesketh went to tell Dorothy that he was finally
free; tearfully she revealed that she had lost confidence in his promises,
the wedding date had been fixed, and that it was now too late. After
several hours of recrimination alternating with tenderness, Hesketh left
and spent the night pounding through silent streets. 'When I reached
home early in the morning Gladys gave me more sympathy than I
deserved. My behaviour to her was unforgivable but she forgave it, and
the rest of our life together was relatively harmonious. My request for a
divorce at that particular time was the only action in my life of which I
am wholeheartedly ashamed. I have said and done many deplorable
things in my life, but I have forgiven myself for everything except
this.'

Meanwhile Hesketh's only son, Henry, had proved to be a good student. From St Paul's he had won scholarships to both Oxford and Cambridge, choosing Clare College, Cambridge, to study classics. Cambridge in the Thirties was a hotbed of communism and Henry soon caught the virus, switching from classics to economics. Once, when Hesketh and Basil Harvey were chatting about poetry, Henry interrupted: 'The trouble with you two is that you haven't had a Marxist education.' Such sentiments were not calculated to cement the bond between father and son. Harvey noticed that Gladys doted on Henry, but that Hesketh seemed 'almost indifferent'.

In June 1934 the Pearsons spent a holiday in Somerset. Henry shared his father's love of walking and most days father and son wandered in lovely weather through the glorious countryside. In such pleasant circumstances Hesketh tried to chide Henry out of his belief that life was intolerable in a capitalist society. To no avail. Hesketh controlled his temper as well as he could but, when Henry said that Shakespeare would have been a better writer had he read *Das Kapital*, the provocation proved too great. Hesketh exploded, avenging this sin against the Holy Ghost in 'violent and personal' language. In that moment what still existed of the 'old confidential relationship' between father and son ruptured; Henry never again confided his thoughts to his father, and Hesketh never again felt close to his son.

On their return to London, Hesketh learned from his sister, Elsie, that their mother was dying. He went to Bedford and found her bed-ridden and barely conscious. She appeared to know he was there but was unable to speak. Just before he left, 'in a strange, deep and ghostly voice' she managed to say: 'Goodbye, darling.' A few days later Amy Pearson died at the age of seventy-nine. The bed she had occupied during her last illness was never moved from the foot of the four-poster she had shared for fifty years with her husband.

Hesketh now spent more weekends in Bedford relieving Elsie of the burden of looking after their increasingly senile and cantankerous father. His pleasures had shrunk to the cricket results and a card game called coon-can which had to be played daily. Never much of a talker, he became silent and morose. He never took the slightest interest in Hesketh's books. Although he had loved the music of Gilbert and Sullivan, he did not acknowledge Hesketh's biography. Once Hesketh forgot himself and quoted a remark the local vicar had dropped about 'the extraordinary conduct of Judas Iscariot'. Instead of chuckling Henry Pearson looked puzzled and then said: 'But it *was* extraordinary.' When Pearson passed this on to Kingsmill, Hughie replied that Henry Pearson's response was every bit as good as the original remark. 'How much more at home Judas would have been in Worcestershire round about 1760 than in Judaea round about 30. Comfortable armchairs, and Archdeacon Pearson and Judas over the port. No ungentlemanly insistence or Boswellianism but just, with a pleasant smile – "A very singular episode, that of the crucifixion, I make no doubt from what you have let fall, with attendant circumstances full, I hazard, of instruction for the curious in such matters."'

In his final year at Cambridge, Hesketh's son had suddenly gone off to Paris. From there he sent his mother a telegram saying that he had decided to join the Republican side in the Spanish Civil War. Hesketh later received one or two reports indicating that, despite his poor eyesight, Henry had fought bravely. Then, nothing. In January 1939 word filtered back that Henry Pearson had been killed in the final days of fighting on the Ebro.

For Gladys it was an irreparable loss made worse because it coincided with Hesketh's request for a divorce. To outward appearances, Hesketh hardly reacted at all. His memoirs gloss over his son's death in a single, unsentimental paragraph. Inside, however, he was devastated. 'I have been terribly unhappy lately,' he wrote to Muggeridge, 'I would welcome Hitler and his bombs; they would at least relieve the void and sickness of my heart.' To Kingsmill he wrote that he was as close to suicide as he was ever likely to be. When Basil Harvey visited 88 Abbey Road not long after Henry's death he noticed a picture of a soldier; he asked: 'What's that?' 'That's our little boy,' Hesketh replied. Pearson now took to wandering the streets alone, often for most of the night, saying to himself over and over again Johnson's lines from *The Vanity of Human Wishes*:

> Yet hope not life from grief or danger free,
> Not think the doom of man reversed for thee.

He continued to grieve, as is evident from this diary entry written on April 8, 1940, after Pearson had walked through Alma Square where Henry and Gladys had stayed when Hesketh was in Mesopotamia. 'I again felt the loss of Henry keenly and I tried to visualize his unknown grave on the banks of the Ebro where he died fighting; a shocking waste of a fine intelligence in a damnable cause. He was such a splendid companion before he went Red and I saw "red". Religion, whether it be of church or state, is the curse of mankind. He and I got on famously before he went mad and became a communist, which made him impossible; which made me impossible. I haven't the temperament to endure this sort of thing and we quarrelled . . . we became utterly incompatible and estranged. The pity of it overwhelmed me once more.

I wish I could have died in his place. But there it is. I suppose I should be just as unsympathetic, be just as pig-headed, if it were to happen all over again.'

CHAPTER TWELVE

Success

'A man's life of any worth is a continual allegory – and very few eyes can see the mystery of his life . . . a life like the scriptures, figurative.'

John Keats

From the first moment Pearson began to write biographies, he cast away the jejune theories he had expounded in *Ventilations*. He paid little heed to formula, less to style. He strove instead to understand his subject, to grasp his inward essence, and then, through anecdote and narrative, to communicate that understanding to the reader. Format and technique vary from book to book because they are secondary to the purpose, which is to bring a man's character to life.

In choosing a subject Pearson looked for 'wit, humour, good nature and invincible gaiety of spirit'. When he discovered these qualities, it mattered little what the subject did or was. With equal facility, he wrote of actors, authors, eccentrics, statesmen, playwrights and generals. He admired individuality. 'More than any other art,' he wrote, 'biography enshrines and encourages the spirit of individualism.'

Money was never his principal motive. He turned down lucrative proposals. In fact, Malcolm Muggeridge owed his most successful book to Pearson's refusal to write for money. In 1938 Hamish Hamilton proposed three subjects to Pearson: Mark Twain, Dornford Yates, or a short history of *Punch*. Pearson refused all three and wrote on John Nicholson instead, which Hamilton declined to publish. Anxious to maintain relations, Hamilton then suggested that Pearson write a social history of the decade. A similar book about the Twenties had been successful. Pearson considered the suggestion profitable but out of his line and he suggested Muggeridge instead. The publisher agreed and Muggeridge's *The Thirties* became his first commercially successful book, a Book of the Month Club choice, which has been more or less continually in print since 1940. Conversely, publishers often turned down subjects proposed by Pearson (including Thackeray and Sheridan) because of doubts about sales. Pearson once asked a publisher if he considered there might be a lingering public interest in the life of Jesus Christ.

Pearson did not begin to write full-time until he was middle-aged. Once begun, he discovered that writing allowed him to live with a minimum of fuss, intrusion, and subservience. It also left time for talking, walking and quaffing. Although a disciplined writer, he would always abandon his work for a talk or stroll with Muggeridge, Hurry, or Kingsmill. 'If I had enough money,' he told Kingsmill, 'I would never again put pen to paper.' Every writer says this and it is always untrue. The itch to write is inborn and must be scratched. But it is not, equally, untrue. For Pearson money was less important than the opportunity that writing biography gave him to satisfy an insatiable curiosity about his fellow human beings and to indulge a love of anecdotage.

Once he had hit upon a subject, Pearson began by skimming through previous biographies, not making notes, but trying to get an overall impression. Next he would read the subject's literary output – books, letters, articles, diaries – typing out on onionskin paper under rough headings such passages as might later prove useful. He would then comb quickly through reminiscences and memoirs of contemporaries in search of incident, anecdote, and gossip. If anyone was still alive who could shed light, he or she would be interviewed. From this Pearson would derive 'a generalized and somewhat blurred' picture. At this stage his purpose was to establish the right *relation* to his subject. No amount of reading, collating, assembling or interviewing will give a biography its shape until the author knows his relation to his subject. Like artist and sitter, the angle of vision is crucial to the finished portrait.

The second stage was one of 'concentration and clarification'. This involved an intense scrutiny of the subject and his time. The man's writings would be condensed and analysed, preliminary hypotheses would be verified against social histories of the period; preliminary opinions would be tested; secondhand material would be cross-verified; the difficult task of pruning the true from the apocryphal would begin. At this stage he made a point of visiting any locale which had been significant in his subject's life. These literary pilgrimages combined the two forms of recreation, walking and searching for literary landmarks, which Pearson most enjoyed. This diary extract, written on March 24, 1940 while at work on his life of Shakespeare, is typical:

We went on a pilgrimage to the City, a regular habit of ours at about this time of year, though it is usually towards the end of April – Shakespeare's Day. As a rule too we visit Southwark, the George, the Cathedral, the site of the Globe, the river bank, etc. But today we kept to Shakespeare's haunts this side of the river. We bused to

Kingsway, walked through Lincoln's Inn Fields, New Square (where we had a look at No. 2 where poor old Butler used to call and ask after Pauli), down Chancery Lane, Fleet Street, taking Gough Square and Johnson's house enroute, and so passed St Bride's Church to Blackfriars and the Wardrobe. Chambers says that the property Shakespeare bought in 1612, known as Blackfriars Gate House, was situated in what is now Ireland Yard 'to the north of and over the entrance to which from St Andrew's Hill the Gate House probably stood'. We duly placed this and then went on via Carter Lane, Cheapside and Cornhill, to Bishopsgate where we viewed St Helen's, in which I had often sat as a youth during lunch hours when I was in the city. Shakespeare lived in the ward of St Helen's probably when he was creating Falstaff. Eastcheap and the Boar's Head Tavern were not far off. After that we repaired to the Great Eastern Station for light refreshment, then walked down Middlesex Street (Petticoat Lane) which was being cleaned up after the market, and finally tried to find the spot in Cripplegate, where Shakespeare had stayed with the Mountjoy family. We went hither and thither; the police, being wartime 'temporaries', had never heard of St Olave's or Silver Street. With the assistance of a resident out for an afternoon stroll in his Sunday best, we at last found Monkwell Street, at the juncture of which with Silver Street we discovered the site – marked, rather to our annoyance, with a plaque – a bit of St Olave's church-yard just opposite, the Church itself having been burned in the great fire. A cup of tea in Ludgate Hill, a walk back to the top of Kingsway, via Fleet Street and Carey Street, the Old Curiosity Shop, thence home by bus.

The next stage was a 'gestation' period. Pearson described this as 'a time to walk a great deal and smoke an immoderate number of pipes in my armchair, while the imagination is busy selecting, rejecting, criticizing, cutting'. Since his biographical subjects inevitably became his friends, they were naturally included in the talk at the Silence Room of the Authors' Club or the Horseshoe in Tottenham Court Road. When Pearson was at work on a book Kingsmill and Muggeridge had to steel themselves to unending speculation about what X would have said or done in a thousand real and imagined circumstances. Gladys Pearson once burst out: 'All you and Hughie talk about are Dr Johnson's toenails.' Incidentally, Gladys appears not to have been over fond of Kingsmill nor, as we have seen, Dorothy Kingsmill of Pearson; perhaps wives cannot be expected to like male friends who absorb their husband's attention and in whom intimate confidences are reposed.

The final stage, writing, appears to have been quite effortless. As he used up the onionskin paper notes, he would draw a line through them, but the notes were preserved. Pearson generally wrote by hand in pencil in bound notebooks, down the right hand side and leaving the left side free for interlineations and corrections. The scarcity of these suggests that all that stood between a first and a final draft was an envelope. His prose was assertive, sometimes bellicose.

Pearson never confused life-writing and literary criticism. Literary criticism (what he called 'the assessment of the once-living by the ever-dead') is absent. He was interested in a man, not a critique of a man's work. Since he chose only subjects sympathetic to his own nature, this is hardly surprising. The creative element in all his biographies is the vivid expression of his own personality through that of his subject. Sympathy for one's subject does not preclude objective biography. If it did the three finest biographies – Plato's account of Socrates, the Gospel writers' Christ, and Boswell's Johnson – would not exist. Indeed truth that is concealed to antipathy may be revealed to sympathy. Pearson considered the 'ultimate perfection in biography' to be Johnson's *Lives of the Poets*; specifically his lives of Richard Savage and of Edmund Smith. Yet Johnson was an intimate friend of the first and sympathetic to the second. Pearson made no bones of the fact that he *liked* his subjects. It is to his credit that he tried to write objectively about them.

The one area in which Pearson's biographies noticeably lapse is when he dealt with his subject's sexual misconduct (e.g. Oscar Wilde's pederasty). His inclination was to gloss over or to minimize anything that was distasteful to him. Muggeridge recalled that when a disclosure of an unpleasant sort was forced upon Pearson his usual reaction was to puff hard on his pipe and stare fixedly out a window, 'wearing an expression reminiscent of a country rector considering whether there may not be a preponderance of vegetable marrows at the Harvest Thanksgiving display'. Although Pearson praised 'reminiscential candour' in biography, his own work falls short. He once acknowledged this, admitting an aversion to considering 'the intimate details of a man's sexual life' even though, by omitting this, one runs the risk of omitting 'quite half the man, and sometimes a very important half'. Such reticence was foreign to Pearson's robust nature and did not spring from prudery or censoriousness, still less from any sense of moral indignation. Quite the opposite. Rather, he was reluctant to delve too deeply into areas where he felt himself vulnerable. For all his bluster and bravado, Pearson was a product of a Victorian upbringing, and a grandson of the Manse, a man who did the honourable thing by marrying the women he got in trouble, and he greatly feared 'discussing something about a subject that I should hate to be discussed about myself'. His reluctance to disturb skeletons in a subject's cupboard originated in fear of rattling bones in his own. This is a charitable, indeed a biblical (as in the mote and the beam parable), attitude, but it is damaging to the biographer's art.

Pearson was also hypocritical about preserving the biographical record. At least three of his subjects (Tree, Johnson and Wilde) had in common the fact that intimate letters and papers, which could have proved invaluable to a future biographer, were destroyed. Pearson roared against this. 'To me there is no crime so wicked as the wanton destruction of a person's private papers and manuscripts, or their partial obliteration . . . Herod the baby-killer seems to me a harmless gentleman compared to the vandal who, for respectability's sake, sends a legend and a lie down the ages.' Yet Pearson was guilty of exactly this. In several letters to Kingsmill (fortunately not acted upon) he urged Kingsmill to destroy his letters. 'Kindly destroy *all* my letters,' Pearson wrote on one occasion. 'Otherwise I will start an Edgar Wallace train of conspiracy and you will end up with a green arrow, or something equally harmonious, through your gizzard.' From 1940 to 1945 Pearson kept a diary. It is heavily censored, both in initial content (e.g. the January 18, 1940 entry begins: 'Colin arrived in the morning and we discussed a matter that is too private even for a private diary') and after the fact. Several passages, which could have shed light on an affair Pearson had with the wife of a friend, have been meticulously obliterated. The manner of obliteration is precisely Pearson's practice in his letters and notebooks (except that the diary has been gone through more thoroughly to ensure total illegibility) which confirms that the destruction was done by Pearson himself. At the end of his life, Pearson sent a manuscript copy of his memoirs to his friend, Michael Holroyd; Holroyd was surprised to discover no mention of Pearson's affairs. Also, he had portrayed his marriage to Gladys in conventional Church of England terms. With difficulty Holroyd persuaded Pearson that times had changed and that he must at least acknowledge those affairs which had been significant to him. Some are briefly mentioned in *Hesketh Pearson by Himself*; apparently others were too private and were omitted.

Modern 'warts and all' biography began with Boswell. Before that most biographies were an unpalatable stew of tedious panegyric and orthodox obituary. Pearson would have been honoured to claim Boswell as his spiritual progenitor, although he considered Johnson a superior biographer even to Boswell. About Johnson's *Life of Savage* Pearson wrote: 'In less than forty thousand words he gives us the life and character of his strange subject with an honesty and charity not previously brought to the art of biography and not often to be found in the work of his successors.' When Boswell wrote Johnson's life he was writing the biography of a biographer. To that difficult task Boswell brought a lawyer's accuracy, a grasp of essentials, a love of first-hand anecdote, simplicity of narrative, frankness, and above all a sense of purpose. He also revelled in the sheer fun of the enterprise. Boswell would journey across London to verify a date, trek halfway across England or Scotland to hear a fresh story. Like Boswell (and also John Aubrey) Pearson was an anecdotal biographer, unafraid to delineate minor or obscure characters if they shed light on his subject. This is evident in his very first biography (*Doctor Darwin*). Also like Boswell, he used dialogue extensively and effectively. He understood that the biographer's art is to be judged as much by what he leaves out as by what he puts in. In 1921, before he had written a biography, Pearson had learned that '. . . selective condensation, dramatic use of significant detail – these are the essentials. He must know when the trivial is vital and when the imposing is redundant.'

If the challenge of biography is to recreate a subject's character by a process of judicious selection and arrangement, to bring a scene to life as vividly in the reader's imagination as anything he has actually experienced, then Pearson should be considered a worthy descendant of Boswell. Unlike Boswell, who was a lawyer, Pearson was an actor and he had absorbed the instincts of the dramatist. He knew he had a story to tell and he knew how to tell a story. The story was less about significant events or achievements, more about human character. 'Singularity of character is the flesh and bones of enduring biography.' If the story was to grip it must have its climax in the right place. The portrait must be illuminated by light and shadow. The wellsprings of action must be examined. The soul of the subject must be exposed to view. Pearson once defined the 'born biographer' in this way: '[He] is interested in human character beyond anything else in the world. He is absorbed, to the exclusion of everything except the objectionable necessity of earning a living, in the oddities, the humours, the emotions, the antagonisms, the curiosities of human nature. He is stone cold to types, to people who conform to the standards of their class; he instantly warms to eccentrics, to folk who are fundamentally different from their fellows.'

In his excellent lecture series published as *The Nature of Biography* (Heinemann, 1978) Robert Gittings has pointed out that every true biography is a commentary on the human spirit. As such a biographer's first requirement is enthusiasm. The second is a relative contentment with life. Pearson had both, although his enthusiasms sometimes got the better of him. Since this happens just as often in his late (e.g. *Charles II* and *Henry of Navarre*) as in his early (e.g. *Darwin* and *Smith*) biographies, it must be considered an inherent, lifelong weakness. It was a failing Pearson was quick to criticize in others (e.g. he wrote of Carlyle that 'he first touched the right key, but he refused to see the weaknesses and faults in his heroes, and ruined his portrait by over-emphasis') but which he seemed unable to correct in himself. In 1955 Pearson delivered the Tredegar Memorial Lecture on Biography to the Royal Society of Literature; in it he described himself as 'a hero-worshipper who likes to take his heroes off their pedestal and to know them as fellow men'. When enthusiasm got the upper hand, Pearson reverted to what Kingsmill called his 'sunstroke style'; his prose became bombastic and dogmatic. At his best Pearson wrote in a brisk, mildly ironic style exemplifying (quoting Kingsmill again) 'a jollity of mind pickled in a scorn of fortune'.

Most academic reviewers sneered at Pearson's biographies, dismissing them as 'popular' and 'readable', signifying thereby that their own writing was neither. For his part Pearson was contemptuous of critics ' . . . who always confuse an appearance of laboriousness with profundity of thought or feeling, until their judgments are upset by time'. He usually ignored the dons, but he did once go after Charles Williams who had savaged his *Shakespeare* in *Time and Tide* (September 19, 1942). Pearson wrote to the editor: 'The critic who reviewed my Life of Shakespeare has the lifeless attitude of literature of the typical don and the usual classroom habit of making one joke go a very long way.' When several academics wrote to protest against this slight on their classroom humour, Pearson wrote again: 'I can only apologize for suggesting that a man of Williams's "very great genius" should have been guilty of making a joke.'

For the most part, through twenty-four full-length biographies and another half-dozen collections of shorter portraits, Pearson's work exemplifies Gittings' definition of biography – 'the welding of scientific observation with imaginative art'. His biographies are accurate but not pedantic, lively but seldom flippant, informative yet not scholarly. Free of pomposity and the curse of the footnote, Pearson gave the reader a clear (though sometimes romanticized) view of a man, not necessarily the last word but all the words that most readers wanted to know. His portraits are drawn in primary, sometimes lurid, colours but he never loses control. Michael Holroyd has noted: 'It is only when you look closely that you can see how solid is the underlying draughtmanship.'

By drawing on firsthand records of contemporaries, by including only that which illuminates character, and by letting the subject speak for himself whenever possible, Pearson combined the journalistic vividness of Boswell and the autobiographical intimacy of Pepys. Never preachy, never didactic, except in the sense that life itself is didactic, his books are a quite unique blend of instruction and entertainment. Perhaps the most remarkable feature of all is that they manage to tell just what one wanted to know about the subject. Neither pot-boilers nor brief lives, they make the difficult task of being informative, accurate, lively, sympathetic, and succinct, appear easy.

While the audience for Pearson's biographies steadily expanded through the Thirties, Kingsmill's fortunes plunged ever lower. 'I wish I could do something for you,' Pearson wrote, 'do you think prayer would help? Or fasting? If I knew for certain that God took a personal interest in supplications, I would spend a considerable portion of the time between meals on my knees.' Kingsmill's books continued to be ignored and, unlike Pearson, he had no regular employment income to fall back on. In an attempt to help, Pearson met J. V. Kitto, chief librarian of the House of Commons, in an attempt to persuade him to give Kingsmill a part-time job as an assistant librarian. Kitto promised to consult with the Speaker. On January 21, 1938 Pearson wrote to Kingsmill: 'It would impress the Speaker, who nominates everything in the House from the cat to the canary, if you could enclose a letter of recommendation from some bigwig. Do you know a leading soldier or an eminent saint? I mention this because (1) they would impress the Speaker, and (2) they know nothing about anything. Go careful with the politician because he may be a radical and the Speaker, who is descended from a mistress of Charles II (name of Fitzroy), is sure to be a conservative.' Kingsmill applied and an interview was scheduled. Obviously worried about his friend's haphazard appearance and dress, Pearson dispatched the following letter to Kingsmill one day before the interview:

Dear Hughie:

A few hints for your forthcoming appearance at the House of Commons:

Haircut.
Shave.
Hat.
Respectable lounge suit.
Socks to match ditto.
Shirt to match ditto.
Tie to match ditto.

Collar fastened to stud.
Shining shoes with laces to match.
Soft speaking voice.
False teeth in position.
No satchel or book encumbrances.
Remember you once held His Majesty's commission.
Clean vocabulary.

Yrs,
H.P.

In the end more exalted strings were pulled and the job went to someone else. Kingsmill eventually found temporary employment as a schoolmaster but his financial circumstances remained ruinous.

Pearson's money worries came to an end with his biography of George Bernard Shaw. This is ironic because he had written (in *Ventilations*) that Shaw would be 'a bad subject' for biography. Also he had contended that 'no biography worth the name can be written of a living person'. Pearson had first met Shaw when he appeared in *Androcles and the Lion* in 1913. He had exchanged letters since, collected materials, and once or twice raised the idea of a biography. Shaw forbade it. In August 1938 Kingsmill raised the possibility in a letter to Shaw, almost as an aside. Shaw sent Pearson a one-word postcard: 'Don't!' But he also invited Pearson to call. On October 21, Pearson took up the invitation. At first Shaw was adamant. 'I am delighted to see you again, but you are wasting your time,' he began. 'There is nothing to be told about my life that isn't to be found in the Henderson and Harris books. Give it up, and let us talk of something else.' Pearson was not easily deterred. After an hour or two of sustained fusillade, Shaw capitulated. 'All right. Go ahead. You have my blessing.' He later confirmed this by letter. Pearson left floating on air. He informed his agent who approached Collins as a prospective publisher. Collins offered an advance of £1,500. None of Pearson's advances had ever exceeded £100; he considered £1,500 'a sum of which I could form no very accurate numerical notion'. In fact the advance was to prove barely commensurate with the aggravation which lay ahead.

Shaw proved co-operative – much too co-operative. At first Pearson called on him once a week, either at his London flat in Whitehall Court or at his country retreat at Ayot St Lawrence in Hertfordshire. Then Shaw began sending letters and cards. Pearson was allowed access to Shaw's correspondence and he badgered Shaw into confessing more about his private life than ever Shaw had intended. 'Lost to all sense of decency and good taste, I forced him to come clean, or if you prefer it, dirty; but in the process I had to endure the usual succession of Shavian shocks delivered to all who could not see eye-to-eye with him. He called me a simpleton, an idiot, a fathead, a lost soul, and other terms of endearment, but as they merely expressed his feeling of comradeship I didn't mind.' Eventually Pearson left London and went to Colin Hurry's farm near Chipperfield to write in peace. By now Shaw had demanded prior approval of the manuscript. Though it went against his principles, Pearson had no choice but to agree.

The autumn of 1939 was spent in a rented cottage on the Teme near Ludlow. In a tiny orchard hut, Hesketh wrote through the mornings and spent the afternoons walking in the countryside, denuded by the war of motor vehicles, deriving such pleasure from the tranquillity that 'for the first time we perceived a virtue in war'. By the end of the year the manuscript was half finished and Pearson returned to London. With the money from the Shaw advance, they moved from 88 Abbey Road to a ground floor flat at 144 Goldhurst Terrace. Another six months completed the book.

Pearson took the manuscript to Shaw and asked him how long he might take with it. Shaw replied that this depended on how much there was to correct; it might take five years. Pearson thought he must have meant five weeks and said so. 'Good heavens, no!' said Shaw. 'It takes me more than that to write a play. Shall we say six months?' Pearson left disheartened. As it turned out, six months was optimistic.

While he waited for Shaw, Pearson wrote articles and book reviews, even an occasional letter to the editor. Though he usually avoided these as 'violent irruptions of diseased minds', he was moved to dispatch the following letter on the issue of nudity in the public theatre:

Sir:
   Is nudity disgusting? If so the Creator, who omits to clothe human beings when creating them, is disgusting.
   Those who regard such a notion as blasphemous are revolted, not by the exposure of decent bodies on the stage, but by the exposure of indecent minds in print.

He mulled over future biographical subjects and tramped away his impatience in Regent's Park. Since the beginning of the war four 3.7 anti-aircraft guns had taken up occupancy of Primrose Hill; this necessitated a change of route but it did not deter Pearson from covering five to ten miles each afternoon. His diary entry for January 22, 1940 records: 'Today, as so often, my head was full of the biography I am preparing to write and the biographies I hope to write. My head is nearly always in the clouds, which explains why my feet seldom deviate from their accustomed route. Often enough I finish the walk without being conscious of having noticed anyone or anything in particular on the way, though I usually know what the weather has been like and have a vague sense of having passed people and seen the usual things.'

In 1940 the Pearsons' flat was damaged by a German incendiary bomb. For several months they rented a farm house at Washington near Amberley. It was here that Pearson began his biography of Shakespeare ('the most stimulating and exalting influence of my life') to fill up the time until Shaw returned the manuscript. Dribs and drabs, with extensive alterations and suggestions, eventually began to arrive by post. Early changes were in pencil and could be easily erased; but, as Shaw warmed to the task, he used ink, saving red ink for his 'unpublishable comments'. Pearson was apparently expected to pass these revisions off as his own work. Shaw also disowned or objected to most of the anecdotes Pearson had been at pains to compile and verify. Shaw preferred the strict Greek meaning of the word anecdote – not published.

Meanwhile Kingsmill had temporarily moved into the Pearsons' vacated London flat, drowning out the blitz by playing Beethoven's Emperor Concerto on the gramophone. When Pearson returned he discovered that the grooves in the slow movement had been worn away. 'When he arrived at our flat,' Pearson recalled, 'he had no ration book, and used to wash his underwear in the bathroom. When Beatrice [Pearson's sister-in-law] took his old ration book to the shop to see if anything could be bought with it, the woman said, "You can put that in the British Museum".' Kingsmill simply ignored the manifestations of collective insanity all around him; one letter to Pearson concludes thus: 'The walks home by search light or simply by starlight are a pleasing end. The siren has just started, a wearisome noise which might remind a primeval medicine man of an ichthyosaurus in childbirth, but has no old associations for me.'

A combination of Shaw's delay and a persistent fever reduced Pearson to a state of nervous exhaustion. He felt sufficiently mortal to have a will drawn up, naming Gladys and Kingsmill joint beneficiaries. Kingsmill wrote: 'It was very nice indeed of you to include me in your will . . . what in my present mood would appeal to me most would be to look down in your company from some poetic, non-biblical paradise, and observe my infants and Dorothy cheering the latest returns on your Shaw from America.' As winter yielded to spring and still the manuscript had not been returned, Pearson contemplated going direct to the publishers without waiting any longer. This would mean, he knew, that Shaw would renounce permission to quote from his letters. Already Shaw had warned him: 'If a word is said to connect me with the authorship of the book, or its first proposal or its commercial profits, I shall be driven to the most desperate steps to disclaim it.' Kingsmill counselled patience – never Pearson's strong suit. 'It is impossible to approach Collins till the old ruin has exhausted his narcissistic frenzy.' In the meantime Pearson could only fume and walk. By spring his health and spirits had revived and he was back to ten-mile afternoons. Even when Shaw dispatched a note saying that he might be 'years more', Pearson managed to control his temper. His diary records: 'I have written to inform Shaw that though, like God, a thousand ages are to him but as yesterday, a single day of uncertainty is to me, a mere human, as a thousand ages.'

Despite the blitz and the grim outlook for England, the war seldom rates a mention in Pearson's diaries; one exception is this entry on February 12, 1940: 'This war, like the last, is to me simply a bore. War can only appeal to wretched people suffering from arrested development. To vital, intelligent folk it is just a tedious intrusion, silly, puerile, imbecile. What a bore Napoleon must have been to the intelligent men of his time! What an unutterable bore Hitler is now! I hope someday he will be put in a padded cell and made to listen for hours a day to records of speeches by Neville Chamberlain, such treatment to last for as many years as people have been bored by him . . . "Are you doing work of national importance?" someone asked me at the Club. "No, I am doing work of international importance," I replied; which happened to be the sober truth, as I was then finishing my life of Shaw.'

Malcolm Muggeridge had enlisted and was for a time billeted in London. He and Pearson met most days for drinks. On July 17, 1940 they paid a visit to the House of Commons. 'Malcolm wanted to see the revolting swine in session for the last time,' Pearson told Kingsmill. They sat in the Distinguished Strangers' Gallery, looking down on the assembled parliamentarians, and 'tried hard to pick out a face that hadn't crook or fool written all over it'. Pearson's diary entry concludes: 'We came to the conclusion that only one face was passably civilized: it belonged to a man who would be cast for the comic in a musical show at the Gaiety. The Mother of Parliaments has reached such a stage of imbecility and corruption that I shall not be sorry to see the end of it.'

Shaw's revisions became ever more finicky. When Pearson referred to his 'puritanical strictness', Shaw changed this to 'country lady strictness', adding the comment: 'Keep this word "puritanical" out of the story. Irish Catholicism is inhumanly puritanical. Irish Protestantism is snobbish and violently political; but it is not puritanical beyond the entirely irreligious Mrs Grundyism of the bourgeoisie.' Six months after giving Shaw the manuscript, Pearson had received less than a quarter of it back. His diary entry for June 20, 1940 notes: '"Here is a scrap to go on with", writes Shaw, returning twenty odd corrected pages. He has excised my remarks on his religion and written his own version.' A month later Shaw responded to yet another appeal: 'Have not done any. Overburdened with other work.' To this Pearson replied on a postcard: 'You are terribly trying. Damn your other work. Do mine.'

In November Pearson wrote to Shaw: 'You will have had my Life of you exactly one year on the 29th of this month: that is almost as long as I took to write it. As I cannot get any more cash from it until it is published, and as I am hopelessly hard up, will you either (a) let me have it back with whatever corrections are of real importance or (b) advance me £300 which I will repay when the book comes out?' Shaw replied: 'I am full of pressing work and ruined by war taxation. As for £300, you might as well ask for three hundred millions.' In his diary, Pearson commented: 'What an old liar he is! However the request for cash has jollied him up and I shall expect the balance of the book before the month is out.' His expectations were again dashed. At the end of the year, Pearson's diary records: 'The present Shaw-Pearson situation may be described as follows: Shaw is playing variations on a theme by Pearson, who is orchestrating the variations.'

Pearson did not receive final corrections until the late spring of 1941. When he did send the last instalment off Shaw grumbled that he could have written three comedies in the time that it had taken to make changes. Pearson replied that posterity would be grateful he had spent his time on the manuscript instead. 'His comment on that lacked restraint.'

The book appeared in October 1942. The reviews were superlative. In *The Times* Desmond MacCarthy called it 'most entertaining and illuminating'. James Agate said it was 'an almost flawless book . . . this masterpiece of biography'. Edwin Muir wrote: 'This is a book which calls for a general thanksgiving.' The *Daily Telegraph* reviewer considered it 'witty, well planned, very knowledgeable and extremely readable'. The *New York Times* and the *Irish Times* compared Pearson's Shaw to Boswell's Johnson. The book sold thirty thousand copies in the original hardcover edition, and another hundred thousand copies in a cheaper reprint. As a consequence of this success, Pearson had offers for film rights but Shaw refused permission. 'He had made up his mind that no one on earth could play the part of G.B.S. except himself, that none of his living contemporaries could endure being impersonated, that there was no story to tell, and in fact that his life would be burlesqued and his teachings parodied.' Pearson also had a request from Shaw's American publishers, Dodd Mead, to edit a two-volume edition of Shaw's letters. Shaw vetoed this proposal as well. But Shaw was enormously pleased by the book's success. He wrote to Pearson:

'The success of your book has driven the whole trade mad. They all want a book about me, a film about me, anything about me.' And, having cautioned Pearson before publication that not a word must ever connect him with the book, Shaw took to speaking openly of the enormous assistance he had given the author. On seeing Pearson's copy during a visit, Shaw opened it at the title page and underneath the author's signature wrote: 'Also his humble collaborator – G. Bernard Shaw.'

CHAPTER THIRTEEN

Talk and Travel

... A merrier man,
Within the limit of becoming mirth,
I never spent an hours talk withal.'
Love's Labour's Lost, Act II, Scene I

Of all his books Pearson most enjoyed the three talk and travel books –
Skye High (1937), *This Blessed Plot* (1942), and *Talking of Dick
Whittington* (1947) – written in collaboration with Kingsmill. Looking
back on them Pearson wrote: 'There never was a more stimulating and
agreeable companion than Hughie and the days we spent together were
among the most delightful of my life. I am quite sure that no books
could have been written with greater pleasure than those we wrote
jointly.'

The idea originated innocuously. In the Thirties Kingsmill lived in
Hastings. One afternoon, as he and Pearson walked along the cliffs
towards St Helen's Cemetery, where one can look over the Sussex weald
in one direction and Romney Marsh in the other, Pearson casually
remarked: 'Wouldn't it make a very amusing book if you and I followed
Johnson and Boswell round Scotland and wrote an account of our own
adventures in their wake? We love the lads and every place they visited
would interest us.'

A week later they called on their publisher, Hamish Hamilton, where
the following dialogue ensued:

Pearson: Hugh and I have a brilliant idea for a book we want to do
together.
Hamilton: Good. I welcome ideas. The more brilliant the better.
Pearson: Then you're in luck this morning. As you know Boswell's
original *Journal* of his visit to the Hebrides with Johnson is coming
out in a week or so. It's his day-to-day account of the round and
there is a lot of stuff in it which he cut out when he published his
Tour – the only version the public has yet had.
Hamilton: Yes?
Kingsmill: Hesketh and I want to follow Johnson and Boswell round

Scotland and write an account not only of our own adventures but of theirs as reconstructed by us on the spot.

Pearson: Or rather spots. Up to date Scotland to most Englishmen means the country of Burns, Stevenson, and Walter Scott, and no one seems aware that Johnson and Boswell covered more ground than they did.

Kingsmill: The whole of the east coast from Berwick to Inverness, right across Scotland to the west, half a dozen of the Hebrides, and back through the Lowlands.

Hamilton: Funnily enough –

Pearson: And it is not only the spots they visited; it's themselves. Wherever they went, humour and incident crowded upon them.

Kingsmill: And, assuming that humour and incident also crowd upon us, the combination ought to make a very amusing book.

Hamilton: Funnily enough –

Kingsmill: Part of the humour consisting in the contrast between the glory and discomfort in which Johnson and Boswell travelled –

Pearson: And the lesser glory and greater comfort in which we shall travel.

Hamilton: Funnily enough I discussed this very idea with James Agate and Jock Dent.

Kingsmill: Oh?

Hamilton: Jock seemed keen on it, but I have heard nothing further from them. I suppose they are too busy.

Pearson: Well, as you're bursting to have this book written, I don't see why Hugh and I shouldn't help you. Do you, Hugh?

Kingsmill: I'm perfectly game. Hamish's idea strikes me as a very sound one.

To travel required transportation (neither Kingsmill nor Pearson owned a car) and transportation meant wheedling a free railway pass and lodgings. Pearson wrote to several companies. The Advertising Manager of the London and North Eastern Railway Company replied that it was kind of Pearson to have written but '. . . at the moment we are not in need of any articles on the lines suggested'. Hesketh read this to Kingsmill with the comment that it was apparently as easy to please railway companies as publishers; at one time or another, half the publishers in London had written to acknowledge the happiness which his proposals had conferred on them and it now appeared that his capacity to distribute felicity was to be extended to railways. Eventually the London, Midland and Scottish Railway produced two first class passes, the Steamship Company, Caledonian MacBrayne, followed

suit, and Kingsmill mapped out a route, not remarkably similar to
Johnson and Boswell's itinerary, but one which allowed them to stay
free in hotels associated with his father's touring agency. With these
obstacles behind them, it remained only for Pearson to suggest that
Kingsmill obtain Birkbeck Hill's *Footsteps of Dr Johnson* as a guide. On
May 23, 1937 Kingsmill wrote to his friend: 'I got Birkbeck Hill's
Footsteps from the London Library. When I say 'I got', I mean that the
book was lowered by a crane from the attic in which it is housed, and
transported by Harrods to Hastings, where a shed has been erected for
it, in which, by an ingenious system of ladders and platforms, I can read
it with some comfort. I imagine that in Brobdingnag it would pass for
rather a dainty piece of bookmaking. I want to make it quite clear that,
as yours was the happy thought of procuring it, you are fairly entitled to
its possession during our journey, and more particularly when we are on
foot.'

The travellers departed from Euston on the morning of May 31. As
the train pulled out Kingsmill produced from his pocket a notebook and
a pen, 'a noble example' commended by Pearson. The train entered
Rugby Station. 'It is a hundred years old,' said Pearson. Kingsmill: 'I
will make a note of that.' Pearson: 'Which, unless amplified, will hardly
send the book into a second edition.' Kingsmill: 'We can amplify it with
short sketches of all the famous men who stood on that platform – Dr
Arnold, Matthew Arnold, Arnold Bennett and so on.'

The train next approached the Potteries which seemed promising of
material until each discovered that the other knew nothing about the
intricacies of china-making. Pearson: 'Let us keep a look out for
Lichfield. It was, as you have so finely said in your book on Johnson, the
place where Johnson was born. Ah, there it is.' Kingsmill pulled
himself to his feet and gazed with particular interest, seeing it for the
first time. As the train crossed the Scottish border Pearson raised the
topic of immortality, with regret disclaiming any belief in it.

> Kingsmill: I believe in immortality because I have felt immortal, just
>   as I believe in mortality because I have felt mortal, and I do not see
>   why the part of me which feels immortal should not survive when
>   the part of me which feels mortal crumbles away.
> Pearson: Yes, I've had that immortality feeling, too, usually after a
>   few double whiskies; and it has always been a mystery to me why
>   the church advocates temperance, though of course, many ortho-
>   dox Christians, Hilaire Belloc and G. K. Chesterton for example,
>   have praised the virtue of certain intoxicants. But don't let's waste
>   another precious minute of this mortal life arguing about a future

life; because if there is no hereafter our argument is futile, and if there is we'll have all eternity in which to appreciate it.

Kingsmill: As you raised the subject, you have the right to say when you have had enough of it. I will only add that my belief in immortality is sustained on tea, and that I believe it is being served at this moment.

At which point they adjourned to the restaurant car.

From Edinburgh they commenced a leisurely pilgrimage up the east coast through Stirling, St Andrews and Aberdeen, talking as they went along of such topics as which writer would be the greatest help in a street-fight (Johnson according to Kingsmill; Fielding according to Pearson), where did Hazlitt stand to look upon Ben Ledi through tears 'that fell in showers'; do vergers think and, if so, about what; would the Church of England extend Christian burial rites to a pirate; and why does the cuckoo in Scotland actually say 'wuckoo'?

On the train from Aberdeen to Elgin, Pearson told Kingsmill how he had first read Shakespeare as a young man in a country house in Shrewsbury and how Falstaff, Shallow and company had saved his life in Mesopotamia. Kingsmill: 'The best tribute to the knight I have ever heard. But what would have happened to you if that rainy day there had been a Bible, but no Shakespeare?' Pearson: 'I would be wheeling myself about in Hell, minus two legs.'

At Elgin, where Johnson and Boswell had found their food unappetizing and did not linger, Pearson and Kingsmill spent two relaxed days. On emerging from their hotel rested and anxious for a stroll, they stopped an elderly woman and inquired the nearest way to the sea?

Elderly Woman: The sea?
Kingsmill: The harbour.
EW.: The harbour?
Pearson: The front.
EW: The front?
Kingsmill: The beach.
EW: The beach?
Pearson: The promenade.
EW: The promenade?
Pearson and Kingsmill: Isn't Elgin on the sea?
EW: No.
Pearson and Kingsmill: Oh.

From Elgin they travelled to Inverness, thence by MacBrayne's motor coach down the north shore of Loch Ness to Invermoriston.

From Invermoriston they walked the forty-five miles to Glenelg in two days. Pearson, who considered this little more than a pleasant outing, outdistanced Kingsmill who found a satisfactory explanation for the ever-widening gap between them in the thought that his own practical difficulties of late years had been even more exhausting than those of his friend. At Glenelg they put up at a hotel whose proprietor, Captain Redmayne, bristled with interest on learning that, if not exactly retracing Johnson and Boswell's footsteps, they were travelling in roughly the same direction. He would, he said, 'welcome a talk with them'. Worn out and wanting nothing but an early bed, Pearson sighed to Kingsmill: 'We are clearly in for a lengthy session with one of the world's leading bores.' The Captain, having returned with a file of press cuttings about himself, settled to a monologue to which Pearson made the occasional polite interjections of 'Ha', and 'Do say', and 'Indeed'. The contrast between his friend's prediction and this ostensible show of interest was straining Kingsmill's patience. When Pearson, removing his pipe, affirmed: 'All three parties. God bless my soul. Capital!', it was more than Kingsmill could bear. Pearson described what happened next to Muggeridge: 'Hughie was seized with uncontrollable laughter and hurried from the room. I can still see his heaving back and his hand pushing a handkerchief into his mouth as he walked unsteadily to the door. Exercising considerable self-control, my belly muscles aching with the contraction necessary to prevent myself from exploding, I remained for over two hours with Redmayne, continuing these courtly interjections so necessary to a one-sided conversation. On the way to my room I looked in to see if Hughie was asleep. He was lying on his bed, gasping for breath, his body occasionally shaken by convulsions, and a long-drawn sound, something between a groan and a howl, escaping from his lungs at intervals. He was suffering from the after-effects of over two hours of continuous laughter, and as the mere sight of me produced further spasms I deemed it expedient to retire. The next day he was not fit for human society; but unfortunately we met Canon Fowler, the vicar of Rye in Sussex, who was in the smoking room of the hotel. He described the place in a rich parsonic manner as 'ma-gic', the pause between the two syllables being too much for Hughie, who rushed from the room, said to the steward outside: "Where on earth d'you get them from?", tottered down the corridor emitting curious cacaphonies that were quite audible to us, and left me once more to contract my belly muscles and try to maintain a civilized conversation about nothing in particular.' They left the Glenelg hotel that morning telling the manageress, Miss MacDonald, that they had enjoyed their stay; she said she knew that for she had often heard them laughing.

A tiny fishing boat carried them from the beach at Glenelg to the middle of the Sound where they were picked up by a MacBrayne steamer making the crossing to Skye. The passengers on the steamer crowded the side to watch the travellers ascend, from their expectant look apparently hoping for some mishap, but the two men mounted the ladder 'with firm dignity', and the passengers dispersed. From Portree, the capital of Skye, they motored to Elgol, then by boat across Loch Scavaig to the Black Coolins, described by Boswell as 'a prodigious range of mountains, capped with rocks like pinnacles in a strange variety of shapes'. Kingsmill and Pearson lost the track on their ascent but eventually descended into a valley through which a stream flowed into a little loch. Halfway down the glen, they overtook several people, one of whom happened to be the sole inhabitant of the Isle of Skye with whom Pearson was acquainted. The man, a Baptist, was critical of the Church of England and its wealthy endowments. 'I'd like to ask the Archbishop of Canterbury what Christ would say about his fifteen thousand a year,' he said. 'If that question could stump the Archbishop,' replied Kingsmill, 'he'd still be a curate.' After a stay at the Sligachan Hotel they went to Dunvegan Castle where they were hospitably received by Flora, Mrs McLeod of McLeod. On June 19 they left Dunvegan, returned to Portree, thence to Mallaig.

When torn between convenience and fidelity to the Johnson-Boswell route, the travellers invariably chose convenience, inventing the term 'yarrowing' (from Wordsworth's poem 'Yarrow Unvisited') to accommodate such choices. Having already yarrowed Ellon, Banff and Cullen en route to the western islands, the island of Raasay, where Johnson and Boswell met Flora MacDonald, posed no difficulty. As the boat passed Raasay, Pearson said: 'There is Raasay.' 'Oh,' said Kingsmill. Pearson: 'Our thirst for broadening our minds with new scenes seems to be diminishing.' They comforted themselves with the thought that knowing which places to yarrow and which places not to yarrow was the beginning and end of the art of travel.

From Mallaig, they journeyed by train to Fort William, thence to Oban where they put up comfortably for three days. After a day's work writing up their journals, they strolled along the seafront at sunset. 'This,' said Pearson, 'is the refuge I am looking for. There are plenty of trees here, and however repulsive the Hebrides may be at close quarters they are beautiful far away when the sun is setting behind them.' They next went by ferry to the Island of Iona where Columba and his missionaries brought Christianity to Scotland. Boswell preached a sermon in the abandoned cathedral of Icolmkill, even in 1773 a ruin of 'antiquity and remoteness'. Pearson was not impressed, telling Kingsmill that it was only love of Boswell that induced him to set foot on 'this leprous island'. Rejoining the steamer, they sailed to the Isle of Staffa where all the other passengers disembarked to inspect Fingal's Cave. Kingsmill was inclined to join them but Pearson was adamant, maintaining that inside or out a cave was only a heap of basaltic rock. 'We must stand firm and prove that we are serious yarrowers; men who can make a sacrifice in the cause of yarrowing; men who do not merely yarrow out of indulgence or caprice; men who, in short, with Fingal's Cave on one hand and lunch on the other, unswervingly decide for lunch.' The boat continued on to Tobermory and then, as night fell, they sailed over placid waters back towards Oban. Was it not here, Kingsmill inquired, where Johnson and Boswell hit a gale and nearly drowned?

> Pearson: I was only thinking a moment ago how funny it would be if we were shipwrecked and drowned while following Johnson and Boswell through these waters. What would your last words be before going under?
> Kingsmill: Hard on Hamish.
> Pearson: I am sure your sympathy will touch him. Anyhow, apart from the fact that there is no sign of dirty weather, this is not the stretch where Johnson and Boswell encountered the gale. I think it was off Coll. Didn't you see Coll someway back, a long low island?
> Kingsmill: I must have yarrowed it unconsciously. One gets the knack after a time and it becomes second nature. One does it like breathing.

Pearson felt compelled to remind his companion that, since Johnson and Boswell spent ten days on Coll and wrote more about it than any other place except Skye, to unconsciously yarrow Coll was much the same as doing an English pilgrimage in Johnson's footsteps and absent-mindedly missing out Lichfield. Kingsmill appeared chastened. Pearson insisted on making good the omission by reading aloud particulars of Boswell's account, including his 'mortal aversion' to having to sleep in the same bed with another man. 'Hardly in the modern spirit,' Kingsmill murmured, at which a fellow passenger who overheard conspicuously shifted his deck chair in protest. As the steamer approached the harbour lights of Oban, Kingsmill pronounced that, thanks to Pearson's recital, he now knew all he had ever wished to know about Coll. As they departed from Oban the following day, 'they experienced some regret that there were no more Hebrides left to yarrow'.

Pearson and Kingsmill concluded their tour at the Boswell home at Auchinleck. They walked the three miles from the railway station to the house, a splendid stone structure built in Boswell's youth by the Adam brothers. When Johnson walked up the front steps in 1773 he described the house as 'of hewn stone, very stately and durable'. So it has proved. Pearson and Kingsmill were cordially received by Miss Boswell and her sister, who had purchased the house from the last direct Boswell descendant, Lord Talbot de Malahide. The two men searched out the ruins of the former castle over which Johnson and Boswell had also clambered, with Johnson reflecting how ruins afford 'striking images of ancient life'.

From Auchinleck Pearson and Kingsmill went directly to Glasgow; then, after excursions to Pitlochry and Gullane, they returned to England. Johnson and Boswell had gone to Edinburgh, then, after ten days during which they were 'harassed by invitations', Johnson had returned alone to London. On November 27, 1773 Johnson wrote to Boswell: 'I came home last night without any incommodity, danger or weariness and I am ready to begin a new journey.' Johnson and Boswell never made another journey. A decade later, only a year before his death, Johnson asked Boswell: 'Shall we ever have another frolick like our journey to the Hebrides?'

Pearson and Kingsmill were to frolic twice more. But first they completed an account of their Scottish ramble. Hamish Hamilton objected to the proposed title (*The Road They Went*) because it would not convey to the reader what the book was about; however he agreed to Pearson's alternative, *Skye High*, although it is not immediately apparent how this title is any more informative. After reading the proofs, Pearson wrote to Kingsmill: 'I do not think it right to conceal from you my considered judgment that it is one of the major masterpieces of the world, which means of course that it will not sell a copy.' Kingsmill replied: 'A book which will confer pleasure on the few sane persons in each of the generations to come, as long as English is used.' Both men were correct. Sales were abysmally low, which Pearson attributed to the high price but which Hamish Hamilton attributed to public bewilderment at a travel book which contained no travel information and at levity displayed towards literary subjects. However the book has given pleasure to a handful of readers, even from its first publication when it was highly praised by Evelyn Waugh, David Garnett and Harold Nicolson – 'A book which will, I know, for long remain among my favourites'.

Shakespeare was their next subject, a talk and travel book to be called *Falstaff's Ghost*. Early in 1939 Pearson and Kingsmill called on Hamish Hamilton's office in Great Russell Street. Stunned by the poor sales of *Skye High*, Hamilton listened in silence as the plan was explained.

Hamilton: It's – It's very good of you two fellows to bring me this idea, but I am afraid that at the moment people won't read anything but politics.
Kingsmill: And that is getting you down a bit?
Pearson: Hence our desire to lift you into a cleaner atmosphere.
Hamilton: Thanks . . .
Kingsmill: But not so clean as to deprive you of all hope of profit.
Hamilton: Yes, but . . .
Pearson: Pull yourself together, Hamish, and listen carefully to me. Since Munich the English have begun to stir themselves. They are getting sick of being barked at by all the Yahoos on the continent. Shakespeare went through exactly what we are going through now – 'Bragging horror' is what he calls it. And it was the spirit of Shakespeare that beat Spain, just as it will be the spirit of Shakespeare that will smash these Nordic dagos.
Hamilton: Are you two proposing a patriotic pamphlet?
Pearson: Of course not. All we want is a short holiday in Shakespeare's country.
Kingsmill: Hesketh has never been to Marlborough so that is to be our starting-place. We are just going to wander about that part of the world, drifting gradually towards Stratford, and piecing Shakespeare together as we go.
Hamilton: Piecing . . . Shakespeare . . . Together?
Kingsmill: Well, Hamish, we mustn't take up your time. You have been very good to us in the past.

They shook hands cordially and Hamilton said they must have lunch some day. Pearson and Kingsmill walked thoughtfully to the Horseshoe where, over a drink, they decided 'there was nothing for it but to let Hamish go his own wild way'. Shortly after Hamish Hamilton's offices were severely damaged by fire and Kingsmill wrote to Pearson: 'The place looks battered and exhausted, but not more so than if Hamish had published *This Blessed Plot* or *Talking of Dick Whittington* in addition to *Skye High*. The whole business has merely been the Deity's way of letting Hamish know that a man cannot evade his duty and hope to escape the consequences.'

Pearson's relations with authors' agents were as troubled as his relations with publishers. Watt, Watson, Pollinger, Watkins and

Higham each acted for Pearson at one time or another. When a Swedish publisher sought translation rights in his *Shaw*, Pearson turned down the proposal rather than pay Pollinger the 19% commission demanded. He sacked Pollinger instead and wrote in his diary: 'These dirty agents do no work, ask one to sign rotten contracts, and then sting one good and proper. The unproductive middleman is the curse of our civilization. What can be worse than an incompetent parasite?'

Falstaff's Ghost was temporarily put on the shelf. In 1941 Kingsmill wrote to Pearson: 'How delightful it would be to do another book, at ease in the English meadow with nothing to disturb one except a dozen Nazi Aerodromes ten minutes away.' Later that summer, Kingsmill stayed with Pearson in Sussex. They agreed to begin their new book with or without a publisher, even though this meant no advance to finance their perambulations. Pearson could cover his share but Kingsmill was destitute as usual. Since Pearson was then at work on Shaw it occurred to Kingsmill that a connection, however frail, existed between himself and Shaw. In due course, he called at Whitehall Court. Kingsmill subsequently related their conversation to Pearson:

G.B.S.: Well, and how is Hesketh? Is it about him that you wished to see me?

H.K.: He is not very fit at present, and wants to go into the country. He has asked me to go with him, and I thought that as you are interested in Hesketh –

G.B.S.: I am not interested in Hesketh. Hesketh is interested in me.

H.K.: I really can't go on with my preposterous errand unless you are willing to listen to me.

G.B.S.: Quite so, quite so.

H.K.: Hesketh is my host, and I can't ask him to support my family while I am away. I have just published a book on D. H. Lawrence which has fizzled out, and I have no cash at the moment.

G.B.S.: T.E. finished D. H. Lawrence off. There is no interest in D.H. anymore.

H.K.: So I have found. I wondered therefore if you would care to come to my assistance?

G.B.S.: But what about Sir Henry? He is still alive, isn't he?

H.K.: He is on a cruise, and in any case, apart from other complications, the travel business isn't what it used to be.

G.B.S.: That is a fine hotel your firm has up in Scotland. And there is that one at Hastings. I have stayed there myself.

H.K.: So have I. None the less . . .

G.B.S.: I'm a poor man, too. I've just had to borrow two thousand from my wife.

H.K.: I'm so sorry. (Rising) In that case . . .

G.B.S.: Would a tenner be of any use?

H.K.: (Sinking back) Certainly. It's extremely good of you.

Afterwards Kingsmill regretted that he hadn't held out for more. Clutching Shaw's cheque, he departed 'conscious of a very warm feeling towards the old man, but unable to find words in which to express it'.

This time their pilgrimage started in Marlborough, thence through the Cotswolds. Near Bibury they were almost trampled by scarlet-clad huntsmen in pursuit of a solitary fox; to Kingsmill's surprise, Pearson unleashed a volley of oaths in the general direction of the hunters and continued muttering imprecations as they made their way to the village hotel. Over scones and jam, Pearson explained: 'There are two types of men who get my goat; those who damn the sins they have a mind to, and those who damn the sins they have no mind to. The first is the puritan who suppresses his natural instincts, and whose sex goes rancid with him. Of such was W. T. Stead. The second is the ex-rake and debauchee who after a lifetime of guzzling like a hog, drinking like a fish, and copulating like a stoat, turns over a new leaf when he can no longer gorge, soak and womanize, and preaches temperance, sobriety and chastity. Of such was Tolstoy. Compared with these two, the idiot of a fox-hunter strikes me as a relatively harmless cad.' Kingsmill: 'A powerful speech, but haven't you rather confused the issue?' Pearson: 'I hope so.'

Impecuniosity cut short further travel at that point. Meanwhile the Pearsons rented a part-Tudor, part-Georgian farm house, Woods Place, at Whatlington in Sussex which had been vacated by its owner. It was remote, accessible only by a long winding lane, the nearest habitation being the Mill House where the Muggeridges lived. On their first night in the house, Pearson's diary records: 'Hun aeroplanes passed and repassed most of the night, but the solitude was otherwise unbroken.' Kingsmill spent several holidays from his wartime school-mastering duties at Woods Place and, when Pearson was not tenaciously digging the overgrown garden, they talked of Shakespeare. In June 1941 Pearson went to Harrow to visit scenes of Kingsmill's childhood. They found the place much altered but Kingsmill was able to identify a bit of wasteland where, at sixteen, he had had his first sexual encounter. The lady in question was an experienced woman many years his senior; having only fourpence with him and feeling that in such matters payment should be made generously or not at all, no money changed hands. That evening, after an admirable dinner at the King's Head Hotel, the two men sat on the terrace smoking pipes and planning their book. Pearson suggested that they consider broadening the theme to embrace England.

Kingsmill: Excellent. And much more likely than Shakespeare to appeal to a publisher, especially as England is at the moment so much in the air. Well put, that.

Pearson: And of course we can drag in Shakespeare as often as we like.

Kingsmill: We can start with our Cotswold journey, and then proceed with no settled plan. It would be unEnglish to deal with our subject systematically. As we are both English it is reasonable to assume that England will emerge from the book. I don't say the whole of England, but much more than if we were French. It will be a book from which a sensitive reader will be able to infer England. That gets it. *Infer* England.

A fortnight later, Pearson and Kingsmill dined at the Authors' Club with Alan White of Methuen. 'It is difficult to give a cut-and-dried idea of the book,' Kingsmill began, adding tentatively. 'Our aim is to write a book from which the reader will be able to *infer* England.'

White: Infer?

Kingsmill: Gather.

Pearson: The book is bound to contain a lot about us. That can't be helped. Every man is his own England.

Kingsmill: Always provided that he is an Englishman.

White: What are you going to call it?

Pearson: Why not *Between You and Me*?

White: Or, more simply, *The Gatepost*.

Kingsmill: I think that the title, at least, should have something to do with England. There must be something suitable in the poets.

Pearson: There is only one poet and most of his patriotic phrases have already been pinched . . .

'This happy breed of men, this little world,
This precious stone set in the silver sea . . .'

Kingsmill: 'This precious stone', – I like that.

White: Isn't it a little too –

Kingsmill: Precious? Perhaps you are right. Forge ahead, Hesketh.

Pearson: 'This blessed plot, this . . .

Kingsmill: Stop! 'This Blessed Plot' – you can't beat that.

White: Yes, that's not at all bad.

Kingsmill: It expresses our feeling, it will ensnare readers of thrillers, and it will give you, Hesketh, an opportunity to recur to your recent exploits with fork and spade.

Pearson: Not that I have ever called any of the plots I've been digging 'blessed'.

White: Have you been digging for victory, too?

Pearson: No, for gluttony.

Kingsmill: Strange – it never occurred to me before that digging for victory had its compensations. Well, Alan, you have the title, and I can guarantee that none of our readers will guess the plot, even when they have reached the end of the book.

Perhaps that was a problem because sales of *This Blessed Plot* were modest, although they exceeded those of *Skye High*. *This Blessed Plot* has more conversation and less travel; what travel there is occurs mostly between pubs in villages around Whatlington. The book, published by Methuen in 1942, included drawings by Maurice Weightman which Kingsmill considered '. . . good, but not quite what I had expected'. Pearson, however, was his usual ebullient self: 'The book is, in my unbiased view, very much better even than *Skye High*.' Although most readers ignored it, the *Manchester Guardian* reviewer claimed that the authors had 'invented the conversation – travel book as a new art form', an assessment with which the authors saw no reason to quarrel.

Pearson returned to biography, choosing for his next subject his boyhood hero, Arthur Conan Doyle. A diary entry on November 18, 1941 explains: 'I think he wants "placing" in the literary firmament, and so far he has been regarded as an elaborate joke by highbrows, who patronize him but funk a real assessment . . . when the object of reading is to rest, refresh or recreate the mind, no volumes in our literature are so welcome as those which constitute the *Holmes* saga, the *Gerard* stories, and *Rodney Stone*. We could better spare an equivalent output by any better writer of fiction, if such there be.'

Adrian Conan Doyle gave permission to quote from his father's papers. Early in 1942 Pearson and Doyle lunched at the Savage Club. Pearson came away convinced Doyle was 'a charming fellow who offers to do everything for me to help in my life of his father'. They corresponded amiably for months, Doyle concluding one letter: 'I know you will write the book as you yourself see the facts, unswayed by any but your own powers of perception and I neither expect nor desire anything more fair than that.'

The gist of Pearson's portrait of Arthur Conan Doyle was that he was 'the man in the street', an author who gave articulate voice to the instincts and prejudices, the longing for action and excitement, which the average man feels but cannot express. When he came to Doyle's final years, seeing fairies in the garden and communing with spirits in darkened rooms, Pearson was humorously tolerant. The only critical note he sounded in an otherwise sympathetic portrait was this: 'Like all spiritually undeveloped folk, Doyle was greatly attracted to such subjects as telepathy, theosophy, hypnotism, and anything else that went beyond the borderland of normal experience . . .'

On September 21, 1943 Pearson forwarded the manuscript to Adrian Doyle with a covering letter. 'You will not agree with some of my opinions,' he wrote, 'but I think you will find my portrait of your father as sympathetic as I can assure you it is sincere.' Adrian Doyle liked the book, or so it seemed. Three days later, he responded: 'May the book prosper as it deserves. Already I have dipped extensively and I am now settling down to the contents with great interest.'

Methuen published on September 23, 1943. Reviews were favourable, sales were brisk, and all went smoothly until November 5 when Adrian Doyle wrote an article in *John O'London's Weekly* claiming that his father *was* Sherlock Holmes, a fact unappreciated by Hesketh Pearson, 'for whom I have the highest regard as a writer and a friend'. Silence then descended until February 20, 1944 when, suddenly, a dam of pent-up hostility burst. It began with a letter from Adrian Doyle castigating Pearson and the book. Doyle claimed to have received a glut of correspondence from perfect strangers blaming him for this 'travesty' of a biography. In the *News Review* Doyle claimed not to have read more than ten pages of Pearson's book prior to February 1944; also, that Pearson had interviewed none of his father's acquaintances and 'none had substantiated his "portrayal"'; finally, 'of the papers lent to this man by the family there is not one that gives a tittle of substance or authority to this self-created conception of my father'.

Pearson immediately drafted a reply demolishing these false assertions and calling into question Doyle's sanity. Before sending it, however, he showed it to George Bernard Shaw, who dissuaded him. 'Let nothing persuade you to argue with this man,' Shaw counselled, 'it could do no good and be an expensive and very wearing waste of time.' Instead Shaw dictated this measured rebuke which Pearson eventually sent:

Dear Adrian Doyle,

I am very sorry to hear that you have changed your first friendly opinion of my book; but what can I do? The book is out, and two editions are in the hands of the public. I could not withdraw nor suppress it even if I had changed my own opinion of it, which I have not. You must not forget that it would be a miracle if a professional biographer's opinion were an echo of a son's opinion; and I have cleared you and your brother of all responsibility for my judgments in the note of Acknowledgement.

There is nothing for me to discuss. But if you can throw a new light on your father, do so in print by all means; nobody will be more interested than

Yours Sincerely,

A year later Adrian Doyle took up the challenge, producing a pamphlet (which he later, accurately, called a 'monologue') entitled *The True Conan Doyle*. He began by disowning an 'alleged biography of my father by a Mr Hesketh Pearson', and went on: 'In its portrayal of my father and his opinions, the book is a travesty and the personal values therein ascribed to him are, in effect, the very antithesis of everything that he represented, believed in, and held dear.' This pamphlet, which gives fresh meaning to the word hagiography, has become something of a collector's item. Doyle sent Pearson a copy which he promptly sold for nine shillings, with difficulty resisting the temptation to write and ask the author for more. For twenty-five pages, in tones of pained indignation, a son praises his father and chastises his biographer, finishing up with the conclusion: 'Conan Doyle was the perfect pattern of a gentleman.' This time Pearson had the sense to rein in his temper and do nothing, letting the pamphlet reap the contempt it deserved. None wielded the scalpel more delicately than George Orwell, who, after calling it 'a labour of piety', added: 'One would gather from it that Conan Doyle came nearer to perfection than it is given to ordinary mortals to do.'

When Pearson's biography went into paperback in 1947, Adrian Doyle threatened criminal proceedings against both author and publisher. Nothing came of this threat but the war of words continued, albeit intermittently, for years afterwards. In 1959, on the centenary of Conan Doyle's birth, the BBC invited Pearson to give a radio talk. When Adrian Doyle got wind of it a solicitor's letter was sent to the BBC warning that if Pearson's talk was broadcast they would be denied permission ever to broadcast another Sherlock Holmes story. The BBC caved in and the talk was cancelled, although Pearson was paid his fee (£18).

Pearson and Kingsmill projected three more talk and travel books (tentatively called *Cloak and Rapier*, *After Cromwell*, and *Rest and Be Thankful*). Meanwhile, Pearson's attentions were diverted by his father's ill health. Ever since his wife's death in 1934, Henry Pearson had become more cantankerous, his loneliness exacerbated by osteo-arthritis. Like many elderly sick, he became obsessed with his health and took to carrying a thermometer from room to room, recording his temperature at frequent intervals. By 1941 he could move only with the aid of sticks, then crutches. When he could no longer negotiate the chancel steps at St Martin's, he gave up reading the lessons and going to church. When a landmine exploded near the house, he sat up in bed and asked a nurse: 'What's that?' She told him it was probably a bomb. 'I disapprove of all this gallivanting in the air,' he muttered. At the very last he became pathetically violent, feebly hitting out at all who came within striking distance. He died on Easter Sunday, 1942. Three days later a funeral service was held in St Martin's. It was a rainy, blustery day and the vicar was blown about at the graveside. Hesketh's last recorded reference to his father is this diary entry: 'Oh, how I hate these services which always make me cry. Strange and sad to think of the old man, so much in command of his circumstances throughout life, left up there on the top of the wind-swept hill, willy-nilly.'

In 1944 Hamish Hamilton proposed that Pearson write the text for a series of line drawings of London by Marjory Whittington. Pearson signed a contract but failed to produce the text. Meanwhile he and Kingsmill were deliberating another talk and travel book. Age and increasing indolence ruled out anything like the territory covered in *Skye High*; they were reluctant to cope even with the more limited geography of *This Blessed Plot*. 'However we should be able to manage London,' Kingsmill asserted, 'something topographical, reaching back into the past, I suppose.' 'And forward into the present, perhaps,' added Pearson. 'I was at Highgate the other day,' Pearson continued, 'and thought of Dick Whittington with his cat – a young chap with a jerkin, you know, a stick over his shoulder, and hanging down from it a handkerchief with a few belongings. What about "Talking of Dick Whittington" for our title?' Kingsmill: 'An admirable title. It commits us to nothing, neither of us knowing anything about him.'

Hamish Hamilton did not approve this plan for simultaneously satisfying inclination and contractual obligation but, thanks to Graham Greene's intervention, the firm of Eyre and Spottiswoode did. Greene had enjoyed *Skye High* and *This Blessed Plot* and wanted to know how the actual writing was done. Pearson explained: 'We take notes as we go around, from time to time putting down anything that has struck us as interesting or amusing, and recording the details of chance encounters as soon after as possible. So far as our own conver-sations are concerned, they are sufficiently faithful reports. Then when enough material has been accumulated, we put it together, Kingsmill holding the pen, and I striding up and down, or seated, as the case may be.'

In 1945 the owner of Woods Place returned and the Pearsons moved to 14 Priory Road in London. He and Kingsmill began what was to be their last book by taking afternoon walks, usually originating at the Authors' Club and sufficiently short that they could be back in time for tea. One summer afternoon they strolled from Cockfosters Station through a pleasant wood of scattered trees with a little lake below them. Hardly had they passed the lake when a young couple asked to be directed to it. 'That is perfectly simple,' said Pearson, 'you . . .' and at some length proceeded to tell them to continue in the direction they were going. At one point Kingsmill attempted to supplement this information but without deflecting from Pearson the gratitude evident on the girl's face. 'We shall pass this way but once,' Pearson sighed, 'any good thing that we can do, let us not neglect, for we shall not pass this way again.'

Over the following months they made literary pilgrimages around London and as far west as Worcester to talk to Stanley Baldwin, as far east as Yarmouth to commemorate Charles Dickens, and as far south as Horsham to call on Hilaire Belloc. They also resolved to pay Shaw a visit and Pearson wrote to ask about a convenient date. Receiving no reply, Pearson wired: 'What the hell! Unless you forward doctor's certificate, expect us on Monday.' On November 5, 1945 they motored to Ayot St Lawrence. They found Shaw sitting immobile in a chair in the dining room, in no hurry to receive them. Eventually he did and Pearson asked him: 'How are you?' 'Ninety.' 'Yes, but how are you feeling?' 'How does anyone feel at ninety!' After two hours of pleasant talk, the travellers took their leave, repeating how delightful it had been to see him. 'And why wouldn't it be?' said Shaw. It was dark; Pearson said there was no reason for Shaw to see them out. But he insisted on doing so and stood by the gate, drooping and motionless, until they were out of sight. 'I am afraid I shall never be able to attack the dear old boy again with real gusto,' said Kingsmill.

Early in 1946 Kingsmill fell ill. In fact he was suffering from a duodenal ulcer and the continuing failure of the medical profession to make a proper diagnosis eventually cost his life. By March, though, he seemed to have recovered and the two men met to review progress on their book. Finding that they had accomplished little, and what little they had did not match Marjory Whittington's drawings, their editor, Douglas Jerrold, questioned their industry and methodology. He was not entirely reassured by Kingsmill's response: 'Our book may not be of much use to Stalin if he wants something for street-to-street fighting, but it will preserve the essence and spirit of London for our Patagonian readers a thousand years hence.'

The travellers now concentrated on some of the better known London landmarks, beginning with Westminster Abbey which they entered by the west entrance to avoid having to pass the statues of politicians located in the north transept. In the west porch they came upon a notice: '*Lunch Hour Addresses* – April 3. Prayer – What Is It For? April 10. Prayer – How Is It Done?' Kingsmill considered this odd: 'Considering all the money spent on this building, they might have settled these elementary points before now.' In Poets' Corner they stood before the Nollekens bust of Dr Johnson and Kingsmill recalled Johnson's remark: 'I think my friend, Joe Nollekens, can chop out a head with any of them.' Pearson, who was then at work on a life of Wilde, allowed that he might someday 'polish off' Johnson and Boswell.

In Worcester, the travellers strolled through the Cathedral Close and came upon an elderly woman lying in a drunken stupor. They wondered what Dr Johnson would have done? Pearson inclined to the view that Johnson would have shouldered her and carried her home; Kingsmill pointed out that the incident Pearson had in mind was an isolated one where the woman had been evicted by her landlord and was crying out for help. 'Johnson staggering along Fleet Street with a woman on his back was not a nightly spectacle.' Having debated the question over the recumbent and now snoring form, Pearson yielded; the travellers passed by on the other side. They assuaged their consciences with the thought that the old woman had sought the open of her own free will and she might not be grateful to be forced back from oblivion to reality.

Apart from a final pilgrimage around Hampstead Heath, the travellers finished off London with visits to St Paul's, where Pearson told the taxi driver to wait, assuring him 'we won't be so long as the size of the building might lead you to expect'; Southwark Cathedral, where Pearson insisted that the only thing worth recalling about it was that Shakespeare's feet had actually touched these stones; and, finally, Dr Johnson's house in Gough Square. Kingsmill recalled how he had often come here during the black-out when the house was in darkness but clearly outlined against the night sky; he would imagine Johnson, sitting in an upper room, writing *Rasselas* at a feverish pace in order to pay off debts from his mother's funeral. Kingsmill said that Johnson had finally reconciled himself to the pain and disappointment of life and, as proof, he quoted to Pearson the sage's valediction to Imlac:

My retrospect of life recalls to my view many opportunities of good neglected, much time squandered upon trifles, and more lost in idleness and vacancy. I leave many great designs unattempted, and many great attempts unfinished. My mind is burdened with no heavy crime, and therefore I compose myself to tranquillity; endeavour to abstract my thoughts from hopes and cares which, though reason knows them to be vain, still try to keep their old possession of the heart; expect, with serene humility, that hour which nature cannot long delay, and hope to possess in a better state that happiness which here I could not find, and that virtue which here I have not attained.

Talking of Dick Whittington appeared in 1947. It is more wistful than their two previous books. Kingsmill was dying and, although Pearson could not have known it, perhaps he sensed it. This exchange, as they listened to the Cathedral bells of Winchester, captures the melancholic mood of the book:

Pearson: One of the reasons why they move me so much is that their sound is unchanging from age to age, and Chaucer and Lady Jane Grey and Shakespeare and dear old Anna Seward all heard those chimes just as we hear them, and they accompany one's own journey in the same unchanging way. One's tastes take different forms from year to year, but church bells are always the same.

Kingsmill: And so they both recall the transitory expectations of the past and, being unchanging themselves, promise something that does not pass away.

CHAPTER FOURTEEN

Nothing to Repent

'Night hangs upon mine eyes; my bones would rest,
That have but labour'd to attain this hour.'
Julius Caesar, Act V, Scene V.

On March 30, 1948 Hugh Kingsmill had a severe haemorrhage. The ambulance which delivered him to the Royal Sussex Hospital in Brighton had to make an emergency stop at a doctor's office en route so that he could be given a blood transfusion. The doctor's name, fittingly, was Dickens. Dickens asked the local vicar, who happened to be visiting, to wrap a muffler round his neck so that Kingsmill would not see a clerical collar and suspect that extreme unction was about to be administered. In hospital surgery was performed but neither the ulcer, nor any other cause, was diagnosed. On April 4 Pearson wrote:

My Dear Hughie,
   You have given us anxious moments: to which you will naturally reply that our anxiety cannot have equalled yours. Which is true. All the same . . . how unutterably (to use the *mot juste*) sickening it has been for you! . . . Poor old lad! I am really so sorry for you that I can't pass ten minutes of the day without thinking of you. Which suggests the hideous thought that if one wishes permanently to occupy the mind of a friend one must be seriously ill. That, I suppose, would be the extremest form of egotism. Anyhow, I beg you to dismiss yourself from my thoughts by getting well as soon as you possibly can. If you want to make me comfortable, make yourself comfortable.

Dorothy Kingsmill rang Pearson the next day to say that her husband was worse; she thought he might be more comfortable in a private room. Hesketh agreed and insisted on paying the additional cost. Unfortunately, no private room was then available.

Before his illness, Kingsmill's only regular income was as literary editor of the *New English Review*. Determined that he should not lose this meagre lifeline, Muggeridge and Pearson met at the Authors' Club to plan a strategy; afterwards they strolled through Regent's Park where Muggeridge remarked that if Kingsmill should die half the joy of living would be gone at a stroke. Pearson agreed. To Kingsmill, Pearson wrote: '[Malcolm] tells me to set your mind at rest concerning the *New English Review*, which is going steadily forward on its appointed mission. I doubted whether its mission had ever lain near to your heart; but he assured me that its main mission was to pay you a salary, with which I heartily agreed, and what he wanted you to know was that the salary position was sound and secure.' Throughout Kingsmill's hospital confinement and his later convalescence, Muggeridge turned out articles and reviews under Kingsmill's name, apparently without editor or reader noticing the difference.

Pearson offered to go to Brighton. Kingsmill declined. 'I think it would be a great mistake for you to come down; either we shall laugh in which case I shall immediately pass out or we shall not laugh, and for you to take a considerable journey to safeguard me from laughing seems over-complicated.' However Kingsmill rallied and on May 4 was discharged from hospital.

Meanwhile Gladys Pearson had fallen ill and, after three weeks in a nursing home, Hesketh took her to the Esplanade Hotel in Folkestone for rest and sea air. Kingsmill joined them there and, for a fortnight, Hesketh played nurse to his wife and his friend. Kingsmill enjoyed the rest, always referring to Folkestone afterwards as 'paradise'. The weather was splendid, the sea air bracing, and Kingsmill could gratify his passion for rich cakes and ices in the sweet shops along Sandgate Road. Through the summer and autumn Kingsmill came up to London once or twice a week, usually meeting Pearson for lunch at the Authors' Club, a walk in the late afternoon, dinner, then talk and music at 14 Priory Road; Kingsmill now wanted to hear only sad and soothing music, particularly Mozart's Clarinet Concerto, the slow movement from Elgar's Violin Concerto, and Beethoven's A Minor Quartet and Mass in D Major.

Early in 1949 Kingsmill was strong enough to revise proofs of *The Progress of a Biographer*, his last book, a collection of wonderfully shrewd literary criticism. Pearson considered the book a masterpiece. '[It] contains the very best literary criticism in the language; at least if there is anything to compare with these essays for imaginative insight, unfailing commonsense, spiritual illumination and sustained humour, I should like to hear of it.'

In February Kingsmill suffered more internal bleeding. He managed to come to London on February 23 when the two men dined at the Authors' Club for the last time. 'The doctors told me some weeks ago that if these haemorrhages go on, I won't,' he told Pearson, 'so I have spent a pensive weekend.' On April 10 (the same day he inscribed a copy of *The Progress of a Biographer* to H.P. in the hope that 'we shall yet have many laughs together'), Kingsmill was re-admitted to the Royal Sussex Hospital in Brighton. Four days later he wrote: 'To see you in this belching, groaning cave of wind and water would be wonderful.' He counselled Hesketh to tell the hospital authorities that they were literary collaborators and that the purpose of any visit would be business not pleasure; that way the regulations would be bent. 'Christ could have sat by Saint John's side for double the ordinary time if stock exchange tips had been his ostensible theme.'

Pearson drove to Brighton on May 4, arriving at three o'clock. He was kept waiting for an hour while Kingsmill was given another blood transfusion. When he entered the room Kingsmill took his hand and held it, an unusual thing for him who was, by nature, undemonstrative. 'You're a good colour,' Pearson said. 'Not mine, old boy,' Kingsmill laughed. 'It belongs as of right to others who have kindly contributed to my present appearance.' Kingsmill wanted to talk of Shakespeare. After an hour, a nurse came and told Pearson he must leave. When Pearson turned at the door to say goodbye, Kingsmill was crying. He was recalling, he said, their laughter together on their literary rambles; 'About three years since Winchester, isn't it? How well I remember the old walled garden and the chimes!'

His courage lasted to the end. In the last letter Pearson received, Kingsmill wrote: 'Balmy spring breezes blowing in from the sea outside, and all past springs revive, but I hope that this decaying old husk will release me at not too long a date to recover all the beauty of those old days in some other form.'

On May 15, 1949, about midday, Kingsmill fell into a coma. Twice he seemed momentarily to rally but on both occasions he was too weak to speak. He died about 9 p.m. Dorothy rang Muggeridge and Pearson. Hesketh said that 'a very large part of myself died with him'. He, in turn, notified Colin Hurry who showed up a short while later with the following epitaph:

> Hugh, I am sure, will find salvation,
> Join celestial conversation,
> Meet the celebrated dead
> Know at last what each one said;
> Death, for him, could have no sting
> Save in all our sorrowing.

A memorial service was held at St Paul's, Covent Garden on June 9. The Reverend Vincent Howson officiated and Pearson and Muggeridge read the lessons. Shortly after, they began to exchange reminiscences of

Kingsmill by letter. In preparation for this, Pearson re-read his diaries
in search of Kingsmill's bon mots and was appalled to find that he had
recorded so few. 'Monstrous, when one remembers that he said something either funny or profound almost every time he opened his mouth.
Oh, dear! Why on earth didn't I Boswellize him? I suppose because I
was enjoying his company so much. And now the best of him is lost
forever, because of my laziness. I always thought I would die first.' The
Pearson-Muggeridge letters, under the title *About Kingsmill*, were
published by Methuen in 1951. Like everything connected with
Kingsmill the book was a commercial failure, but the letters have an
immediacy and charm that somehow brings their subject to life in a
unique way. Some critics have suggested that this slight volume
contains the very best writing of both Muggeridge and Pearson.

Kingsmill's death brought to an end a friendship of nearly thirty
years, the closest of Pearson's life. But, like Johnson, Pearson made a
practice of keeping his friendships in good repair. Also like Johnson,
he preferred the friendship of younger men; he saw more now of
Muggeridge, Basil Harvey and Michael Holroyd, all his juniors. These
men found Pearson generous, unassuming and amusing, his company a
guarantee of good cheer with or without the stimulation of drink. For
Pearson there was also the consolation of literature; for the rest of his
life he seldom turned over the pages of a book that had not been
illuminated by talk with Kingsmill. In his diary he wrote: 'Friendship,
love, nature and art: these are the only four things that matter in life,
and I have never been able to determine the order of importance. Each
has at different times meant more than the rest to me. But whereas
friendship fluctuates; and love dies; and nature is intermittent in its
appeal, depending so much on one's state of mind, art continually
fascinates and increases its hold on the mind and spirit of man; that is, if
man does not stagnate. In the long run Shakespeare wins.'

Pearson returned to biography, choosing, oddly enough, a politician,
Benjamin Disraeli, for his next subject (*Dizzy*, Methuen, 1951). In
England V. S. Pritchett proclaimed the book 'picturesque, witty,
sympathetic, perceptive, and very readable'; in America the *New York
Times* called it 'fascinating', their reviewer (Orville Prescott) adding:
'Mr Pearson has a pretty wit himself. Dizzy contains nearly as many
examples of his terse and cynical wisdom as it does of Disraeli's.' The
book sold well in England and better in the United States. One rum
consequence was that Pearson received speaking invitations from Conservative constituency groups; the suggestion was even made that he
might be persuaded to stand as a Tory candidate. For a man who had
voted on but three or four occasions in his life, and then 'only because

the people who gained my vote seemed a little less dishonest then their opponents', such proposals were bizarre. He soon convinced his would-be patrons that the only things about Disraeli he admired were his wit, character, and persistent efforts to write poetry, and that Disraeli's particular brand of political partisanship was the least interesting thing about him.

Until Disraeli, Gladys had been a partner in her husband's books, usually assisting with the inevitable drudgery of research. She often worked in the Reading Room of the British Museum, tracking down dates, sources or references, while Hesketh wrote at home. But a crippling, progressive illness restricted her first to home, then to bed. By degrees she lost the use of both legs and, in the end, had to be lifted from bed to chair and back again. Hesketh could not have provided the care she needed without the assistance of Joyce Ryder who, with her sister Jean, occupied the ground floor flat at 14 Priory Road. Gladys bore her afflictions stoically. In his memoirs, Pearson chose to remember her in these words: 'During the whole of her illness she never uttered a word of complaint, and the only thing that worried her was the inconvenience which she believed her enfeeblement caused me. She loved reading and talking to her friends, and she never seemed in the least depressed. When she thought she was dying she told me that I had been a good husband and that she had been happy with me. But she spoke from the goodness of her own heart, which made me weep. Aware that I had not been a good husband, I could believe that she had been happy, for we had had grand times together, never ceasing to love one another. She died quite suddenly on March 8, 1951, and forty years of a deeply affectionate relationship closed with her last breath.'

Almost immediately Hesketh married Joyce Ryder. When he proposed to Joyce she told him that the last wish Gladys had expressed was that they might marry. Pearson was sixty-four, twenty years Joyce's senior, but she told him that, since he habitually acted more like six than sixty, it scarcely mattered. The truth of this remark was borne out shortly after when Pearson was confronted in Regent's Park by a boy of about seven who took aim at him with a toy gun, squeezed the trigger, and popped. Hesketh executed a realistic stage-fall backwards, coming to rest motionless on the ground. The boy screamed, then lapsed into hysterics, which brought his nurse bundling over. She upbraided the recumbent Pearson most severely as a grown man who should know better. The boy wailed and keened. Thinking any explanation of his action in altruistic terms would prove pointless, Hesketh picked himself up with what dignity he could muster and made off. 'Since then I have not attempted to amuse small children.'

Through the 1950s Pearson's literary reputation blossomed, bringing him invitations to lecture and broadcast. Apart from one lecture tour to Iceland (undertaken at the instigation of a friend) and occasional appearances on the BBC's Brains Trust (which he said, in his case, should be called Brains Rust) he turned down such invitations, preferring the solitude of writing to the false bonhomie of the crowd or the camera's unseeing eye. It was one of his charms that he could never pretend to an interest he did not feel. Politics, science, sport or religion – these were fripperies. Only one subject was worth discussing – human nature in life and literature – and this subject was inexhaustible. Benny Green recalls seeing one Brains Trust programme in which, while the rest of the pundits on the panel were setting the world to rights, Pearson sat smoking in silence. 'Eventually on being pressed by a despairing Chairman, he calmly shattered the sepulchral quietude of the proceedings by announcing that, with regard to the subject under discussion – some piffling geopolitical frivolity – he knew nothing about it and cared even less, and therefore declined to say anything, with which he cheerfully resumed cleaning out his pipe with the wrong end of a pencil.'

In 1953 Pearson experienced severe abdominal pain, perhaps the earliest manifestation of the cancer that would kill him. Rest and a bland diet appeared to cure him, however, and that year he produced a well-received biography of James McNeill Whistler (*The Man Whistler*, Methuen).

Sir Walter Scott, whose *Lay of the Last Minstrel* Hesketh had botched in a Bedford classroom half a century before, was his next subject. The research for this book provided one of those rare strokes of fortune which every biographer dreams of but seldom encounters. Hesketh and Joyce were staying in Scotland, casually searching out places which had been associated with Scott. Before building Abbotsford, Scott had lived some miles away at Ashiestiel, a farm house on the Tweed River. It was now hidden by trees and there was nothing by which to determine its exact locality. However Pearson found it and walked down the lane to take up a position on the lawn for a good stare. His reveries were interrupted by a voice from behind sharply inquiring: 'Is there anything I can do for you?' Realising he had been caught in the act of trespass, there was nothing for it but the truth. He explained to the gentleman that he was a biographer masquerading as a literary sleuth, and he tried to soften the impression that his sole interest in the house was that it had once been inhabited by someone more interesting than his interrogator. The owner, Admiral Abel-Smith, listened with interest and then offered to show him through the house. As they walked from room to room, the Admiral mentioned that he had bought the place lock, stock and barrel, including an old desk which turned out to be full of old manuscripts. Would Pearson care to inspect these? Needless to say, he would. The manuscripts turned out to be contemporaneous reminiscences of Sir Walter Scott, hitherto unknown, written by his cousin which revealed, along with much else, that several incidents in Lockhart's classic *Life of Scott* were incorrect.

Walter Scott: His Life and Personality was published by Methuen in 1954 and dedicated to Joyce – 'who made it possible'. Although sales were respectable, Pearson never again approached the commercial success of his *Shaw*, *Wilde* or *Disraeli* books. But he later became President of the Sir Walter Scott Society of Edinburgh and delivered their annual oration on March 4, 1960. The Scott biography brought praise from Max Beerbohm who wrote of Pearson's 'shining skill in narrative', and asked him if he would consider writing a biography of his old stage mentor, Max's half-brother, Beerbohm Tree. Beerbohm died before the book (*Tree*, Methuen, 1956) appeared. The W. S. Gilbert estate next requested Pearson to expand the portrait he had limned in *Gilbert and Sullivan*; this became *W. S. Gilbert: His Life and Strife* (Methuen, 1957).

Pearson had left but one subject close to his heart – a dual biography of Johnson and Boswell. He and Kingsmill had corresponded about this since the Twenties. Originally Pearson had been dismissive of Johnson, regarded him as a dour moralist and a prig whose conversational sparkle was the creation of James Boswell. In 1923 he told Kingsmill: 'Johnson is Boswell's creation or he is nothing, just as Socrates is Plato's creation and Falstaff Shakespeare's creation'. By the time Pearson wrote *Ventilations* (1930) his view had softened; 'Johnson served Boswell as an excellent rough model; his position, his tricks, his rudeness, his circle of friends, his blunt common sense, all helped the artist to create something as good as Falstaff.' But it was only under Kingsmill's tutelage that he came to see Johnson in a larger frame, excusing his earlier prejudice with the tolerant and accurate comment that 'a true understanding and appreciation of Johnson does not begin until one is middle-aged.'

It is typical of Pearson that, once his view had changed, he tended to overlook even the rough spots on Johnson such as his obdurate rudeness. Wraxall had said of Johnson that whom he could not vanquish by intellect he silenced by rudeness. When once his wife upbraided Hesketh for being rude to people, he quoted Wraxall's remark to her and said that he wanted carved on his tombstone: 'He was nothing if not a gentlemen,' then, under that, 'And he was not a gentlemen.' The only

aspect of Johnson's character which Pearson did not grow to appreciate
was his melancholia. This derived, Pearson considered, from unre-
solved religious doubts. Several books have been written on the subject
of Samuel Johnson's religion; in two sentences Pearson says all that
needs to be said on the subject: 'He longed for absolute truth, for
spiritual anchorage, for something by which the validity of all things
could be tested; yet the obstinate rationality which prevented him from
embracing the Roman Catholic religion made him uncomfortable in
any other. His congenital scepticism was at war with his yearning for
what was durable, and the yells he admitted when his faith was
questioned were caused by his inner doubts.' Against Johnson's
dyspeptic view of the human condition, Pearson set his own credo: 'The
most sensible and satisfying philosophy of life would comprise a
recognition of three essential elements: the sheer joy of existence; a
constant sense of the miraculous, and the perception of the impossibility of fulfillment in a temporary state that should never detract from
present obtainable happiness.'

Although not the last of Pearson's biographies, *Johnson and Boswell*
is the last to exhibit him at the peak of his form. For a biographer whose
territory was temperament, he had the two richest characters in English
literature. How many biographers, from Sir John Hawkins in 1787 to
Jackson Bate in 1977, have stumbled over the immensity of Johnson.
Yet Pearson produced a lucid, comprehensive and lively portrait
of both Johnson and Boswell. By the art which conceals art, he
made it appear easy. In *Time and Tide* Laurence Meynell wrote:
'Hesketh Pearson writes as a man should write about Johnson, as
one feels Johnson himself would have written had he ever penned an
autobiography.'

There are several reasons why *Johnson and Boswell* succeeds. First,
as an anecdotal biographer, Pearson had a treasure trove to draw upon.
Second, he was not afraid to challenge Johnson's interpretation of
events. For example, as proof of his father's madness, Johnson had
cited the fact that his father would lock the front door of his dilapidated
tanning factory, even though a thief might easily gain entry through the
tumbled-down back. Pearson contended that this was habit, not madness, adding: 'If everybody who acted in a thoughtless manner and did
unnecessary things were to be adjudged mad, a large majority of the
world's population could be certified as mentally unfit.' Nor is Pearson
reluctant to poke fun at great men of the past; of Edmund Burke ('a
born politician') he wrote: 'He had the politician's love of information
for its own sake, addiction to rhetoric, bursts of righteous indignation,
spasms of moral fervour, and flair for collecting money from mysterious

sources.' Also, distance and inclination allowed the biographer to take up and continue a quarrel with his, by nature, disputatious subjects; *à propos* Johnson's remark that Sir Isaac Newton could have applied equally to poetry as to science because 'the man who has vigour may walk to the east just as well as to the west if he happens to turn that way', Pearson wrote: 'He should have provided a few more illustrations: e.g. if Shakespeare had applied himself to navigation he could have smashed the Spanish Armada as effectively as Drake; if Marlborough had concentrated on literature, he could have written satire as well as Swift, if Garrick had studied draughtsmanship he could have vied with Sir Joshua Reynolds as a portrait painter. At which point it might have begun to dawn on Johnson that he was talking nonsense.'

After *Johnson and Boswell*, it is sad to note a falling off in the quality of Pearson's last three biographies. Now in his seventies, his strength was failing and he was straining for sympathetic subjects. *Charles II* (Heinemann, 1960) and *Henry of Navarre* (Heinemann, 1963) are flat and boring. The third book, *The Pilgrim Daughters* (Heinemann, 1961), is a disgrace, the product of a man who for the first and only time violated his principles by accepting a commission to produce a book for money. The topic held no intrinsic interest for him. He later told Michael Holroyd that, alone of all his books, he disowned *The Pilgrim Daughters*.

But like a runner who could no longer complete a marathon, Pearson could still sprint and he did produce two excellent volumes of short portraits: *Lives of the Wits* (1962) and *Extraordinary People* (1965).

It is a subjective, and ultimately pointless, exercise to debate which is Pearson's finest biography. Muggeridge prefers *Hazlitt*. Kingsmill chose *Tom Paine*, then later preferred *Labby*. Pearson himself chose *Sydney Smith* or *Scott*. Harold Nicolson wrote that *Wilde* was Pearson's great accomplishment. Graham Greene had high praise for his *Conan Doyle* ('Mr Pearson as a biographer had some of the qualities of Dr Johnson – a plainness, an honesty, a sense of ordinary life going on all the time.'); Anthony Burgess praised his *Shakespeare*; Benny Green for his *Whistler*; Desmond MacCarthy and Richard Ingrams for his *Shaw*. But Pearson's great achievement is none of these, excellent though each is in isolation. Rather, his achievement is synoptic – a panorama of eccentricity, wit and genius unique in British literature. Consistency of treatment over an astonishing array of subjects is Pearson's accomplishment. By reading through his biographies one may obtain, with remarkably few gaps, an accurate and lively cultural and literary history of England. Pearson was once asked what he really believed in? He replied: 'I believe in the miracle and the mystery of

Creation.' Through the lives of others, Pearson explored the mystery and celebrated the miracle.

In 1961 Pearson fell ill again, this time a burst blood vessel, and he spent a month recuperating in France and Belgium. Just before returning to England he wrote to Michael Holroyd of the 'excellent claret' and 'superb weather, sometimes even too hot'; when Holroyd saw him again, he appeared restored to his old form. His routine was unchanged; writing for four hours in the morning; answering letters, reading and walking in the afternoon; listening to music, mostly Beethoven, in the evenings. He worked hard to put the final touches to an autobiography (*Hesketh Pearson by Himself*, Heinemann, 1965). He had no regrets. 'I have enjoyed the experience of living so much that I now ask nothing of life but a quick death.'

In March 1964 he entered hospital where, after exploratory surgery, a diagnosis of terminal cancer was made. This was kept from him, although his wife was told. He returned home, weak and tired, but convinced that nothing more was wrong with him than a stomach ailment. He was supposed to address the annual meeting of the Sir Walter Scott Club in Edinburgh on March 6 but he was too weak to go; he asked Muggeridge, as a personal favour, to fill in for him. Muggeridge did, and four days later received this letter from Joyce Pearson:

> Hesketh wants me to thank you so much for sending him the script of your Scott speech. I read it to him and he pronounced it really excellent. He finds any physical effort (even reading) terribly tiring, but his mind is perfectly clear and receptive.
>
> I often ask him if he would like to see any of his old friends but he says he is too tired. He dozes and sleeps most of the time and mercifully so far does not seem to be in any pain. He is depressed by his weakness but still thinks it is the result of the operation. We all pray that he won't have time to realize that there is any other cause.

On April 8, 1964 Muggeridge went to see him for the last time. Hesketh was in bed with the gramophone hooked up next to him, the pick-up arm pre-set to play over and over again the andante of Beethoven's Razumovsky Quartet and the scherzo from the Ninth Symphony. From under the bed Pearson produced a bottle of champagne which Colin Hurry had brought and he proposed that they drink a toast to Shakespeare. Muggeridge noted that Pearson talked of Shakespeare as though he were a friend in the room. He was serene and cheerful. He told Muggeridge that he found his spiritual life in

Shakespeare, Beethoven, the English countryside and a limitless interest in his fellow human beings. As to immortality, he said he neither believed nor disbelieved, not having been privileged with any special revelation on the point. Truth, beauty, and love survived; he said this was enough, even if individual consciousness did not. When Muggeridge got up to go, Pearson said that he would not object to drifting out of life on bubbles of champagne while listening to Beethoven.

Pearson died the next day, April 9, 1964, at the age of seventy-seven.

Writing his friend's obituary, Muggeridge remembered him in these words:

> Pearson loved the English countryside, and English bells sounding across it, the English language, and all who tried in however humble a capacity to use it worthily . . . He could never manage to finish reciting Wordsworth's verses upon the death of James Hogg. The closing lines –
>
> 'How fast has brother followed brother
> From sunshine to the sunless land'
>
> were too much for him. I shall always think of him stumbling over the poignancy of those exquisite verses, and hope that the land will, after all, turn out not to be sunless.

A memorial service was held at St Paul's, Covent Garden on April 27, 1964. Because 'nothing would have excited his derision more than a contrived eulogy' the Order of Service consisted of a brief organ recital, then silence during which mourners were invited to remember that 'although it is a man's mortality that has brought you together it is also an expression of the love which alone gives to life its meaning'. As the mourners left the church they were given a memorial card on which were printed two stanzas from a poem, *Elegy for a Man*, written of Hesketh Pearson by Colin Hurry:

> Leave nothing to repent
> Richly did he live.
> Prodigal of life, he spent
> All that life could give.
>
> Sing no dirges, ring no knell;
> All his spirit spurned.
> He who loved this earth so well
> Is to earth returned.

Bibliography

Modern Men and Mummers, George Allen and Unwin, 1921
A Persian Critic, Chapman and Dodd, 1923
The Whispering Gallery, The Bodley Head, 1926
Iron Rations, Cecil Palmer, 1928
Ventilations: Being Biographical Asides, Lippincott, 1930
Dr Darwin, J. M. Dent, 1930
The Fool of Love, Hamish Hamilton, 1934
The Smith of Smiths, Hamish Hamilton, 1935
Labby: The Life of Henry Labouchere, Hamish Hamilton, 1935
The Swan of Lichfield, Hamish Hamilton, undated
Tom Paine, Hamish Hamilton, 1937
Thinking It Over, Hamish Hamilton, 1938
The Hero of Delhi, Collins, 1939
Bernard Shaw, Collins, 1942
Conan Doyle, Methuen, 1943
The Life of Oscar Wilde, Methuen, 1946
Dickens, Methuen, 1949
A Life of Shakespeare, Carroll and Nicholson, 1949
The Last Actor Managers, Methuen, 1950
G.B.S.: A Postscript, Collins, 1951
Dizzy, The Life and Nature of Benjamin Disraeli, Methuen, 1951
The Man Whistler, Methuen, 1952
Sir Walter Scott: His Life and Personality, Methuen, 1954
Beerbohm Tree, Methuen, 1956
Gilbert: His Life and Strife, Methuen, 1957
Johnson and Boswell, Heinemann, 1958
Charles II: His Life and Likeness, Heinemann, 1960
The Pilgrim Daughters, Heinemann, 1961
Lives of the Wits, Heinemann, 1962
Henry of Navarre, Heinemann, 1963
Extraordinary People, Heinemann, 1965
Hesketh Pearson By Himself, Heinemann, 1965

With Hugh Kingsmill
Skye High, Hamish Hamilton, 1937
This Blessed Plot, Methuen, 1942
Talking of Dick Whittington, Eyre and Spottiswoode, 1947

With Malcolm Muggeridge
About Kingsmill, Methuen, 1951

Index